The Return of Tarzan
The Screenplay

A complete adaptation of the classic
novel by Edgar Rice Burroughs

Oscar Cintronmarina

Printed in the United States of America

First Printing, 2017

ISBN 978-0-9967875-1-2

The Return of Tarzan
The Screenplay

Psalm 115:17, Douay

"*I will sacrifice to thee the sacrifice of praise,
and I will call upon the name of the Lord.*"

In memory of Edgar Rice Burroughs

BLACK SCREEN

A blaring whistle and moments later the screeching halt of a
locomotive.

FADE IN:

EXT. WISCONSIN - TRAIN STATION - MORNING

Hissing like a gigantic constrictor, steam spouts from its
sides covering the ground and some of the waiting passengers,
while the sky above covers them all with smoke from the
ongoing forest fires.

Before boarding, ESMERALDA looks over at PROFESSOR ARCHIMEDES
Q. PORTER.

Prof. Porter is stopped from his incessant pacing by a
courtesy tug at his frock coat by the ever vigilant MR.
SAMUEL T. PHILANDER.

Esmeralda shakes her head and then takes a gander at TARZAN,
JANE PORTER and WILLIAM CECIL CLAYTON who are talking
together further up the platform.

She shrugs her shoulders and then caught by the encroaching
smoke from above, she coughs and tries to brush it away.
Unable to endure it, she hastens into the train with the
assistance of a porter.

The two men are facing Jane and her face is attentive but her
eyes are listless, almost lifeless.

Bothered by the smoke, Clayton squints as he looks at his
watch and then at the still steaming train.

                    CLAYTON
          I say, I think it's time we boarded
          before -- by Jove, I've forgotten
          my ulster!

                    JANE
          Did you leave it inside?

                    CLAYTON
          I must have. I won't be long,
          dear.

Clayton trots off towards the waiting room.

Tarzan and Jane look into each other's eyes.

                          JANE
               You're not coming with us... are
               you?

Tarzan shakes his head.

                          TARZAN
               It wouldn't be safe for Clayton.

Jane makes a poor attempt at a smile.

                          TARZAN
               Please let the others know?

                          JANE
               I will.

Tarzan extends a hand.

                          TARZAN
               Good luck, and God bless you. I
               wish you all the best that life can
               offer.

Jane responds in a low, soft voice.

                          JANE
               Goodbye? This can't be happening.

Tarzan looks down to the ground as if searching for words and
then looking at her with steady grey eyes...

                          TARZAN
               I don't understand it myself, but
               it's happening. I had hoped you'd
               be riding back with me.

Jane turns her head to one side and checks a tear with the
base of her palm.

                          JANE
               I can't believe I'll never see you
               again.

                          TARZAN
               Please, don't cry.

                          JANE
               I won't... not here...

With trembling lips and tear-filled eyes she faces him.

                          JANE
               ... But I will.

Tarzan takes her in his arms.

                    JANE
          O God... I love you so.

Tarzan breaks the gentle embrace and slipping his hand into
his side coat pocket pulls out the golden, diamond studded
locket.

                    TARZAN
          Please take this... it could never
          be mine, not now. It was meant for
          you... it belongs to you.

Jane hesitates, but Tarzan gently takes one of her hands and
lowers the priceless bauble into her palm and closes it with
the caress of his other hand.

Jane nods her acceptance and Tarzan let's go.

                    JANE
          Will you be going back to France?

                    TARZAN
          I'll spend some time in New York
          first... then return to France.

His eyes pierce her soul for a moment and then he smiles,
gently.

                    TARZAN
          Remember the night you sat writing
          to Hazel in my cabin?

                    JANE
               (blushes)
          You were watching me?

Tarzan grins and then nods.

Jane smiles, a little embarrassed at the confession.

                    JANE
          That wasn't very polite.

                    TARZAN
          I wasn't civilized, then. Do you
          remember?

Jane nods not knowing where he's going.

                    TARZAN
          That's when I loved you, and I
          still do... and I always will.

                         JANE
          I --

                         TARZAN
               -- Goodbye, Jane.

Tarzan tears himself away and heads towards his convertible,
his face like a groom left at the altar.

The engine, of the Rolland-Pilain E Ventoux, blasts and Jane
watches her heart zoom away from the train station and from
her life.

INT. WAITING ROOM - MORNING

Clayton scratches his head as he tries to remember where he
laid his ulster. He moves around the room, then stops and
snaps his fingers.

He steps to a group of chairs near the windows where he sat
for awhile talking to Jane the night before and there he
finds it on the floor between two chairs.

He bends down to pick it up and as he rises he notices a
cablegram on the floor several feet away from him.

Curious, Clayton walks over to see what it says and being
face down, he picks it up. Flipping it, he gives it a quick
glance and his world turns upside down.

The ulster in the perch of his arm falls to the floor and his
eyes open up in fear and disbelief. He shakes his head once,
then again and rereads the cablegram.

INSERT - CABLEGRAM

               "The fingerprints confirm you're
               Greystoke. My sincerest
               congratulations!

               Your friend,

               Paul D'Arnot."

BACK TO SCENE

Clayton reels backward as if punched in the gut. Swaying, he
holds on to one of the chairs to support his crumbling legs
and forces himself to take in a deep breath.

Two long, piercing whistles jar Clayton's mind awake.

He picks up his ulster, shoves the cablegram into one of its pockets and rushes awkwardly out from the waiting room.

EXT. TRAIN STATION - MORNING

As the train begins to creep and chug forward, building its momentum, Clayton, urged on by the others from the windows and Jane from the coach platform, sprints quickly towards the steaming and accelerating monstrosity and taking hold of a handle, jumps up beside Jane.

INT. TRAIN - PASSENGER CAR - MORNING

After taking their seats, Clayton begins to scan the passengers until...

                    JANE
          What took you so long?

Clayton attempts to disguise his troubled mind with an attempt at being debonair.

                    CLAYTON
          An ulster, my dear, is not as easy
          to find as one might think.

Jane gives him a suspicious but weak smile.

                    JANE
          Is that a fact?

                    CLAYTON
          Oh, believe me, I speak from vast
          experience -- by the way where's
          our jungle friend, Tarzan? I don't
          see him. I thought he was suppose
          to be in the same car with us.

                    JANE
          He asked me to tell you and the
          others, that he changed his mind.
          He'll see New York first and
          then... return to France.

Plagued by the cablegram, Clayton pries a little deeper.

                    CLAYTON
          He said nothing else?

Jane shakes her head.

                         JANE
              What else could he say?

Clayton can't meet Jane's questioning gaze, and dropping his
eyes, he turns away looking downward and covers his
conscience with a nervous reply.

                         CLAYTON
              That's too bad. I would have very
              much liked to have said goodbye.

In a melancholy mood she replies.

                         JANE
              It's alright. I said goodbye...
              for all of us.

They both try to settle into their seats next to each other.

Jane with a lifeless beauty.

Clayton in a state of high anxiety.

EXT. BALTIMORE - OUTSKIRTS - PORTER HOUSE - DAY (LIGHT RAIN)

SUPER: "2 WEEKS LATER"

A soft, steady rain falls on the grand, old Porter house.

The trees sway lightly before a gentle wind.

A 1909 Pierce-Arrow and a 1909 Buick Model F are parked on
the road in front of the house, patiently enduring the rain.

INT. PORTER HOUSE - LIVING ROOM - DAY

Raindrops pitter-patter the rooftop like falling pebbles that
seem to strike everywhere at once.

Jane sits alone on a couch engrossed in a novel ignoring the
vociferous chess match between her father and Mr. Philander.

                         PROF. PORTER (O.S.)
              Checkmate?! Nonsense!

                         MR. PHILANDER (O.S.)
              I said "gardez!" I warned you that
              your queen was in danger!

                         PROF. PORTER (O.S.)
              What's the score?

                        MR. PHILANDER (O.S.)
               It's my two games to your one.

                        PROF. PORTER (O.S.)
               Not for long, Mr. Philander... not
               for long! Set up the board, while
               I make the drinks.

Esmeralda enters the living room humming away and, like a
mother hen, places an extra pillow behind Jane.

Jane looks up from her book and greets her with a smile.

                        JANE
               Thank you, Esmeralda.

                        ESMERALDA
                   (in Southern black accent)
               A cup of coffee?

Jane's eyes head for the ceiling at her indecision.

                        ESMERALDA
               With a little brandy?

Jane gives in and Esmeralda smiles big and chuckles.

                        ESMERALDA
               I'll be right back, honey child.

Esmeralda's large rolling body disappears behind the swinging
doors and into the kitchen.

Clayton wanders in and seats himself next to Jane.

She knows it's him but continues reading.

                        CLAYTON
                   (re: book)
               Any good?

Jane stops reading and turns her head to regard him.

                        JANE
               I like it.

She waits for him, knowing something is on his mind. Her
eyes follow him as he gets up and paces.

He then sits back down next to her again and confesses his
mind.

                         CLAYTON
             Jane, there's really no reason why
             we should wait. Let's get married
             right away.

                         JANE
             Right away as in ...

                         CLAYTON
             ... next week.

She stares at him as if he's just escaped from an asylum.

                         JANE
             A week! My goodness, Cecil, a girl
             needs more than a week to prepare
             for a wedding... at least I do.

                         CLAYTON
             I know it's sudden, but I have a
             good reason for wanting an early
             wedding. England beckons, and I
             must return as soon as possible...
             and I want to leave with you as my
             wife.

Jane, looking for loophole, doesn't give in. She puts her
book on the end table and rising, walks over and watches the
soothing shower through a blurred window.

                         JANE
             I'll need at least a month, if not
             more time to prepare. It only
             happens once, you know... and I
             don't want to rush it. Why don't
             you go on to England and when you
             return, everything will be ready.

Clayton closes his eyes and grabs his head with his right
hand, bearing the large Greystoke ring upon his right ring
finger. It's not what he wanted to hear.

                         CLAYTON
             Very well then...

The pressure falls from her face as a horse-drawn buggy
crosses her view.

                         CLAYTON (O.S.)
             ... I'll put off my trip to England
             for a month.

Jane winces, shuts her eyes and bites her lower lip. That's
not what she wanted to hear.

Esmeralda breaks through the swinging doors with Jane's steaming, spiked coffee. She puts it down beside the book and reading the situation at a glance, shakes her head and returns to the kitchen humming a cheerful tune.

EXT. ATLANTIC - DAY

On the great dark-blue ocean, the stacks, of a French ocean liner, blow steam and smoke into the clouds that sail the cerulean skies.

The powerful liner plows the tranquil waters at a strong and steady pace.

EXT. FRENCH LINER - UPPER DECK - DAY

Well dressed and elegant passengers stroll the deck while several ship officers and stewards chat with a few of them. Others look out over the rail, while a family poses for a photo session.

In another section of the upper deck, gentlemen putt golf balls down putting lanes and a group of young couples laugh gaily as they play shuffleboard.

COUNTESS OLGA DE COUDE, 20, a Russian brunette several shades lovelier than beautiful, relaxes with a magazine in a steamer chair.

As she reads, she happens to glance up. Her eyes widen, her ample lips part and the magazine falls onto her lap. Whatever caught her eye captivates her and takes her breath away, under which she involuntarily exclaims...

The dialogue begins in French with subtitles and then transitions seamlessly into English without the French accent.

                    OLGA
          Superb!

Her husband, COUNT RAOUL DE COUDE, 40, attached to the French Ministry of War, looks up from his book.

                    RAOUL
          What is superb?

Raoul's eyes scour the deck for the object of interest.

                    OLGA
          It was nothing, my dear. I was
          just remembering those tall and
          imposing buildings of New York
          City.

                    RAOUL
          But you said you detested those
          cold and artless skyscrapers only
          three days ago. What's gotten into
          you, Olga?

Caught, her already cherubic cheeks redden slightly more.

                    OLGA
          Yes, I know, darling... but I've
          changed my mind. It just dawned on
          me -- that -- they are a wonder to
          behold, after all.

He smiles shaking his head and goes back to his book.

Olga, likewise, picks up her magazine and resumes where she
left off.

Raoul unable to continue the book, puts it away, exasperated.

                    RAOUL
          I'm sorry, my dear, but I am
          mentally exhausted. I cannot sit
          here another minute with this
          lifeless book. I think a game of
          cards will do the trick.

                    OLGA
          You know, it's not very polite to
          leave a young lady alone... yet, I
          understand exactly how you feel.

She gives him a loving smile and stretches out her hand. He
takes it, gives it a gentle squeeze, grins and leaves with
her encouraging support.

After his departure, Olga's attention reverts back to their
object of interest. Her catlike eyes fall upon Tarzan
lounging in a chair not too far from her. Her bosom rises
and under her breath she exhales...

                    OLGA
               Superb!

As her eyes rest upon his unmatched symmetry, Tarzan rises to
leave the deck and the countess stops a FRENCH STEWARD.

                    FRENCH STEWARD
          Yes, Countess?

She nods towards Tarzan.

                    OLGA
          Who is that man?

                    FRENCH STEWARD
          He's registered as Monsieur Tarzan
          of Africa.

                    OLGA
          Thank you, Steward.

                    FRENCH STEWARD
          Not at all, Madame.

EXT. FRENCH LINER - SMOKING-ROOM - DAY

As Tarzan nears the smoking-room just outside the entrance he
surprises two men who are whispering and gesturing in a
heated discussion. One of them shoots him a suspicious,
guilty barb.

Tarzan notes the guilty glance and, dismissing it, enters the
smoking-room.

INT. SMOKING-ROOM - DAY

Within, ostentation of elaborate design and decor abound. A
high ceiling is supported by pillars and between them and
about them are many small card tables surrounded by four
heavy chairs, cushioned for passenger comfort.

Against the walls are various couches occupied by men
drinking and conversing while others make use of the snug
single chairs for reading books, magazines and periodicals.

Stewards weave in and out among them satisfying their every
whim, need and desire.

Tarzan selects an unoccupied table facing away from the
activity. He summons a steward and is brought a drink.

Tarzan, moody, sips his drink in contemplation. On the wall
before him is a mirror and as he casually glances at it he
notices a card game in progress. One of the foursome gets up
and leaves, but another man offers to join the trio.

Tarzan recognizes him as the SHORTER of the two dark-visaged men, who was whispering so nervously with the taller man outside the smoking-room.

As a new game begins, TALLER, casually walks up and stands behind Count de Coude, who's one of the four playing cards.

Tarzan's eagle, grey-eyes watch as the man behind the count scans the room and with an adroit, sleight of hand slips something into Count de Coude's coat pocket.

INT. SMOKING-ROOM - DAY (15 MINUTES LATER)

Tarzan continues to watch the reflection of the card game, when suddenly he spots Taller -- still standing behind the count -- give Shorter, a barely perceptible nod.

On cue, Shorter stands up and accuses Count de Coude.

                    SHORTER
          Had I known, Monsieur, that you
          were a card sharp, I would never
          have joined this table!

Standing up to his full height and joined by the other two men, Count de Coude blanches at the unexpected and uncalled for accusation.

Controlling his righteous anger the count counters his accuser with unwavering, burning eyes.

                    RAOUL
          How dare you, Monsieur. Do you
          know who I am?

With a voice full of arrogance and a smirk of disrespect, Shorter replies.

                    SHORTER
          I don't care who you are, Monsieur.
          All I know is that you are a
          cheater.

Count de Coude steps up closer to the table and strikes him resoundingly across the face.

                    CARD PLAYER 1
               (to Shorter)
          You have made a grave error,
          Monsieur. The man you have accused
          is Count de Coude of France.

                         SHORTER
          I will gladly tender any apology
          required to the count if I am in
          error. All he need do is explain
          the extra cards I saw him place in
          his coat pocket.

TARZAN

watches Taller turn about and attempt to slither from the
smoking-room.

EXIT

Taller's way is barred by a very tall and powerful man. With
a quick glance at the stranger and a peremptory voice he
commands the man to step aside.

                         TALLER
          Excuse me -- let me pass.

                         TARZAN
          I think not.

Surprised and with a mounting temper of desperation.

                         TALLER
          What?! Let me pass I say!

                         TARZAN
          You may pass once I am through with
          you.

Taller tries to shove Tarzan out of his way, only to find
himself easily manhandled.

Tarzan catches the man's arm with a grip of steel causing a
cry of pain, turns him about locking the man's arm into the
small of his back and seizing him roughly by the back of the
neck, forces him towards the count's table, futilely
resisting and casting invectives at his tormentor.

BACK TO SCENE

At the card table, interested spectators have gathered to
witness the ongoing accusation.

                         RAOUL
          ... The man is mad, I tell you.

                         CARD PLAYER 2
                    It's an absurd charge.

                         SHORTER
                    Absurd you say? Search his coat
                    pocket and what you so adamantly
                    call "absurd" will turn out to be
                    the truth.

The other card players do not move to comply with Shorter's
request.

                         SHORTER
                    If you gentlemen are afraid... I'll
                    search him myself.

The count thrusts out an open, bold palm stopping Shorter in
his tracks.

                         RAOUL
                    Only a gentleman, may search me.

A strong voice breaks into the quarrel.

                         TARZAN (O.S.)
                    Count, there is no need to have
                    anyone search you.

All eyes turn towards Tarzan and the struggling man in his
control.

The count's demeanor demands an explanation from the
stranger.

                         TARZAN
                    The cards are, indeed, in your
                    pocket. I saw them placed there.

                         RAOUL
                    Impossible! Here, I will prove to
                    everyone that there is nothing in
                    my pocket but --

Count de Coude reaches quickly into his pocket only to freeze
with mortification. Slowly his hand pulls out several
playing cards.

The crowd of men around him gasps and the faces of the two
other players are in full shock. The count's face flushes
with shame.

                         TARZAN
                    It was planned, Monsieur.

And then turning to the audience.

> TARZAN
> Gentleman, the Count de Coude did
> not know that the cards were
> planted in his pocket. I saw the
> whole affair in the reflection of a
> mirror across my table. This man
> and the accuser plotted the whole
> affair.

An audible relief is palpable in the crowd.

Count de Coude notices the man in Tarzan's grip for the first
time and surprise usurps his countenance.

> RAOUL
> It is not possible! Rokoff! But --

Count de Coude turns quickly to face his accuser and studies
the man's face.

> RAOUL
> I should have guessed it was you!
> Paulvitch, you're a different man
> without your beard. But I see you
> now... even through your clever
> disguise.

The other two card players move to apprehend the accuser
while the rest of the spectators begin to disperse.

> RAOUL
> No, let him be.

> TARZAN
> And this one?

Count de Coude turns and gives NIKOLAS ROKOFF a contemptible
stare.

> RAOUL
> Please, release him, Monsieur.
> This is a private affair which I
> will settle at a later date...
> permanently.

Tarzan releases Rokoff who quickly tramps off to join ALEXIS
PAULVITCH, who is anxious to depart from the smoking-room.
Before reaching the exit, Rokoff, with a vindictive sneer
turns and threatens Tarzan.

                    ROKOFF/TALLER
          You will regret your interference
          in my affairs, Monsieur. I will
          not forget!

                    RAOUL
          You have made a terrible enemy,
          Monsieur. Nevertheless, I owe you
          a great deal. You have cleared my
          name and restored my honor before
          ample witnesses against these vile
          vermin. Please take my card. If
          ever I can be of service, do not
          hesitate to call upon me.

Tarzan retrieves a calling card case from his coat pocket,
pops the top open like a cigarette lighter and hands one to
the count, who reads...

INSERT - TARZAN'S CARD

"M. Jean C. Tarzan"

BACK TO SCENE

With a thankful smile Raoul pockets the card.

                    RAOUL
          It is a pleasure and an honor to
          meet you, Monsieur Tarzan.

Tarzan bows to the count.

                    TARZAN
          As is mine to meet you, Monsieur.

                    RAOUL
          Those two are notorious villains
          and my recommendation is for you to
          remain fully on your guard while
          they are aboard this ship.

                    TARZAN
          I will take your advice...

Tarzan looks toward the exit but the two are already gone.

                    TARZAN
          ... But I've had deadlier enemies.

                    RAOUL
          Perhaps, but do not underestimate
          them or you will come to regret it.
          Come, enough about them. Please,
          join us.

Tarzan accepts the count's invitation. The other two card
players AD LIB their thanks for his timely appearance and
rescue of Count de Coude's good name.

Raoul stops a steward and orders drinks for the table.

INT. TARZAN'S STATEROOM - EVENING

Tarzan enters his cabin and turning on the light discovers a
folded note on the floor.

Unfolding it, he reads it.

                    ROKOFF (V.O.)
          Monsieur Tarzan,

          you have inadvertently become
          involved in my affairs and as such
          I am willing to forego my threat if
          you apologize to me and refrain
          from ever again meddling in matters
          that do not concern you.

          I am certain that you will want to
          make amends.

          Sincerely,

          Nikolas Rokoff

Tarzan smiles, crumbles up the letter and tosses it in the
trash bin. He takes off his coat, loosens his tie, and
removing the bed covers prepares to call it a night.

INT. DE COUDE'S STATEROOM - EVENING

Raoul is sitting on a sofa grappling with internal forces and
his wife is troubled to see him so.

                    OLGA
          Darling, what is wrong? You've
          been silent and unapproachable all
          night. Is it something I said --
          or did, my sweet?

Raoul's face shines as he gazes at his beautiful wife and shakes his head to her query.

> RAOUL
> You? No, my dear.

Finally, he releases the thoughts that have been galling him most of the day.

> RAOUL
> Rokoff and Paulvitch are onboard.

> OLGA
> What?! But, how? I thought they were in prison somewhere in Germany.

> RAOUL
> So did I. But believe me... they are here. In fact, while I was playing cards they both almost succeeded in destroying my family name... my very honor.

Olga rises from her vanity confused and unsure of what to say.

> RAOUL
> Olga, I'm going to have those two wretched criminals arrested by the captain. I will no longer tolerate their attacks on my person. This has gone on long enough!

Raoul drops his head into his hands and fear clouds the beauty of his wife as she falls to her knees at his side.

> OLGA
> Please no! You swore you would not!

> RAOUL
> Some promises must be broken, when it endangers the one you love. Yes, for you I swore to be lenient with your brother but now, for your very safety and mine, I must break that promise.

Teardrops fall from her eyes as she beseeches her husband to stay his hand.

> OLGA
> Please, Raoul... for me -- for us!

Raoul lifts his head and taking her gentle hands, gazes into her gazelle-like eyes, moist with fear and sorrow.

                    RAOUL
          I cannot understand your zealous
          support for such a cruel creature.
          But, let it be as you wish. Yet, I
          fear you may live to regret your
          decision to protect him.

                    OLGA
          It's not him, it's -- oh please,
          trust me and do nothing that will
          entangle us deeper into his web.

                    RAOUL
          So be it, but if it were not for
          the help of Monsieur Tarzan, you
          would be lamenting your decision
          this very moment.

Olga is surprised by her husband.

                    OLGA
          Monsieur Tarzan?

                    RAOUL
          Yes, it was he who foiled their
          plot. He saw them plant the cards
          in my coat pocket.

Raoul is puzzled at his wife's demeanor.

                    RAOUL
          Why? Do you know him?

                    OLGA
          No -- I've never met him. Only --
          a steward pointed him out to me.

                    RAOUL
          Did he? I didn't realize that
          Monsieur Tarzan was a man of note.

She kisses her husband and wipes her watery eyes from one side of her face and he wipes them from her other side.

                    RAOUL
          There now, feel better?

She nods, smiles and looks into his eyes.

                    OLGA
          Thank you... you're so good to me.

She embraces him and returns to her vanity. Raoul leans back into the sofa and picks up the lifeless book.

EXT. UPPER DECK - NEXT DAY

With hands in his pockets, Tarzan strolls the upper deck like a restless soul. As he walks his eyes are upon the deck -- his mind busy with thoughts.

Heedless of where his path takes him, he approaches a deserted part of the deck and he inadvertently comes upon Rokoff, 30, and Paulvitch, 29, arguing with a VEILED WOMAN.

Tarzan advances towards them but they are so enmeshed in their dispute that they're unaware of his close proximity. He notices her finely dressed voluptuous, slender figure.

They speak in Russian, a language unfamiliar to Tarzan, and her pleading voice vibrates with fear and anguish as Rokoff and Paulvitch increase their verbal assaults.

Rokoff, angry, seizes her wrist and begins to twist and a large ornate ring, on one of her slender fingers, catches Tarzan's eye as with a powerful hand he collapses one of Rokoff's shoulders sending him crumbling to the deck.

Paulvitch backs away in awe and the Veiled Woman places one of her hands to her lips.

Rokoff, meanwhile, attempts to shake off the effects of the human sledgehammer and to his consternation, finds Tarzan confronting him with a grim smile.

Incredulity and rage suffuse his black mustached and bearded face.

                    ROKOFF
          You pig! Did I not warn you! Did
          you not receive my letter?!

                    TARZAN
          I did, and now you've received my
          answer.

Rokoff charges Tarzan with madness and murder in his heart. His throat collides into Tarzan's hand and he finds himself lifted from the deck and then roughly shaken and thrown against the rail.

Rokoff howls and curses in pain and humiliation and with evil eyes reaches into his coat pocket.

                    VEILED WOMAN
          No, Nikolas!
               (to Tarzan)
          Fly, Monsieur, before it is too
          late! Run!

Rokoff pulls out a revolver and fires a dud into the chest of
his nemesis but before he can fire another shot Tarzan's
quick, powerful hand slaps the gun from his grasp sending it
into the depths of the Atlantic Ocean.

Rokoff, fearful, yet filled with humiliation and hate lashes
out against the ape-man with words.

                    ROKOFF
          I will kill you for this! There
          will be no more letters. You do
          not yet know who I am... but soon
          you shall curse the day you met me.

                    TARZAN
          I know who you are. You're a base,
          wretched coward who threatens and
          assaults women.

Tarzan turns to face the girl but she and Paulvitch are no
longer there and forgetting Rokoff, continues his stroll as
cool and unperturbed as a serene and shaded pool of water.

EXT. UPPER DECK - DAY (30 MINUTES LATER)

Tarzan, finding his steamer chair, sinks into it. The past
crowds his mind and he shuts his eyes.

QUICK FLASHBACKS - BAD MEMORIES

-- Tarzan mourns Kala

-- Cannibals torture a victim

-- Snipes shoots King in the back

-- A pickaxe is buried into Snipes' skull

BACK TO PRESENT

Tarzan opens his eyes, sits up and under his breath...

                         TARZAN
          Lower than beasts... all of them.
          Killing, lying, cheating, abusing
          women... and for what?

Tarzan, feeling watched, turns his head too quickly for Olga
to avoid his steel-grey eyes.

She drops her lids from his penetrating look and with
blushing cheeks turns her face away.

Tarzan smiles at his own impoliteness and releases the
countess from his grip and leans back into his chair.

Olga rises from her steamer chair and as she passes Tarzan,
his eyes follow the beauty.

Placing a hand to the nape of her swan-like neck, she pushes
up and underneath her raven locks and summons a steward.

Tarzan's quick eyes recognize the large ornate ring on her
slender finger.

EXT. UPPER DECK - NIGHT

Around the singing full moon an arm of the Milky Way dots the
heavens with infinite luminaries.

Next to a davit Tarzan stops his night saunter and leans over
the rail to look out upon the deep waters reflecting the
wonders from above.

Hidden by the davit, two men pass by already in conversation
unaware of his presence.

                         ROKOFF
          ... If she cries out, do with her
          as you will.

Upon hearing those words, Tarzan familiar with Rokoff's
voice, turns and follows him and his side-kick, Paulvitch.

EXT. SMOKING-ROOM - NIGHT

Tarzan trails them stealthily and watches them stop before
the entrance to the smoking-room.

Paulvitch opens the door, pokes his head in for a few moments
and then returns nodding his head. The pair then quickly
departs.

Close behind, Tarzan follows as they descend the stairs down to the promenade deck.

INT. FIRST-CLASS PASSENGER CORRIDOR/INT. DE COUDE'S STATEROOM - NIGHT

Using the shadows, passageways and niches along the way, Tarzan escapes detection.

The pair stops before a stateroom and Rokoff knocks upon the door.

Tarzan slips into one of the passageways near the two men. Watching. Listening.

> OLGA (O.S.)
> Yes? Who is it?

> ROKOFF
> It's only me, your brother. Please let me in. I wish to speak to you.

> OLGA (O.S.)
> No, Nikolas. Why can't you leave me in peace? Go, and leave me alone.

Rokoff changes his gruff voice in deception.

> ROKOFF
> Please, dear sister... it's your brother. Can I not have a single word with --

> OLGA (O.S.)
> -- I'm listening.

> ROKOFF
> I've come to apologize...

He smiles and winks at Paulvitch.

> ROKOFF
> ... But not to a door. I promise to behave and I won't enter your cabin.

Olga unlocks and opens the door.

Rokoff takes a step and stands on the threshold while Paulvitch flattens his back against the panel next to the door. At first, Rokoff's voice is indistinguishable but hers is not.

                    OLGA
          No, Nikolas, I will not be your
          pawn. You are wasting your time.
          I will never go along with your
          plans. Leave this instant!

                    ROKOFF
          Very well, but remember that I gave
          you the opportunity to help me
          freely. But if not freely...

Rokoff gives her a disappointed look, turns his head and
signals his tag-team partner.

                    ROKOFF
          ... Then by force!

Paulvitch rushes in and slams the door shut while Rokoff
eavesdrops with a wicked sneer on his lips.

INT. DE COUDE'S STATEROOM - NIGHT

                    OLGA
          Get out! Get out or I shall call
          my husband.

                    PAULVITCH/SHORTER
          There's no need for you to call
          him, for the purser has already
          been dispatched to inform your
          husband that another man is within
          his cabin... with his lovely wife.

                    OLGA
          He will not believe it.

                    PAULVITCH
          He won't, but the purser will.

Paulvitch looks over his manicure as he continues with the
blackmail.

                    PAULVITCH
          And once we've landed, the
          newspapers most assuredly will hear
          of it.

                    OLGA
          You wouldn't dare! I know
          something that will keep you from
          my door forever. Let me but
          whisper it, and you'll understand.

Paulvitch comes near and the whisper transforms his face into a maniacal frenzy of rage.

With an oath, both his hands grip her fair throat stifling her scream and, throwing her back upon her bed, he begins to throttle her mercilessly.

INT. FIRST-CLASS PASSENGER CORRIDOR - NIGHT

The momentary silence is pierced by a scream and Tarzan dashes like a bullet towards the door.

Rokoff tries to flee but Tarzan tackles him, yanks him up by the scruff of the neck with terrific force, drags him back to the door and rams it open.

INT. DE COUDE'S STATEROOM - NIGHT

Tarzan bursts into the room and finds Paulvitch strangulating the countess who's struggling and striking him with all her might.

Paulvitch wheels about caught in the act, while the countess rises up gasping for air. Though faint and shaken-up Tarzan recognizes her.

Rokoff is helpless in his grasp and Paulvitch, cornered like a rat, can do nothing but threaten with his foul face.

Tarzan drags Rokoff along with him towards Paulvitch. Before Paulvitch can speak Tarzan is squeezing his windpipe with his other arm.

Savage fierceness fills Tarzan's features and the scar across his forehead becomes vividly visible.

                    TARZAN
          How does it feel, coward!

Tarzan lifts him straight up into the air, like an empty suit, and just before he passes out Tarzan slams him into the cabin floor.

Dazed, Paulvitch crawls away from Tarzan and manages to sit up against the wall.

Tarzan then turns his attention to Rokoff.

                    TARZAN
          This ends tonight.

He turns to Olga.

> TARZAN
> Please ring for the captain. These
> two must pay for what they've done
> to you.

Olga runs towards him pleading.

> OLGA/VEILED WOMAN
> Oh, Monsieur, please, do not. It
> was just a misunderstanding and I --

> TARZAN
> -- A misunderstanding? Madame,
> that man,
>   (indicates Paulvitch)
> was just trying to kill you. What
> is going on here?

> OLGA
> Please, do nothing, I beg you.

Tarzan catches the sneers and smiles upon the features of the
two villains.

> TARZAN
> And what would you have me do,
> release them so they can assault
> you again on another day?

Olga cannot answer him but her desperate appeal is
unmistakable.

> TARZAN
> So be it. I'll let this incident
> pass,
>   (faces both men)
> but from now on I'll be watching
> both of you. If I hear so much as
> a whisper out of you concerning
> this woman -- if I see either of
> you even glancing at her, you will
> both have to deal with me,
> personally. Now get out of here!

INT. DE COUDE'S STATEROOM/INT. FIRST-CLASS PASSENGER CORRIDOR
- NIGHT

Tarzan grabs them both by their necks and throws them out
through the entrance, one at a time, to land like two heaps
of deadweight.

He then turns his attention to the awe-struck woman.

                    TARZAN
          Madame, if these two men ever
          trouble you again, all you need do
          is call upon me.

Olga pretends not to know his identity.

                    OLGA
          You are most kind, Monsieur...

                    TARZAN
               (bows)
          ... Tarzan -- forgive me.

Olga is genuinely concerned.

                    OLGA
          I owe you my life, Monsieur
          Tarzan... and I am deeply grateful
          to you for saving it, but I fear
          you have only brought their
          vengeance upon your head. Be
          careful, Monsieur. These are
          wicked, evil men.

                    TARZAN
          You're the second person who's
          given me that warning, but fear
          not, Madame, they will not leave my
          sight for the remainder of the
          voyage.

                    OLGA
          I am in your debt, Monsieur.

With an alluring and illuminating smile, she curtsies.

                    TARZAN
               (bowing)
          Good night, Madame.

After Tarzan leaves, Olga closes the door as best she can and
leaning her back against it, slides down to the floor. She
drops her chin and, covering her face, weeps silently.

EXT. UPPER DECK - DAY (2 DAYS LATER)

Passengers are busy roving about the deck and Tarzan is among
them.

As he nears the steamer chairs, he spies Countess de Coude
approaching from the opposite direction.

She greets him with an exotic, radiant smile and Tarzan's winsome smile is not overlooked by the countess.

Drawn to each other, Olga begins the conversation -- a little nervous and not certain how to begin.

> OLGA
> I'm glad to find you here. I -- I
> just wanted to explain -- I hope
> you don't think less of me for my
> association with those two men.
> And I so do apologize for
> inconveniencing you and -- well --
> ruining your evening.

Tarzan, a perfect gentleman, bows.

> TARZAN
> It was the least I could do,
> Madame. My journey, on the
> contrary, has been better than I
> had hoped. And as for those two
> scoundrels... can a flower be
> blamed for the surrounding weeds?

Olga is put at ease by his steady, strong voice and his charming point of view and with her soft, aristocratic voice...

> OLGA
> That's very sweet of you,
> Monsieur... and elegantly put. You
> sound like a poet. Are you a poet,
> Monsieur Tarzan?

Tarzan is enchanted by her quizzical smile.

> TARZAN
> Not intentionally, but I speak of
> the things I'm familiar with and of
> things I know. And I don't make
> the comparison lightly, because I
> have already encountered their
> corrupt nature in the smoking-room
> during a card game, only a few days
> ago.

Olga turns slightly, about to leave.

> OLGA
> Yes, I know. My husband told me
> all about it. He was very
> impressed by you and feels greatly
> indebted to you, as do I.

Tarzan is taken by surprise.

> TARZAN
> The count is your husband? Then,
> if you knew --

Olga postpones her departure and faces him.

> OLGA
> -- Yes, I am the Countess de Coude.

And then she lies.

> OLGA
> My husband mentioned your name and
> though I've seen you before...

Tarzan grins, a little embarrassed remembering his brazen
stare at the beautiful girl the previous day.

> OLGA
> ... I was unaware that you and
> Monsieur Tarzan, were one and the
> same.

> TARZAN
> Ah, I see. Please forgive my
> misunderstanding.

> OLGA
> But there is nothing to forgive. I
> would have asked the same question.

> TARZAN
> You're very kind, Countess, and may
> I say that it was an honor and a
> pleasure to serve not only the
> count, but his wife as well.

With a graceful curtsy and a breathtaking smile, she takes
her leave.

Tarzan follows her swaying motions, wondering at the
unexpected revelation.

EXT. PORT OF MARSEILLE - DAY

The steam whistle of the French liner blares its lungs as it
nears the harbor where it is met by a pair of tugboats.

UPPER DECK

From the crowded rails, Tarzan looks out at the vista of the port city.

BACK TO SCENE

The albatross, the seagull and many other sea birds welcome the steamship back home.

INT. D'ARNOT'S APARTMENT - LIVING ROOM - DAY

SUPER: "PARIS"

In sumptuous surroundings, Tarzan and LIEUTENANT PAUL D'ARNOT are in a discussion.

Tarzan is stretched out on the couch and D'Arnot is pacing the floor and upbraiding his friend.

The dialogue begins in French with subtitles and then transitions seamlessly into English without the French accent.

> D'ARNOT
> ... I can't believe it!

D'Arnot stops his pacing to glance down at Tarzan.

> D'ARNOT
> How can you give up your birthright
> so easily? Don't you realize that
> you're the son of the two noblest
> houses in England? And what do
> you? You toss it away as if it
> were nothing.

> TARZAN
> (almost laughing)
> Come now, Paul, it's not the end of
> the world and besides it's my title
> and if I don't care why should you?

D'Arnot is annoyed at Tarzan's nonchalant attitude.

> D'ARNOT
> Why?! Because it's wrong. To
> renounce your name, title and
> fortune is just plain madness. No
> man in his right mind would do such
> a thing.

Tarzan sits up, yawns, stretches and then shifts his eyes
towards D'Arnot.

> TARZAN
> Tarzan is the only name I need --
> or want.

> D'ARNOT
> May I remind you, that Tarzan is
> destitute and that Lord Greystoke
> is wealthy. How are you going to
> live your life?

> TARZAN
> I don't plan on remaining
> impoverished. Help me find some
> employment. I'll make the money I
> need plus it'll keep me busy.

> D'ARNOT
> That's not what I meant. Coming
> into your own is what I'm referring
> to. Anyway, all that I have is
> yours. I have more money than I
> know what to do with. You saved my
> life -- you sacrificed more than I
> knew at the time. I can never
> repay you, but in this, I can be of
> help.

Tarzan laughs.

> TARZAN
> Anyway, enough about money.
> Besides, my birthright is in good
> hands. Clayton, has been groomed
> since childhood to be the next Lord
> Greystoke and I for one am content.

Tarzan looks out of one of a windows.

> TARZAN
> Besides, what do you think would
> have happened if I would have
> claimed my right?

He looks back at D'Arnot and continues.

> TARZAN
> It would have taken all that my
> birthright entails from the woman I
> love and made her cleave even more
> to Clayton during his downfall.
> (MORE)

> TARZAN (CONT'D)
> No, I could never have put her
> through that.

D'Arnot doesn't share his decision.

> D'ARNOT
> The day will come when you may want
> to claim your right and the longer
> you wait the more difficult it may
> become.

> TARZAN
> Perhaps, my friend, but without her
> none of it matters to me.

MONTAGE - TARZAN IN PARIS

1) Tarzan sits in a library going through a stack of books
late into the evening.

2) Tarzan browses the museums and sites.

3) Tarzan and D'Arnot hit the nightlife, attending music
halls, cabarets, gambling houses, operas and are trailed by a
shadowy figure.

4) Tarzan and D'Arnot step out along the Champs Elysees and
stop at cafes and theaters and are stalked by a shadowy
figure.

INT. PORTER HOUSE - LIBRARY - DAY

Prof. Porter sits in his chair smoking a pipe and reading a
very thick volume.

Mr. Philander reads the paper in a another chair.

Jane lounges on the couch knitting.

Esmeralda's joyful voice brings life into the library as she
waltzes in with a large platter filled with food.

> ESMERALDA
> (in Southern black accent)
> Smile everybody! It's time to eat.

As one, they all stop what they're doing and obeying her
command, smile to varying degrees.

                    MR. PHILANDER
You're just in time. My stomach
was beginning to interrupt my
reading.

                    PROF. PORTER
        (puffing pipe)
I can vouch for that!

Jane gets up chuckling and helps Esmeralda. She grabs her
order.

                    JANE
Which one's Mr. Philander's?

                    ESMERALDA
        (in Souther black accent)
The roast beef sandwich.

Jane hands Mr. Philander the sandwich on a small platter.

                    MR. PHILANDER
Thank you, me dear. If only your
father were as kind.

Jane laughs.

                    ESMERALDA
        (in Southern black accent;
         to Prof. Porter)
Here's your food, and a letter.

                    PROF. PORTER
A letter? From who?

                    ESMERALDA
        (in Southern black accent)
From Mr. Clayton.

Prof. Porter puts his food aside and pushing back his
spectacles, scans the envelope.

                    PROF. PORTER
Ah! And so it is! It's been a
month since he left. Hopefully,
he'll be coming back soon.

Prof. Porter puffs his pipe as he reads.

Mr. Philander munches on his sandwich as he watches the
professor.

Jane and Esmeralda do likewise from the comfort of the couch.

Finishing, Prof. Porter stands up and taps his pipe on the
side table, like a gavel.

                    PROF. PORTER
               Our esteemed friend and Jane's
               fiance, has invited us all to
               London, and that includes you too,
               Esmeralda.

                    ESMERALDA
                    (in Southern black accent)
               As long as it's not to a jungle,
               it's fine with me.

Jane laughs and nudges the big, warm-hearted woman with a
delicate shoulder.

                    PROF. PORTER
               He says it's time his future bride
               became acquainted with her future
               home.

Jane's smile subsides as she pretends to focus on her meal.

                    PROF. PORTER
               I for one agree and I am glad for
               the opportunity to do some
               travelling again. He advises us to
               bring only what we absolutely need
               because everything and anything
               will be provided.

Prof. Porter looks around the room.

                    PROF. PORTER
               Does anyone have any questions?

                    MR. PHILANDER
               Yes, when do we leave?

Prof. Porter is forced into a smile by his dear friend.

                    PROF. PORTER
               You're a man after my own heart,
               Mr. Philander. Next week, we sail
               for London.

The ever watchful Mr. Philander doesn't miss Jane's downcast
reaction to the news.

INT. MUSIC HALL (PARIS) - NIGHT (2 WEEKS LATER)

Drinking alone, Tarzan watches a Russian dancer. The music
hall is well lit with tables filled with patrons enjoying the
show.

As he puts down his glass, his sixth sense kicks in and
turning about spots a WATCHER with a pair of villainous eyes.

The man quickly mixes with the people in the back and
disappears through the exit.

The momentary sighting stirs up his memory, but unable to
place it, he picks up his glass and takes another sip. The
thought fades as he casts his eyes back on the performer.

EXT. MUSIC HALL - NIGHT

The Watcher takes to the shadows across from the music hall
as Tarzan exits the entertainment venue.

Tarzan begins his journey back home along his customary route
and the Watcher moves quickly ahead of him.

EXT. PARIS - RUE MAULE - NIGHT

On a dark and quiet street Tarzan strides leisurely to his
apartment through a dilapidated neighborhood. He threads
along the obstacle course, skirting around trash and thrown
trash cans and leaping over potholes in the cobblestone
street.

Alley cats dash out of his way and watch as the intruder
passes by. Human shapes slink into dark recesses to avoid
detection.

A few blocks into the street and SCREAMS from a woman fill
the night air. He looks up towards the source and dashes
into an apartment building.

INT. APARTMENT BUILDING - NIGHT

Tarzan leaps up an unlighted

STAIRCASE

to reach the distress call. Her desperate cries lead him
through a dark

THIRD-FLOOR CORRIDOR

and finally to a

DOOR

that is partially open.

INT. SCREAMER'S APARTMENT - NIGHT

Once inside Tarzan finds himself surrounded by twelve
sinister goons in a dingy room.

Four candles in sconces, distributed to the four corners of
the room, cast their feeble, amber light on their sneering,
malevolent mugs.

The SCREAMER, though young, wears a wasted face from a life
of dissolution.

                    SCREAMER
          Oh, Monsieur, thank heaven you've
          come. These men --

Movement draws Tarzan's attention behind him to discover
Rokoff stealing out of the room and simultaneously from the
corner of his eye Tarzan detects a huge rogue with a matching
cudgel about to brain him.

Tarzan dodges the club and crushes the man's skull with his
anvil-like fist and as one, the rest fall upon him, but
Tarzan turns the tables.

Dropping the thin curtain of civilization, Tarzan reverts
back to his savage roots and lashes out with all the bestial
ferocity imbued within his powerful body and resourceful
mind.

ROKOFF/WATCHER

waits outside in the corridor as the horrible growls and
snarls and the sounds of shrieking men reach his dumbfounded
ears. Realizing that his plan has backfired, he flies from
the corridor and into another

APARTMENT

where he places a call.

BACK TO SCENE

With unmatched speed and fighting like the bull-ape, Tarzan
is everywhere tearing out throats with his powerful jaws,
breaking arms, legs and faces as he rips and rends in all
directions with the fury and the power of a lion.

Tarzan roars, freezing the blood of several of the men who
swiftly fall mangled under his mighty and merciless muscles.

One, he hurls through a window with the shattered glass and
splintered wood trailing him as he screeches to the street
below.

Tarzan lifts up an apache high above his head and launches
him into the backs of the fleeing men helping them out of
door and into the black corridor.

MOMENTS LATER

A sudden rush of footsteps moving up the staircase keeps
Tarzan prepared and at bay.

Instead of thugs, four policemen enter the apartment and find
multiple, broken bodies moaning or motionless on the floor
and the Screamer cringing against the wall in wide-eyed
terror.

                    POLICEMAN 1
          What happened here, Monsieur?

Tarzan recognizing the police, relaxes his posture somewhat
and explains.

                    TARZAN
          This woman screamed and when I ran
          up here to help her, I was attacked
          by these men.

The policemen look at Tarzan and then at all the bodies on
the floor.

                    POLICEMAN 2
          You did all this?

                    TARZAN
          I had no choice.

Tarzan nods towards the Screamer.

                    TARZAN
          She will corroborate what I've just
          told you.

                    POLICEMAN 1
            Well, Mademoiselle?

                    SCREAMER
            He's a liar!

Tarzan is bowled over by her countering outburst.

                    SCREAMER
            This man broke into my apartment
            and tried to kill me and when I
            screamed these men came running to
            my aid.

                    POLICEMAN 2
            Well, Monsieur, what have you to
            say against her accusation?

                    TARZAN
            I've told you the truth but I
            cannot explain why she would lie to
            you.

                    SCREAMER
            Are you going to do your job or are
            you going to let him get away with
            attempted murder?

The policemen unable to make heads or tails of the incident
that just took place, do what they're trained to do.

                    POLICEMAN 1
            I'm afraid you're both under
            arrest.

They cuff the woman and then one approaches Tarzan.

                    TARZAN
            Wait, I've committed no crime. You
            cannot arrest me for defending
            myself.

                    POLICEMAN 1
            Don't make it difficult for us,
            Monsieur. Since we do not know
            what happened here we must take
            both of you into custody.

POLICEMAN 1 makes a costly mistake and puts a hand on him and
Tarzan grabs him swiftly with one arm and flings him across
room into a wall and Policeman 1 collapses, like a spiritless
corpse, to the floor.

The other three jump into the maelstrom and Tarzan knocks one into oblivion. He then lifts the other two, like rag dolls, and sends them flying through the air to kiss the same wall their partner just encountered.

As one of the policemen recovers, Tarzan jumps onto the window sill with the agility of a great cat and leaps outwards towards a telegraph pole, chased by a missing bullet.

EXT. PARIS - ROOFTOPS - NIGHT

Tarzan trots among the rooftops and leaps across wide gaps as he negotiates the higher altitudes of Paris.

With a short burst of incredible speed Tarzan leaps far out from the edge of a building to nab another pole and quickly descends.

EXT. PARIS - STREET - NIGHT

Tarzan touches down on a dark street and speeds towards a lighted boulevard. As he nears the lights he slows to a quick walk.

EXT. PARIS - BOULEVARD - NIGHT

Once on the boulevard, Tarzan heads for the nearest open cafe.

INT. CAFE - NIGHT

Smiling and nodding, he makes for the bathroom.

BATHROOM

Tarzan cleans the blood stains from his hands and puts the rest of himself and his suit in order.

EXT. BOULEVARD - NIGHT

Tarzan stands under the lights of the boulevard waiting for the cars to pass.

At the end of a train of cars, Tarzan sees a beautiful 1909 Rolls-Royce Silver Ghost.

INT./EXT. SILVER GHOST - NIGHT

As the limousine nears Tarzan, Olga seated within, catches
sight of him.

She peers out of the window and greets him with a wondrous
smile, and waves.

                    OLGA
          Monsieur, Tarzan!

Tarzan bows as the limousine continues on it's way and rising
up, wonders.

                    TARZAN
          Rokoff and the countess... the same
          night. Coincidence, or chance?

INT. D'ARNOT'S APARTMENT - BREAKFAST ROOM - MORNING

D'Arnot eats and listens as Tarzan sums up the events of the
previous evening.

                    TARZAN
          ... After it was all over, I
          hurried back here as fast as
          humanly possible. Paris, is much
          more treacherous and dangerous than
          the jungle.

D'Arnot takes a drink of his morning coffee to help push down
the food.

                    D'ARNOT
               (in a French accent)
          Yes, I quite agree, especially when
          you wipe the floor with the French
          police.

D'Arnot finishes his coffee and then makes use of the napkin.

                    D'ARNOT
               (in a French accent)
          They won't forget, you know? And
          we must pay them a visit before you
          and they, meet again.

                    TARZAN
          I rush to a woman's aid and now I'm
          the villain? Is that the kind of
          justice I am to expect from
          civilization?

                    D'ARNOT
               (in a French accent)
          I understand why you did it. They
          don't. Furthermore, there are very
          precise procedures which they must
          follow in their daily routines as
          policemen.

Tarzan eyes his friend.

                    TARZAN
          They tried to lock me up... and
          that was not going to happen.

Tarzan's serious tone draws a concerned look from D'Arnot.

                    D'ARNOT
               (in a French accent)
          There are laws in your jungle, and
          there are laws in Paris.

D'Arnot gets up and grabs his coat.

                    D'ARNOT
               (in a French accent)
          And besides, I warned you not to
          take the Rue Maule... and for good
          reason.

                    TARZAN
               (smiling)
          Well, you're wrong. Last night was
          the best time I've had since I've
          been back. I will make it a point
          to go through there as often as I
          can.

D'Arnot laughs at his friend's grim humor.

                    D'ARNOT
               (in a French accent)
          Come, let's be on our way. It's a
          good thing for you that the
          inspector and I have become quite
          good friends since our first visit.

Tarzan gets up, gulps the rest of his coffee, wipes his mouth
with a napkin, slips on his coat and follows D'Arnot out of
the room.

INT. POLICE STATION - INSPECTOR'S OFFICE - MORNING

Tarzan and D'Arnot are seated before the INSPECTOR's desk.
He listens calmly as D'Arnot recounts Tarzan's episode of the
previous night.

After he finishes, the Inspector smiles, looks down at his
desk, shuffles through a few papers for a specific report and
finding it, he presses a button and a clerk enters.

                    INSPECTOR
          Joubon, take this and have these
          men report to me immediately.

The clerk takes the paper, leaves and closes the door behind
him.

The Inspector addresses Tarzan with an understanding
attitude.

                    INSPECTOR
          Monsieur Tarzan, your actions last
          night would normally merit an
          uncompromising sentence; but, in
          light of Monsieur D'Arnot's
          summation of the events in question
          and the reasons for your abuse of
          my police officers, I will do
          nothing.

He looks from Tarzan to D'Arnot and then resumes.

                    INSPECTOR
          You left quite a mess in the Rue
          Maule. Many of those men are dead
          and I thank you... Paris thanks
          you. For many years they plagued
          our city and you have done us a
          great service, but assaulting
          police officers is a serious
          matter. I will let the men you
          assaulted decide what is to be done
          with you after they hear what
          Monsieur D'Arnot just told me.

Several knocks pull their eyes to the door and when the four
police officers enter, Tarzan and D'Arnot rise and turn to
face them.

Rattled and surprised, the four take an involuntary step
back, beholding the very man who so easily bested them the
previous night.

After formally being introduced, D'Arnot retells the tale.

INT. POLICE STATION - INSPECTOR'S OFFICE - LATER

                    D'ARNOT
          ... And so you see, gentlemen,
          Tarzan was guided by animal
          instinct, and not by any attempt on
          his part to evade our laws.

The four policemen look at one another for some kind of
mutual decision.

                    D'ARNOT
          I know your pride has been wounded
          but you have nothing to be
          humiliated or ashamed about. This
          man you fought with last night
          fights lions and other powerful
          creatures in his jungle on a daily
          basis... and overpowers them. How
          then can you feel offended when he
          is able to overcome you?

The four men are silent, but Tarzan, humbled by their
crestfallen expressions, approaches them.

                    TARZAN
          Gentlemen, please pardon my
          ignorance... I'm truly sorry for
          what I did.

Warmed by Tarzan's humble repentance the men forgive him.

                    POLICEMAN 1
          It's an amazing story, Monsieur.
          Nevertheless, we hope we never have
          the pleasure of meeting you again,
          if it entails a disturbance.

His remark draws laughter from everyone in the room and the
rest of the policemen with their pride restored, AD LIB the
events that brought them all together.

INT. D'ARNOT'S APARTMENT - LIVING ROOM - LATE MORNING

Tarzan lies on the couch without coat, tie or shoes reading
the newspaper.

D'Arnot plops into his armchair and scans his mail until he
comes across a certain letter.

                    D'ARNOT
              (in a French accent)
          Ah! A letter from our mutual
          friend, Clayton.

                    TARZAN
          You mean, your friend... he's not
          mine.

D'Arnot, ignoring Tarzan's comment, cons the letter and
finishing...

                    D'ARNOT
              (in a French accent)
          He says they're to be married in
          London in two months time.

Tarzan's tranquil countenance tightens ever so slightly over
the news.

EXT. PALAIS GARNIER - NIGHT

Limousines, taxis and horse drawn carriages pull-up before
the majestic facade of the opera house.

Dressed for the occasion, men, with women at their sides,
enter the renown edifice.

INT. PALAIS GARNIER - NIGHT

Like a beacon from a lighthouse, the stage lures the eyes of
nearly two-thousand audience members, except one pair.

Beneath the golden glow of the chandelier, hanging overhead
like a gigantic jewel, Tarzan's eyes stare straight ahead,
but not at the extraordinary dancers, but within -- and then,
he nods off.

NIGHTMARE - EXT. JUNGLE - DAY

A fair face crowned with golden locks mixes and dissolves
within swirling clouds.

Dressed in suit and tie, he forces his way through the
choking jungle after the fleeing beauty.

His clothes begin to shred -- to be torn to ribbons -- the
further he chases her into the bosom of the unforgiving
jungle.

The tumultuous sound of rolling thunder begins to dissolve the elusive doe before him and he melts into the realm of drowning mists.

Thunderous applause awakens Tarzan back to reality as he rejoins, reluctantly, the exuberant audience.

His uncanny sixth sense, sends his eyes into the lofts above to meet the glittering eyes of the Countess Olga de Coude smiling down upon him -- beckoning him to join her.

The intermission begins and D'Arnot and Tarzan stand-up to leave.

                    TARZAN
          Forgive me, but I'll have to leave
          you for awhile. My presence is
          requested.

D'Arnot follows his eyes and catching her gaze, he smiles and bows to the fanning countess who acknowledges his courtesy.

                    D'ARNOT
          The lovely Countess de Coude. I
          know her and her husband well, but
          when did you meet them?

                    TARZAN
          Aboard the steamer.

                    D'ARNOT
          I see you skipped a few important
          details from your voyage.

                    TARZAN
               (grinning)
          Remind me to tell you someday.

INT. PALAIS GARNIER - OPERA BOX - NIGHT

Dressed in blue and glittering diamonds, Olga waits impatiently for Tarzan.

The door opens and, rising like a decked out column, she faces the door.

Tarzan with a wide shaft of light behind him enters and closing the door, squelches it.

With a winsome smile, he bows.

                    TARZAN
          Good evening, Countess, it's good
          to see you again.

                    OLGA
          Likewise, Monsieur Tarzan...
          please, let us sit.

BALCONY

In the lowest balcony across from the high opera box where
Tarzan and Olga sit and hidden by the shadows, Rokoff and
Paulvitch watch with glee.

Wicked grins wrinkle their faces. They regard one another
for a moment and Rokoff tapping Paulvitch on a shoulder,
sends his cruel countenance towards the box in exultation.

                    ROKOFF
          Perfect!

BACK TO SCENE

                    OLGA
          ... I see that you and I have a
          mutual friend.

                    TARZAN
          No better friend can a man have,
          than Paul D'Arnot.

                    OLGA
          We are both fortunate in that
          respect... and unfortunate in
          another.

Fanning herself nervously with a matching fan, she looks
across into the almost empty auditorium. She rests her
partially folded fan on her lap and faces her invited guest.

                    OLGA
          I've been very anxious to see you
          again. I suppose you don't think
          very much of me or my husband for
          allowing those two vile creatures
          to torment us as they do.

                    TARZAN
          On the contrary, I hold you and
          your husband in the highest regard.

Olga's radiant smile lights up the box.

                         OLGA
          You are very gracious with your
          compliments, Monsieur, yet I feel I
          owe you an explanation.

                         TARZAN
          As I mentioned on the ship, I was
          honored to have been able to serve
          you. You owe me nothing. I hope
          they've not been a thorn at your
          side lately -- have they?

                         OLGA
          Not of late, but if only you knew
          them as I do -- they're merciless
          wolves. They never cease in their
          evil plots. Again, I advise you to
          look out for them, for they will be
          after you. I have some information
          that may help you against Rokoff --
          but not here. Will you be able to
          visit me at five tomorrow?

Tarzan stands up.

                         TARZAN
          It will be an honor, Countess.

                         OLGA
          Do you know where we live?

                         TARZAN
          I don't but I believe are mutual
          friend does.

Olga nods.

                         TARZAN
          At five then?

                         OLGA
          Yes, please. I'll be expecting
          you.

                         TARZAN
                (bowing)
          Good night, Countess.

Tarzan closes the door behind him and Olga puts her fan to
work.

The auditorium begins receiving its audience anew, as Olga watches from on high.

                                        FADE TO BLACK:

KNOCK.   KNOCK.   KNOCK.

INT./EXT. DE COUDE'S PALACE - SERVANT'S ENTRANCE - NEXT DAY (4:30 PM)

The door opens and the footman is struck by the presence of Rokoff, who's foul smile spreads his face unevenly.

Pressed for time, he begins to haggle with the footman in low tones. The footman shakes his head, but after an exchange between hands, the footman motions for Rokoff to follow in silence.

INT. DE COUDE'S PALACE - DRAWING ROOM - AFTERNOON (5 PM)

Tarzan is ushered into an empty, luxuriant but cozy drawing room. With his arms behind his back, he looks at the paintings upon the walls and other museum pieces that attract his attention.

A sweet-sounding voice permeates the air and stops his inspection of the room.

                    OLGA (O.S.)
          Welcome, Monsieur Tarzan.

Tarzan turns to find the ravishing countess hurrying towards him with outstretched arms.

Taking her hands, they greet.

                    OLGA
          I'm so pleased that you were able
          to come.

Tarzan smiles.

                    TARZAN
          I wouldn't have missed it for all
          of Paris.

Sitting on a couch next to each other, Olga commences to speak only to be interrupted by the maid who sets the coffee on the table before them, pours it and bows out of the room.

Once the door is closed she begins again.

                    OLGA
          I'll try to explain everything to
          you before I lose my courage...
          Nikolas, as you may already know is
          my brother; he and Paulvitch are
          also Russian spies.

Olga sips her coffee and continues as Tarzan listens on
patiently.

                    OLGA
          My husband works for the Ministry
          of War with access to many state
          secrets that a spy would kill to
          possess... that is why he tried to
          blackmail first my husband and then
          me. You, thank God, ruined his
          plans.

                    TARZAN
          I was glad to do it.

Tarzan puts down his coffee.

                    TARZAN
          Perhaps I'm not following all you
          say. If this is the problem, I
          still cannot understand why you and
          your husband don't have them
          arrested. With the information you
          already have and my testimony, they
          could be thrown in jail for a very
          long time... perhaps even executed.

ALCOVE

Hidden behind a curtain, Rokoff watches and listens to the
pair. His malignant features twist as he salivates at the
scene before him.

BACK TO SCENE

Like the wings of a hummingbird, the fan strives to cool the
cherubic cheeks of her mistress.

                    OLGA
          Paulvitch would be the first.
          That's why he tried to kill me.
          For I know something about him that
          merits the gallows in Russia. My
          husband does nothing, because I've
          begged him not to and I --

Her fan picks up speed as she searches for the reinforcements needed to tell her tale. She stops fanning and takes a long sip.

> OLGA
>
> I'm not sure why, but I feel that I can trust you with what I'm about to tell you... something I dare not tell my own husband.

Putting down the coffee and resting her lovely hands on her lap she continues.

> OLGA
>
> When I was younger my father, a count, sent me to a convent for my education and there I met a man I thought I loved. Well, we eloped for a whole of three hours time. All, in public places. But as he disembarked from the train he was arrested for desertion from the army and many other crimes. Once they found out who I was, I was sent back to the convent. All this was kept quiet by the convent and forgotten.

Olga stands up and Tarzan with her. She walks a few paces back and forth and finally approaches him and looks up into his handsome, noble face.

> OLGA
>
> Somehow Rokoff met this very man who held back nothing in the telling of what had transpired between us. This is what he's been holding over my head... threatening to tell my husband unless I comply.

Tarzan begins to laugh lightly and she not understanding, smiles with questioning eyes.

> OLGA
>
> What is it?

> TARZAN
>
> My dear Countess, your pure heart is the only thing holding you back. Otherwise, you would see that you're not to blame.
> (MORE)

                    TARZAN (CONT'D)
          Tell your husband what you've just
          told me and I assure that he will
          be but amused at your
          unsubstantiated fears. Tell him.
          Tell him all as soon as you can and
          you'll be free of this pestilence
          once and for all.

Olga puts her hand to her full lips to calm the apprehension
creeping upon her countenance.

                    OLGA
          I wish I could be sure. Do you
          think -- no but I couldn't. He
          would never --

                    TARZAN
          -- Countess, if I understand... the
          count will undoubtedly understand
          even more.

                    OLGA
          Oh, I wish I could, but I fear him.

Tarzan expresses concern at such a comment.

                    TARZAN
          I do not believe a woman should
          fear her husband. A woman should
          feel safe and secure with her man,
          not fear. I would not like it if
          my woman feared me.

Olga stares at him with a hint of anxiety.

                    OLGA
          I'll try, Monsieur Tarzan.

Tarzan takes her hands to strengthen her.

                    TARZAN
          Lose your fear, Countess, and you
          won't have to try.

                    OLGA
          You must drop by tomorrow for
          coffee... say you will.

Tarzan thinks for a moment and not wanting to disappoint
her...

                    TARZAN
          Far be it from me to go against
          your wishes, Madame... until
          tomorrow, then.

Olga smiles and, pressing a button, summons the butler.

Tarzan bows and departs with the butler leading the way,
leaving her in the drawing room to ponder his advise.

Olga's thoughts are invaded by the sudden slide of a curtain
being drawn to one side.

Wheeling about she finds herself face-to-face with Rokoff!

The countess is furious.

                    OLGA
          You!

She sees the drawn curtain and the exposed alcove.

                    OLGA
          How long have you been here?

Rokoff winds his way towards her, smiling like a hyena.

                    ROKOFF
          Since before you two entered.

                    OLGA
          Get out this instant or I'll have
          you thrown out.

                    ROKOFF
          Dear sister, your own brother?
          Come now, let us come to an
          understanding.

                    OLGA
          You've been wicked since I can
          remember. There can never be any
          understanding between us and
          tonight Raoul will learn of my
          elopement and your hold over me
          will be broken.

Like a crocodile, Rokoff takes hold of his victim.

                    ROKOFF
          Bah, that was intangible. But now,
          this affair with Monsieur Tarzan,
          is very real.

> OLGA
> How dare you suggest such a thing.
> You were here and you saw. There
> was nothing improper in our
> meeting. Now get out!

> ROKOFF
> Perhaps not in your words or
> actions, but your eyes and voice
> said otherwise. Any other man...
> well....

He opens his hands to rest his case.

> OLGA
> Regardless of what you may think, I
> will tell Raoul all and --

The crocodile begins to pull his prey underwater.

> ROKOFF
> -- You will say nothing! One word
> from me and one of your servants
> will whisper a few words into your
> husband's ear.

> OLGA
> He wouldn't believe it.

> ROKOFF
> Really? You. Alone. With a
> young, tall, and handsome man? Are
> you willing to take that risk. I
> think not.

Laughing, he sees himself out.

> ROKOFF
> Goodbye, my dear little sister, and
> thank you.

> OLGA
> You beast!

Olga drops into the couch, defeated.

INT. DE COUDE'S PALACE - DRAWING ROOM - AFTERNOON (NEXT DAY)

Tarzan is announced and ushered in, where Olga is
entertaining a clique of close friends. Tarzan is introduced
and joins the conversation in step.

MONTAGE - FRIENDS AND ENEMIES

1) Tarzan and D'Arnot visit De Coude's palace and the four dine together.

2) Tarzan and Olga sit in the drawing room drinking coffee, talking and laughing.

3) Rokoff and Paulvitch keep tabs on Tarzan's visits and outings with Olga.

4) Tarzan and Olga sit in the Opera Box enjoying each other's company and the opera.

5) Tarzan, Olga, and D'Arnot converse at an upscale cafe on the Champs-Elysees.

6) Rokoff watches in disgust as Tarzan leaves the countess at the entrance of her home after a night venue.

                                        FADE TO BLACK:

SUPER: "1 MONTH LATER"

INT. ROKOFF'S APARTMENT - LIVING ROOM - DAY

Rokoff and Paulvitch are sitting at a table brainstorming.

                    ROKOFF
          ... He'll never go in after dark
          when the count is not at home! We
          must find a way to get him inside
          and alone with Olga.

                    PAULVITCH
          But how? He's too much of a
          gentleman.

                    ROKOFF
          There's always a way, my friend.

Rokoff picks up the paper and Paulvitch likewise takes a break from plotting by leaning back and drinking his cold coffee.

Grinning, Rokoff folds the paper to focus on a particular section. He places it on the table oriented to Paulvitch's view, and pushes it towards him.

                    ROKOFF
          Did I not tell you that there is
          always a way?

Paulvitch still drinking his coffee picks it up but can't find whatever it is that caught Rokoff's eye.

                    PAULVITCH
          What am I looking for?

Rokoff irritated.

                    ROKOFF
          Must I do everything? Read the one
          about the German ambassador.

Paulvitch scans the newspaper article. The article shows a picture of the German ambassador and speaks of a smoker to be given by him the following day -- at his place -- with a list of invited guests. Count de Coude, is one of them.

Paulvitch looks up from the paper.

                    PAULVITCH
          Finally! This is exactly what
          we've been hoping for.

He throws his head back and finishes the coffee.

                    ROKOFF
          Yes, but will he attend? We must
          know for certain.

Paulvitch nods and starts chomping on a crusty croissant.

INT./EXT. PAULVITCH'S CAR - NIGHT (NEXT DAY)

Parked along the curb at the German ambassador's residence, Paulvitch, narrow-eyed, watches as the invited guests exit their limousines and other means of transport.

Soon his patience is rewarded as Count de Coude steps out of his limo.

Paulvitch, grinning from ear-to-ear, hurries back to Rokoff.

                                        FADE TO BLACK:

A telephone receiver is lifted and a number is dialed.

                    PAULVITCH (V.O.)
          Yes, good evening... I have a
          message for Monsieur Tarzan...
          thank you.

Silence. Then...

                    PAULVITCH (V.O.)
          Monsieur Tarzan? I am Francois...
          a servant of the Countess de
          Coude... she says that it is
          imperative that you come at once...
          no, Monsieur, I do not know why...
          she says it is critical and begs
          your presence... yes, Monsieur, I
          will tell her... thank you,
          Monsieur Tarzan, we shall expect
          you shortly.

INT. ROKOFF'S APARTMENT - LIVING ROOM - NIGHT

The receiver is hung back onto a wooden, wall phone.

Paulvitch turns and glances at Rokoff with a fiendish grin
and sits down at the table.

Rokoff strokes his Vandyke beard as he thinks.

                    ROKOFF
          It will take Tarzan no more than
          thirty minutes -- you have the
          note?

Paulvitch pulls it out partially from his inner breast coat
pocket.

                    ROKOFF
          Good. Go now. It should take you
          fifteen minutes to the German
          ambassador's home and from there,
          it will take the count...

Rokoff gestures with a hand, as he calculates.

                    ROKOFF
          ... About the same amount of time
          as Tarzan. So, thirty minutes.
          Olga will give us the rest of the
          time we need.

                    PAULVITCH
          What if she doesn't? What if --

                    ROKOFF
          -- Don't worry, she will. She
          won't permit Tarzan to leave her
          side after just arriving. Trust
          me. Now off with you, there's no
          time to waste.

Paulvitch leaves Rokoff alone at the table and as the door closes, Rokoff takes note of the time.

INT./EXT. GERMAN AMBASSADOR'S RESIDENCE - NIGHT

A car brakes and its door is left open as Paulvitch hustles to the ambassador's front door.

It's opened by a footman, who's not given an opportunity to speak.

>   PAULVITCH
>   Give this to the Count de Coude.
>   It is crucial that it be put into
>   his hands.

Paulvitch drops a pair of silver coins into the Footman's hand and without looking back scoots into his horseless carriage and darts away.

INT. GERMAN AMBASSADOR'S RESIDENCE - DRAWING ROOM - NIGHT

Cigar and pipe smoke, conversation, and laughter rise above men spread throughout the room, drinking, playing cards or eating.

One group of men is standing in a circle talking, laughing and joking as they smoke cigars.

The footman enters and after looking about the room sees Count de Coude among the men in the standing circle. To make himself heard above the bedlam, the footman nears the count on the left side and speaks almost into his ear and then hands him the envelope.

Count de Coude excuses himself from the group and as he walks in the direction of the bar, he opens the envelope and reading, stops dead in his tracks.

The letter morphs from French into English.

INSERT - ROKOFF'S LETTER

>   "Count de Coude,
>
>   a man you know is at this very
>   moment with your wife in her
>   boudoir. I beg you, Monsieur, to
>   hurry before all is lost.
>
>   An Old Friend."

BACK TO SCENE

Count de Coude never makes it to the bar. Like a dead man,
all the blood drains from his face.

He staggers a step backward as if mortally wounded, shakes
his head lightly, closes his eyes and when they reopen,
crumbles the letter in his fist.

Excusing himself, Count de Coude rushes out of the rumpus,
smoked-filled, drawing room.

INT. DE COUDE'S PALACE - BOUDOIR - NIGHT (5 MINUTES LATER)

On a small, elegant table draped with an intricate cloth,
stands an exquisite lamp over an artesian telephone. Two
matching figurines decorate each side of the table.

Serene silence reigns in the room until the delicate ringing
of the phone draws a feminine hand a few moments later.

A YOUNG MAID picks up the cradled receiver.

                    YOUNG MAID
          Hello?

INT. ROKOFF'S APARTMENT - LIVING ROOM - NIGHT

                    ROKOFF
          I wish to speak to the Countess de
          Coude.

INTERCUT - TELEPHONE CONVERSATION

                    YOUNG MAID
          I'm sorry, Monsieur, the countess
          has retired for the evening.

                    ROKOFF
          Please tell her that this is an
          emergency and that I will call back
          in five minutes.

END INTERCUT

Rokoff drops the receiver on the hook.

INT. ROKOFF'S APARTMENT - LIVING ROOM - 10 MINUTES LATER

Paulvitch enters.

> ROKOFF
> Did he get the message?

> PAULVITCH
> I'm sure of it.

Paulvitch removes his coat.

> ROKOFF
> Excellent!

Rokoff begins to laugh as he moves to the table.

> PAULVITCH
> At this very moment he's sure to be
> racing home to save his precious
> honor.

> ROKOFF
> Olga should be up and awaiting my
> call by now and dressed in a most
> becoming, and I might add, sheer
> negligee that will outline her
> charms rather nicely.

Paulvitch throws the coat on the couch and joins Rokoff who
is now sitting at the table with a bottle of vodka and two
glasses.

Rokoff smiles as he pours the liquor.

> ROKOFF
> And Jacques will soon escort our
> esteemed Tarzan into her boudoir,
> unannounced.

Rokoff gloats in unsuppressed laughter.

> ROKOFF
> I would give my right arm to be
> there and see it myself, but
> enough. Let us drink to our sweet
> revenge.

> PAULVITCH
> To our sweet revenge.

Two glasses crash above the table.

EXT. DE COUDE'S PALACE - NIGHT

Before the great facade of the palace, a black Rolland-Pilain
E Ventoux comes to an abrupt stop.

Tarzan hops out and trots up the stairs to be met by JACQUES
who's standing outside the door.

                    JACQUES
          Good evening, Monsieur. Please
          follow me, the countess is
          expecting you.

INT. DE COUDE'S PALACE - NIGHT

Jacques escorts Tarzan up the wide, marble staircase
straddled between two sets of marble bannisters supported by
elegantly designed balusters standing side by side, like
decorated soldiers.

Above the circular, bottom posts of the staircase, hang two
small lightly lit, resplendent chandeliers.

Moving through a gallery punctuated with priceless art,
Jacques stops at a door, opens it, draws a rich curtain aside
and bows, motioning for Tarzan to enter.

BOUDOIR

Dressed in a diaphanous negligee covered by a clinging robe,
Olga sits before the little table waiting for the phone to
ring.

As she flips through the pages of a fashion magazine she's
unaware that anyone but her is within the room until...

                    TARZAN (O.S.)
          Olga, what is the matter?

Olga's face is struck with shock as she's jolted to her feet
by Tarzan's unexpected, surprise visit.

                    OLGA
          Jean, what are you doing here?!

She ties off her robe around her narrow waist, but it only
accentuates her curves all the more.

A shadow of suspicion descends upon Tarzan.

                    TARZAN
          Didn't you wish to see me, at once?

                    OLGA
          I didn't send for you.

                    TARZAN
          Someone did... a servant of yours
          named Francois.

Olga shakes her head a little confused.

                    OLGA
          But I have no such servant under
          that name.

A delicious smile begins to spread across her face.

                    OLGA
          Someone has played a practical joke
          on you this night.

Placing a gentle hand over her lips, she begins to laugh
politely.

Tarzan sees it for what it is and doesn't share her humor.

                    TARZAN
          I'm afraid, Olga, that it was not a
          mere joke -- where is the count?

Olga's laughter subsides.

                    OLGA
          He was invited to a smoker this
          evening... at the German
          ambassador's. But you don't
          imagine --

                    TARZAN
          -- I'm not imagining, this is your
          brother's handiwork and somehow
          your husband will hear the wrong
          version of the story just as Rokoff
          would have it.

Filled with anxiety and uncertainty, Olga floats closer to
Tarzan with her alluring robe flowing behind her.

                    OLGA
          But what can we do?

She looks up at him with fear and vulnerability and with
doleful, teary eyes and with trembling full lips she places a
hand on his broad chest to steady her nerves.

                    OLGA
          I know Nikolas. He'll inform the
          papers and tomorrow the whole city
          will....

Tarzan instinctively puts a comforting arm about her and both
become instantly electrified beyond their control.

Unable to resist, Olga clasps her arms around his neck with
her bosom rising and falling rapidly.

Tarzan melts into her wondrous eyes and covers her parted
lips with burning kisses.

EXT. COUNT DE COUDE'S PALACE - SAME TIME

A limousine stops and Raoul, with cane in hand, exits and
jogging up the stairs, finds the door already open.

INT. COUNT DE COUDE'S PALACE - NIGHT

Up the low lit staircase he moves with caution and
deliberation, tiptoeing through the gallery for his wife's
boudoir.

BOUDOIR

Count de Coude enters to discover his wife in the arms of
another.

As she parts her lips from Tarzan to catch her breath, Olga's
eyes open in fear as she sees her husband striding towards
them with retribution etched on a merciless face.

                    OLGA
          Jean!

Tarzan, alarmed, turns in time to ward off the first blow
from Count de Coude's heavy cane.

In quick succession two more powerful strikes follow and
Tarzan transforms into a very savage bull-ape.

Tarzan snatches away the cane and snaps it as if it were a
mere matchstick.

Snarling, he casts the two pieces aside and with blinding
speed he shoots his hands for the Frenchman's throat and body
lifting him high above his head like a babe and begins to
crush the life out of him.

Olga rushes to the ape-man's side and tries desperately to save the life of her husband.

                    OLGA
          Stop, Jean, you're killing him!

She pulls at his arms but to no avail. Tarzan is lost in the berserker rage of the great anthropoids.

Tarzan's scar, running from above his left eye to his right ear, comes to life as in mad rage he shakes the count until he hangs limp and throwing him to the floor stamps his foot on his vanquished enemy.

Tarzan raises a snarling, savage face upwards and bellows out the powerful, long drawn-out, eerie roar of the victorious bull-ape, reverberating throughout the palace like aftershocks.

Olga, horrified, falls at her husband's side and endeavors to revive him while uttering a low desperate prayer. Then with a low cry she falls on his still body.

The wave of sudden savage instinct ebbs from Tarzan's eyes and the flaming scar recedes to its barely noticeable state. His mind clears and reason resumes control of his perception.

He sees Olga for the first time since the fight. As if waking from a dream he utters her name.

                    TARZAN
          Olga.

She rises slowly from the body with a mournful face streaked with light tears.

                    OLGA
          You've killed him Jean... he is
          dead.

Tarzan focuses and detects a strong heartbeat.

                    TARZAN
          He's not dead. Get some brandy.

Olga unsure of Tarzan's statement, nevertheless, does as she's told while Tarzan carefully lifts the count and lays him on the couch.

Olga hurries to him with the medicinal brandy and Tarzan forces it through the count's lips.

Count de Coude coughs for a spell and then groans, though still unconscious.

> TARZAN
> I'm truly sorry, but I had to
> defend myself... I could not go
> against my nature and do nothing.

> OLGA
> He would have killed you... you had
> very little choice. I've never
> seen anyone fight like you... such
> strength and ferocity is unheard
> of. I thought for certain he was
> dead and I'm so relieved for my
> sake as well as yours that he
> lives.

> TARZAN
> As, am I. You may not believe me,
> but I'm barely civilized, having
> lived most of my life in the
> jungle... change and control come
> painfully slow. I should have told
> you earlier.

> OLGA
> I believe you, Jean, and though
> this is a sad affair, I know that
> you would not lie to me. Hurry,
> you must leave before he regains
> consciousness.

Tarzan nods and puts a strong hand on her shoulder and she, in turn, places an understanding and forgiving hand on his.

He gives her a wane smile and turning his powerful broad back upon husband and wife, Tarzan makes a speedy departure.

EXT. DE COUDE'S PALACE - NIGHT

Once outside and with the palace standing tall behind him, any guilt or sorrow he may have felt, disintegrate. With a set jaw and grim determination, his eyes light-up in righteous indignation.

Tarzan hops into the convertible with a slight spring and roars into the Paris streets.

EXT. POLICE STATION - NIGHT (20 MINUTES LATER)

An empty, black Rolland-Pilain E Ventoux is parked in front
of the police station reflecting the city lights arrayed
along the sidewalks that cast a glowing mist among the
pedestrians still strolling the cool streets of Paris, as
Tarzan makes his way towards the building.

INT. POLICE STATION - NIGHT

A quiet atmosphere reigns within. The graveyard shift is
preoccupied with much of the day's paperwork.

Policeman 1 is no exception.

The front door opens and seeing who's just dropped in, he
smiles.

                    POLICEMAN 1
          Monsieur Tarzan, what brings you to
          us at this hour?

Grinning, Tarzan extends his hand.

                    TARZAN
          Good evening, Monsieur. I've come
          hoping that you could perhaps help
          me.

                    POLICEMAN 1
          In trouble are we?

                    TARZAN
          No, nothing like that. I'm looking
          for information on two men. One is
          Nikolas Rokoff and the other is
          Alexis Paulvitch. Do you know
          them?

                    POLICEMAN 1
          Quite well. They've been charged
          numerous times but nothing seems to
          stick to them... they have powerful
          friends, so it would seem.

                    TARZAN
          Do you know where they can be
          found?

                    POLICEMAN 1
          But of course. Their location is
          known to us as are many other
          criminals in our fair city.
                    (MORE)

                    POLICEMAN 1 (CONT'D)
          But why would you be interested in
          such men as these?

                    TARZAN
          We have unfinished business that
          must be resolved this evening and I
          would be grateful if you could
          point me in the right direction.

Policeman 1 gets up and goes to a filing cabinet near the
desk and slides open a drawer.

He flips through the folders until he finds the one he's
looking for and leaving the drawer open, places the folder on
the counter before Tarzan.

He opens the folder and after a few pages, writes down an
address on a piece of paper.

                    POLICEMAN 1
          I do this against my better
          judgment. I hope that I will not
          come to regret it.

He hands Tarzan the piece of paper.

                    TARZAN
          You won't... of that I am sure...
          until we meet again, mon ami.

Policeman 1 nods and watches until the door closes behind
Tarzan.

He places the folder back in the filing cabinet and returns
to his desk, looks at the stack of papers piled high, lets
out an audible sigh, and sits back down to the grind wheel.

INT. ROKOFF'S APARTMENT - LIVING ROOM - NIGHT

Laughing and still toasting, Rokoff and Paulvitch continue to
celebrate their sinister plot.

Several knocks on the door interrupt their two-man party.

They both face the door with vile visages filled with glee.

                    ROKOFF
          Ah, that must be the reporter from
          Le Matin.

                    PAULVITCH
          And on time.

> ROKOFF
> Come in!

Rokoff and Paulvitch rise to greet the expected guest but are met instead by the terrible, steel-grey eyes of Tarzan.

Both are dumbfounded beyond words, but Rokoff manages to spit out a few.

> ROKOFF
> What are you doing here?!

With a deadly whisper Tarzan commands.

> TARZAN
> Sit, down... both of you and stay
> there.

Sensing the edge of a sword at their throats, they sit back down.

> TARZAN
> You know very well why I am here.
> Normally I would kill you both, but
> because of the countess I will
> spare your lives this once... but
> only if you do as I say.

The air is tense with the ape-man's presence and death stands next to both Russians.

> TARZAN
> First you will confess in writing
> as being fully responsible for
> tonight's conspiracy against the
> count, the countess and myself --
> and you will omit nothing. Second,
> you will not breath a word of this
> to any newspaper... now or ever or
> I will kill you both.

Like a restrained hungry lion, Tarzan glares at both men. A terrible low growl rumbles from his chest.

> TARZAN
> Life or death, you choose.

Defiant, Rokoff's nature gets in the way of common sense.

> ROKOFF
> Who are you to come into my home
> and threaten me, pig!

In a blink of an eye Tarzan's powerful hand has Rokoff by the throat.

Paulvitch, tries to escape but is lifted high and thrown into far side of the room.

Tarzan loosens his crushing grip on Rokoff's windpipe and shoves him back into the chair.

With an empurpled face he coughs and gasps as Paulvitch walks back to his seat on unsteady legs.

                    TARZAN
          Start writing!

Rokoff, still recovering, opens a drawer from the table and takes out a pad of paper, a pen and begins to write.

A knock at the door shifts Tarzan's attention.

                    TARZAN
          Come in.

A neat, young man enters.

                    REPORTER
          I was sent by Le Matin -- a
          Monsieur Rokoff, supposedly has a
          story for me.

                    TARZAN
          Unfortunately, Monsieur Rokoff, no
          longer has a story for your paper --
          do you?

With a subdued, hateful glance he answers in a forced voice.

                    ROKOFF
          No, I do not have a story for you
          today.

                    TARZAN
          Not today, not tomorrow or ever,
          correct?

Rokoff is assaulted by Tarzan's blazing eyes which the REPORTER is not privy to and Rokoff swiftly amends his statement.

                    ROKOFF
          Yes, that is correct... there will
          never be a story.

Rokoff faces the Reporter.

                    ROKOFF
          Ever.

Tarzan smiles at the Reporter.

                    TARZAN
          I'm sorry, Monsieur, that you
          wasted your valuable time coming
          here. But as you heard, there is
          no story. Allow me.

Tarzan escorts the Reporter to the door.

                    TARZAN
          Good night, Monsieur.

Tarzan closes the door and goes back to supervise the
confession in progress.

INT. ROKOFF'S APARTMENT - LIVING ROOM - SOMETIME LATER

Tarzan finishes the last page of the confession, folds it and
slides it into his inner breast pocket.

At the door he gives Rokoff parting advise.

                    TARZAN
          If you remain in France, sooner or
          later, I will kill you.

INT. D'ARNOT'S APARTMENT - LIVING ROOM - MORNING (NEXT DAY)

Restless bare bronzed feet pace the floor.

                    TARZAN (O.S.)
          ... I should have left the moment I
          suspected foul play. Now I've
          ruined what was once a wonderful
          friendship and possibly their
          marriage.

A hand lifts up a coffee pot and begins filling a cup.

                    D'ARNOT (O.S.)
          Come over here and have your
          coffee... you'll feel better.

Tarzan joins D'Arnot at the coffee table with yesterday's
affair still nagging his mind.

                         D'ARNOT
          Don't be so hard on yourself.
          Considering what happened, you
          demonstrated remarkable restraint
          and resourcefulness. Any other man
          could not have done more.

D'Arnot begins pouring himself a cup of coffee.

                         D'ARNOT
          Do you love each other?

Drinking his coffee, Tarzan gives D'Arnot a quick glance.

                         TARZAN
          It was a moment of intense passion.
          But it was not love. The low
          lighting, her clothing, her beauty
          and her need for comforting, all
          came together like an electric
          storm... it was unstoppable.

D'Arnot chuckles lightly.

                         D'ARNOT
          That is life, my friend. And you
          are learning it fast, and the hard
          way.

                         TARZAN
          This is no place for me. The
          jungle I understand. This city has
          more ambushes, traps, and pits than
          I have ever encountered... and your
          rules and laws are suffocating me.
          I need to leave. The sooner the
          better.

                         D'ARNOT
          I'm afraid the Count de Coude would
          not like that. This affair is not
          quite over, yet, I fear.

D'Arnot sips his coffee and glances, solicitously, at his
troubled friend.

INT./EXT. D'ARNOT'S APARTMENT - MORNING (A WEEK LATER)

The door opens to the face of MONSIEUR FLAUBERT, who bows
with great ceremony.

> FLAUBERT
> Good afternoon, I am Monsieur
> Flaubert. I come on behalf of
> Count de Coude. Would you be,
> Monsieur Tarzan?

D'Arnot smiles pleasantly.

> D'ARNOT
> Good afternoon, Monsieur Flaubert.
> No, I am Lieutenant Paul D'Arnot.
> Please come in and I'll introduce
> you to the man you seek.

> FLAUBERT
> Thank you, Lieutenant D'Arnot.

Flaubert bows again and follows D'Arnot.

> D'ARNOT
> We were just breakfasting... would
> you care to join us?

> FLAUBERT
> No thank you. I've already eaten
> and my time is limited.

Flaubert follows D'Arnot into the breakfast room.

BREAKFAST ROOM

> D'ARNOT
> (addressing Flaubert)
> This is Monsieur Tarzan...

Flaubert is taken aback at the power and size projected by
Tarzan as he rises to meet him.

> D'ARNOT
> (addressing Tarzan)
> ... and this is Monsieur Flaubert.

They both bow to each other -- Tarzan a short, curt one and
Flaubert a low, long one.

> FLAUBERT
> Monsieur Tarzan, I've come on
> behalf of the Count de Coude to
> challenge you to a duel. Do you
> accept this challenge?

                    TARZAN
          I accept Count de Coude's
          challenge.

                    FLAUBERT
          Do you have a second?

                    TARZAN
          Yes. Lieutenant D'Arnot will
          represent me.

                    FLAUBERT
          Excellent.

Bowing to Tarzan he turns his attention to D'Arnot.

                    FLAUBERT
          Would you be available to discuss
          the terms, at two, this afternoon?

                    D'ARNOT
          I will be there at two.

He bows towards D'Arnot.

                    FLAUBERT
          Thank you, Monsieur... I look
          forward to our meeting.

And turning towards Tarzan...

                    FLAUBERT
          Good day to you, Monsieur Tarzan.

Bowing, he's escorted by D'Arnot's valet to the door while
Tarzan and D'Arnot sit back down and continue with their
morning repast.

With a good appetite they both eat for a few moments, with
D'Arnot watching the ape-man for any reaction. Finally,
D'Arnot breaks the silence.

                    D'ARNOT
          Well?

Tarzan looks up at him.

                    TARZAN
          Well, what? I accepted didn't I?

                    D'ARNOT
          I mean, what weapons? Pistols or
          swords?

Tarzan stops eating for a moment to consider.

> TARZAN
> Pistols.

> D'ARNOT
> Count de Coude is a top swordsman
> and a great shot... that is to say,
> he's deadly with either weapon. I
> recommend you select swords... a
> wound may be enough to satisfy him.

> TARZAN
> You think wounding me will satisfy
> him?

> D'ARNOT
> One can never say.

> TARZAN
> It really doesn't matter since I'm
> familiar with the use of neither
> one... and if he's going to kill
> me, I would prefer it done with
> great dispatch.

D'Arnot raises one hand, palm out, and looks down and to one
side.

> D'ARNOT
> I've already given you my counsel,
> but if that's your decision, let it
> be so.

Tarzan smiles and resumes eating.

D'Arnot considers his friend and shaking his head with a sad
face, leans back with a frothing cup of coffee.

INT. D'ARNOT'S APARTMENT - LIVING ROOM - DAY (HOURS LATER)

Tarzan is busy looking through D'Arnot's record collection
for a particular song.

A little fatigued, but glad to be home, D'Arnot arrives from
the meeting and enters upon Tarzan shuffling his vinyls.

> D'ARNOT
> It's all settled. We meet tomorrow
> at an isolated place near Etampes.

Tarzan, still busy looking for his song, responds.

                    TARZAN
          That's good news.

D'Arnot is bothered by Tarzan's indifferent attitude.

                    D'ARNOT
          Is that all you have to say on
          this, your possibly last day?

Tarzan focuses on his current objective.

                    TARZAN
          Where is that record, you know, the
          one that -- never mind, here it is.

Tarzan dusts it off a little with his sleeve and settles it
on the gramophone. The grinding needle follows the spinning
grooves and releases the music, light and low throughout the
living room.

Tarzan looks at D'Arnot with a childlike smile and drops into
the couch and picks up the newspaper, the duel already
forgotten.

INT. D'ARNOT'S APARTMENT - TARZAN'S BEDROOM - PREDAWN

The door to Tarzan's bedroom opens and a hand flips a light
switch.

D'Arnot's valet rouses him from slumber.

Tarzan awakens to find D'Arnot framed by the doorway, fully
dressed and wearing a grave countenance.

                    TARZAN
          Not even the apes wake up this
          early. It's inhuman to be awakened
          at this hour.

D'Arnot is not in a jocular mood.

                    D'ARNOT
          Did you sleep well?

Tarzan doesn't miss the undertone.

                    TARZAN
          I take it, you did not.

                    D'ARNOT
          How could I? You sound like you're
          going to a ball instead of a duel.
                    (MORE)

>   D'ARNOT (CONT'D)
>   It's infuriating that you can take
>   this so lightly against such a
>   deadly opponent.

>   TARZAN
>   But, I don't, and it's why I chose
>   the pistols, because he doesn't
>   miss.

D'Arnot is shocked by his attitude.

>   D'ARNOT
>   Is that what you wish?

>   TARZAN
>   It's not what I wish, but the odds
>   are against me surviving this
>   encounter. I touched his mate,
>   Paul... he has the right to kill me
>   and erase the stain I've put on his
>   house and honor. It's what I would
>   have done.

EXT. D'ARNOT'S APARTMENT - DAWN

Without a word, the two men enter D'Arnot's white 1909 Rolls-
Royce 40/50 limousine.

INT./EXT. 40/50 LIMOUSINE - DAWN

Through the morning twilight the limo cruises, each man with
his own private thoughts to keep him company.

Transparent scenes spring up around and about Tarzan as he
remembers his childhood and invariably end with the
incomparable loveliness of Jane Porter. This last memory
brings a fond smile to his strong, handsome face.

EXT. FIELD OF HONOR - MORNING

Along a lonely road by a field covered with low lying fog,
D'Arnot's valet stops the limousine.

After taking the field, Count de Coude's limo arrives with
Monsieur Flaubert and a another man.

Flaubert brings the other man to Tarzan and D'Arnot.

>   FLAUBERT
>   Good morning, Gentlemen. Allow me
>   to introduce Doctor Poisson.

Tarzan and D'Arnot greet him with a bow.

Flaubert and D'Arnot, along with the doctor, move aside and begin to converse in low voices.

Tarzan and Count de Coude stand on either side of the field.

Count de Coude, relaxed and confident.

Tarzan, dispassionate.

Finished, they call both principals.

Tarzan and Count de Coude bow to each other in peremptory fashion, and then focus their attention on their seconds who are examining the pistols.

The examination complete, the pistols are handed to the principals.

Flaubert recites the rules.

> FLAUBERT
> Gentlemen, you will stand back-to-back. When I give you the command to "march," you shall both move forward in time with Lieutenant D'Arnot's pace count. At the count of ten, you will turn and fire at will until one falls or until you exhaust your three rounds.

Flaubert looks from Tarzan to Count de Coude.

> FLAUBERT
> Are there any questions, Gentlemen?

Not receiving a reply, he motions for D'Arnot and together they position them back-to-back.

The three men retire from the line of fire and once in position...

> FLAUBERT
> Gentlemen, are you ready?

> RAOUL
> Ready.

Tarzan gives a short nod to Flaubert.

Flaubert checks with D'Arnot who responds with a curt nod that he's ready and then...

                    FLAUBERT
          March!

D'Arnot's is awash with emotion as he begins the pace count.

                    D'ARNOT
          One, two, three...

Tarzan and Count de Coude march off in sync with D'Arnot's
measured count, like two large, toy soldiers.

Sorrow grips D'Arnot's eyes.

                    D'ARNOT
          ... Four, five, six, seven...

A surreal fog hangs above the field of honor swirling around
the legs of the duelists as if trying to stop them.

                    D'ARNOT
          ... Eight, nine, ten!

Count de Coude spins about and fires!

IN SLOW MOTION

The bullet explodes from the barrel traveling swiftly,
ripping through the air and adjusting its path ever so
slightly as it encounters the invisible hand of Nature.

As the bullet rushes towards him, Tarzan stands like a stone
statue, his pistol hanging motionless -- like its master --
at his side as the bullet penetrates his left shoulder
effecting a slight movement and then exiting from the back of
the shoulder, deformed.

BACK TO NORMAL SPEED

Like a pillar, in face and body, Tarzan does not register the
hit in any other way. Standing straight and broad, his keen,
grey eyes are focused on the count.

The count pauses to watch the effect of the hit, but seeing
that Tarzan is still standing, he fires again; but, ruffled
by his opponent's calm disposition, the bullet strikes Tarzan
on the left side -- off target.

This time there is no appreciable motion that can be detected
by the eye.

Reminiscent of a Greek statue, Tarzan stands tall and
fearless with the pistol still hanging at his right side.

Though the morning is cool, a sweat breaks forth upon the count's forehead.

Unnerved by Tarzan's strange and deliberate inaction, the count fires his last remaining shot and misses!

The echo of his last bullet slowly melts into the quiet, foggy morning.

With the low lying fog clinging to their legs, the two men stare at each other. Tarzan's countenance depicts an expression of a dashed hope while that of the count is filled with high anxiety and apprehension.

Unable to bear the terrible pressure any longer, the count explodes.

                    RAOUL
          Monsieur, fire and be done with it!

Tarzan moves towards the count and the two seconds misconstruing his intention, run forward to intervene.

With a look and a motion of his hand Tarzan stops them as he continues and stops before the count.

D'Arnot holds back Flaubert who is still uncertain of Tarzan's motives.

In a humble and respectful manner, Tarzan addresses Count de Coude.

                    TARZAN
          Your weapon must have
          malfunctioned... please, try again,
          Monsieur.

Tarzan raises his weapon for the first time and, butt-first, proffers it to the count.

Relief and an expression of incredulity enliven the face of Count de Coude.

                    RAOUL
          Monsieur, have you lost your mind?
          What you ask, I cannot do... it
          would be murder.

                    TARZAN
          Death is a fair price for the wrong
          I committed against your wife.

The count confused.

                    RAOUL
          What wrong? She swore --

                    TARZAN
          -- That's not what I meant,
          Monsieur. What you witnessed is
          all that transpired between your
          wife and myself. Nevertheless, for
          coming between you and your wife, I
          deserve to die. I only, am to
          blame.

The three other men gather about the two principals.

The count quickly grasps the meaning.

                    RAOUL
          You only?

Tarzan continues the white lie.

                    TARZAN
          Yes, I am solely to blame,
          Monsieur. Your wife is innocent of
          the whole affair...

Tarzan pulls out a folded paper from his inner coat pocket
and extends it to Count de Coude.

                    TARZAN
          ... But Rokoff is not.

The count bewildered, takes the document and after scanning
its contents...

                    RAOUL
          I thank Almighty God, that your
          blood is not on my hands.

Before Tarzan can respond, the emotional Count de Coude
embraces him like a dear friend.

Following his principal's example, Flaubert embraces D'Arnot.

Somewhat irked at being left out...

                    DR. POISSON
          Alright. Enough of this. I must
          examine Monsieur Tarzan. I saw him
          hit at least once --

                         TARZAN
                    (grins)
              -- Twice. The shoulder and the
              side.

Tarzan points out the entries of the bullets to the fussy
doctor.

Using the cloaks from the seconds -- one as a blanket and the
other as a pillow -- DOCTOR POISSON has Tarzan lay upon the
moist sward where he proceeds to dress his wounds.

INT./EXT. 40/50 LIMOUSINE - A HALF HOUR LATER

Count de Coude and Flaubert ride back to Paris in D'Arnot's
limousine, all in good spirits.

Laughter and good cheer flow from within as Count de Coude's
valet follows from behind with the count's limo.

EXT. LONELY ROAD - MORNING

A two-limo convoy moves out in a northeasterly direction, at
a leisurely pace, upon a foggy road.

INT. D'ARNOT'S APARTMENT - TARZAN'S BEDROOM - DAY (3 DAYS
LATER)

Tarzan lies in bed -- naked from the waist up -- with Dr.
Poisson and a nurse changing the bandages around his left
side and left shoulder.

                         DR. POISSON
              ... Stop fidgeting and stay still,
              Monsieur. The bandages must be
              changed daily.

Sitting, D'Arnot watches with amusement.

                         TARZAN
                    (looking at D'Arnot)
              This is ridiculous... bedridden for
              two scratches. I've suffered much
              worse in the my jungle without the
              comfort of a bed, a doctor or a
              nurse.

                         DR. POISSON
              You want to recover don't you?

                    TARZAN
          I am recovered and if you'd --

                    DR. POISSON
          -- You'll be recovered when I say
          so, and for the last time stop
          complaining and stay still.

Tarzan acquiesces and as they begin to work his shoulder, he
glances at D'Arnot.

                    TARZAN
          Anything yet?

                    D'ARNOT
          No, nothing. But, I happened to
          mention it, in passing, to Count de
          Coude -- that you were seeking
          employment -- and he said he would
          see if there was anything who could
          do to help you.

Tarzan snarls under his breath and stares at the doctor.

                    TARZAN
          What are you doing?

                    DR. POISSON
          You see?

                    TARZAN
          If you'd stop poking it --

                    DR. POISSON
          -- Be quiet and don't move.

Tarzan grinning spreads his hands out in surrender as he
looks at D'Arnot who's chuckling at Tarzan's ordeal with the
medical staff.

INT. MINISTRY OF WAR - COUNT DE COUDE'S OFFICE - DAY (A FEW
DAYS LATER)

Count de Coude is at his desk reading a document. He then
signs it, hands it to his clerk -- standing by -- and grabs
another one from an inbox and begins to read it.

Someone pounds on the door and without looking up...

                    RAOUL
          Enter.

An ESCORT enters and reports.

                    ESCORT
        Monsieur, Monsieur Tarzan is here
        to see you.

                    RAOUL
        Excellent, show him in.

Count de Coude dismisses his clerk and stands up as the
Escort ushers Tarzan inside and closes the door leaving the
two alone.

Count de Coude goes around his desk and extends his hand in
greeting.

                    RAOUL
        Welcome, Monsieur.

                    TARZAN
        It's an honor, Monsieur.

Tarzan performs a succinct bow.

                    RAOUL
            (proffers a chair)
        Please.

Both take a seat and the count continues.

                    RAOUL
        I believe I've found a position
        that was made to order. It's for a
        man with your attributes... someone
        with physical and mental
        strength... a man with a sharp mind
        that can think on the go. You will
        be assigned as an agent working for
        the Ministry of War. Needless to
        say, a great deal of travel, trust
        and responsibility are attached to
        this commission. Plus, it carries
        with it a stepladder into the
        diplomatic realm.

Count de Coude stands up, followed by Tarzan.

                    RAOUL
        I'll escort you to General Rochere.
        He will fill you in on the details
        of the assignment. Afterwards, you
        can decide whether or not to accept
        it.

INT. MINISTRY OF WAR - CORRIDOR - DAY

Count de Coude leads Tarzan just a few doors down. He knocks
and then without waiting for a reply sticks his head inside.

                    RAOUL
          General, I've brought you Monsieur
          Tarzan.

                    GEN. ROCHERE (O.S.)
          By all means, Monsieur, let him in.

The count pops back out.

                    RAOUL
          Good luck, and I hope, you accept
          the position.

                    TARZAN
          Thank you, Monsieur, I am in your
          debt.

They shake hands, Count de Coude waits for him to enter and
then closes the door.

GEN. ROCHERE'S OFFICE

GENERAL ROCHERE, sporting a large mustache moves to the front
of the desk and greets Tarzan.

                    GEN. ROCHERE
          I bid you welcome, Monsieur Tarzan.
          Please have a chair.

After Tarzan accommodates himself, Gen. Rochere sits on the
edge of the desk, facing the ape-man.

He pulls the pipe out of his mouth, crosses his arms and
regards Tarzan for a moment.

                    GEN. ROCHERE
          How much do you know about the
          assignment?

                    TARZAN
          Only that it would involve
          traveling.

The general continues to eye Tarzan with an air of
satisfaction as he puffs his pipe a few times.

                    GEN. ROCHERE
          We need a man to shadow a
          Lieutenant Gernois. We suspect that
          he is in the process of dealing
          with an unknown foreign power for
          the sale of sensitive information
          now in his possession as a French
          military officer.

                    TARZAN
          Is that all... to spy on a man for
          possible treason?

                    GEN. ROCHERE
          Yes, but to make it easier for you,
          you'll go undercover as an American
          Hunter. We were informed that you
          have an American accent, so you'll
          be ideal.

                    TARZAN
          True... thanks to a dear friend.

The general nods and puffs a few.

                    GEN. ROCHERE
          That's the job in a nutshell. If
          you accept the assignment you'll
          receive more detailed briefings,
          proper clothing, weapons and
          anything needed to play the role in
          the next day or so. Well,
          Monsieur?

Tarzan stands up -- a head taller than the general -- and
extends a powerful hand.

                    TARZAN
          The answer is yes, General.

After the handshake and in-between Gen. Rochere's pipe
puffs...

                    GEN. ROCHERE
          How does Africa sound to you?

Tarzan beams.

EXT. MEDITERRANEAN SEA (UNDERWATER) - DAY (3 DAYS LATER)

Beneath the blue sheath of the Mediterranean, a lonely
predator circles a sunken galleon.

The filtered, soft light from above bounces from the scales of schools of fish that swim and dart in harmony.

An eel bites a fish in half.

A pod of dolphins swims through bubbles from an unknown source that travel upwards towards the surface of the sea.

Suddenly, the dolphins change course and chase the bubbles upwards towards the bottom of a huge vessel.

EXT. MEDITERRANEAN SEA - DAY

The dolphins leap out alongside a steamship matching it stride for stride like honorary escorts on both sides of the vessel.

A steam whistle blows as it passes another steamer heading in the opposite direction and the other turns her whistle loose in reply.

EXT. STEAMSHIP - UPPER DECK - DAY

Tarzan along with many other passengers take advantage of their steamer chairs and stewards at their disposal.

Tarzan relaxes with a drink and a book, while the steamer puffs its gigantic frame towards the coast of Africa.

A superimposed map appears with an animated, dotted line that begins at Marseilles, stops at Oran, and ends in the Algerian city of Sidi Bel Abbes.

EXT. SIDI BEL ABBES - 2ND SPAHI REGIMENT HQ - 4 DAYS LATER

SUPER: "2ND SPAHI REGIMENT HEADQUARTERS"

The French flag along with regimental colors flutters above the arched gateway with the name of the regiment following the curve of the arch.

Tarzan's black hair is covered by a wide-brimmed felt hat matching his hunter's khaki outfit tapered with puttees.

With papers in hand he approaches one of two guards on either side of the gate entrance. The guard goes over his papers and after talking in indistinguishable tones, Tarzan is permitted to enter, where a specific building is pointed out to him by the sentry.

INT. 2ND SPAHI REGIMENT - DAY

Tarzan stops at the counter behind which a mix of French officers, enlisted and spahis go about their duties.

An officer, CAPTAIN GERARD, 30, notices the tall foreigner watching the clutter of soldiers criss-crossing in all directions.

The dialogue begins in French with subtitles and then transitions seamlessly into English without the French accent.

                    CPT. GERARD
          May I help you, Monsieur?

                    TARZAN
          I beg your pardon, Monsieur. I was
          told to make myself known here
          before I begin hunting.

                    CPT. GERARD
          Your papers, please.

Cpt. Gerard reads the papers of introduction. Impressed, he greets the ape-man with a friendly smile.

                    CPT. GERARD
          Any friend of General Rochere is a
          friend of mine. Monsieur, Tarzan,
          I am Cpt. Gerard, at your service.

Cpt. Gerard bows locking his heels together and Tarzan likewise minus the heel clicking.

                    TARZAN
          Likewise, Cpt. Gerard and I look
          forward to some great hunting in
          the coming days.

                    CPT. GERARD
          For an American, your French is
          excellent.

Tarzan grins.

                    TARZAN
          I had a remarkable Frenchman for a
          teacher.

Cpt. Gerard laughs.

                    CPT. GERARD
          Ah, I should have guessed it. Have
          you found accommodations already?

Tarzan nods.

                    TARZAN
          I'm staying at the Hotel de Ville.
          What I haven't found is a good
          place to unwind... any
          recommendations?

                    CPT. GERARD
          I can do better... I'll take you
          there myself.

Cpt. Gerard has a few words with a clerk and then moves to
the front of the counter.

                    CPT. GERARD
          Follow me to the best tavern in
          town.

Laughing, Cpt. Gerard, at six feet and robust, escorts Tarzan
along the wide corridor with decorated walls covered with
swords, carbines, unit colors, standards, pictures and
portraits.

The administrative din is unbroken as they step outside and
shut the door behind them.

INT. TAVERN - EVENING

Native music floats in the background as a mixture of spahis,
legionnaires, French officers and civilians fill the tavern
with a cacophony of voices.

Berber and Arab waiters wearing fezzes and long tunics walk
the floor taking orders for food and drink.

The spahis dressed in their colorful garb are busy drinking
strong, black coffee.

Near the center of the tavern is a group of French officers
dressed in red jackets and blue breeches and, with Tarzan and
Cpt. Gerard among their group, they encircle a table with
camaraderie and laughter.

With a glass of red wine in his hand, Cpt. Gerard indicates
soldiers at other tables.

                    CPT. GERARD
          ... Many of us here tonight are
          from the Second Spahi Regiment.

Tarzan spots LIEUTENANT GERNOIS, sitting alone at a small
table with a drink.

Cpt. Gerard notices Tarzan's interest in Lt. Gernois.

                    CPT. GERARD
          And that is one of my
          lieutenants... Lieutenant Gernois.

                    TARZAN
          Why is he drinking alone?

                    CPT. GERARD
          He's not the social type. Plus his
          personality helps to keep him that
          way.

Cpt. Gerard chuckles and sips the red wine.

                    CPT. GERARD
          But, he's an able officer and
          follows orders... in the end that's
          all that matters. Now then, let us
          drink to the Second Spahi Regiment!

Tarzan, with the other officers, raises his glass, toasts and
then steals a glance at the dark and lonely figure of Lt.
Gernois.

MONTAGE - TARZAN HUNTS AND SHADOWS

1) Tarzan trails Lt. Gernois into restaurants and bars.

2) Playing his part, Tarzan hires porters and guides and
returns with two large red deer.

3) He shadows Lt. Gernois in the public gardens and even to
the church but he's either alone or his interactions with
others are ordinary.

4) Tarzan returns late in the day with the carcasses of a
leopard and a wild boar.

5) Through the streets of the city and to the train station
Tarzan prosecutes his mission, but through no act or word
does he detect any suspicious activity. Tarzan begins to
wonder if it's all for naught.

INT. COFFEEHOUSE - DAY (A MONTH LATER)

SUPER: "1910"

Daylight illuminates the interior through large front
windows.

Next to one of these windows, Tarzan and Cpt. Gerard are
having a conversation over coffee and a small meal.

> CPT. GERARD
> ... Some of my men are going to
> miss your hunting excursions. The
> fresh meat you've been supplying us
> with, has boosted the men's morale
> immensely.

Tarzan, after a drink of his java...

> TARZAN
> Tell them not to fear... I'm not
> leaving yet.
>   (takes another sip)
> In a day or two I'll be going out
> again.

> CPT. GERARD
> It's not that. Our detachment has
> been ordered to relieve a unit
> stationed in Bou Saada and I will
> be leading it with the assistance
> of Lieutenant Gernois.

Tarzan's agile mind moves in quickly.

> TARZAN
>   (smiles)
> That can be easily remedied, if you
> let me tag along. I hear lions are
> plentiful in that area and I have
> yet to see one here.

Finishing his coffee...

> CPT. GERARD
> My friend, you need say no more.
> You're welcome to join us, if that
> is your wish. We leave the day
> after tomorrow by train, to Bouira.

EXT. BOUIRA - TRAIN STATION - DAY

A lazy stream of smoke escapes from a locomotive's
smokestack, as it chugs slowly into the train station and
screeches to a painful halt with its top and sides exploding
with pent up steam.

Cavaliers and their mounts disembark from the hissing train.
Nervous and irritable horses rear up and neigh while others
are composed as their masters lead them away from the
exhausted train.

EXT. BOUIRA - BAZAAR - DAY

Dry, dusty, dirt roads, crowded with the life of the
marketplace, become gauntlets with hands and voices vying for
those caught in their web.

Tarzan is among them and barters with a ragged Arab for a
paltry horse.

Over the Arab's turban, Tarzan's eagle-eyes descry an odd
man's attention focused on him, who vanishes into a
coffeehouse once he realizes he's been discovered.

A certain familiarity about the man strikes the ape-man, but
the thought fades as he's dragged back into the haggling
arena by the earnest Arab.

EXT. VALLEY - DAY

Two long columns of spahis ride through a green, rugged
valley surrounded by low hills with mountains far in the
distance.

With saber on one side and a revolver on the other, Cpt.
Gerard, wearing a French red, short jacket with blue
breeches, topped-off by a blue kepi, leads the cavalry with
Tarzan riding beside him.

Tarzan is garbed in a khaki outfit and shaded from the sun by
a wide-brimmed hat. Puttees wind wrapped around his legs
down to thick, leather shoes. On his hips are a brace of .45
Colt revolvers.

On his saddle are two scabbards. One for a scoped Rigby
Mauser and one for an express rifle.

Lt. Gernois, dressed similar to his commander, brings up the
rear of the disciplined formation.

Astride their gray mounts of various shades, each spahi is covered with a scarlet burnous lined with a white interior. The hood is tied securely around their foreheads with plaited camel hair.

A short, red jacket embroidered in black, followed by a red sash, blue pantaloons and ending in Moroccan leather boots, constitutes their official uniform.

Armed with a saber and their backs strapped with an 1892 carbine, they ride stoically and silently behind their leader.

EXT. AUMALE - HOTEL GROSSAT - NEAR SUNSET

(NOTE: Today, Aumale is known as Sour El Ghozlane.)

SUPER: "AUMALE"

Before the large veranda of the Hotel Grossat, a weary Tarzan, unaccustomed to horseback riding, dismounts as the spahi detachment continues on towards the garrison further up the road.

INT. HOTEL GROSSAT - TARZAN'S BEDROOM - MORNING

While dressing, Tarzan is pulled to the window by the sound of heavy hoofbeats.

Moving in a single column, the spahi detachment is leaving the fortress Aumale.

Tarzan picks up the pace and finishing donning on his outfit, grabs his hat and gear and slams the door behind him as he rushes out of the room.

INT. HOTEL GROSSAT - DINING ROOM - MORNING

A wristwatch is quickly turned and read on a powerful left wrist.

Tarzan wolfs down his breakfast to make-up for lost time and as he's about to gulp down some coffee, he spots through the door of an adjoining barroom, Lt. Gernois speaking with another man in hushed tones.

Unexpected, Tarzan puts down the cup carefully so as not to make a sound and fixes his eyes on the pair. The back of the other man is towards Tarzan and the ape-man's brows come together as his memory is jogged.

QUICK FLASHBACK

From a distance, a staring odd man, in European clothes, darts into a native coffeehouse.

BACK TO PRESENT

The steady pressure of Tarzan's interest is suddenly met by Lt. Gernois' startled face, who quickly whispers to his associate effecting a swift departure from the field of Tarzan's vision.

EXT. SIDI AISSA - AFTERNOON

Tarzan crawls into the dusty village with his aging mount.

SUPER: "SIDI AISSA"

It's market day in the village and the

MARKETPLACE

is overrun with caravans and a river of humanity. Burdened camels and horses stand patiently by as the din of the haggling Arabs takes over the airwaves in a constant babbling melody of madness.

Tarzan finds the spahis dismounted, resting and watering their horses at the troughs on the

OUTSKIRTS

of the colorful and lively Arab mall.

As he rides in through their midst, Tarzan spies Lt. Gernois among them minus his earlier companion.

He finds Cpt. Gerard taking stock of his mount.

                    CPT. GERARD
          I'd thought we'd lost you. What
          happened?

                    TARZAN
          I was delayed and with this poor
          wretch, it took me awhile to catch
          up... but here I am.

                         CPT. GERARD
              Well, you'd better rest up... we're
              leaving within the hour.

                         TARZAN
              That's what I wanted to talk to you
              about... I've decided to stay a day
              or two in this town... it interests
              me. Plus, I need to get another
              horse before this one dies under
              me.

Cpt. Gerard looks at the small worn out mount and then at
Tarzan's huge body and laughs.

                         CPT. GERARD
              I think you're right, and the
              sooner the better.

He pats the horse on the side of the neck as it stares with
dull eyes towards the ground.

                         CPT. GERARD
              In a few days, then.

                         TARZAN
              Until, then.

Tarzan wheels his mount about with no little effort drawing a
few comments and laughter from some of the nearby men and
trots away towards the pandemonium, trailed by the unamused
countenance of Lt. Gernois.

EXT. SIDI AISSA - INN - AFTERNOON

Tarzan parks his dilapidated mount before an inn and removing
all his gear, enters within.

INT. INN - AFTERNOON

A servant greets Tarzan at the entrance and taking his bags
leads him to the INNKEEPER at the

FRONT COUNTER

The dialogue begins in French with subtitles and then
transitions seamlessly into English without the French
accent.

                    INNKEEPER
          I bid you welcome, Monsieur. How
          may I be of service?

                    TARZAN
          I need a room for a day or two.

The Innkeeper claps his hands and a bellboy hustles to take
hold of Tarzan's gear.

Tarzan signs in and is given a key.

                    INNKEEPER
          Would their be anything else,
          Monsieur?

                    TARZAN
          Yes, where can I hire a a guide?

The Innkeeper smiles broadly.

                    INNKEEPER
          Say no more, Monsieur.

And turning his gaze towards the lobby...

                    INNKEEPER
          Abdul!

He turns his attention once again to Tarzan.

                    INNKEEPER
          Abdul is my most trusted guide. He
          will not fail you.

ABDUL, 18, with an intelligent face, stops on a dime, from
his dash to the front counter, before the Innkeeper.

                    ABDUL
          Yes, Master?

                    INNKEEPER
          Abdul, you will be this man's
          guide. Take good care of him.

                    ABDUL
          I will, Master.

And turning to Tarzan with a contagious smile...

                    ABDUL
          It will be a pleasure to guide you,
          Monsieur.

EXT. SIDI AISSA - MARKETPLACE - LATE AFTERNOON

Tarzan holds the reins and strokes the mane of beautiful
horse he's just bought from a distinguished, older Arab.

>   SHEIK BEN SADEN
>   You have bought a fine animal at a
>   bargain price. I am Kadour Ben
>   Saden, sheik of a tribe south of
>   Djelfa.

Tarzan looks at SHEIK KADOUR BEN SADEN, and smiles.

>   TARZAN
>   I am glad to meet you, Sheik Ben
>   Saden. I am Tarzan, an American
>   hunter. I must tell you, there is
>   no comparison between this horse
>   and the one I gave away.

He looks at Abdul with a big grin.

>   TARZAN
>   Abdul, would agree with me, when I
>   say, it was a horse in name only.

Abdul, smiling broadly, looks at Sheik Ben Saden.

>   ABDUL
>   It is true... it was not a horse.

Amused.

>   SHEIK BEN SADEN
>   Then, I am glad, that I sold you a
>   true horse.

Abdul takes the reigns from Tarzan and strokes the horse's
neck, softly speaking to him in hushed Arabic.

>   TARZAN
>   Would you dine with us? You would
>   honor us by saying yes.

>   SHEIK BEN SADEN
>   (smiling)
>   How can I say no?

EXT. SIDI AISSA - STREET - LATE AFTERNOON (15 MINUTES LATER)

Tarzan, Sheik Ben Saden, and Abdul walk among the chaotic din
of the populace with Abdul casting his eyes occasionally
behind them.

EXT. SIDI AISSA - RESTUARANT - LATE AFTERNOON (MINUTES LATER)

Before a bustling restaurant, Abdul stops them.

                    ABDUL
          Here, Monsieur.

Tarzan and the sheik are about to enter when...

                    ABDUL
          Wait, Monsieur.

                    TARZAN
          What is it?

                    ABDUL
          All day, a man has been following
          us.

He turns and points.

Tarzan's sharp eyes lock onto a FURTIVE MAN wearing a turban
with a half-veiled face and covered in a dark-blue burnous.

Spotted, the man vanishes with the crowd.

                    TARZAN
          The one in the blue burnous?

                    ABDUL
          Yes, Monsieur. I'm afraid he means
          us no good.

Tarzan ponders the problem.

                    ABDUL
          Who would have reason to follow
          you?

                    TARZAN
          That's what I was thinking. It's
          my first time in your country...
          who could possibly have anything
          against me?

                    ABDUL
          Thieves don't need an excuse,
          Monsieur.

Tarzan continues to scan the crowd for the slippery figure
without any success.

                    TARZAN
         In any case, thanks to you, we're
         onto him.

And with a meaningful smile...

                    TARZAN
         It's his move.

INT. RESTAURANT - EVENING

Tarzan, Abdul and Sheik Ben Saden sit around a table with
empty plates and empty cups.

Sheik Ben Saden pats his flat abdomen and turns to Tarzan.

                SHEIK BEN SADEN
         My thanks, Monsieur, for an
         excellent dinner. My land is
         always open to you. There you may
         hunt the lion, leopard, boar and
         antelope at your pleasure.

                    TARZAN
         Don't mention it, Sheik Ben Saden.
         The honor was mine... and who
         knows, I may yet take you up on
         your offer.

With that, Sheik Ben Saden takes his leave from his host and
Tarzan, curious in the ways of the Arab, departs shortly
thereafter into the nightlife of Sidi Aissa.

EXT. SIDI AISSA - STREET - NIGHT

In the cool evening, the lamplights along either side of a
large street cast an eerie glow upon the mixture of night
owls walking along the boulevard or sitting against the walls
on mats or chairs near the entrances to Arab cafes.

On both sides of the street these cafes, like nighclubs, are
patronized by Arabs and Europeans alike seeking diversion and
entertainment to round out their day.

The loud blaring flutes and drumbeats of an elusive and
exotic sound beckon Tarzan and Abdul to a large cafe maure.

INT. CAFE MAURE - NIGHT

In a very large and subtly lit room, the walls are decorated
with tapestries and arabesque embroidery depicting the past.

A round stage is set in the middle with the musicians blowing and beating skillfully upon their instruments against a further wall.

Surrounding the stage are mainly men sitting at tables with either chairs or benches. Others sit without the convenience of a table and others stand without the convenience of either.

Many with hashish pipes puff away their kif, while others sip their hot, dark coffee.

The combination of loud music, voices and smoke fill the atmosphere with a stifling, palpable heat.

Despite the oppressive aura, all eyes are held by the OULED NAIL dancing upon the stage.

Towards the center of the room Tarzan and Abdul find seats to accommodate them and then cast their eyes on the jeweled, desert beauty twirling before them.

Covered with bracelets, anklets, earrings, and coins woven together to decorate her forehead, the lithe and taunting figure snaps and thrusts her mesmerizing hips effortlessly to the delight of her audience as parts and bits of clothing slide, fall or are thrown from her wriggling, tantalizing body.

Left only with a a sheer top and pantaloons, she slows her dance and with her inexplicable motions, she draws their breaths into her maddening and intricate web of desire.

The musicians, immune to her breathtaking charms, suddenly increase the tempo of the music and her long, lustrous, black undulating locks sweep the air around her as lights flash from her kohl outlined eyes, like wild moonlight striking two, hypnotic pools.

Catching Tarzan's eyes upon her, she nimbly drops from the stage and caressing him with a hip, she brushes one of his broad shoulders with a silken handkerchief earning a well deserved franc from the ape-man.

Smiling with her elongated darks eyes, she sweeps the colorful handkerchief over his head and twirls around to call upon another European patron.

Another sleek girl takes her place upon the stage to continue the seductive, desert dance.

The light-eyed Abdul notices as Ouled Nail is drawn aside by two men near a side door. He recognizes one of them as the Furtive Man. Abdul is intrigued at this interaction.

The men, while speaking to her, look in Abdul's general direction followed by a quick glance from the desert gem aimed at Tarzan. Then, the two slip through the side door exit leaving the lightly clad girl alone.

INT. CAFE MAURE - NIGHT (30 MINUTES LATER)

With shouts of approval and applause, a dancing girl drops from the stage to mingle with the customers while Ouled Nail once again takes center stage.

She arouses the approval of the men yet her sultry smiles and teasing, black lashes are for Tarzan alone.

The other patrons realizing her focus is on the ape-man begin to curse and scowl at their neglect.

Pure as pearls, her full lips expose glistening white teeth as she moves closer to her prey.

With jaw-dropping motions of her body, she slithers around behind Tarzan and back-to-back she lowers and eases the back of her head onto his shoulder and turning her full lips to his ear she whispers...

                    OULED NAIL
          Monsieur, two men in the outer
          court would do you harm.

Ouled Nail rises with gyrating hips and breasts, spellbinding and leading her masculine audience deeper into captivity.

Still behind the unruffled Tarzan, she wheels around with a twist and slips her shapely, soft, cinnamoned arms around his neck resting her ringed fingers upon his expansive chest.

She coos into his ear as she chokes the life out of the men devouring her, with heart bursting movements.

                    OULED NAIL
          They wished me to lead you to
          them... but I will not... leave
          this place.

She stands as her hips, with a will of their own, ceaselessly move in sync with the sweating musicians hidden in the shadows near the walls.

Dancing before him, she stares into his eyes and then passes her handkerchief over his shoulder and Tarzan rewards her uncanny performance with an ecu -- a five-franc silver coin.

Tarzan bows his head slightly in gratitude.

                    TARZAN
          Mademoiselle, what is your name?

                    OULED NAIL
          Asilah.

With a beautiful flash of her teeth, she puts the coin to her
forehead, bows, and swiftly scurries from the room on dainty
feet, leaving the others dumbfounded and eager for more, as
the next girl takes the stage.

INT. CAFE MAURE - NIGHT (20 MINUTES LATER)

A large RUFFIAN enters the cafe and targets Tarzan with his
vulgar, dark eyes.

Tarzan and Abdul are approached from behind by the Ruffian as
they continue to enjoy the unabashed dancing of the desert
flowers.

Ruffian stands behind Tarzan and begins to speak aloud
drawing Abdul's undivided attention.

                    RUFFIAN
               (in Arabic)
          You are a dog, Frenchman... your
          mother is a dog and so is your
          father.

Tarzan, unfamiliar with the Arab tongue, is shielded from the
insults, but not Abdul who looks around the room only to find
anxious men waiting in the eaves for the axe to drop.

With mounting concern, Abdul leans closer to Tarzan and
speaks from the corner of his mouth.

                    ABDUL
          Monsieur, the man behind you has
          just called you and your family
          dogs... and he's brought friends.
          I suggest we leave immediately.

Tarzan turns and looks up at Ruffian who's still shooting off
his mouth with his arms crossed over his chest.

                    ABDUL
          Except for myself... you have no
          friends here, Monsieur.

Ruffian raises his voice even more.

                              RUFFIAN
                         (in Arabic)
                    ... You Christian pig! For
                    insulting one of the dancing girls,
                    I will have your head. I will tear
                    your heart out with my bare hands.
                    But you dare not fight me like a
                    man because you are a weakling and
                    a great coward!

Many of the other Arabs begin to laugh and to hurl unwanted
taunts at Tarzan.

                              ABDUL
                    He says, you insulted one of the
                    dancing girls and that you are a
                    weakling and a great coward... he
                    wants to hurt you, very much.

Tarzan rises and faces Ruffian with a grim smile evident on
his face.

Ruffian is big, but Tarzan is much bigger.

Ruffian licks his sun-baked lips and grins with a mouth full
of rotting teeth, as his allies look on itching for the fight
to commence.

In a blink of an eye Tarzan plows his right fist into
Ruffian's face and drops him like a bag of cement releasing a
horde of armed Arabs crying out for his blood.

A dancing girl scampers from the stage and the music switches
from flutes and drums to angry voices cursing and yelling, as
they rush headlong towards Tarzan and his faithful guide with
swords and knives.

Tarzan grabs a chair and uses it as a shield and with his
free arm, two more Arabs find themselves unconscious at
Tarzan's feet. Notwithstanding, the swarthy, blood-thirsty
crowd, pushes Tarzan and Abdul backwards.

Like a cornered lion, Tarzan rips into any coming within
range of his powerful arm.

Abdul, with a long, curved knife, stabs and cuts helping to
keep them at bay.

Meshed together like matches, the motley mob of swearing
Arabs is unable to avail itself of its superiority in
numbers; hence, at the most, only three are able to engage
the duo.

Pushed near the side door, Tarzan ensnares a bold, desert son and discarding the chair, uses him as a shield instead, while Abdul opens the door and exits the cafe.

With Abdul safely out of the way, Tarzan lifts the struggling man above his head and hurls him with his mighty muscles into the buzzing swarm of hornets, taking down a great number of them and disappears to join Abdul in the inner courtyard.

EXT. CAFE MAURE - INNER COURTYARD - NIGHT

The darkness of the courtyard is alleviated only by the candlelights shining dimly from before the doors of the dancing girls above the cafe.

Each room above the cafe is reached by a staircase along the wall.

Beneath one of the staircases, the report of a revolver turns the two men around to face two robed figures with half-covered faces, running towards them while taking aim anew.

Within the cafe, the unexpected shots stop the horde at the threshold.

A woman's shrill voice causes all the women to douse their candles.

In a single bound, Tarzan's fury engages the foremost, and a howl of pain escapes the attacker as his left wrist is snapped and then thrown to the ground groaning in pain.

The other assailant with his revolver only inches from Abdul's forehead misfires and Abdul eviscerates him.

Unable to find the revolver, Tarzan grabs a sword from one of the disabled men and he and Abdul turn to face the group, now peering cautiously into the courtyard.

A weak light from the doorway strays into the inner courtyard giving the enemy within little if any advantage.

A slender hand alights on Tarzan's shoulder from behind.

                    FEMALE VOICE (O.S.)
          Monsieur, follow me quickly.

Tarzan wheels about and though it's dark he recognizes ASILAH, the dancing girl.

With a grin.

                         TARZAN
                Why, hello again.

                    ASILAH/OULED NAIL/FEMALE VOICE
                Come, time is precious!

Tarzan taps Abdul, who's focused on the side door, on the
shoulder.

                         TARZAN
                Let's go.

Abdul obeys the ape-man without hesitation.

Asilah leads the two men up a flight of stairs.

At the summit of the stairs, the noise of the search below
commences.

                         ASILAH
                Soon they will search our rooms.
                You are strong and brave, but they
                are too many and will kill you.
                You can escape them through my --

An excited alarm at the bottom of their staircase draws the
rush of feet and shouts from another quarter of the courtyard
to their location.

The handful of men, having discovered them, charge up the
dilapidated stairs followed by the rest of the shrieking mob.

Tarzan shoves the sword into the first man and separates him
from the blade with a powerful kick taking down all those
behind him, like bowling pins.

The combined weight of the hostile, cursing Arabs is no match
for the stairs as it disintegrates beneath their feet,
dropping them like rocks to the ground below.

                         ASILAH
                Make haste, they will reach us
                through another girl's room. Come!

INT. CAFE MAURE - ASILAH'S ROOM - NIGHT

Angry voices and feet clamber up the stairs next door and
voices in the courtyard alert Abdul and the girl.

                         ASILAH
                It's over.

Tarzan looks from Asilah to Abdul.

                    TARZAN
          What?

                    ABDUL
          They've sent men to the other side
          to cutoff our retreat!

Tarzan looks down at the distraught girl and lifting up her
chin...

                    TARZAN
          It's not over... not yet.

Tarzan sticks his head out of the window but instead of
looking down his eyes gaze upward towards the roof.

He turns to the girl.

                    TARZAN
          Come here.

Once next to him, Tarzan crouches and has the shapely girl
wrap her arms about his corded neck and turning to Abdul...

                    TARZAN
          Bar the door with whatever you can
          to slow them down -- and be ready
          when I call for you.

With the girl secured to his broad back, Tarzan exits the
window and disappears.

Abdul is about to barricade the door when the howling nomads
start to slice and dice the door with their heavy swords.

                    TARZAN (O.S.)
          Abdul!

Abdul sticks his head out, raises an arm and is whisked
upwards into the night air like a hanging rope, just as the
Arabs crash into an empty bedroom.

EXT. CAFE MAURE - STREET - NIGHT

Oaths and fists are directed upwards towards men with heads
poked out of a window, who return the insults railed against
them.

EXT. CAFE MAURE - ROOFTOP - NIGHT

Near the edge of the roof, Tarzan, Abdul and Asilah lie prone listening to the expostulations and recriminations being exchanged between their pursuers.

Tarzan turns to Abdul.

                    TARZAN
          What are they saying?

                    ABDUL
          The men in the room are chastising
          the men in the street for allowing
          us to escape them so easily.

Abdul stops translating to listen-in some more and then begins to chuckle beneath his breath.

                    ABDUL
          The men in the street are
          maintaining that we never came down
          from the window and that we are
          still in the building. They're
          calling the others cowards for not
          continuing the search.

                    TARZAN
          Good... the more confusion, the
          better.

                    ABDUL
          Soon they will be fighting one
          another.

EXT. CAFE MAURE - ROOFTOP - NIGHT (5 MINUTES LATER)

Peering over the edge of the roof Tarzan can see a few men still in the street below them smoking and chewing the cud, but the room beneath them is dead quiet, the men having left.

Lying between Abdul and the girl, Tarzan props himself up on his elbows and faces Asilah.

                    TARZAN
              (in a low voice)
          Thank you for helping us from this
          unruly bunch... you didn't have to,
          you know?

Asilah studies his face for a moment, her eyes along with the golden discs woven together across her brow and underneath her chin, reflecting the faint light from the night sky above.

                    ASILAH
          I wanted to... you're not like the
          others. You treated me kindly and
          with respect. Most men give me
          money in an offensive manner, you
          did not... you seemed... grateful.

                    TARZAN
          How can any man behold you and not
          be grateful?

She drops her head for a moment after Tarzan's bold compliment and then raises it again with a shy smile suffusing her lovely countenance.

                    ASILAH
          You are too kind, Monsieur.

                    TARZAN
          Not at all... I only speak the
          truth.
               (concerned)
          You'll have to leave this cafe --
          perhaps the village. It cannot be
          safe for you here after helping us.

                    ASILAH
          I am in no danger and by tomorrow
          it will be forgotten... yet with
          all my being I long to leave here,
          but I dare not.

                    TARZAN
          Why not? If you do not like it
          here, just leave.

                    ASILAH
          He would kill me.

Tarzan does not like what he's hearing.

                    TARZAN
          Who?

                    ASILAH
          My owner. You see, Monsieur, I am
          a prisoner... a slave, truly, and I
          cannot leave.

A snarl almost escapes the ape-man's throat.

                    ASILAH
          Two years ago, marauders stole me
          from my father's douar during the
          night and sold me to the owner of
          this cafe.

                    TARZAN
          If you wish to leave, stay with me.
          I will take you to Bou Saada and
          from there it will be quite easy to
          send you back to your people.

Filled with hope and excitement, Asilah, with great
difficulty, replies in a subdued voice.

                    ASILAH
          You would do this for me?

                    TARZAN
          Could I do any less for a brave
          girl who has done so much for us?

Thrilled, her face is alive with suppressed joy.

                    ASILAH
          My father, Kadour Ben Saden, is a
          great sheik and he will surely
          reward you for my return.

                    TARZAN
          Your father? Sheik Ben Saden is
          your father?

                    ASILAH
          Yes, that is what I said and --

                    TARZAN
          -- He's here.

The girl is stunned.

                    ASILAH
          My father, is here?

Grinning with the good news, he nods.

                    TARZAN
          I bought a horse from him and we
          dined together earlier today...
          he's here in Sidi Aissa.

                              ASILAH
                    How can it be? Oh, I am truly
                    fortunate this night.

Suddenly their conversation is interrupted by the alert
Abdul.

                              ABDUL
                    Shh!

The men on the street below are joined by a few others and
their voices carry loud and clear through the cool clear
night.

A conversation takes place between them and abruptly they all
depart.

                              ASILAH
                    It is you they seek, Monsieur.
                    They said that the man who offered
                    the reward for your death is at
                    Akmed din Soulef's house with a
                    broken wrist and has offered even
                    more money for them to ambush you
                    on the road to Bou Saada.

                              TARZAN
                    That must be the man who attacked
                    me in the courtyard...

                              ABDUL
                    ... and it's the same man who
                    followed us throughout the day. I
                    saw him with another man earlier
                    talking with her in the cafe... I
                    thought they had left.

                              ASILAH
                    Why are they trying to kill you?

                              TARZAN
                    I really don't know -- unless --
                    no, it couldn't be.

Tarzan shakes his head to dispel the thought that was
beginning to form in his mind.

With the cafe, courtyard and streets now empty, Tarzan lowers
himself carefully into the room below.

Looking over the side, Abdul and Asilah await Tarzan's
return.

MOMENTS LATER

A hand grabs the roof edge and soon he's at their side again.

Tarzan lowers Abdul down to the window and then the girl into Abdul's arms.

EXT. CAFE MAURE - ASILAH'S BEDROOM WINDOW - NIGHT

Hanging from the sill, Abdul drops down to the street below.

Tarzan takes the girl in his sinewy arms and, as he jumps out, she cries out involuntarily.

EXT. SIDI AISSA - STREET - CONTINUOUS

Impressed and filled with admiration, she looks up into his noble, handsome face with her supple arms still clinging around his neck.

                    ASILAH
          Such strength! Monsieur, is truly
          a powerful man... more so than even
          el adrea, our black lion.

                    TARZAN
          I've heard much about el adrea.

Tarzan lowers her down to ground gently.

                    TARZAN
          I'd like to see one.

INT. INN - FRONT COUNTER - NIGHT

Sitting behind the counter, the Innkeeper dozes. His head drops slowly forward and then jerks backward as he wrestles with the z monster.

ENTRANCE

Tarzan, Abdul and Asilah, burst through the doors!

                    TARZAN
          Innkeeper!

FRONT COUNTER

The sound of the commanding voice turns the tide in his sleepy battle, and the Innkeeper awakens with a start.

> INNKEEPER
> Who -- what?

Still a little befuddled, he eases into reality.

> INNKEEPER
> (reluctantly)
> Oh, it's you, Monsieur Tarzan. How
> may I serve you?

> TARZAN
> I'd like for you to have Sheik
> Kadour Ben Saden awakened
> immediately and brought here --
> it's important.

Raising both hands as if to stop any further words...

> INNKEEPER
> That, Monsieur, I cannot do. The
> hour is late and I do not wish to
> incur the wrath of my guests.

Tarzan plops a 20-franc gold piece on the counter.

> INNKEEPER
> But of course if it's urgent, I
> will see to it immediately.

INT. INN - LOBBY - NIGHT (15 MINUTES LATER)

With a bellboy in the lead, Sheik Ben Saden is ushered into their presence.

Calm, though riddled with questions, the distinguished sheik recognizes Tarzan as they stand to greet him.

> SHEIK BEN SADEN
> Monsieur Tarzan, what can be so
> urgent that you --

His eyes alight upon Asilah standing at the ape-man's side and he lets out an emotional cry.

> SHEIK BEN SADEN
> Daughter! My child!

                    ASILAH
          Father!

He takes his daughter in his arms as tears of joy well up in
his eyes while Asilah weeps gently.

                    SHEIK BEN SADEN
          Fate has been kind to an old man.

INT. INN - LOBBY - NIGHT (LATER)

Rising from the couch with his daughter at his side, Sheik
Ben Saden comes before Tarzan with an outstretched hand.

                    SHEIK BEN SADEN
          Monsieur, Tarzan, all that I have
          is yours... even my life.

Tarzan bows his head at thus being honored and as Sheik Ben
Saden turns to take his leave, he's stopped by a thought and
turning back towards Tarzan takes hold of his arm...

                    SHEIK BEN SADEN
          At first light we depart for Bou
          Saada... you will ride with us,
          yes?

Tarzan, with a questioning glance, looks at Abdul who quickly
acquiesces to take part in the journey.

                    TARZAN
          Abdul and I, both.

EXT. PETIT SAHARA - MORNING

Split in two by the horizon, the weak, orange face of the sun
mounts an ascent.

Seven horses move along a harsh terrain with scant vegetation
made up of sparse grass and tufted, miniscule shrubs as far
as the eye can see.

The view of the horizon stops at the rugged, Saharan Atlas
mountain range, far into the distance.

Riding together are Sheik Ben Saden, his daughter, his
entourage of four horsemen, Tarzan and Abdul.

Abdul, watchful, scans the terrain to their rear.

EXT. PETIT SAHARA - AFTERNOON

A light wind lashes them with desert dust as the horses struggle through fetlock-deep sand.

Following the example of his desert friends, Tarzan covers his lower face with a handkerchief as they continue their trek southward towards Bou Saada.

The barren landscape is now accentuated by low rocky hills all about them.

As they reach the summit of a hillock, Abdul reins in his horse and turning about spots six horsemen on their trail.

                    ABDUL
               (pointing)
          We're being followed!

White-shrouded, mounted figures disappear and reappear, like desert phantoms, as they follow the lay of the land.

                    SHEIK BEN SADEN
               (looking at Tarzan)
          Friends of yours?

                    TARZAN
          Unfortunately, yes. I regret
          having brought this burden upon
          you.

                    SHEIK BEN SADEN
          It is no burden... not from a
          friend.

                    TARZAN
          Nevertheless, it is my problem and
          I will stay behind and deal with
          these men... for the last time.

The sheik stops his horse, and everyone else does likewise. He considers Tarzan for a moment with his proud, regal countenance.

                    SHEIK BEN SADEN
          I will not allow you to fight these
          men alone. If you stay, we stay.
          There's nothing more to be said.

Sheik Ben Saden spurs his splendid horse forward and the march resumes.

The shrouded riders keep their pursuit at a prescribed
distance, never coming too close or straying too far from
their quarry.

EXT. PETIT SAHARA - HILLOCK - LATE AFTERNOON

Upon another hillock Tarzan's party rests.

Tarzan, Sheik Ben Saden and Abdul stand together regarding
the pursuers as they too rest at the same distance on another
rise of the desolate land.

Without looking at either one of them.

                    SHEIK BEN SADEN
              When darkness falls, they will
              come.

EXT. BOU SAADA - OUTSKIRTS - NIGHT

The city lights of Bou Saada shine brightly in a moonless
night as the column of seven horses approaches the fringes of
the isolated town.

Abdul coaxes his horse beside that of Tarzan's and speaks to
him in hushed tones.

                    ABDUL
              By sunset, they had closed the gap
              between us. I fear they'll be upon
              us before we reach the city.

                    TARZAN
              Ride up ahead and say nothing to
              the sheik. I will deal with these
              characters.

                    ABDUL
              If you stay, I stay.

Tarzan doesn't argue the point and watches the column ahead
of him as it descends upon Bou Saada.

                    TARZAN
              Let's go.

Together, moving slowly, so as not to alert the rest of the
company, they ride back towards a rocky hillock.

EXT. BOU SAADA - OUTSKIRTS - HILLOCK - NIGHT

On the sloping backside of the hillock they tie-off their mounts to the low growing shrubs.

Tarzan gives Abdul his belt with the revolvers and takes a carbine from his saddle holster with ammunition, for himself.

Armed, they take-up advantageous positions among the large boulders as they await the shrouded riders.

With the city lights behind them, the night before them leaves little to their vision.

The sound of galloping horses amplified by the cold, clear and moonless night reaches them long before Tarzan first catches sight of the ghostly shrouds of the riders.

With his powerful voice Tarzan challenges them.

> TARZAN
> Halt or we'll open fire!

The unexpected challenge causes the white-shrouded figures to rein in their mounts to skidding stops.

Without warning one of the riders opens fire on Tarzan's location and then all of them dash in from different directions.

Tarzan and Abdul fire at the muzzle flashes only, as the assault commences.

From all sides, bullets are laid into them ricoheting and echoing far into the reaches of the starry sky.

Slowly, the shrouded riders begin to encircle them as they tighten the net.

One rider comes in a little too close and Tarzan's night-eyes spot him and so does his carbine.

Crying out, the rider falls to the ground and his horse, spooked, darts off into the wilds of the night.

Angered by the fall of one of their number, the shrouded riders, charge.

The fusillade from the hillock repels the mad rush and as they retreat, a bullet rams through one of their skulls.

Like a man in shock, the unlucky one drops from the saddle.

Silence reigns as the thwarted riders retreat into the haven of darkness.

Tarzan and Abdul take advantage of the lull and reload.

                    ABDUL
          Perhaps they have gone.

Tarzan shakes his head.

                    TARZAN
          No, there's still out there.

                    ABDUL
          I see nothing... I hear nothing...
          most assuredly they have left.

                    TARZAN
          I can hear them... get ready.

                    ABDUL
          How --

Yelling riders renew their assault on their position.

Firing as they charge, Tarzan and Abdul reciprocate but their bullets are not the only ones targeting the riders.

From the direction of Bou Saada a shouting band of riders charges in firing into the enemy.

Out numbered and effectively defeated, the shrouded riders shoot one last volley and hightail it from the field of battle.

                    SHEIK BEN SADEN
          Tarzan! Abdul!

                    TARZAN
          Who are you?

                    SHEIK BEN SADEN
          It is I, Sheik Kadour Ben Saden.

                    TARZAN
          We're coming down.

At the foot of the hillock the party reunites.

                    SHEIK BEN SADEN
          I feared we would not be in time.
          Why did you not tell us you were
          going to ambush these men?

                    TARZAN
          The thought crossed my mind but for
          your daughter... I did not want to
          risk her life.

                    SHEIK BEN SADEN
          Nevertheless, the odds would have
          been better.

                    TARZAN
          True, but it's over now.

                    SHEIK BEN SADEN
          Perhaps... perhaps not. Let us go.

EXT. BOU SAADA - OUTSKIRTS - NIGHT

Near Bou Saada, the group encounters a cavalry of soldiers
who at the orders of the officer in charge surround the small
party of late travellers.

                    OFFICER
          Who are you?

                    SHEIK BEN SADEN
          I am Sheik Kadour Ben Saden and
          these are family and friends.

                    OFFICER
          We're investigating the sound of
          gunfire. Were you involved?

                    SHEIK BEN SADEN
          Yes, Monsieur. Two of my friends
          stayed behind to find out why six
          men where following us and when we
          went back seeking them, we found
          them engaged with the marauders and
          managed to run them off. We
          suffered no casualties, but I am
          told that at least two of their
          number are dead.

                    OFFICER
          Where are the bodies?

                    SHEIK BEN SADEN
          Near a rocky hillock... a few miles
          from here along this very path.

                    OFFICER
          In case there are more questions,
          I'll need your names.

                    SHEIK BEN SADEN
          We are at your disposal, Monsieur.

                       OFFICER
               Sergeant!

The sergeant tags another cavalryman, who ignites a lantern;
the sergeant then whips out a pad and pen, and begins
gathering their names.

MINUTES LATER

The lantern goes out.

The Officer cries out a few commands and the cavalry,
outlined by the myriad stars above, reforms and resumes its
march onward.

EXT. BOU SAADA - SOUTHERN PASS - EARLY MORNING (2 DAYS LATER)

Tarzan sits on his proud and lively mount.

His steel-grey eyes follow Sheik Ben Saden, his alluring
daughter and their entourage as they file through the pass
far in the distance, descending as they move further and
further away like a mirage on the verge of dissolving into
the desert air.

Regret mixed with longing reflect his state of mind at their
departure.

He tugs lightly on the reigns, turns the horse's head in the
direction of Bou Saada, taps the sides of his mount with the
stirrups and gallops away.

EXT. BOU SAADA - HOTEL DU PETIT SAHARA - MORNING

A large two-story hotel stands alone enclosed with a low
masonry wall surmounted by an iron fence with small pillars
at intervals similar to the ones upon the roof of the
building.

A six-horse diligence before the hotel unloads baggage,
customers and mail.

Several camels are parked outside the enclosure with their
handlers nearby.

Arabs and Berbers in burnouses are gathered in various areas
of the hotel grounds, while European tourists, soldiers and
other natives stroll to and fro before the tall edifice.

118.

A few enter and others exit in the routine life of an inn.

One of those exiting the inn is Abdul with a big youthful grin on his bright face.

Near the diligence he opens a fist filled with ten gold coins. He drops them into a leather bag, secures it to his waist and after exchanging a few words with the driver climbs into the diligence.

INT. HOTEL DU PETIT SAHARA - BAR - MORNING

Tarzan orders breakfast and while he waits, his roving eyes fall on Lt. Gernois who is still breakfasting in the officer's dining room.

An Arab in a white burnous negotiates his way through the dining room to stop at Lt. Gernois' table.

He leans over and speaks to Lt. Gernois and as he rises to leave, the parting of his burnous exposes an arm in a sling.

Tarzan's eyes narrow and stick to the Arab as he exits the dining room through an alternate door.

The BARTENDER brings Tarzan coffee and a sealed envelope on a small tray.

                    BARTENDER
          You are Monsieur Tarzan?

                    TARZAN
          Yes, that's me.

                    BARTENDER
          This letter has just arrived on the
          diligence for you... your breakfast
          will be here shortly.

The Bartender sets the tray down before Tarzan.

                    TARZAN
          Thank you.

As the Bartender continues his duties, Tarzan sips the welcome hot coffee and glances at the letter.

After a few more sips, he puts the coffee down and opens the sealed envelope.

He picks up his coffee cup, takes another sip, and his eyes shift as they take in the letter.

                    D'ARNOT (V.O.)
Dear Tarzan,

I hope this letter finds you well.
Recently, I visited London on a
business trip and was pleasantly
surprised when I bumped into, of
all people, Mr. Philander and he
did not come alone. At his
invitation, I met the rest of the
group at the Greystoke mansion
(your mansion, mon ami) where I was
warmly greeted by Professor Porter,
Miss Porter, Clayton, Esmeralda,
and a friend of Clayton's by the
name of Tennington.

From what I was able to gather,
Clayton and Miss Porter are to be
married rather soon in a subdued
wedding ceremony due to his
father's recent death. Mr.
Philander, however, maintains that
Jane has no real desire to go
through with it and that she has
already postponed the marriage
three times. Nevertheless, it
seems that the wedding will take
place this time.

I was bombarded by questions
concerning you especially by Miss
Porter and I gladly obliged them.
I informed her that your wish is to
ultimately return back to your
jungle. This upset her not a
little, though she believes it a
better life for you than the life
of civilization where nothing is as
it seems. Looking directly at me,
she said that despite her ordeal in
the jungle, that they were the best
days of her life and she will
always cherish those memories in
her heart. I believe she suspects
my knowledge of the marriage that
could not be and wanted me to
impart to you her thoughts.

Clayton, on the other hand,
appeared agitated by the mere
mention of your name, though he was
kind in his regards for you.
                    (MORE)

                    D'ARNOT (V.O.) (CONT'D)
          Could it be that he realizes your
          true identity?

          Meanwhile, his friend, Lord
          Tennington, wants to circumnavigate
          Africa and asked the others and me
          to join him in this mad voyage. I,
          of course, declined.

          Once back at Paris, I met the Count
          and the Countess De Coude at the
          races. They asked about you and
          wish you well in your career. They
          both hold you in high esteem and
          hope for your return to Paris.
          Olga informed me that she forced
          her brother out of France with
          20,000 francs because he was
          looking to do you harm.

          She and the count feared there
          could be only one outcome and she
          did not want his blood on your
          hands. Orders have just come in
          and I'm to report to my ship.
          Write to me when you can, in care
          of my vessel. It may take some
          time, but the letter will get to me
          in the end.

          Your friend,

          Paul D'Arnot.

A dark mood settles over him for a moment, but only for a
moment and then he folds the letter and stows it away in one
of his many pockets with a half, meditative smile.

                    TARZAN
          You wasted your money, Countess.

Tarzan takes another sip of his coffee and his breakfast
arrives.

MONTAGE - TARZAN HUNTS AND SHADOWS SOME MORE

1) From a fruit stand across a street, Tarzan spies on Lt.
Gernois as he talks with the white-robed Arab in an outdoor
cafe.

2) Gazelles graze on the low grasses of the dry landscape
surrounded by hills and mountains. Tarzan removes the scoped
rifle from its boot and takes aim while still mounted.

He takes his eye from the scope and shaking his head with a distasteful look on his face, returns the rifle to its holster.

3) Strolling back to his hotel, he finds the white-robed figure exiting the very hotel and shadows him, but loses him in the crowded street.

EXT. BOU SAADA - OUTSKIRTS - RAVINE - DAY (3 WEEKS LATER)

Through a rocky ravine, Tarzan's horse picks its way. The sun is high in a clear sky. A slight wind disturbs Tarzan's handkerchief tied around his neck.

A bullet explodes from the barrel of a rifle and the sound echoes as it travels towards Tarzan's back, but the trajectory is foiled by the wind as it's lifted off its target.

The impact of the bullet goes through Tarzan's cork helmet knocking it off his head.

He wheels his mount around and gallops back along the trail but after searching and finding no one he goes back and leaning low to one side of the saddle he recovers his cork helmet.

Tarzan examines the hole putting a finger through the perforation.

> TARZAN
> Olga, you most <u>definitely</u> wasted
> your money.

INT. OFFICER'S CLUB - EVENING

A gramophone plays classical music filling the medium sized dining room with atmosphere.

Tarzan along with several officers are seated and feasting. Opposite Tarzan sits Cpt. Gerard, who's busy drinking red wine, and to the right of the captain, Lt. Gernois.

Cpt. Gerard, puts down his glass and looking at Tarzan...

> CPT. GERARD
> (smiling)
> How's the lion quest progressing?
> Any luck?

                         TARZAN
             Not good. I haven't so much as
             heard a lion's cough, much less
             seen one. In fact, I've been
             considering moving further south
             for better hunting grounds.

                         CPT. GERARD
             Then you must come with us!
             Lieutenant Gernois and I will be
             moving out tomorrow with a hundred
             men for Djelfa to patrol that
             marauder infested region.

Cpt. Gerard begins cutting his venison.

                         CPT. GERARD
             You'll have our company, at least
             until we reach the city. Will you
             join us?

Lt. Gernois' face tightens at the unwelcomed invitation.

Tarzan is surprised but not lost for words.

                         TARZAN
             You certainly know how to make a
             man feel wanted.

Tarzan raises his wine glass.

                         TARZAN
             I could not have hoped for a better
             opportunity.

Tarzan and Cpt. Gerard clink their glasses together and
drink.

                         TARZAN
             And now that I have a real horse,
             the trip will undoubtedly be more
             bearable.

Cpt. Gerard, remembering his previous horse, laughs along
with a few others.

                         CPT. GERARD
             Who knows, I and a few of my men
             may join you on one of your hunting
             excursions.

                         TARZAN
             Just say the word... good company
             is always welcome.

Cpt. Gerard raises his glass in acknowledgment of the
compliment and takes another drink.

                    CPT. GERARD
          You know... these lions are not to
          be taken lightly. They'll give you
          more than a run for your money...
          they're not antelopes.

                    TARZAN
          But even antelopes can be dangerous
          especially if one hunts them alone.
          But, unlike some, the antelope is
          not a cowardly animal... it's in
          its nature to run away.

Tarzan drops a cursory glance on Lt. Gernois who's face
flushes as he tugs uncomfortably at his collar.

EXT. PETIT SAHARA - DAY

A high temperate sun spreads its warming arms over six Arab
horsemen following the coattails of two columns of elite
spahis, from a quarter mile back.

Their faces are half-covered with only their sinister eyes
denouncing them.

Riding in the rear of the two columns is Lt. Gernois, who
occasionally throws a glance over his shoulders towards the
trailing riders.

Tarzan and Cpt. Gerard head the columns.

                    TARZAN
          You realize we're being followed.

Cpt. Gerard, keeping his eyes ahead, smiles a knowing smile
and then glances at Tarzan.

                    CPT. GERARD
          They asked permission to tag along.
          It seems the reports of the
          marauders have spooked them.

Tarzan's brow contracts and his grey eyes narrow as he
considers the new information.

He refocuses far out into the desolate plains mixed with
mountains and isolated hilltops, as he and Cpt. Gerard
followed by a long train of cavalry and the trailing Arabs,
push through an inhospitable and thankless land towards
Djelfa.

EXT. DJELFA - OUTSKIRTS - DAY (2 DAYS LATER)

Tarzan riding in from a hunting trip, discovers the spahis striking camp.

Merchants with their beasts of burden and goods begin to pack up their belongings.

Further away Tarzan sees Cpt. Gerard in talks with Lt. Gernois.

Before Tarzan's approach, Lt. Gernois departs to carry out his instructions.

With his hands on his hips, Cpt. Gerard, who's always in a positive mood, waits for Tarzan to get to him.

                    TARZAN
          Leaving already?

                    CPT. GERARD
          Duty calls.

And noticing that Tarzan has returned empty handed...

                    CPT. GERARD
          What, no luck?

                    TARZAN
          Nothing, and I thought this was
          lion country.

                    CPT. GERARD
          Ride with us, if you're up to it.

Cpt. Gerard grunts as he throws a saddle over his horse.

                    CPT. GERARD
          You can help us hunt men, instead.

Tarzan's rambunctious mount wheels about and as he steadies his animated horse, with light reins and a low voice, he spots Lt. Gernois conversing with a burnoused Arab.

                    TARZAN
          Captain, I accept your invitation.

The Arab leaps onto his horse and rides off kicking up sand as his horse races away.

Cpt. Gerard finishes cinching his saddle to the horse, mounts and Tarzan and he trot towards the forming columns of the cavalry.

EXT. MOUNTAIN RANGE - MORNING

Near the base of the mountains, Cpt. Gerard with a raised
hand and a commanding voice, halts the patrol.

He looks over his shoulder to one of his men.

>   CPT. GERARD
>   Sergeant, tell Lieutenant Gernois
>   to come up here.

MOMENTS LATER

Galloping horses rush past the column with the sergeant
retaking his place and Lt. Gernois reporting to Cpt. Gerard.

>   LT. GERNOIS
>   Yes, Captain?

Cpt. Gerard stretches out an arm to indicate which column Lt.
Gernois is to take and what area he's to cover.

>   CPT. GERARD
>   Take half the men and cover that
>   side of the mountain range... I'll
>   take other.

He turns to Tarzan.

>   CPT. GERARD
>   Well, my friend, choose with whom
>   you will ride today.

Tarzan raises an eyebrow and then looks over at Lt. Gernois
and then back to Cpt. Gerard. He's about to reply when he's
interrupted by the lieutenant.

>   LT. GERNOIS (O.S.)
>   Captain...

Cpt. Gerard and Tarzan turn to the taciturn and aloof man
that is, Lt. Gernois.

>   LT. GERNOIS
>   ... I'll consider it a great favor,
>   if Monsieur Tarzan would do me the
>   honor of riding with my patrol.

Both, surprised by the unexpected offer, look at each other
and Cpt. Gerard unable to explain his lieutenant's change of
character, simply shrugs.

                    TARZAN
          He doesn't leave me much choice,
          does he?

Grinning, Cpt. Gerard shakes his head.

EXT. MOUNTAIN RANGE - DAY

With Tarzan at his side, Lt. Gernois leads the spahi
detachment through rough, rocky terrain as they ascend into
the mountains.

Lt. Gernois, no longer in the presence of his commander,
resumes his unsocial and gruff persona ignoring the ape-man
altogether.

CANYON

Filing through a narrow canyon, they force their reluctant
steeds upwards until they reach a rivulet.

Lt. Gernois stops the patrol.

                    LT. GERNOIS
          We'll rest here for an hour.
          Dismount!

EXT. MOUNTAIN RANGE - VALLEY - DAY (A FEW HOURS LATER)

Exiting the canyon, they come upon a valley with divergent
gorges.

Lt. Gernois brings his binoculars to bear and studies the
terrain.

                    LT. GERNOIS
          We'll save time if we break up with
          each group searching a different
          gorge.

After forming two patrols, Lt. Gernois rides up to Tarzan
who's been sitting on his mount quietly and patiently
watching the preparations being made.

                    LT. GERNOIS
          And you, Monsieur, will remain
          here.

Tarzan's tranquil mood disappears.

                        TARZAN
          Lieutenant Gernois, I did not ride
          all this way to --

                        LT. GERNOIS
          -- I'm sorry, Monsieur, but your
          safety is my responsibility and my
          patrols may encounter fighting.

                        TARZAN
          I joined your patrol to fight
          marauders and not to sit here doing
          nothing.

Lt. Gernois curls his lip and, expressing his true nature,
puts his foot down.

                        LT. GERNOIS
          That is exactly what you will do,
          Monsieur... nothing. You are under
          my authority and you will stay put
          until we return.

Not waiting to hear whatever Tarzan has to say, he quickens
his horse back to his column.

The two patrols split-off towards their assigned gorge,
leaving the ape-man alone within the isolated valley.

Tarzan leads his horse and tethers the energetic mount
underneath a nearby tree to shield it and himself from the
rays of the sun. Piqued at the deception employed by Lt.
Gernois, he snarls suddenly, startling his horse.

The horse sensing that all is not well with his master,
pushes his generous muzzle gently into Tarzan's shoulder.

Tarzan's anger melts into a smile at his horse's affection
and he in turn strokes the long, strong neck of his loyal
mount.

                        TARZAN
          It's alright, boy... he wins this
          one.

Composed, Tarzan removes the express rifle from the saddle
and checks the ammo for it and the revolvers and sitting down
with his rifle next to him, he studies the terrain of the
valley.

EXT. MOUNTAIN RANGE - VALLEY - LATE AFTERNOON

Tarzan scans the gorges as the sun begins to slip beneath the tops of the mountains, yet there is no sign of the spahi patrols.

He looks at his watch and then returns to the cover of the tree. He takes a canteen from the saddle, drinks and shares the water with his horse.

Sitting back down against the tree he inspects his rifle once again and leaning his head against the bole, closes his eyes.

EXT. MOUNTAIN RANGE - VALLEY - NIGHT

Tarzan's eyes open abruptly to the sound of fearful neighing, snorting and his horse's all-out effort to free itself from the tree.

But Tarzan is deaf to his horse's terror. His eyes are focused straight ahead of him.

Underneath the brilliance of a sterling full moon, an immense black-maned lion with a waving tail behind it, regards the ape-man with two burning orbs.

An involuntary smile marks Tarzan's lips and rising ever so slowly, he presses the rifle butt to his shoulder.

The lion crouches, belly down to the ground, the tail twitching nervously.

Tarzan's feet shift for a better position as two fiery coals follow his every move.

With a desperate pull the horse snaps the tether and races into the canyon from whence they entered the valley.

Tarzan takes aim and squeezes the trigger and as the rifle erupts, a huge mass of fangs and claws launches itself, with a tremendous roar, at the hunter.

Like a blur Tarzan is no longer there and the huge lion crashes into the tree.

Tarzan, several paces to it's flank, sends another round into it's hide and an angry, vicious roar echoes through the valley as the lion wheels bristling with unfettered rage.

Tarzan pumps two more quick, explosive shots into the leaping beast and it lands dead upon the valley floor quite close to the ape-man.

The the spirit of jungle savagery taking over, Tarzan stamps
his foot upon the neck of his mortal enemy and roars forth
the savage, eerie victory cry of the bull-ape.

The long, drawn-out cry bounces, like ricocheting bullets,
all over the valley escaping into the beyond.

EXT. MOUNTAIN RANGE - SAME TIME

A lone, hunting leopard freezes in place and then darts off
to disappear among a pile of boulders.

EXT. PETIT SAHARA - SAME TIME

Aroused Arabs rush out of their tents turning their faces
towards the mountains as their goats bleat in fright.

EXT. MOUNTAIN RANGE - GORGE - SAME TIME

A short distance from the valley, twenty white-robed figures
armed with long rifles, stop dead in their tracks at the
uncanny sound of the bloodcurdling roar.

Once it subsides, they look at one another as if seeking an
explanation and after a few whispering words among each
other, continue the silent thread through the gorge.

EXT. MOUNTAIN RANGE - VALLEY - NIGHT

A cork helmet is picked up at the base of the tree.

Tarzan reexamines the hole and then flings it out among the
rocks.

He reloads and straps the rifle to his right shoulder and
following the horse's example, disappears into the canyon.

EXT. MOUNTAIN RANGE - VALLEY - NIGHT

From the opposite side of the canyon a score of sneaky, white-
robed Arabs enter the valley and take cover behind boulders
scanning the area for their objective.

But realizing that their quarry is no longer present, they
move out towards the canyon and come upon the huge carcass of
the slain lion.

Surrounding the king of beasts, the men utter suppressed
exclamations at the rare sight.

They search the immediate area around the creature, but finding nothing, one by one, they slip into the canyon.

EXT. MOUNTAIN RANGE - CANYON - NIGHT

Moving quietly through the rock strewn canyon, like a jungle cat, Tarzan's acute ears are alive to the sounds of the night.

His ears pick up the familiar coughing of a leopard. They then, pick up the unmistakable sound of many bare feet moving quickly but cautiously upon the canyon floor.

Aware that he's being followed he takes cover behind a group of boulders and awaits the wolves on his trail.

Soon Tarzan's night eyes spot the burnoused stalkers emptying into his line of vision.

                    TARZAN
          Who goes there?!

A bullet careens off a boulder, and Tarzan fires back.

Scurrying from boulder to boulder the Arabs move in closer around him and as Tarzan takes a bead on a moonlit Arab, another white-robed figure's long rifle explodes and Tarzan is thrown backward by the force of the bullet into unconsciousness.

Peaking over their cover the Arabs move-in cautiously and soon surround the body of the fallen ape-man. A STALKER moves in closer to inspect the body and puts his ear to the man's massive chest.

                    STALKER
               (in Arabic; subtitled)
          He still lives!

Another, places the barrel of his long rifle to Tarzan's head.

                    STALKER
               (in Arabic; subtitled)
          Do not! The reward will be much
          greater if we bring him alive.

EXT. PETIT SAHARA - NIGHT

The high searing moonlight falls upon a group of Arabs
burdened with the body of another man as they exit the canyon
and begin their track across the desolate terrain of the
Petit Sahara.

Bound and unconscious Tarzan rides upon the shoulders of four
of his captors.

Blood oozes from his temple leaving a dripping blood trail
behind them.

EXT. PETIT SAHARA - MORNING

Tarzan awakens with his face and the side of his head covered
in dried blood.

With the rising sun full in his face, Tarzan squints and
lifts his aching head.

Up ahead he makes out two Arabs with a small herd of saddled
horses.

Feeling movement, the four Arabs lower him to the ground and
cut the bindings from his feet. He is then herded to one of
the horses, goaded to mount and his hands tied to the saddle.

Once Tarzan is secured, the white-robed cavalry sets off at a
brisk pace with their prisoner in tow.

EXT. PETIT SAHARA - DOUAR - NOON

A light, sandy wind whips the flaps of a tent village.
Thirty large tents are spaced creating streets within the
desert community.

Before the tents, old men and women sit with their children --
talking or partaking of food.

Before this village a cavalcade of burnoused riders comes to
a halt with a prisoner. No sooner do the riders dismount
than Tarzan is surrounded and beset by veiled curmudgeons who
fling varied insults at the helpless ape-man, while others
resort to sticks and stones.

After conferring with one of the riders, an enraged SHEIK ALI
BEN AHMED, scatters the women back to their tents and turning
to his men he lays down the law speaking in a loud voice so
that not only the men, but also the dispersed women, can hear
his edict.

                         SHEIK BEN AHMED
                      (in Arabic; subtitled;
                       pointing to Tarzan)
                  I don't know what the stranger
                  wants with this man, but while
                  under my tent he will be respected
                  and treated just. A man who kills
                  el adrea single-handedly at night,
                  deserves no less.

INT. TENT - AFTERNOON

A large ornate carpet covers the interior of an empty tent.
The entrance flaps are tied off allowing the light to push
most of the shadows aside.

Framed by the entrance, Tarzan grows in size as he nears the
tent with the prodding of two guards behind him.

After entering, Tarzan is forced to sit and the bonds from
his wrists are removed.

A veiled woman enters with food and drink, sets it before him
and departs.

Tarzan rubs his chafed wrists as he looks around. His
curiosity sated, he takes advantage of the free meal.

INT. TENT - AFTERNOON (5 MINUTES LATER)

No sooner is he finished eating, than the guards force him to
his belly and tie his feet and the hands behind his back.

Tarzan positions himself so that he can look out as he leans
to one side.

Only one guard sits outside the entrance facing away.

Tarzan tests his bonds, but no amount of effort can snap the
tough strands binding his wrists together.

Realizing the futility of it, Tarzan desists and getting into
as comfortable a position as possible, he waits.

INT. TENT - SUNSET

Several burnoused men enter the tent and with the light
waning, a lantern is lit.

One of them, Furtive Man, with the lower part of his face covered crouches low near Tarzan and removes the veil from his face.

Rokoff sneers into Tarzan's unaffected countenance. His short, pointy beard and thin mustache only enhance his wicked visage.

His identity established, Tarzan ignores him.

                    ROKOFF/FURTIVE MAN
          Greetings, Monsieur Tarzan. It is
          very gratifying to see you again.
          Do you not agree?

Aware that Tarzan is purposely ignoring him, his short temper erupts.

                    ROKOFF
          Look at me when I speak to you,
          pig!

Inflamed with blind rage, Rokoff's stands up and kicks Tarzan in the side with a heavy boot.

                    ROKOFF
          That's for the first time we met.

He kicks him again.

                    ROKOFF
          And that's for the second time...
          and these... these, are for all the
          others.

Rokoff goes berserk and begins kicking Tarzan viciously all over his body.

Sheik Ben Ahmed, who is among them, is provoked to anger by the abuse.

                    SHEIK BEN AHMED
          Enough! If you're going to kill
          him, then kill him. But I will not
          stand for this mindless abuse... in
          fact it would be interesting to see
          how you fared against him were I to
          turn him loose.

Rokoff's anger morphs into fear and the abuse stops.

                    ROKOFF
          I'll kill him now.

Rokoff pulls out a large, wicked knife and kneels next to
Tarzan.

                    SHEIK BEN AHMED
          Not now and not here. You shall
          not kill this man in my douar.
          You'll take him a day's ride from
          my territory and there you may do
          with him as you please.

Standing back up, with his eyes full of hatred still full
upon the helpless man, Rokoff reluctantly puts the blade away
and then faces this host.

                    SHEIK BEN AHMED
          And to ensure you do so, several of
          my men will accompany you.

                    ROKOFF
          Tomorrow morning, then.

                    SHEIK BEN AHMED
          You will be gone by dawn.
          Unbelievers and cowards are not
          welcome here.

Rokoff is stung by the sheik's last remark, but holds his
tongue.

Together the men turn to leave, but Rokoff unable to resist
hurling one more taunt, turns towards Tarzan, who throughout
the whole ordeal did not look at him or utter a sound.

                    ROKOFF
          Soon, Monsieur, I will kill you.
          It will be very painful and very
          slow... and then...

Rokoff snuffs out the lantern and exits.

EXT. PETIT SAHARA - DOUAR - NIGHT

From the towering mountains that watch over the douar, a
lion's thunderous roar challenges the Milky Way and the
zenith full moon.

The striking light of the moon and the splendor of infinite
heavenly candles, combine to illuminate the desert village
with a supernatural glow.

INT. TENT - NIGHT

Like a faulty bellows, moon rays sneak into the tent riddled with cracks, gaps, tears and rips throughout, producing a semi-darkness.

These rays of light give Tarzan's night eyes a weird glow as he fights to free himself from the strands binding his wrists.

The lion roars again. Tarzan stops his exertions to listen. The roar is closer this time.

A bedlam of uninterrupted roars ensues, with each roar strengthening as it closes in on the douar.

The roars suddenly stop and silence reigns.

Tarzan's ears pick up stealthy movements towards his tent. The sounds stop and the dead silence that follows screams for release.

Tarzan lies motionless on his side with his back only a few feet from the panel separating him from creature without.

Tarzan parts his lips in a barely perceptible smile as the rear panel behind him, like a dark spectre, rises slowly allowing the head and shoulders of the creature ingress, exposing the interior, momentarily, with a touch of moonlight.

The panel drops and the semi-darkness prevails.

Tarzan, knowing the end is near, keeps his eyes steady and staring straight ahead.

He can hear the creeping of the creature. It stops next to him breathing quickly.

Instead of a clawed paw, a hand gropes in the dark and lands gently on the side of his face.

And instead of fetid muzzle, a pair of soft lips whisper his name.

                    ASILAH
          Tarzan?

                    TARZAN
          Yes, it's me, but who in blazes are
          you?

                    ASILAH
          It is I, Asilah... now be still. I
          am going to cut your bonds.

She works quickly and soon Tarzan is free.

                    ASILAH
          Follow me.

Through the same panel she used to enter, they crawl out into
the compound of the douar leaving the semi-darkness behind.

EXT. PETIT SAHARA - DOUAR - NIGHT

Crouching low, they move swiftly and quietly towards a group
of shrubs outside the douar and take cover behind them.
Peering over the shrubs and detecting no activity, the girl
relaxes her guard.

Tarzan stares at her with a mystified expression.

                    TARZAN
               (whispering)
          How is it that you're here... and
          how did you know I was a prisoner
          in that tent?

                    ASILAH
               (whispering)
          Come, let us go. I will explain
          along the way.

Asilah grabs the ape-man's hand and leads him after her.

EXT. PETIT SAHARA - NIGHT (15 MINUTES LATER)

The resplendent light of a mute moon lights their way as
Asilah -- dressed in a light tunic that falls just below her
knees and wrapped in a sash that accentuates her small,
supple waist -- leads Tarzan towards the rugged mountains
through desolation and the dead stillness of night.

Asilah looks up at the tall and powerful man with a soul
stirring smile.

                    ASILAH
          I have travelled far to find you
          and I feared I would not be in
          time. But now, I am filled with
          joy, for I have found you alive and
          well. We have a great distance yet
          to go before we are out of danger.

She lapses into silence and looks in different directions
ahead as they continue their trek through the wasteland.

> ASILAH
> I was afraid that I might not reach
> you because of el adrea. I hope
> the scent of the horses did not
> reach him. We should be nearing
> them soon.

Tarzan regards the lithe figure with admiration.

> TARZAN
> You're a brave girl to risk all for
> a man you hardly know... an
> unbeliever, no less.

Asilah, stops and faces him standing proudly to her full
height.

> ASILAH
> I am Asilah, the daughter of Sheik
> Kadour Ben Saden. Should I not
> attempt to save the man who saved
> me?

> TARZAN
> Still, what you did took great
> courage -- but tell me, how did you
> know where to find me?

Asilah studies the face of the impending mountain range.

> ASILAH
> My cousin, Achmet Din Taieb, was
> there when they brought you into
> Sheik Ali Ben Ahmed's douar. And
> when he told us of a large
> Frenchman that had been captured
> for another Frenchman, I knew it
> was you. My father was out hunting
> so I tried to enlist other men from
> my tribe but none wished to help an
> unbeliever much less start a
> quarrel with another tribe. So,
> when the night came, I rode out
> with an extra horse for you.

Asilah stops and does a quick sweep of the area and then with
a troubled look creeping over her face, she turns to Tarzan.

> ASILAH
> They are gone! Here is where I
> tethered both horses.

Tarzan easily finds the disturbed ground and the tracks of
the horses and more.

He crouches near the find and the girl next to him.

>   ASILAH
>   What is it?

>   TARZAN
>   This is where the shrub you tied
>   your horses was before it was
>   pulled from the ground... and these
>   are their tracks.

Tarzan glances at the worried girl.

>   TARZAN
>   (pointing)
>   And those are el adrea's tracks.

With sad eyes she looks into the ape-mans face and dropping a
gentle hand on his shoulder...

>   ASILAH
>   (in a mournful whisper)
>   Please say it is not true.

Before he can stop her, she buries her sad, sweet face in his
neck in preparation for tears, but Tarzan stems them from
fully flowing and comforts her with his arms.

>   TARZAN
>   Fear not, Asilah. The lion has not
>   feasted this night.

Slowly, she lifts her head from his neck and faces his noble
countenance with a recovering smile, wiping away the wet
corners of both eyes.

>   ASILAH
>   (sniffles)
>   I am glad to hear it. It would
>   have been difficult to bear the
>   loss of my beautiful stallion... it
>   was a gift from my father.

>   TARZAN
>   Odds are you'll see your stallion
>   again. A lion is no match for a
>   horse in open country... lions are
>   no good at long distances.

Tarzan rises bringing her up with him and holds her by the
shoulders.

                         TARZAN
               And now, my intrepid young lady,
               where to?

She grins and with a feminine gesture points towards the
looming mountain range.

EXT. MOUNTAIN RANGE - NIGHT

A light, cool wind caresses Asilah's long locks as she leads
Tarzan upwards along a spur.

High up along a known trail they pause and Tarzan and the
girl take in the night vista of the Petit Sahara punctuated
by shrubs, rocks, and lonely hills that sit upon a barren
flatness that goes on and on.

Far below them, the brilliant moonlight bounces off the tents
of the douar.

Tarzan's chest swells as he takes a deep breath of the
enlivening night breeze.

The girl touching Tarzan's arm to attract his attention,
resumes the trudge up the steep and rocky mountain trail.

EXT. MOUNTAIN RANGE - NIGHT (LATER)

In silence they follow the trail on level ground and as they
skirt an outcropping of rocks, they're met by a pair of bared
fangs and ominous, glowing eyes.

An enormous black-maned lion bars their way with a wicked
snarl that spreads wrinkles over its massive face.

Tarzan and Asilah instinctively freeze in place and the maned
monster shatters the night with a deafening and reverberating
roar.

The lion, unmoving, glares at its puny prey with smoldering
eyes.

Tarzan with a snarl creeping up on his face and burning eyes
of his own, extends an open hand to Asilah without turning
his head, his full concentration on the malevolent creature
before him.

                         TARZAN
               Give me the knife.

Asilah slaps the hilt into his open palm.

Tarzan pushes her back behind him carefully.

                    TARZAN
          Walk back slowly, then run back
          down the mountain once you're out
          of sight.

                    ASILAH
               (hopeless)
          It will make no difference... it is
          the end.

The lion's tail stops swaying from side to side and dropping
its grimacing muzzle to the ground it begins to edge forward.

                    TARZAN
          Go! He's going to charge.

Galvanized by the suddenness of his command, the girl takes
several awkward steps behind him but, horror-stricken, she
stands petrified with eyes glued on the nightmare before her.

Yet, her eyes open even wider when she realizes that the
rumbling growls near her are those of Tarzan.

Tarzan crouched, cautiously changes his position with a few
steps to keep the girl out of its charge.

The lion's fiery eyes follow the moving man and releasing a
thunderous roar it hurls its massive body full at the ape-
man.

In a blink of an eye, Tarzan flanks the engine of
destruction, grabs the mane with his right hand and pulls
himself onto its back.

Roaring horribly, the lion rears up on its hind legs and
Tarzan loses no time in wrapping his mighty right arm around
its throat and locking his long legs beneath the belly of the
ferocious cat before it can recover.

With parted lips and both hands pressed to her cheeks, the
girl's bosom falls and rises uncontrollably at the spectacle
being played out before her beautiful, bewildered eyes.

The deafening roars of the lion are matched only by those of
the man as the blade plunges fast and deep into the side of
the frantic and raging el adrea.

Its fangs and claws useless, the lion leaps high into the air
landing on its back again and again, but Tarzan is
entrenched.

No amount of jumping, twisting, falling or roaring can dislodge the ape-man as the blade, glinting in the moonlight, drinks deep into the lion's side to sate its inexorable thirst.

One last bellowing roar escapes the cavernous mouth of the lion before it collapses dead on the little mountain plateau.

Splattered in blood, Tarzan rises and shakes himself, unconscious of the girl's presence.

With the silver giant in the starry sky showering the tableau with an eerie light, Tarzan puts a foot on the lifeless body of the lion, and rips the mountain airwaves with the victory cry of the bull-ape.

The terrific roar shakes the poor girl into a state of uncertainty and fright as she watches what once she believed to be a man.

Turning his face from the heavens, his eyes fall upon the disquieted countenance of Asilah and with a winsome smile, the savage madness disappears.

Asilah reassured by the return of his normal demeanor moves up to Tarzan and the dead lion.

She blinks her eyes and shakes her head attempting to verify what she's seeing.

She changes her gaze, filled with awe and wonder, towards Tarzan who's kneeled and is busy wiping the bloody blade on the lion's hide.

>   ASILAH
>   What kind of man are you, that can
>   kill el adrea with nothing more
>   than a knife? Who are you,
>   Monsieur?

Tarzan stands up.

>   TARZAN
>   I'll say this... I'm not normal.

He sees her face cloud with confusion.

>   ASILAH
>   And that most terrible roar... it
>   was the cry of a beast, not of a
>   man.

                    TARZAN
          If I told you the truth, you
          wouldn't believe it.

Tarzan hands her the knife.

                    ASILAH
                 (grinning)
          I think it best, if you keep it.

Tarzan laughs.

                    TARZAN
          I'll keep it... as a gift.

He slides the blade into his side between his leather belt
and khaki trousers.

She looks down at the dead lion once again and giving the ape-
man a thoughtful glance...

                    ASILAH
          Come, we must cross before
          daylight.

With the girl slightly ahead of Tarzan, they renew their trek
across the mountain range.

EXT. MOUNTAIN RANGE - DRAW - MORNING

The fragile fingers of the sun's rays caress the sides of the
mountain range.

As they descend, Tarzan's sharp, grey eyes spot a pair of
horses feeding near a rivulet.

EXT. PETIT SAHARA - MORNING

Near the horses, the girl calls out to them and faithfully
they obey their mistress.

They mount and gallop, side by side, towards her father's
douar.

EXT. PETIT SAHARA - SHEIK BEN SADEN'S DOUAR - MORNING

In the mist of black and red striped tents, a grief-stricken
Sheik Ben Saden is busy assembling fifty of his Berber
warriors for a search and rescue of his missing daughter.

With all the riders mounted, Sheik Ben Saden takes hold of his stallion's reigns but his eyes are abducted by the shimmering, morning horizon as a pair of blurred shapes make their way towards them.

From a blur, the shapes become more tangible and the dust of the horses begins to shoot out and spread from beneath the driven animals.

A smile of grateful relief spreads over the sheik's face as he recognizes his daughter and her escort. Raising his hands and eyes upwards he breathes a silent prayer.

MONTAGE - GUEST OF THE SHEIK

1) Sheik Ben Saden embraces his daughter and then Tarzan in gratitude.

2) With voice, hands and beautiful face, Asilah narrates Tarzan's feat against el adrea.

3) Tarzan becomes the center of respect and esteem among the Berbers.

4) Tarzan is given native clothing to wear while his clothes are washed and then returned with only a slight hint of bloodstains.

5) Tarzan sits at Sheik Ben Saden's right during dinners and discussions.

6) Sheik Ben Saden and many of his men bestow Tarzan with gifts.

EXT. LONDON - GREYSTOKE MANSION - DAY

Like twin statues, two large deerhounds rest on the landing of the marble staircase yet their loyal eyes and nostrils scour the grounds for their master.

A stately, uncovered 1909 Rolls-Royce, Silver Ghost stands regally, adjacent to the pristine, white staircase.

INT. GREYSTOKE MANSION - DRAWING ROOM - DAY

Servants move about the room serving the fashionably dressed company.

All eyes are riveted upon LORD TENNINGTON, 30, tall and debonair.

                    TENNINGTON
          ... Imagine sailing through the
          Strait of Gibraltar on a clear and
          glorious day... then cruising on
          the bosom of the Mediterranean and
          then dropping anchor in the Red Sea
          to visit an exotic port you've only
          read about.

Tennington pauses to see the affect of his spellbinding
enchantment that promises more than just mere adventure.

                    TENNINGTON
          Think of it! Breakfast in the Gulf
          of Aden, lunch as we cruise the
          Arabian Sea, followed by an outdoor
          dinner as we watch the sun dip
          below the horizon on the Indian
          Ocean... these are memories you
          will never forget.

Clayton cuts in and breaks the spell.

                    CLAYTON
          I'd like to forget I ever invited
          you to tea.

A friendly burst of laughter erupts among his guests
including Tennington.

                    MR. PHILANDER
          It sounds tempting. I've never
          been to that side of the world.

                    PROF. PORTER
          It does indeed. But wouldn't we be
          crowding you?

                    TENNINGTON
               (smiles)
          Tell them, Cecil.

                    CLAYTON
          Not in the least. You can take my
          word for it... although she's a
          yacht, he thinks of the Lady Alice
          as a four-funneled, passenger
          steamship.

                    TENNINGTON
          Oh, but she's far better than any
          old steamship. First, she's
          faster.
                         (MORE)

                    TENNINGTON (CONT'D)
          Second, she's luxury personified
          and third she's better looking.

Tennington gives Jane a quick, smiling wink.

                    MR. PHILANDER
          This trip, as I understand it, will
          involve circumnavigating the
          continent of Africa?

                    TENNINGTON
          Correct. But as you've gathered,
          I'll be stopping at various places
          along the way.

                    JANE
          It sounds wonderful, Papa! Why
          can't we go?

Prof. Porter looks at his daughter a little surprised.

                    PROF. PORTER
          When did I intimate that the voyage
          was off limits?

Prof. Porter turns to Mr. Philander.

                    MR. PHILANDER
          I have no reservations.

Esmeralda not wanting to be left out...

                    ESMERALDA
                (in Southern black accent)
          If my honey child goes, Professor,
          I'm going... jungle or no jungle.

Jane jumps up and gives her mother hen a hug and a kiss and
Esmeralda reacts with a jolly grin.

Clayton watching the turning of the tide, becomes a little
vexed at everyone's lack of consideration.

                    CLAYTON
          Jane, haven't you forgotten
          something?

Jane feigns memory loss but Clayton deigns to remind her.

                    CLAYTON
          It's a little something called a
          wedding.

Jane pushes the charade forward.

                    JANE
          Oh my goodness! That's right.

She glances from Clayton to Tennington and then back to her
fiance.

                    JANE
          Why, we can marry afterwards. It's
          a once in a lifetime opportunity,
          Cecil.

Clayton eyes her a little hurt at her stance.

                    JANE
          Call it... a pre-wedding gift. My
          last trip as a single girl -- we
          won't be apart.
               (smiling)
          We'll be together the entire
          voyage.

Clayton shakes his head knowing he's been defeated and breaks
a smile.

                    CLAYTON
          You win. Have it your way, my
          dear. Anyway, I can't well fight
          all of you, can I?

He's met by approving hails and smiles.

                    CLAYTON
          And I certainly don't want to
          dampen anyone's spirits.

He takes a drink and glances at Tennington.

                    CLAYTON
          I've known Tennington for a long
          time... when it comes to sailing
          he's one of the best.

Tennington is pleased at the unanimous decision.

                    TENNINGTON
               (to Clayton)
          Thank you, old friend.

He sweeps the room with a smile and raises his glass.

                    TENNINGTON
          To God, king, country, and a safe
          voyage!

Everyone raises their glasses.

> OTHERS
> To God, king, country, and a safe
> voyage!

EXT. SHEIK BEN SADEN'S DOUAR - DAY

Tarzan sits astride a spirited mount near an escort of fifty
of Sheik Ben Saden's mounted Berber warriors.

SUPER: "A WEEK LATER"

As Sheik Ben Saden maneuvers his horse inspecting his men
before departure, Asilah comes to take leave of the ape-man.

Asilah's exotic beauty is marred only by the sadness
expressed by the light in her eyes as she looks up at Tarzan
as with one hand she caresses the powerful neck of his horse.

In the background, Sheik Ben Saden gives a command and the
cavalry moves out from the douar.

Asilah's hypnotic eyes follow their departure, only to return
to Tarzan's handsome features.

> ASILAH
> I hoped and prayed with my very
> soul, that you would stay with us.
> After you have gone, I will pray
> all the more for your return... my
> friend.

> TARZAN
> God only knows, but please don't
> let me leave without your beautiful
> smile.

At that, Asilah releases a gentle but radiant smile and
Tarzan greets it with a noble one.

She raises a delicate hand towards him and Tarzan let's it
fall into his palm.

> TARZAN
> Goodbye, Asilah. I will miss your
> spirit --

The the spirited horse throws back its head and Tarzan
steadies him.

                         TARZAN
          And most of all, your dancing.

Asilah grins and drops her eyes at the compliment.

She then meets his gaze with a pair of dark, beckoning eyes.

                         ASILAH
                    (softly)
          All you need do is ask.

                         TARZAN
          If we meet again, I just might.

Tarzan releases Asilah's reluctant hand and spurring his
excited mount forward, chases his escort, now far ahead of
him.

                                        FADE TO BLACK:

SUPER: "BOU SAADA"

EXT. BOU SAADA - OUTSKIRTS - LATE AFTERNOON

Tarzan and Sheik Ben Saden speak in whispers in a mounted
powwow.

Finished, Sheik Ben Saden jerks the reigns on his horse and
leads his men towards Bou Saada, leaving Tarzan behind.

EXT. BOU SAADA - NATIVE INN - EVENING

With a waning moon beginning it's night climb on the horizon,
A few burnoused Arabs loiter near the entrance.

INT. NATIVE INN - DINING ROOM - EVENING

Sheik Ben Saden and a few of his men lounge on a carpeted
floor around a large low table as they're served by a waiter.

A curtain is thrown aside and Tarzan is shown in by another
servant.

                         SHEIK BEN SADEN
          Were you seen by anyone?

                         TARZAN
          Not by anyone who knew me.

                    SHEIK BEN SADEN
          Come. Sit and join us.

Sheik Ben Saden speaks a few words to the waiter and food is
brought swiftly and placed before Tarzan.

Famished, Tarzan begins to sate his hunger.

Sheik Ben Saden stops eating for a moment and gives Tarzan a
thoughtful gaze with his hawkish face, who, catching the
Sheik's eyes intent upon him, does likewise.

                    TARZAN
          What is it?

                    SHEIK BEN SADEN
          I don't know if this will be of any
          help to you... a tale of a
          Frenchman impersonating an Arab has
          come to my hearing... one, that
          once wore an arm in a sling.

Tarzan's interest is immediately kindled and with a slight
grin Sheik Ben Saden lays a piece of paper before him and
motioning with his eyes...

                    SHEIK BEN SADEN
          There, is where he lives.

EXT. HOTEL DU PETIT SAHARA - NIGHT

Traffic is low at the front of the hotel but Tarzan, in
stealth, makes his way to the rear of the building and enters
through a back door.

INT. HOTEL DU PETIT SAHARA - NIGHT

Standing behind the counter, the CONCIERGE is agape at the
sudden and unexpected appearance of the ape-man.

                    CONCIERGE
          Monsieur, Tarzan!

                    TARZAN
          Is there any mail?

The Concierge stares at Tarzan as if at a ghost.

                    TARZAN
          My mail?

                    CONCIERGE
          Yes, Monsieur, of course -- I just
          -- yes, several pieces of mail are
          in your box. I'll --

The Concierge turns about and draws forth, from one of many
cubicles in the wall, several letters and lays them on the
counter before the ape-man.

Tarzan flings a pair of gold coins on the counter.

                    TARZAN
          Tell no one you've seen me.

The nervous Concierge picks up the coins.

                    CONCIERGE
          My tongue is dead, Monsieur.

Tarzan canvasses the lightly populated lobby and then goes
through the letters quickly and stopping at one, opens it.

The letter morphs from French into English.

INSERT - LETTER

          "Your present mission has been
          postponed until further notice.

          You are to embark on the next
          available steamer to Cape Town
          under the name of John Caldwell,
          London.

          Upon arriving, contact Monsieur
          Diondre Bouchard at 78 Beaumont
          Street, for further instructions.

          Home Office."

BACK TO SCENE

Tarzan folds the letter and secures it inside one of his
pockets.

                    TARZAN
          My key, please.

The Concierge, ready, hands him the key and Tarzan glides up
the stairs to his room.

EXT. BOU SAADA - ALLEY - NIGHT

Tarzan negotiates through a dark, foul alley and follows it
until it intersects another one.

The new alley continues to right but to the left, on the left-
hand side -- just shy of a dead-end -- a stone staircase
rises up onto a small landing before the door of mud-brick
building.

EXT. ROKOFF'S HIDEAWAY - NIGHT

Silent as the padded feet of the great cats, Tarzan ascends
the staircase to the landing before the door.

High above the door and just below the eaves of the roof is a
small dirty window.

Tarzan hears voices within and, stretching his arms up high,
grips the sill with his fingers and raises himself up to peer
within.

INT. ROKOFF'S HIDEAWAY - NIGHT

In a lighted, ugly room, Rokoff and Lt. Gernois sit at a
table.

                    LT. GERNOIS
          ... You dog! If not for Paulvitch,
          I'd strangle you this instant!

Unfazed, Rokoff laughs in his face.

                    ROKOFF
          Very wise, Lieutenant. We wouldn't
          want the Ministry of War to receive
          an anonymous package detailing the
          entire affair... would we?

                    LT. GERNOIS
          I lost my honor the day I met you.

Lt. Gernois looks at his hands.

                    LT. GERNOIS
          You've turned me into a murderer.

                    ROKOFF
          Come, come, now. Your honor is
          intact. Haven't we kept your
          secret? And as for Tarzan... you
          and I did not kill him.

                    LT. GERNOIS
          What do you mean? He lives? Was
          he not killed where I left him?

Rokoff weighs telling the lieutenant the truth and with a
grin and a few shakes of his head...

                    ROKOFF
          We had him as helpless as a babe,
          tied up in a tent. The next
          morning I learn that during the
          night a lion made off with our
          mutual friend. I would have
          preferred to have done it myself,
          but....

Rokoff shrugs with a gleaming, wicked grin.

                    ROKOFF
          So you see, comrade, we did not
          kill him.

Lt. Gernois is hot under the collar.

                    LT. GERNOIS
          When were you going to tell me
          this?

                    ROKOFF
          I've told you! Enough, the money
          and the papers, Lieutenant, and
          we'll be out of your life forever.

Lt. Gernois pulls out two envelopes from a leather satchel.
He hands him a very thick envelope.

                    LT. GERNOIS
          Here's the money.

Rokoff goes through the thick bundle of bills swiftly.

                    ROKOFF
          Ah, I knew you wouldn't
          disappointment me. Now the papers.

Lt. Gernois hesitates.

                    LT. GERNOIS
          You should be paying me for this.

                    ROKOFF
          Your payment is our silence. The
          papers.

Lt. Gernois hands Rokoff the other envelope.

Rokoff inspects the contents going over a few of the documents, grinning all the while.

                    ROKOFF
          Yes, this will do nicely.

Rokoff puts the documents back and slides the envelope into his inner coat pocket.

                    ROKOFF
          Thank you, Lieutenant. Next time --

Cold and deliberate.

                    LT. GERNOIS
          -- Next time, Rokoff, I will kill
          you.

Rokoff's sneering smile disappears as he swallows down the threat.

Without another look or word, Lt. Gernois rises to leave his shaken companion.

INT./EXT. ROKOFF'S HIDEAWAY - NIGHT

Tarzan drops to the landing and with his back pressed against the wall, the door opens and Lt. Gernois marches out in a stern state of mind and does not spot the ape-man.

Rokoff stands inside, close to the entrance threshold, with Tarzan about a foot away from him.

As Lt. Gernois descends the staircase he abruptly stops and half-turns as if to return, but changing his mind continues down the steps to vanish into the dank, dark alley.

Rokoff exhales a sigh of relief and a moment later shuts the door.

INT. ROKOFF'S HIDEAWAY - NIGHT

Rokoff sits down and wipes the perspiration from his forehead.

The door is thrown open and there before him stands his nemesis, Tarzan!

Rokoff's eyes bulge in incredulity and his faces turns a deathly gray.

                    ROKOFF
          You!

Before he's able to move, Tarzan pounces on his prey.
Lifting him from the chair Tarzan slams him against the wall
knocking the wind out of him.

Rokoff dazed, shakes his dumbfounded face only to come face-
to-face with a pair of deadly, steel-grey eyes.

                    TARZAN
          What's the matter, Rokoff, don't
          you trust your own eyes?

Panic seizes Rokoff.

                    ROKOFF
          Don't kill me, please d --

                    TARZAN
          -- Why not? I owe you for the warm
          welcome you gave me in the tent,
          remember?

Feeling the aura of death, Rokoff attempts to dart past
Tarzan, but before he can get to the other room Tarzan has
him by the scruff of the neck.

Fearing death imminent, Rokoff begins squealing like a stuck
swine.

Tarzan cuts off his shrill cries with a crushing grip around
the throat and lifting him up and off the floor with one
hand, he carries the choking, gagging and struggling man back
to the table and lowers him slowly down into the chair.

Before Rokoff can be saved by unconsciousness, Tarzan opens
his vise-grip.

Rokoff coughs and wheezes as his lungs struggle to breath
normally again.

                    TARZAN
          That was but a sample of what I
          will do to you and worse, if I ever
          see your filthy face again.

Rokoff is visibly relieved.

                    TARZAN
          Because of your sister, I will not
          kill you... but cross me once more
          and I will destroy you.
                    (MORE)

                    TARZAN (CONT'D)
          If ever I learn that you've
          harassed your sister or her husband
          or that you're back in France or in
          any of her possessions, I will find
          you and finish what I started here
          tonight.

Realizing that he is not to be killed, his surly, sneering
demeanor makes a halfhearted return but, playing it safe, he
keeps his trap shut.

                    TARZAN
          I believe you have something that
          doesn't belong to you.

Tarzan reaches into Rokoff's inner coat pocket and produces
two envelopes and tapping the larger one on his palm...

                    TARZAN
          My, this one's heavy.

He then examines the documents and his eyes open in unfeigned
surprise. He gives Rokoff a quick look and after returning
the papers puts both envelopes into his pocket.

                    TARZAN
          The chief of staff will be very
          pleased.

As the door slams, Rokoff, elbows on the table, drops his
head into his trembling hands.

                    ROKOFF
          You'll pay for this Tarzan...

He raises his rabid face with a clenched fist.

                    ROKOFF
          ... Do you hear me, you French
          pig?! You will pay!

EXT. HOTEL DU PETIT SAHARA - NEXT DAY

Tarzan strolls by mounted on his horse and meets Lt. Gernois
riding in the opposite direction.

In shock surprise, Lt. Gernois reins in his horse to a sudden
stop.

Tarzan nods and smiles pleasantly as he passes the astounded
soldier who unconsciously returns the greeting.

Lt. Gernois wheels his mount about and watches as Tarzan continues his leisurely pace out of Bou Saada.

                              FADE TO BLACK:

SUPER: "ALGIERS"

EXT. HOTEL ST. GEORGE - DAY (4 DAYS LATER)

A white, long and rectangular hotel several stories high basks in the sunlight.

Well dressed patrons, mostly European, haunt the hotel.

Many in the back partake of an outdoor dining terrace.

INT. HOTEL ST. GEORGE - DAY

Tarzan comes down a flight of steps with a bellboy behind him carrying his luggage.

At the counter, he waits as the CLERK attends to another guest.

Finished he turns to Tarzan.

                    CLERK
          Checking out, Monsieur?

                    TARZAN
          Yes, please.

The Clerk begins preparing the bill, then stops and looks up at the towering Frenchman.

                    CLERK
          Forgive me, Monsieur, I almost
          forgot, a telegram arrived for you
          this morning.

The Clerk stops the paper work and retrieves the telegram for Tarzan.

Tarzan, wondering, opens it.

The telegram morphs from French into English.

INSERT - TELEGRAM

> "Status of last mission changed
> from postponed to cancelled. Lt.
> Gernois is dead. Suicide.
>
> Home Office."

EXT. PIER - DAY

A large steamer is docked alongside a pier that is strung out
into the yawning mouth of a calm harbor.

A well dressed Tarzan waits with a crowd of passengers at the
base of the ramp as those ahead of them board the vessel.

EXT. STEAMSHIP - UPPER DECK - DAY

Two interested spectators, appareled in the latest fashions,
watch the ape-man from above.

Both are clean shaven and the taller of the two sports a
dirty-blond coiffure with contrasting black eyebrows.

EXT. MEDITERRANEAN SEA - DAY (HOURS LATER)

The smoke stacks, like giant black columns, send up all the
turmoil from the boiler rooms into the sky.

The steamer plows through the white-speckled, dark blue
waters on a steady course bearing West.

EXT. STEAMSHIP - UPPER DECK - LATE AFTERNOON

A black-haired, grey-eyed giant approaches two men who
quickly turn their faces out to sea to avoid his glance.

But Tarzan, deep in thought, does not notice them.

INT. DINING ROOM - CAPTAIN'S TABLE - EVENING

In the middle of a large and elaborate dining room,
surrounded by tables decorating the floor and filled with
finely dressed passengers, is CAPTAIN DONOVAN's table around
which sit a varied number of guests.

To the standing captain's immediate left is an attractive
young woman and at her elbow sits Tarzan decked out in his
dinner attire.

The volume of voices lends to a lively occasion which does not overwhelm as the captain begins to introduce his guests.

                    CPT. DONOVAN
          To my right is the enchanting Mrs.
          Strong from Baltimore, Maryland and
          the gentleman sitting next to her
          is...

His voice tapers off as he continues with the introductions.

MINUTES LATER

                    CAPTAIN DONOVAN
          ... And this is Mr. John Caldwell
          of London... and sitting next to
          him is the lovely, Miss Strong, the
          daughter of Mrs. Strong.

The captain takes his seat and the feast begins.

Tarzan gazes at the young girl beside him, as if trying to grasp a fleeting memory, but then the puzzle is solved by MRS. STRONG.

                    MRS. STRONG
          Oh, Hazel... Hazel, dear.

                    HAZEL
          Yes, Mother?

With the name still echoing in his mind, Tarzan suddenly remembers.

FLASHBACK - INT. CABIN - NIGHT

Jane sits at a heavy wooden table writing a letter with the golden light of the lantern gently illuminating her beautiful face.

                    JANE (V.O.)

          West Coast, Africa
          February 3, 1909

          Miss Hazel Strong
          1729 Whetstone Point
          Baltimore, Maryland

          Dear Hazel,

          I write to you this letter...

Her voice fades away.

BACK TO PRESENT

Tarzan takes in HAZEL STRONG with new eyes realizing that he is sitting next to Jane's best friend!

EXT. STRAIT OF GIBRALTAR - DAY

Below cerulean skies, two crafts approach each other from opposite directions.

One, a very large and spacious steam yacht, glides eastward.

The other, a mammoth, two-stacker, passenger steamship, plows westward with its British ensign flapping in the breeze.

At 250 feet, the sleek Lady Alice is no push-over, yet she is overshadowed by the massive steamer.

Smoke rises from her single funnel. Two masts, one fore and another aft, rise from her deck and four very large lifeboats, two on either side, are secured to her davits.

EXT. LADY ALICE - UPPER DECK - DAY

A golden-haired girl sits alone on deck. She stares ahead, past the looming steamship, far out into the interminable horizon.

Encircling her fine, long neck is a golden chain from which depends a diamond-studded, golden locket. Her mindless fingers toy delicately with the trinket.

As they near, strident whistle blasts erupt from each vessel rudely awakening Jane from her reverie and her sad eyes, like two jewels surrounded by exquisite loveliness, come to life.

EXT. STEAMSHIP - UPPER DECK - DAY

Two, among many, watch the fleet yacht as the vessels begin to pass each other.

One of them is Hazel Strong, 20, a darling, beautiful and generous girl who's trusting to a fault.

                    HAZEL
          What a magnificent yacht! I wonder
          who it could be.

                    TARZAN/MR. CALDWELL
          It has a British ensign, so we know
          that much.

                    HAZEL
          Royalty? A British tycoon? Or
          perhaps a rich financier?

She glances at him and together they laugh a her plausible
remarks.

                    HAZEL
          My, it's a home away from home.

The ships finally pass each other leaving only the ripples in
their wakes to collide.

                    HAZEL
          And so, Mr. Caldwell, you were
          telling me about your impression of
          America.

                    TARZAN
          Oh yes, it's a different culture
          from that of the European... they
          have a certain freedom about the
          way they act and speak that I found
          remarkable.

                    HAZEL
          Yes, we Americans are less subtle.
          Except of course if that American
          happens to be a politician.

                    TARZAN
          I didn't meet any and I'm not very
          interested in politics myself.
          Based on what I've witnessed in
          Europe, they talk much and do very
          little.

                    HAZEL
               (chuckling)
          They're no different in America --
          and speaking of America, I've been
          wanting to ask you... how is it
          that you, a British subject, speak
          with an American accent?

                    TARZAN
          My teacher was American.

                    HAZEL
          Oh?

Tarzan considers and smiles.

> TARZAN
> It's a tale, I think, you'll find
> interesting... and perhaps someday
> you'll be able to persuade me to
> tell it; but, please, I beg you,
> not today.

She chuckles and takes a sip of her cocktail.

> HAZEL
> Did you meet any interesting
> people?

> TARZAN
> Quite a few.

MR. JOHN CALDWELL drops a pebble in the pool.

> TARZAN
> In fact, I met a family from your
> city who appealed to me very much.
> The man is an archaeologist... A
> Professor Porter and his daughter,
> Jane Porter and --

Hazel is instantly electrified.

> HAZEL
> -- Jane Porter! Mr. Caldwell,
> you're joking! You met Jane
> Porter?!

Tarzan smiles politely and gives her a few quick nods.

> TARZAN
> Including Esmeralda and Mr.
> Philander --
>   (feigns surprise)
> Don't tell me you know them?

> HAZEL
> Why yes! Jane's my best friend --
> more like a sister, really. It's
> uncanny... what a wonderful
> coincidence. Oh, just the mention
> of their names makes me homesick.
> Please tell me, how are they and
> when did you last see them?

                    TARZAN
          It's been many months since I saw
          them, but they were doing fine when
          I left them.

Hazel starts to reminisce.

                    HAZEL
          She and I grew up together, you
          know. There's not a kinder soul in
          my entire circle of friends. She's
          a dear and to think I'll be losing
          her soon... it's almost too much to
          bear.

                    TARZAN
          Losing her? What's happened to
          her?

                    HAZEL
          It's not what's happened to her...
          it's what going to happen to her.

Hazel, seeing Tarzan's affected confusion, explains.

                    HAZEL
          She's getting married.

Tarzan plays his part to a tee.

                    TARZAN
          And what's wrong with that?
          Shouldn't you be happy for her,
          instead?

Hazel looks long and hard at Tarzan for a moment.

                    HAZEL
          I tell you this in the strictest
          confidence, Mr. Caldwell... but I
          feel that I can trust you.

Empathy fills her soul and it reflects instantly upon her
very attractive countenance.

                    HAZEL
          She's going to marry a man she
          doesn't love. What can be more
          horrible than that, I ask you?

                    TARZAN
          I don't understand. If she doesn't
          love him why then is she marrying
          him?

                    HAZEL
          Believe me, Mr. Caldwell, I'm on
          your side. Some nonsense about
          family honor was her answer. I
          tried to convince her that marrying
          a man she doesn't love is not
          honorable... it's insane!

Tarzan nods his head in recollection.

                    TARZAN
          I know exactly how you feel.

She lays a hand on his arm and leans in closer.

                    HAZEL
               (whispers)
          And what's worse, the man she
          really loves, loves her and she
          knows it... and yet she plans to
          sacrifice that love on the altar of
          false honor.

Hazel leans back in her chair and shakes her head.

                    TARZAN
          It's a sad affair and I feel bad
          for her.

                    HAZEL
          I don't. It's her fault. She
          could have been happy with only a
          few words. I feel bad for him.
          She told me all about him... a
          veritable super-man who saved all
          their lives while they were
          castaways on the coast of an
          African jungle.

Tarzan becomes a little uncomfortable at the new subject of
discussion.

                    TARZAN
          You don't say?

                    HAZEL
          But I do. What I can't figure out
          is how she can say no to Mr. Canler
          but for some inexplicable reason
          she cannot say no to Lord
          Greystoke.

Mrs. Strong appears and breaks up the conversation saving
Tarzan from personal embarrassment.

                         MRS. STRONG
              Hazel, darling. Oh, please forgive
              me, Mr. Caldwell, but I must have
              my daughter.

Hazel grins.

                         HAZEL
              Please excuse me.

Putting her drink aside she rises to meet her mother.

                         HAZEL
              What is it, Mother?
                 (to Tarzan)
              We'll get together again?

                         TARZAN
              By all means.

As they begin to walk away Mrs. Strong continues.

                         MRS. STRONG
              There's someone I want you to meet
              and...

Tarzan watches the departure of mother and daughter and with
a sigh of relief, takes a long drink and lays back in his
steamer chair.

                         TARZAN
              If she ever discovers who I am....

At the thought, he closes his eyes and a big smile spreads
across his noble face.

MONTAGE - TARZAN AND THE STRONGS

1) Tarzan, Mrs. Strong and Hazel have lunch together over
drinks and laughter on the deck of the steamer.

2) Tarzan and Hazel play shuffleboard against Mrs. Strong and
an acquaintance of hers.

3) Hazel hands her mother a camera -- a No. 3A FPK or Folding
Pocket Kodak -- and coaxes Tarzan into a picture with her and
then with her Mother. The acquaintance then takes a picture
of all three of them together.

4) At sunset Tarzan accompanies the ladies for a stroll upon
the deck.

EXT. ATLANTIC - STEAMSHIP - UPPER DECK - MORNING

A few early-birds walk the deck enjoying the cool Atlantic
air.

Tarzan passes a few of them on his customary morning jaunt.

As he nears the rows of steamer chairs he finds Hazel in
conversation with an unfamiliar man.

Both become appraised of his approach.

Hazel smiles warmly upon recognizing him.

But the man bows in haste and attempts to take his leave of
her, but Hazel stops him just as Tarzan stops at her side.

                    HAZEL
          Monsieur Thuran... please wait. I
          want you to meet a good friend of
          mine, Mr. Caldwell.
               (to Tarzan)
          Mr. Caldwell, may I present,
          Monsieur Thuran.

As MONSIEUR THURAN and he shake hands, Tarzan is assaulted by
a sense of familiarity. Tarzan's grey eyes survey the blond
man's smooth face, but the shifty eyes begin to prod his
recollection.

                    TARZAN
          Haven't we met somewhere in the
          past?

                    THURAN
               (in a French accent;
                uncomfortable)
          If we have, Monsieur, I do not
          recall it.

                    HAZEL
               (excited)
          Monsieur Thuran has been most kind.
          He was explaining the amazing art
          of navigation. I feel like a
          schoolgirl.

Tarzan smiles politely as he takes a steamer chair beside
her. His ears are deaf to the ensuing conversation, but his
eyes track Thuran, like those of a stalking lion.

The searching rays of the sun reach the chairs and Hazel has
Thuran move her chair into the shaded area.

Tarzan's quick eyes catch the slight grimace on Thuran's face as he moves the chair. After placing the chair back on deck, he unconsciously rubs his left wrist.

A sudden light goes off in Tarzan's head and all the pieces fall into place.

> THURAN
> (in a French accent;
> nervous)
> Forgive me, Mademoiselle, but I
> have a previous engagement.

> HAZEL
> Must you?

> THURAN
> (in a French accent)
> Yes, I must... we'll be seeing each
> other again, I'm sure.

As Thuran bows to Hazel, Tarzan gets up from his chair.

> TARZAN
> I will walk with you a little ways,
> Monsieur Thuran.
> (to Hazel)
> There is something I must do.

Hazel gives Tarzan a questioning look.

> TARZAN
> I'll be right back in time to join
> you and your mother for
> breakfast... I promise.

Hazel pretends to be hurt with her full lips forming a discernable pout and then with a forgiving smile...

> HAZEL
> Don't be late.

Hazels watches until they turn a corner.

A powerful hand lands on Thuran's shoulder stopping him.

> TARZAN
> What in blazes are you doing aboard
> this ship, Rokoff?

> ROKOFF/THURAN
> (in a French accent)
> I'm leaving France and her
> territories as you demanded.

Tarzan eyes him with mistrust and suspicion.

> TARZAN
> That's very commendable, but why
> this ship and why the disguise?

> ROKOFF
> (in a French accent)
> How was I to know you'd be aboard?
> As for my disguise, I have my
> reasons... as no doubt you have
> yours, Mr. Caldwell.

> TARZAN
> Whatever they are, you're to keep
> out of my sight and, more
> importantly, away from Miss
> Strong... she's a good woman.

Rokoff's face reddens.

> TARZAN
> If I so much as catch you glancing
> at her, I'll toss you over the
> side.

Tarzan burns his eyes into Rokoff's pusillanimous mug and
turning around, he saunters off, leaving behind a smoldering
man.

INT. ROKOFF'S STATEROOM - DAY (DAYS LATER)

Rokoff, furious, paces the cabin as his associate Paulvitch
listens to his tirade from the comfort of an armchair.

The dialogue begins in French with subtitles and then
transitions seamlessly into English without the French
accent.

> ROKOFF
> ... The pig must die! But I dare
> not dispose of him until those
> papers are in my possession -- I
> must have those papers!

Rokoff glowers at Paulvitch.

> ROKOFF
> And what have you done? Nothing!
> All I've gotten from you since the
> ship set sail are excuses as to why
> you can't break in and search for
> the documents.

                         PAULVITCH
                    (sneering)
          You try it then... it's not that
          easy to enter the man's cabin
          unobserved... besides it's not
          something that can be done on a
          whim... one must be patient until
          the right opportunity presents
          itself, my dear Nikolas.

                         ROKOFF
          Listen you spineless, coward.
          Opportunity or not, I want his
          cabin searched today!

INT. FIRST-CLASS PASSENGER CORRIDOR - EVENING

Passengers walk in opposite directions while others loiter in
the long, spacious corridor.

Tarzan exits his stateroom wearing a dinner jacket, glances
at his wristwatch and hurries off, leaving the door unlocked.

A pair of eyes witness his exit.

A smile spreads across Paulvitch's face from ear-to-ear.

INT. FIRST-CLASS PASSENGER CORRIDOR - EVENING (MINUTES LATER)

Rokoff and Paulvitch walk briskly down the corridor.

Rokoff stops near other loitering passengers, while Paulvitch
moves on to boldly stop before Tarzan's door.

Paulvitch keeps his eyes on Rokoff, who after a casual
inspection of both sides of the corridor, nods.

A quicksilver twist of the doorknob and Paulvitch steals in.

INT. TARZAN'S STATEROOM - EVENING

Paulvitch slinks through the cabin with ease.

Closets are opened and adroit hands slither in and out of
pockets.

Drawers are opened and deft fingers pry through notebooks and
papers.

Luggage is opened and swiftly examined.

Baffled, Paulvitch pauses to think, when his roving eyes happen upon a lone chair acting as a coat hanger for Tarzan's double-breasted coat.

A hand slides into an inner pocket drawing forth an envelope.

Paulvitch confirms its contents and quietly closes the door behind him leaving the cabin in its original state.

INT. ROKOFF'S STATEROOM - EVENING

An envelope is dropped on a table.

Rokoff stands while looking at the envelope and then stares at the triumphant Paulvitch, hoping against hope that it's what he thinks it is.

                    ROKOFF
          The papers?

                    PAULVITCH
          See for yourself.

Rokoff nervously and quickly opens the envelope.

                    ROKOFF
               (elated)
          You see... all you needed was a
          little motivation.

                    PAULVITCH
          My dear Nikolas, it was pure luck
          that he forgot the envelope and
          left his door unlocked, not
          motivation... Lady Luck, and
          nothing more.

                    ROKOFF
          Perhaps, but you would not have
          been there to take advantage of
          this fortune without my persuasion.
          Anyway, let us not quibble. We
          must celebrate!

Rokoff, with the envelope in his other hand, picks up the telephone.

                    ROKOFF
          Have champagne brought up at
          once... yes... one bo -- make it
          two bottles... thank you, Monsieur.

Rokoff hangs up the telephone, sits back down and slides the envelope into an inner pocket.

Paulvitch joins him a little disconcerted.

> PAULVITCH
> Have you considered what will
> happen once he discovers the papers
> are missing?

Beaming with villainous eyes, Rokoff smiles at his sidekick and then, almost manically, begins to laugh.

EXT. STEAMSHIP - UPPER DECK - NIGHT

On a new moon, myriad stars stare down below on an enormous vessel sailing southward near the equator of the Dark Continent.

The last remaining passengers on deck begin to disperse except for one.

Tarzan leans upon the rail staring out into the vastness of the Atlantic, lost in thought.

Directly below him, in her stateroom, is Hazel Strong.

INT. HAZEL'S STATEROOM - NIGHT

Dressed in a nightgown that clings subtly to her supple figure, Hazel brushes her long hair facing the port window.

UPPER DECK

Swirling waves clash against the side of ship below the ape-man, mixing with the sound of the powerful and tireless engines of the steamer that lull Tarzan, like a metronome, into welcome forgetfulness.

Two dark shapes creep up behind Tarzan and then crouch. One whispers a few words to the other.

He raises a hand for a moment, then drops it quickly.

The two shadows charge and, each grabbing one of his legs, heave Tarzan over the side before he can react.

HAZEL'S STATEROOM

Tarzan's falling body plunges past Hazel's stunned eyes drawing a stifled cry from her lips.

Unsure of what it may have been, she rushes to the window and tries to look below and then looking upwards she listens for sounds from above.

Hesitant and unsure of what to do, she moves to a table and lays a hand on the phone receiver, but not hearing any cause for alarm she places the other hand on her forehead and then with a quick shake of her head, shrugs it off.

She sinks into the comfort of her bed and, reaching over to the lamp on the nightstand, switches off the light.

EXT. ATLANTIC - NIGHT

Breathing rhythmically, Tarzan treads water.

Calm and cool, he watches the ship move further away from him and southward, like a lighted Christmas tree in an ocean of blackness.

He gazes up towards the heavens to confirm his orientation and with long, easy strokes begins his swim eastward.

EXT. ATLANTIC - NIGHT (30 MINUTES LATER)

Tarzan stops swimming and lets the shoes go. Then the pants come off.

He checks the inner pocket of his jacket for the envelope, thinking he still has it, but comes up empty, instead. A stern realization surfaces on his brave face.

                    TARZAN
             (piqued; in a low voice)
          Rokoff, you bastard!

No longer needed, Tarzan divests himself of the jacket and with only his union suit, resumes the powerful strokes towards the western coast of the African continent.

EXT. ATLANTIC - PREDAWN (HOURS LATER)

A hint of light slowly rises in the horizon and Tarzan, tireless, pushes on until he descries a black object straight ahead of him.

He stops and treads trying to figure out what it is but, with the light still weak, is unable. Nevertheless, Tarzan is not deterred and swims for it.

Once at its side, Tarzan finds it to be a large chunk of flotsam.

With the dawn about to break, Tarzan climbs aboard the large, wooden piece of wreckage and dropping on his back is soon fast asleep.

INT. STEAMSHIP - DINING ROOM - MORNING

Hazel and Mrs. Strong sit at their table waiting for someone. A chair is noticeably empty. Hazel glances at her wristwatch.

                    MRS. STRONG
          Where could he be?

                    HAZEL
          I don't know. He's usually here
          before we are.

                    MRS. STRONG
          I dislike having to breakfast
          without him, but we can't wait any
          longer, my dear.

                    HAZEL
          I feel the same way, but you're
          right.

Hazel signals for a steward who zips to their table to take their orders.

EXT. STEAMSHIP - UPPER DECK - LATE MORNING

Hazel lounges on her steamer chair, but her face is all but relaxed.

Her angelic eyes are busy sweeping the deck for signs of Mr. Caldwell but instead she finds the smiling face of Monsieur Thuran.

                    ROKOFF
               (in a French accent; in
                high spirits)
          Good morning, Mademoiselle!

                    HAZEL
          Good morning.

Rokoff notices the concern in Hazel's eyes.

                    ROKOFF
               (in a French accent)
          Is anything the matter?

                    HAZEL
          Have you seen Mr. Caldwell, at all,
          today?

                    ROKOFF
               (in a French accent)
          I'm sorry to say, I have not. Why?

                    HAZEL
          It's his custom to breakfast with
          us every morning and for some
          unexplainable reason, he was
          absent.

                    ROKOFF
               (in a French accent)
          Perhaps, he decided to sleep late
          or did not feel the need to
          breakfast. This is normal, no?

                    HAZEL
          Perhaps, but I have this
          overwhelming feeling that all is
          not right with Mr. Caldwell.

                    ROKOFF
               (in a French accent)
          Where could he be? He must be
          somewhere on this ship. There's no
          need to worry. I'm sure he'll turn
          up sooner or later.

                    HAZEL
          I don't know, but I intend to find
          out, rather sooner than later.

Hazel attracts the attention of an ENGLISH STEWARD.

                    HAZEL
          Please find Mr. Caldwell for me...
          tell him, we missed him at
          breakfast this morning.

EXT. ATLANTIC - FLOTSAM - LATE MORNING

A golden orb high in the sky shines upon the ape-man, who's
bed of wooden wreckage moves gently with the soft motion of
calm waters.

Tarzan's eyes open, oriented and alert. Dry, Tarzan gulps
the pain of thirst away. He throws an arm over his eyes and
turning his head to the side is brought to his feet by the
sight.

There alongside his flotsam is a huge mass of wreckage.

Tarzan smiles, not only because of an overturned lifeboat,
but also because far in the distance his sharp, grey eyes see
the feeble outline of the western coast of Africa.

Tarzan looks up into a blazing, blue sky and with a parched,
grateful, whisper...

                    TARZAN
          Thank you, Lord.

Tarzan dives into the water and pulls the small lifeboat near
the raft-like flotsam, he clambers back aboard and drags the
lifeboat onto it. He rights it and examines it inside and
out.

Satisfied, he dives back into the ocean. Searching about the
mass of wreckage, he finds a pair wooden planks to serve as
paddles and pulling himself back up to his flotsam, tosses
them both into the lifeboat.

INT. STEAMSHIP - CAPTAIN'S CABIN - NOON

                    CPT. DONOVAN
          ... You say you left him last night
          on deck?

                    HAZEL
          Yes, we bade each other good night
          and that's the last I saw of him.

                    CPT. DONOVAN
          Had he been drinking?

                    HAZEL
          I don't think I ever saw him drink
          while he was with me and my mother
          and he certainly was not
          intoxicated if that's what you
          mean.

                    CPT. DONOVAN
          Please forgive me, Miss Strong, but
          I must consider all possibilities.
          A man, like him, just doesn't fall
          overboard.

Hazel nods.

                    HAZEL
          I agree, and I realize now why you
          must ask these questions.

                    CPT. DONOVAN
          Good. Now, did he seem depressed
          or was he having any problems that
          may have led him to commit suicide?

Hazel shakes her head.

                    CPT. DONOVAN
          I didn't think so. He seemed full
          of life and gay in his demeanor to
          me.

Captain Donovan gets up and throwing his hands behind his
back paces, then turns again to Hazel.

                    CPT. DONOVAN
          To the best of your knowledge did
          he have any enemies onboard this
          ship?

                    HAZEL
          I don't believe so. I never saw
          him associate with anyone but my
          mother and I. If he had any, he
          never mentioned them to me.

Captain Donovan turns his attention to the English Steward.

                    CPT. DONOVAN
          Where did you search for Mr.
          Caldwell?

                    ENGLISH STEWARD
          I searched his cabin first, and
          when I discovered that his bed had
          not been slept in, I looked
          everywhere, where a passenger might
          be found and I could not find him.

The captain's fears mount as his mind ponders the fate of Mr.
Caldwell. He speaks aloud more to himself than to the other
three.

                    CPT. DONOVAN
          Mr. Caldwell did not strike me as a
          man given to spells and even if he
          did suffer such an attack he would
          have fallen within the ship not
          overboard... although, I'm not
          ruling it out completely.

He looks directly at Hazel in a grave manner.

                    CPT. DONOVAN
          You say you saw a body fall past
          your port last night... is that
          correct?

                    HAZEL
          I don't know what I saw... it
          happened so quickly. I listened
          for an alarm but when I didn't hear
          one, I assumed it had been a bundle
          or refuse being thrown overboard...
          but now....

                    CPT. DONOVAN
          I'll hazard a guess, Miss Strong.
          The reason you may not have heard
          an outcry or an alarm, is because
          he may have, in all probability,
          been already dead when he was
          thrown overboard.

Shocked, Hazel throws a quick hand over her mouth.

                    HAZEL
          Oh, My God! Murder? But who --
          why?

Terribly distraught, Hazel is lost for words.

The captain turns immediately to MR. BRENTLY.

                    CPT. DONOVAN
          Mr. Brently, I want you to scour
          this ship from top to bottom...
          leave no stone unturned.

                    MR. BRENTLY
          Aye, aye Captain!

Mr. Brently immediately departs the captain's cabin to carry
out his orders.

INT. CAPTAIN'S CABIN - AFTERNOON (1 HOUR LATER)

As the door opens, Captain Donovan, Hazel, and the English
Steward turn to meet Mr. Brently.

After closing the door, Mr. Brently looks at the captain and
shakes his head.

> MR. BRENTLY
> The entire ship was searched,
> Captain. Mr. Caldwell is no longer
> aboard this vessel, Sir.

EXT. ATLANTIC - LATE AFTERNOON

Long, powerful arms shove the water back, propelling the
craft forward, ever closer to the coastline.

Tarzan searches the shoreline and a quizzical look etches his
face as he continues to push towards land.

A small mouth leading into an inner harbor beckons him to
enter and recognizing it and the landscape flanking it on
both sides, Tarzan begins a smile.

EXT. LAND-LOCKED HARBOR - LATE AFTERNOON

Through a familiar narrow channel, Tarzan's stroking motion
squeezes his wide, back muscles leading him into a small,
tranquil harbor.

Looking into a clearing past the beach, he gazes, with
unbridled happiness, upon a wooden cabin -- his home!

EXT. LAND-LOCKED HARBOR - BEACH - MINUTES LATER

With one last, strong, stroke, the lifeboat glides in and as
soon as Tarzan hears the scraping sound of the keel on the
sandy white shore, he leaps out before it comes to a complete
stop.

EXT. JUNGLE - RIVULET - LATE AFTERNOON

The cooing sound of the gently flowing rivulet mixes with the
unceasing jungle sounds of animals and nameless buzzing
insects as Tarzan sates his thirst and scatters nearby fishes
every which way.

EXT. CABIN - LATE AFTERNOON

Near the doorway, several curious monkeys watch as with a few
motions of his fingers Tarzan easily springs the catch to the
door and enters.

INT. CABIN - LATE AFTERNOON

Within, nothing has changed since he and D'Arnot left seeking
out civilization so long ago.

Hanging from the wall are several of his loin-cloths and next
to them is a coiled, grass rope.

EXT. CABIN - LATE AFTERNOON

Tall and powerful, Tarzan steps out from the cabin dressed in
a loin cloth and with a grass rope strapped across his back.

His joyous, grey eyes sweep the jungle fringes about him,
where giant trees covered with creepers and blossoming
flowers call out to him, like the voices of long, lost
friends, and throwing back his head, he lets out the
terrific, eerie and long-drawn, victory cry of the bull-ape.

A blanket of silence falls upon the jungle for a time and
then a bold lion roars with a challenge and from far back in
the savage, tropical jungle another bull-ape answers in kind.

Growling sounds emanate from his ripped abdomen. Tarzan,
staring into the thick jungle near the cabin, pats his
stomach a few times to calm it.

                    TARZAN
                (in a low voice)
            Soon, my old friend.

He jogs towards the jungle wall and with a quicksilver leap
disappears into the trackless fastness.

EXT. JUNGLE - LATE AFTERNOON

Nimbler than any monkey and faster than his bull-ape
brethren, Tarzan -- reveling in his regained freedom --
speeds through lower terraces of the crowded jungle.

Instinctively his hands always find the next available branch
and dropping to an enormously wide limb, he runs along it for
several feet before dropping cat-like to an ancient elephant
trail below.

Tarzan's alert, keen grey eyes study the ground for a few moments and then raising his face upwards, he dilates his nostrils seeking scents.

Finding none, he springs back up into the jungle giants.

EXT. JUNGLE - NEAR SUNSET

In the distance, an exhibition of aerial wonder speeds through the forest at dizzying heights.

Below him, the ground yawns more than a hundred feet as Tarzan rushes through the entanglements near the canopy at an incredible pace.

Abruptly, he begins dropping twenty feet at a time without losing his forward momentum until he lands on a low limb, above a trail, leading to a river's ford.

Squatting on his haunches, Tarzan prepares the rope and waits.

EXT. JUNGLE - EARLY TWILIGHT

Motionless as a statue, Tarzan's acute ears immediately spy the sound of heavy, padded feet and the body of a large animal brushing against the thicket and grasses near the ford of the river.

An involuntary smile sneaks up on Tarzan.

Another sound arrests his sensitive ears. They pick up the stop-and-go feet of a cautious animal moving along the trail towards the river.

Soon, to Tarzan's delight, a red river hog appears in the trail.

Another pair of hungry eyes, green and baleful, follow the hog's approach.

The hum of the encroaching night is all that can be heard as the bush pig walks towards the river's edge.

Then a silent noose falls from above settling around the neck of the beast.

Tarzan gives it a mighty tug and the pig squeals in desperation as it's dragged rapidly backwards.

Furious, burning eyes watch as the pig is dragged from him.

A great lion charges out from behind the hidden brush and high grasses towards the red river hog being borne upwards into the safety of the trees.

Looking up, the denied lion meets the laughing and taunting, face of the ape-man.

The king of beasts roars and then leaps up, well below Tarzan and his prize, gripping the giant behemoth with its long and powerful claws.

Unable to climb any higher, it's immense weight drags it downward, shredding bark as it falls to earth.

Tarzan pulls the choking, struggling hog up onto the wide limb and crushes the life out of it with his sinewy hands.

Strong white teeth sink into succulent bush pig meat and Tarzan's fast is over.

EXT. JUNGLE - NIGHT

Tarzan finishes a last chunk of fresh, warm meat and then wipes his mouth in stuffed satisfaction.

He grabs a bunch of leaves from a near branch and settling down against the trunk of the tree, wipes his greasy, bloody hands.

Below him, the angry lion paces back and forth as if expecting for the ape-man with the carcass to fall into its lap at any moment.

Tarzan then gathers up the carcass of the hog and tossing it over his shoulder, leaps up into the branches of the forest and zips away.

                                        MATCH CUT TO:

EXT. INDIAN OCEAN - LADY ALICE - NIGHT

SUPER: "INDIAN OCEAN"

Like a lighted beacon, on the opposite side of the Dark Continent, the Lady Alice sails the calm and dark waters beneath it.

INT. LADY ALICE - DINING ROOM - NIGHT

Tennington and his guests are seated around a table in a large, luxurious dining room.

Esmeralda chats away with Mr. Philander and Prof. Porter keeps himself busy by trying to balance his fork on the tip of his forefinger.

Clayton wipes his mouth with a dainty napkin.

                    CLAYTON
               (to Tennington)
          I've never tasted better. How do
          you do it, old man?

                    TENNINGTON
               (chuckles)
          Short of dry land, you'll find all
          the comforts of home and more
          aboard the Lady Alice.

                    JANE
          She's like a mansion on the high
          seas.

                    TENNINGTON
          I couldn't have said it better
          myself, my dear girl.

He looks around at the other guests and seeing that they're all finished...

                    TENNINGTON
          May I suggest that we all retire to
          the drawing room for a little...
          let us say... libation?

At that, Prof. Porter loses his concentration and drops the fork on the table.

                    PROF. PORTER
          Hear, hear!

The group laughs and Tennington rises from the table and leads his erstwhile, thirsty guests from the dining room.

EXT. JUNGLE - NIGHT

As Tarzan swings through the trees on his way home, he hears the movements of the lion following below him.

Looking down Tarzan spots the glowing, green eyes of the stealthy predator.

But after a few more trees, the lion tiring and still hungry, roars his outrage and turns about in pursuit of easier game.

EXT. CLEARING - CABIN - NIGHT

From the fringe of the jungle Tarzan jumps to the ground below with the burden of his successful hunt.

INT. CABIN - NIGHT

Tarzan dumps the remains on the table and finding one of the cots drops into it.

After stretching out his long, muscular body, he takes a deep breath that transitions into a yawn and closes his eyes.

INT. CABIN - MORNING

Tarzan awakens with the sound of rollicking birds and monkeys.

Sunbeams strike his face and his steel-grey eyes gleam as the pupils themselves tighten.

Tarzan sits up, rubs his sore arm muscles, stands up, stretches and then eyes the carcass on the table.

SERIES OF SHOTS - TARZAN'S MORNING PREPARATIONS

1) Tarzan visits the rivulet and drinks long and deep.

2) At an easy run, Tarzan heads to the beach and dives into the harbor swimming briskly above and below the surface of the water.

3) Revitalized, Tarzan tears into the hog for breakfast.

4) Using a spade, he buries the remains several feet from the cabin.

5) Tarzan grabs his rope, jumps high into the nearest forest giant and vanishes with only a waving branch as a silent witness.

EXT. CANNIBAL VILLAGE - AFTERNOON

Tarzan moves on quiet feet to a tree limb overlooking the village. Instead of a thriving community he discovers it deserted.

Huts, in various states of ruin are evident. Some are burned or torn down, while others are simply empty.

Beyond the weakened and tottering palisade, the once cultivated fields have been reclaimed by the onslaught of the jungle.

Tarzan drops to the base of the ancient giant.

The once boiling cauldron -- containing the concoction to poison arrow tips -- is overturned on its side, but no arrows are present.

He goes from hut to hut searching for weapons. In one he finds a broken bow and in another a few broken arrow shafts.

No spears, no knives, no usable weapons of any kind can Tarzan find in the deserted village.

Disappointed, Tarzan takes to the trees and follows the river in a southeasterly direction, leaving behind the ill-fated cannibal village to the ravages of time.

MONTAGE - TARZAN'S JOURNEY

1) Tarzan lifts a moss-covered log and a good-sized rodent darts out from underneath. Like lightning, Tarzan's hand catches it and crushes its body against the fallen tree trunk.

2) Tarzan swings rapidly in the early morning light and drops down on an unguarded nest filled with eggs. He cracks a few, one-handed, and gulps them.

3) At sunset Tarzan settles down high in the canopy upon a wide bough of a gigantic tree and beds down.

4) An unwary antelope finds itself dangling from a tree. A hand comes down and chokes the life out of it. Once it's still, Tarzan pulls it up onto a roomy branch and feasts.

5) Day and night Tarzan speeds through the jungle highways following the river as he moves further and further away from his normal haunts.

6) On a rainy day under the protective cover of the jungle canopy, Tarzan overturns a huge rock and finding a nest of worms and grubs, gorges himself.

7) High up in the canopy and through the branches, Tarzan discovers far out in the distance an open and majestic country, with mountain ranges at the horizon, filled with various grazing antelopes alongside herds of zebras. Tarzan is taken by the wonder before him.

EXT. STEAMSHIP - UPPER DECK - DAY

Hazel reclines alone in a steamer chair, thinking more than relaxing. She tries to read but cannot.

QUICK FLASHBACK

A dark body plummets past Hazel's port window.

BACK TO PRESENT

She closes the book laying it on her lap and puts a hand to her forehead, her once joyful loveliness marked by sadness.

Listless and uncaring she wiles away the time in an absentminded, blank state, looking at no one or anything in particular.

A shadow falls across her slim figure, but she's unaware of it.

                    ROKOFF (O.S.)
                (in a French accent)
            I'm glad to see you on deck again,
            Miss Strong. I was beginning to
            worry.

Startled, Hazel turns to meet her uninvited guest.

                    HAZEL
            I'm sorry, I seem to be in another
            world... please sit down.

Rokoff slips into a steamer chair beside her.

                    ROKOFF
                (in a French accent)
            But you are distraught,
            Mademoiselle... and I do not blame
            you.
                    (MORE)

                    ROKOFF (CONT'D)
          The fate of Mr. Caldwell has been
          uppermost in my mind these last few
          days as well.

Hazel responds in a plaintive voice, wishing she could turn
back time.

                    HAZEL
          If only I had given the alarm... if
          only -- what's the use, he's
          gone... and it's my fault.

                    ROKOFF
               (in a French accent)
          How could you have known? I will
          not allow you to carry this burden
          any longer.

She looks at him with a sad smile.

                    ROKOFF
               (in a French accent)
          Think, Miss Strong. Even if you
          would have given the alarm, the
          likelihood of the ship turning
          around in time, in those dark
          waters and finding him, would have
          been remote, if not impossible.

She nods at his logic.

                    HAZEL
          Yes, I suppose you're right.

Knowing the truth Rokoff goes to work.

                    ROKOFF
               (in a French accent)
          In fact, you're owed a debt of
          gratitude for your intuition and
          perceptiveness in alerting the crew
          to this terrible tragedy.

                    HAZEL
               (feeling better)
          You're much, too kind.

Cool as a snake.

                    ROKOFF
               (in a French accent)
          Not at all, Mademoiselle. It's
          purely selfish... when you smile, I
          smile.

Rokoff gets her to chuckle and the cloud of despair that hung
over her for the last few days, begins to evaporate.

His greedy, rat-eyes squint as they devour the recovering
beauty.

He motions for a steward, who takes his order and Rokoff and
the girl begin to chat in better humor.

EXT. JUNGLE - DAY

Tarzan sails through the lower levels of the mighty jungle.

Ever alert, his nostrils pick up a scent.

He speeds up and swinging upwards lets go and lands on a
large limb several yards away.

He faces upwind and samples the air again. A smile confirms
the scent and Tarzan dives out into empty space and snags a
sturdy branch in pursuit of his prey.

EXT. JUNGLE - DAY (MINUTES LATER)

From above Tarzan follows a lone warrior.

Tarzan's, grey eyes focus on the man's armament.

BUSULI's sleek, black body is strapped with a bow and a
quiver of arrows. At his hip hangs a knife and a metal shod
spear is in his right hand.

With a ready rope, Tarzan shadows the black savage, but his
conscious rings with D'Arnot's words.

                    D'ARNOT (V.O.)
          We do not kill without a reason.

As Tarzan's mind grapples to find an alternate plan to
separate the man from his weapons, the black

WARRIOR

crosses the threshold of the jungle wall and there before
them, across a clearing, is a

PALISADED VILLAGE

replete with beehive huts.

But they're not alone!

TARZAN'S

quick senses catch the form of a

FAST-MOVING LION

in the warrior's wake. The

LION

charges,

TARZAN

shoots out a wide noose and yells.

> TARZAN
> Look out!

The black

WARRIOR

turns in time to see a noose grip the lion's throat stopping
its claw-rending leap in mid-air.

TARZAN

is yanked from the branch by lion's weight and momentum to
fall only paces from the roaring beast.

Wheeling about, the furious creature prepares to launch into
Tarzan, but -- in a blink of an eye --

BUSULI

throws back his arm and releasing it, buries the

SPEAR

into the lion's tawny hide.

With a thunderous and infuriated roar it turns on the warrior
but not before

TARZAN

secures the rope around the tree. As the

LION

hurls itself at Busuli, it's brought down hard by the choke
hold of the rope, and like a man caught between two bases, it
turns in the other direction towards Tarzan only to feel the
bite of an

ARROW

driven deep into its flesh.

Tarzan sprints to the warrior's side and taking his knife,
motions him to keep peppering the lion with the arrows.

Roaring in pain and sheer ferocity, the lion rears up on its
hind legs attempting to reach Busuli and then Tarzan.

Once the lion diverts its attention fully on the archer,
Tarzan darts in like lightning.

IN SLOW MOTION

Tarzan straddles the roaring beast, encircles its throat with
a sinewy right arm, and sinks the knife in rapid succession
into the mighty heart of the feline until it drops at his
feet, vanquished.

A well formed, rugged foot stomps the lion's neck.

A fierce face, with raging eyes and curled lips, upturns
towards the heavens and the victory cry of the bull-ape
disrupts the tranquility of the day.

BACK TO NORMAL SPEED

As the surge of Tarzan's battle-rage fades, the two men --
with the lion between them -- regard each other.

Busuli makes a friendly sign with his hand and Tarzan replies
in kind.

EXT. PALISADED VILLAGE - DAY

The quaking roars ending with the horrific, long-drawn cry of
the ape-man, draws many of villagers outside the gate and
with a wave of excited voices, armed men hasten towards the
disturbance.

EXT. CLEARING - DAY

Soon, Tarzan, Busuli, and the dead lion are surrounded by a
contingent of sleek, ebon warriors.

Augmented by the women and children, confusion sets in with
much gesticulation, jabbering and a high degree of interest
in the Samson-like stature and physique of the white savage
standing before them.

Busuli raises his hands demanding silence and once peace is
restored he begins to explain.

Many of the villagers murmur in amazement as the story
unfolds. Eyes filled with wonder and respect, move from the
body of the dead lion to the noble figure of the white
savage.

Busuli finishes and the awed villagers move as one taking
turns to touch Tarzan upon the his right shoulder in
gratitude for saving one of their own and for killing the
king of beasts.

EXT. WAZIRI VILLAGE/PALISADED VILLAGE - DAY

Led into the village by Busuli and followed by an adoring
crowd, he's introduced to WAZIRI, the chief.

(NOTE: Waziri is the title given to their king and it is also
the name of the people.)

In an indistinct voice, the heroic event is retold to the
chief.

EXT. WAZIRI VILLAGE - LATE AFTERNOON

Tarzan sits with the chief, Busuli and a handful of warriors
in a semi-circle in the midst of a low burning fire.

Presents of domesticated animals are brought to Tarzan as
well as various plates of native food by many of the
villagers.

Noting Tarzan's interest in their panoply, he is awarded a
shield, a spear, a bow, and a quiver filled with arrows.

Busuli, grateful, presents Tarzan with a knife and its sheath
-- the very one used to stop the savage heart of the lion.

Tarzan is humbled by the people's generosity.

                                        FADE TO BLACK:

The sound of loud, rhythmic jungle drums.

EXT. WAZIRI VILLAGE - NIGHT

A crescent moon watches three tiny lights surrounded by
darkness and zooms in at warp speed on a large bonfire that
crackles and sprinkles sparks of lit ashes into the night
sky.

With the ground stained around them, the heads of an antelope
and zebra watch warriors dancing about the fire -- excited
flames reflecting from their dead eyes.

Two other large fires roast their bodies. Men and women cut
pieces of their roasted flesh from the burning buffets.

Viands, cakes and plantains fill plates among the natives as
they eat and drink the night away.

Tarzan sits among the people surrounded by maidens who attend
to his every whim and desire.

Buzzed warriors sit with their friends or families eating and
drinking their native beer.

Others drink and watch the intense drum dance with glazed,
satisfied eyes.

Before Tarzan are several empty plates with only a few scraps
left on them.

A very attractive woman brings Tarzan some of their homemade
brew.

Tarzan raises his beer towards the chief in a savage toast
and then takes a drink, while the chief drains his.

As he drinks Tarzan notices the fine, clean-cut features of
the dancing warriors dressed in sarong like wraps from the
waist to mid thigh.

Their splendid symmetries gleam in the night fire reflecting
their sleek, ebon bodies in the intensity of the dance.

The good looks of the women does not escape his eager and roving eyes.

While the men keep their heads shaved, the women have stranded coiffeurs that cover their foreheads, ears and fall tapered to the base of their necks.

They are dressed in a toga like garment that runs over both shoulders exposing the upper chest but with the breasts fully covered and is girded around the waist by a simple leather thong. Below the waist it continues down just shy of the knees.

But that's not all he sees.

Glints of yellow on the dancing warriors catch his eye.

But not only them. Armlets and anklets of gold adorn the bodies of both men and women in ubiquitous quantities.

Tarzan turns to one of the women attending him and points to her armlet.

The woman, anxious to please him, removes it and hands it to him with a pleasing smile.

Tarzan bounces it on his palm and finds it to be hefty.

He examines it closely. Pure, virgin gold!

Tarzan addresses the girl and indicates the armlet.

                    TARZAN
          Where? Where does it come from?

The girl misunderstanding him, pushes the golden armlet towards Tarzan expressing her desire that he should keep it.

Tarzan attempts to return it.

                    TARZAN
          No. I don't --

The lovely young girl only smiles shaking her head while pointing at the treasure and then again at Tarzan.

A little frustrated, Tarzan acquiesces and accepts her gift with a smile.

Waziri raises a hand. The drums cease and the dance is over.

Tarzan rises with his entourage of the village beauties at his heels, and approaches the chief who stands to receive him.

> TARZAN
> I must go.

Tarzan looks out beyond the palisade and points in the same direction.

And turning to the chief again...

> TARZAN
> I'll return tomorrow.

The chief indicates a beehive reserved for him, instead.

Tarzan shakes his head and points to the jungle again, but not understanding Tarzan, the chief along with many others try to dissuade him.

Tarzan, however, heads for an overhanging branch within the palisade followed by most of the Waziri tribe.

Exclamations of astonishment erupt from the villagers, as Tarzan leaps and vanishes before their incredulous eyes.

EXT. WAZIRI VILLAGE - MORNING

The Waziri warriors are forming up for a hunting excursion. The leader moves from man-to-man inspecting each one's armament and exchanging a few words in their Bantu dialect.

The women are cooking and performing many other domestic chores while the children laugh and play within the safety of the palisaded village.

Suddenly, out of nowhere, a pair of long, powerful legs lands within their compound destroying the early tranquility.

A few women scream in alarm and several armed men rush to meet the intruder only to discover to their relief that it's only their new friend, Tarzan.

A big grin spreads across the ape-man's face and across the faces of the warriors who challenged him.

INT. STEAMSHIP - DINING ROOM - AFTERNOON

Indistinguishable murmuring voices fill the air bouncing off the various-sized chandeliers with the middle one being the largest.

Stewards are running, serving, and dodging each other as they strive to satisfy the demanding passengers.

At the table occupied by Mrs. Strong, Hazel, and Rokoff a
steward is removing the finished plates and glasses.

Hazel converses with Rokoff while her mother sips her coffee
watching and listening attentively.

>   HAZEL
>   ... I'm afraid this evening will be
>   our last meal together.

>   ROKOFF
>   (in a French accent)
>   Last meal? You've lost me, Miss
>   Strong.

>   HAZEL
>   We'll be leaving tomorrow... mother
>   has a brother in Cape Town and
>   that's where we will be staying for
>   some time.

Mrs. Strong spots Rokoff's shifty eyes.

>   ROKOFF
>   (in a French accent;
>   feigning surprise)
>   Why, that's my port of call!

Hazel is happily surprised but her mother veils her
disappointment with a polite smile as she fans her mounting
concern.

>   HAZEL
>   That's simply wonderful! Isn't it,
>   Mother?

>   MRS. STRONG
>   Yes... it's a most welcome
>   surprise, to say the least.

Rokoff's greed focuses on Hazel and is deaf to Mrs. Strong.

>   HAZEL
>   You must promise to visit us
>   often... once we've settled in, of
>   course.

>   ROKOFF
>   (in a French accent)
>   You do me an unexpected honor, Miss
>   Strong. I will not disappoint you,
>   I promise.

Rokoff stands up after patting his lips with his napkin.

                    ROKOFF
               (in a French accent)
          It was a delightful, lunch, but I'm
          afraid I've overlooked a few
          errands this morning which I must
          attend to. I beg your pardon and I
          hope you will allow me to make it
          up to you this evening, at dinner.

With a greasy, subservient smile, Rokoff bows and hurries
away.

Mrs. Strong's fan stops as she watches him depart.

                    MRS. STRONG
          There's something unsound about
          that man... I don't trust him. He
          seems like a gentlemen...
               (shakes head)
          ... but something in his eyes
          betrays him... it gives me a queer
          feeling.

                    HAZEL
               (giggling)
          Oh, Mother, really.

                    MRS. STRONG
          I know, perhaps I'm overly
          suspicious -- still I regret it's
          not Mr. Caldwell who'll be visiting
          us, instead.

Hazel follows her mother's eyes and joins her to stare at the
retreating form of Monsieur Thuran.

                    HAZEL
               (a little sad)
          So do I.

INT. ROKOFF'S STATEROOM - DAY

                    ROKOFF
          ... She's not only beautiful, but
          also an heiress to a vast
          fortune... and I, Esquire Nikolas
          Rokoff, will make her my wife!

Paulvitch, with a raised eyebrow, watches Rokoff with
interest, as if he were staring at a lunatic.

                    ROKOFF
          Can you see her on my arm, as we
          walk down the streets of Saint
          Petersburg?

Paulvitch, lying in a made bed with hands behind his head and
legs extended and crossed, gives Rokoff a sober look.

                    PAULVITCH
          You're dreaming, Nikolas. She'll
          never marry you.

                    ROKOFF
          She wouldn't, would she?
               (gloating)
          She and her mother will be
          disembarking at Cape Town and when
          she learned that I too was to stop
          there, she threw her doors wide
          open, telling me to call upon her,
          often.

Paulvitch is aghast.

                    PAULVITCH
          Cape Town! Have you gone mad?
          You're on assignment, and those
          papers must be delivered to Moscow
          as soon as humanly possible. You
          cannot go to Cape Town.

Rokoff is unruffled and throws up his shaved chin in
arrogance and defiance.

                    ROKOFF
          I can and I will. This is an
          opportunity that only a fool would
          let go... and a fool, I am not.

Paulvitch, knowing Rokoff, moves ahead.

                    PAULVITCH
          I suppose you'll want me to deliver
          the papers?

                    ROKOFF
          No. I'll deliver them myself.

Paulvitch sits up.

                    PAULVITCH
          But --

                         ROKOFF
          -- Just tell them the trail has led
          me to Cape Town and that within a
          month -- or less, the papers they
          so desperately want, will be in my
          possession.

Paulvitch shakes his head and scowls.

                         PAULVITCH
          I hope, for our sakes, you know
          what you're doing.

Rokoff picks up his cup of coffee from the table, and looking
at Paulvitch with smiling eyes, takes a sip.

                         ROKOFF
          Haven't I always?

                                             FADE TO BLACK:

SUPER: "1 MONTH LATER"

EXT. JUNGLE - DAY

A crowned eagle patrols the jungle tops of the canopy. It
soars fearlessly.

Below the canopy fearful monkeys hidden below the leaves
watch as it passes overhead.

Down on a dismal trail a troop of mandrills cross.

A pair of large, striped bongos move along the same trail
eating, twitching their ears alongside a pair of back-swept,
spiralling horns, taking turns sampling the air with their
moist nostrils for danger.

Twelve deadly arrow shafts, swoosh from an ambush into the
large, plump bodies of the antelopes.

One falls upon its front knees, grunting and collapses on its
side.

The other jumps high into the air only to be struck by six
more merciless shafts that bring it down to the ground, with
a solid thud.

Disturbed forest elephants rumble their displeasure as their
huge bodies are heard trampling vegetation as they plow
through the gloomy jungle.

Sleek, ebon warriors rise slowly from their cover. One, a giant, white savage, bronzed to a nut-brown rises among them.

His rich, black hair is longer and loose. His eagle, grey eyes scan the area, animal-like, for any possible threats.

With quivers and short spears slung across their backs and their powerful longbows in their hands, they move to their fresh kills and remove their arrows.

EXT. WAZIRI VILLAGE - DAY

Tarzan leads the way with one of the bongos across his mighty back.

At the gate he's met by another group of men who take charge of both burdens from the successful hunters.

EXT. WAZIRI VILLAGE - NIGHT

Within the village the evening fires are lit. Families or groups of Waziri begin their evening meal enhanced by meat taken earlier in the day.

Tarzan, Busuli and Waziri sit around one such fire. Busuli is talking to Tarzan but cannot be heard.

A chunk of meat roasts over the fire as they drink from wooden cups and eat plantains, viands, nuts and fruits.

Waziri cuts a generous piece off for himself followed by Busuli and Tarzan.

Busuli takes a few bites from the meat and then continues.

The dialogue begins in a Bantu dialect with subtitles and then transitions seamlessly into English without an accent.

                    BUSULI
          ... They came for slaves and ivory.
          We fought but we could not prevail
          against their death-dealing sticks
          of fire. Our once great tribe was
          reduced by the Arab raids.
          Waziri's father, Chowambi, led us
          far from the North to this land.

                    TARZAN
          Have you found peace here?

Busuli and Waziri exchange glances.

                    BUSULI
          Until a year ago... then a group of
          Arabs and Manyuema found us. We
          killed many of them -- but not all.

Busuli unconsciously slides up his golden armlet and Tarzan's
interest is rekindled.

                    TARZAN
          From where do your people get the
          gold?

                    BUSULI
          It was brought from a stone village
          far from here... a month's march,
          at least. But that was long ago.

                    TARZAN
          Where?

Busuli points to the southeast.

                    TARZAN
          Can you take me there?

                    BUSULI
          I cannot, for I have never been
          there.
               (pointing to Waziri)
          The chief was there. He can tell
          you.

Waziri finishes chewing and takes a draught of his native
beer.

He regards Tarzan for a few moments.

                    WAZIRI
          As Busuli has said, it is near a
          moon's distance from here. I was a
          young man when my father, Chowambi
          set out with a scouting party. We
          followed the river to its birth
          place in a mountain range. On the
          other side we found a rivulet that
          led into a large jungle. Here the
          rivulet becomes a river that
          empties into a larger one in the
          center of a huge valley.

Waziri takes another swig from his beer.

                    WAZIRI
          This large river led us to another
          mountain range. Here the river
          turns into a rivulet. We followed
          this waterway as we ascended the
          range. Inside a cave we found the
          source of the river and there we
          camped for the night.

                    TARZAN
          How long did it take to reach each
          mountain range?

                    WAZIRI
          It took us ten days for the first
          mountain range and twenty for the
          second one.

Waziri pauses, his eyes lost in the steady fire, and then
continues where he left off.

                    WAZIRI
          The next day we climbed the
          mountain range through a steep pass
          and from a flat summit we
          discovered a narrow valley with a
          ruined city of stones.

Waziri grimaces as he remembers the horror.

                    WAZIRI
          Once near the city we were set upon
          by a hostile force of men unlike
          you or I. They were white-skinned
          and hairy. Though we were
          outnumbered we held our ground atop
          a small hill until sunset when they
          suddenly stopped fighting and
          returned to their city.

Waziri points to the golden armlets and anklets adorning his
body.

                    WAZIRI
          These, we took off the dead and
          there were many.

                    TARZAN
          Did you ever return?

                    WAZIRI
          We never went back. Once was
          enough.

                          TARZAN
          I would very much like to visit
          these ruins and get more of this
          gold.

The chief stuffs his mouth with food and then washes it down
with beer.

                          WAZIRI
          I'm an old man, Tarzan, and the way
          is far. Now, would not be wise.
          Perhaps after the rainy season.
          Then we can go.

Tarzan sensing the chief's finality, drops the subject.

The palisaded village is engulfed by the ominous dark jungle,
it's tiny, flickering fires fighting to keep it at bay.

EXT. CAPE TOWN - MORNING

In the distance, Table Mountain stands high over the City
Bowl, like a giant guardian flanked on either side by its two
mountain cousins.

EXT. UNCLE'S HOUSE - MORNING

A large house with a second story balcony stands proudly with
a beautifully landscaped yard before it.

A taxi pulls up into the horseshoe driveway and stops across
the entrance of the home.

The door opens and a man gets out carrying two bags.

As he approaches the doorway, the taxi buzzes off.

At the door, the man shifts the weight of one of the bags and
rings the doorbell.

INT./EXT. UNCLE'S HOUSE - MORNING

Within the foyer the doorbell resounds and then footsteps.

Hazel answers the door and is met by the sleazy and
ingratiating smile of Rokoff standing neat and prim with two
bags from which two loaves of bread protrude upwards.

Hazel is surprised by the unexpected call.

                    HAZEL
          Why, good morning Monsieur Thuran!
          And what's all this?

                    ROKOFF
               (in a French accent)
          Remember the list you and your
          mother made last evening? Well, I
          had a copy made and this morning,
          since I had some business in town,
          I decided to fulfill it.

Hazel is endeared by the man's consideration.

                    HAZEL
          Please, do come in.

Rokoff wipes his feet and steps into the foyer.

KITCHEN

Hazel holds one of the kitchen doors open and Rokoff deposits
the bags on the kitchen counter.

Once at his side, Rokoff starts to empty the bags and hands
her the bread.

                    ROKOFF
               (in a French accent)
          Two loaves of bread, still warm.

Hazel smells the uplifting aroma of the fresh loaves.

                    HAZEL
          Mmmmm! Yes, they are. Leave the
          rest in the bags and come join us
          at the breakfast table. This bread
          is just in time.

Rokoff lifts up an index finger for a moment's respite and
pulls out a thick envelope from one of the bags and hands it
to her.

                    HAZEL
          What is it?

                    ROKOFF
               (in a French accent)
          These, are your photographs.

Hazel, unable to wait, puts the loaves on the counter, opens
the envelope and scans through the photos quickly and
glancing at Rokoff...

                    HAZEL
          Thank you... you shouldn't have...
          but I'm glad you did.

Rokoff bows, takes the loaves and with the envelope in one
hand, Hazel escorts Rokoff from the kitchen to breakfast.

MONTAGE - MONSIEUR THURAN THE GENTLEMAN

1) Rokoff escorts Mrs. Strong and Hazel to a night concert.

2) In a member's only night club, Mrs. Strong, her brother
and his wife, watch as Rokoff and Hazel dance on an
immaculate floor.

3) Standing next to Hazel, Rokoff along with Mrs. Strong,
Hazel's uncle and his wife, attend the horse races.

4) Rokoff drops off Mrs. Strong and Hazel at a local cinema
from his car.

EXT. UNCLE'S HOUSE - GARDEN - EVENING

A gurgling fountain lulls the night air.

Hazel reclines on a bench and stares at the man on the moon
mingling with the stars in the sky.

                    ROKOFF (O.S.)
                 (in a French accent)
          Your mother said I'd find you here.

Recognizing his voice, Hazel doesn't turn but continues to
watch the night lights in the heavens.

                    HAZEL
          It's too nice outside to be
          indoors.

She turns to look up at him.

                    HAZEL
          Why don't you sit and keep me
          company?

Rokoff's eyes squint, like those of a predator as he slides
next to the lovely, rich Hazel Strong.

Unconscious of the beast next to her, Hazel exhales as her
eyes return to the stars.

                    HAZEL
          It's so peaceful here... so
          beautiful. There's nothing like
          this back home in Baltimore.

                    ROKOFF
               (in a French accent)
          I've haven't had the pleasure of
          visiting your city.

                    HAZEL
          I think you'd like it. It's
          different, but beautiful... right
          on the lap of Chesapeake Bay.

                    ROKOFF
               (in a French accent)
          Perhaps I shall... someday.

She looks at him not suspecting anything and then out of the
blue...

                    ROKOFF
               (in a French accent)
          I love you... and I've come to ask
          you to be my wife.

Hazel's eyes pop open and her jaw drops in shock, at Rokoff's
sudden marriage proposal.

Straight as a stalk she shoots up from the bench, suddenly
uncomfortable and unsure as to how to respond.

She places a hand upon her bosom and forces herself to breath
normally again. Her suffused cheeks are hidden by the cool
night.

                    HAZEL
          My goodness, Monsieur Thuran...
          what does a girl say to something
          so -- so unexpected.

                    ROKOFF
               (in a French accent)
          Say yes, and make me a better man.

                    HAZEL
          I must say, I've never thought of
          you in that way... I've always
          regarded you as a friend. Now --

                    ROKOFF
               (in a French accent)
          -- A friend only? Nothing more?

                         HAZEL
          Please don't misunderstand me.
          What I mean to say is that now... I
          must consider you in a different
          light. Perhaps I'll find that you
          mean more to me than just mere
          friendship.

Rokoff scrambles to recover from his brash and hasty
proposal.

                         ROKOFF
                   (in a French accent)
          Forgive me if I have offended you.
          I love you and I must confess it...
          It's beyond my control.

                         HAZEL
          You haven't offended me... you just
          caught me off guard. It's not
          everyday a girl gets asked to
          marry.

                         ROKOFF
                   (in a French accent)
          I understand perfectly and I am
          willing to wait. Please tell me
          just one thing. Are you in love
          with someone else?

                         HAZEL
          I've never been in love, Monsieur
          Thuran.

Rokoff stands up, takes her hand and after raising it to his
lips...

                         ROKOFF
                   (in a French accent)
          You have given me great hope, Miss
          Strong. I will take my leave so
          that you may consider my proposal,
          alone.

Bowing, Rokoff turns leaving Hazel in a state of stupor.

She drops down into the bench, leans back and ponders
Rokoff's offer.

EXT. CAPE TOWN - ADDERLEY STREET - DAY

On a wide street lined with buildings of all shapes and
sizes, a mixture of people, double-decker trams, cars, horse
buggies and carriages come together to create a lively mix.

EXT. ADDERLEY STREET - JEWELRY SHOP - DAY

From an upscale jewelry shop Jane Porter pops out only to
bump into Hazel Strong!

They both behave as if they've just won a beauty pageant.

                    JANE
          Hazel?! Is it really you?!

                    HAZEL
          Jane?! Jane Porter! I must be
          dreaming. What in the world -- How
          in the world did you ever get
          here?!

They're so overjoyed that they temporarily lose their ability
to speak.

The two, star-struck friends embrace and kiss each other on
the cheek.

                    JANE
          You look wonderful. Papa and
          Esmeralda will be so surprised to
          see you.

Excited and giddy like two school girls, they hold each
others arms as they face each other overjoyed.

                    HAZEL
          They're here?!

                    JANE
          Yes, and Mr. Philander too... and
          of course Clayton.

                    HAZEL
          Oh my goodness, I forgot. You're
          married!

Jane shakes her head.

                    JANE
          Not quite... not yet anyways.

                         HAZEL
          But I thought -- your letters --

                         JANE
          -- I -- that is, we postponed the
          marriage until our return to
          England.

The mood drops.

                         HAZEL
          Must you? You know I'm against it.

                         JANE
          I know, but I gave my word...
          though I wish this trip would last
          forever.

Jane shakes the thought, the light springs back into her eyes
and with an endearing smile...

                         JANE
          Oh, we must get together! And here
          I thought you were back home in
          Baltimore suffering from unbearable
          boredom.

                         HAZEL
          Not quite. Mother decided it was
          time to visit her brother so I came
          along to escape that boredom. But
          you....

                         JANE
          Yes, I know. I shouldn't be here
          but I am. Believe it or not, a
          friend of Clayton's got it into his
          head to circumnavigate Africa in
          his yacht and coaxed us to tag
          along, and here I am! His yacht,
          the Lady Alice, is moored at the
          pier. We've only been here a few
          hours.

                         HAZEL
          I am so thrilled to see you! Wait
          till mother sees you... she'll have
          a fit, I dare say.

                         JANE
          Oh, I hope not. Still, I look
          forward to seeing her.

The girls interlock arms and continue to catch-up as they stroll along Adderley Street.

EXT. CAPE TOWN - DAY

Low clouds skim the top of Table Mountain.

EXT. UNCLE'S HOUSE - DAY

Two Panhard et Levassor touring cars are parked along the horseshoe drive before the impressive home.

INT. UNCLE'S HOUSE - DRAWING ROOM - DAY

In a large drawing room, an informal gathering is in progress of family and friends -- old and new.

Seated in a close knit group, Jane, Hazel, Mrs. Strong, Esmeralda and the uncle's wife are chatting, laughing and giggling.

A servant sits by the gramophone keeping the soothing music playing.

A maid keeps the ladies hydrated.

Further away Clayton, Tennington and the uncle sit near the fireplace with drinks in one hand and a cigar or a pipe in the other, conversing.

Near the other men, Prof. Porter and Mr. Philander sit at a small table -- lost to the world -- as they play chess.

Rokoff is at the bar getting a drink from the bartender.

When he turns to rejoin the men, he finds Tennington's eyes riveted on Hazel.

Instead of returning to his seat he leans against the bar sipping and watching.

Tennington gets up with an empty glass and joins Rokoff.

Always in a good mood he tries to rub it off on Rokoff.

                    TENNINGTON
          Ah, so here you are! I say, we've
          got the best seats in the house.
          What are you having?

Rokoff eager to ingratiate himself, feigns a polite smile.

                    ROKOFF
              (in a French accent)
          Vodka... on the rocks.

                    TENNINGTON
          That's a little too stark for me.

Tennington turns to the bartender.

                    TENNINGTON
          A Manhattan, please.

Tennington puts the bartender on hold and then glancing at
Rokoff...

                    TENNINGTON
          And just to show you I'm willing to
          rough it a bit...

He turns back to the bartender.

                    TENNINGTON
          ... Hold the cherry.

The bartender grins, Tennington chuckles and Rokoff smiles
and raises his glass in approbation.

Tennington takes a stool and is soon brought the Manhattan
minus the cherry.

                    TENNINGTON
          To your health.

They clink glasses.

Both men follow Hazel as she leaves the other women to chat
with her uncle and Clayton.

                    TENNINGTON
          Delightful girl, Miss Strong.
          Don't you think?

                    ROKOFF
              (in a French accent)
          I think so... especially since
          we're to be engaged once we arrive
          in America.

Tennington almost chokes on his drink.

                    TENNINGTON
          You don't say! You lucky rascal.
          Congratulations.
                    (MORE)

                    TENNINGTON (CONT'D)
          My dear fellow, this is the first
          I've heard of it -- in fact I don't
          think anyone else knows.

Looking about, Rokoff replies in a hushed tone.

                    ROKOFF
               (in a French accent)
          You're quite right, my friend.
          We're keeping it a secret... but I
          feel I can trust you, so please not
          a word to anyone.

                    TENNINGTON
          You have my word, cheers!

They raise their glasses in covenant and together return to
join the other men.

Tennington's smile fades into a thoughtful expression.

EXT. PIER - LADY ALICE - EVENING (2 DAYS LATER)

INT. LADY ALICE - DINING ROOM - EVENING

                    TENNINGTON
               (disappointed)
          ... I say, Mrs. Strong, you can't
          be serious!

                    MRS. STRONG
               (a little dejected)
          I'm afraid I am.

                    TENNINGTON
          We've only been here a few days --
          you can't abandon us now -- it just
          isn't done.

Mrs. Strong takes a sip of her wine.

                    MRS. STRONG
          It's really out my hands. We --

She looks at Hazel in resignation. Hazel glances at
Tennington with the same expression and shrugs.

                    MRS. STRONG
          We had planned to stay here several
          months; but, one thing you must
          know about my lawyer, and it's why
          I retain him...
                    (MORE)

>   MRS. STRONG (CONT'D)
>   he looks after my finances as if
>   they were his own. If he sends me
>   a cablegram advising me to return
>   regarding a financial matter, it
>   would be foolish of me not to.

The long table is filled with Tennington's guests. On his
left sits Rokoff and on his right Clayton. Mr. Philander and
Esmeralda are chatting away between bites while Prof. Porter
puffs his pipe lost in thought and across the table from Lord
Tennington sits Mrs. Strong.

Next to Clayton and across from Hazel sits the matchless,
Jane Porter.

Clayton chimes in.

>   CLAYTON
>   Come now Tennington, if she has to
>   leave there's nothing you can do.
>   As a matter of fact I think we
>   should follow her example and leave
>   too. This harebrained trip of
>   yours has gone fa --

>   TENNINGTON
>   (beaming)
>   -- I have it! You can sail with
>   us.

Clayton's face wrinkles in disbelief.

>   CLAYTON
>   Are you mad?

>   TENNINGTON
>   On the contrary, my good fellow.
>   It's the perfect solution... and
>   it's all thanks to you.

Clayton gives him a look of confusion and Tennington
clarifies.

>   TENNINGTON
>   Your comment about us leaving too,
>   a splendid idea, old chap!

Tennington chuckles and pats his friend on the back noting
his discomfiture.

Tennington turns to Mrs. Strong.

>   TENNINGTON
>   When do you depart?

                    MRS. STRONG
          The day after tomorrow, if I'm not
          mistaken.

                    TENNINGTON
          That's perfect! We've already seen
          what needed to be seen and we can
          be restocked and refueled by
          tomorrow. Please say you will.

Mrs. Strong looks at her daughter for support.

Hazel peeks at the beautiful and giddy-with-excitement Jane
who nods eagerly for them to acquiesce.

Thinking to sweeten the pot, Tennington glances at Rokoff and
then at Hazel.

                    TENNINGTON
          And of course Monsieur Thuran must
          join us... I'm sure it's what you
          would wish.

Hazel is caught off guard and unsure of what to say.

                    HAZEL
          Why yes -- of course... Monsieur
          Thuran is always welcome.

Rokoff meets Hazel's eyes, smiles and smooths his missing
mustache, from habit, like a hungry wolf.

Mrs. Strong is stung by Rokoff's inclusion, but expertly
dissimulates her annoyance by addressing her host.

                    MRS. STRONG
          You're quite sure we won't be in
          the way?

                    TENNINGTON
          The Lady Alice, is more than a
          yacht... she's a luxury steamer,
          really. I'll venture to say,
          you'll be more comfortable and in
          better company aboard her than on
          most, if not all the steamers that
          now sail the seas.

                    MRS. STRONG
          You've persuaded me, Lord
          Tennington... you now have three
          more guests.

Jane and Hazel are ecstatic and hug each other across the table.

Rokoff stands and bows to Tennington and, turning, levels a crooked smile towards Mrs. Strong, who responds politely with a weak one.

EXT. ATLANTIC - DAY (2 DAYS LATER)

Across blue waters the majestic <u>Lady Alice</u> steams northward.

                                        FADE TO BLACK:

The sound of giggling and indistinguishable girlish banter.

INT. LADY ALICE - HAZEL'S CABIN - DAY

Jane and Hazel, sitting on the bed, rummage playfully through Hazel's numerous photographs.

                    HAZEL
          ... And here we are at the pier in
          New York... look at our hair...
          simply scandalous!

Jane takes a closer look and the girls break out into a fit of laughter.

                    HAZEL
               (calming down)
          The wind was <u>awful</u> that day.

Hazel's hand searches through the scattered photos and stops suddenly on one.

Her joyful face becomes solemn as she stares down upon the photograph between both hands.

                    HAZEL
          I meant to ask you about him... but
          until now, I'd completely
          forgotten.

                    JANE
               (still looking at other
                photos)
          Ask me what? And why so serious?

                    HAZEL
          He said he knew you and your
          father.

Jane cocks her golden head in a questioning pose, her eyes diverted to Hazel's hands.

> JANE
> Who is he?

> HAZEL
> He was an Englishman, named John Caldwell... he boarded the steamer at Algiers.

> JANE
> I don't know anyone by that name... are you sure he meant me?

> HAZEL
> I'm positive, dear... how else could he know of Esmeralda and Mr. Philander without knowing you or your father?

> JANE
> (skeptical)
> Let me see this man who claims to know me.

As she proffers the photograph, Hazel is visibly affected by the memory.

> HAZEL
> He's dead... he was thrown overboard.

Jane takes the photo but seeing her friend's sudden, sad mood, tries to comfort her.

Hazel responds with a gentle smile.

> HAZEL
> I'm alright... it's just that he was such a decent man, that --

Jane glances down at the photograph and her face is transfigured into a state of shock and horror!

Jane faces Hazel with a tormented countenance and tears welling up in her eyes.

> JANE
> Hazel! It can't be. Please tell me it's not true.

Before Hazel can reply or react, Jane faints.

INT. LADY ALICE - HAZEL'S CABIN - MINUTES LATER

Hazel's hands are busy rubbing one of Jane's, in her attempt to revive her.

She then rubs her cheeks gently.

Jane's head moves first and then her eyes open suddenly as if from a bad dream.

Hazel overcome by her friend's unexpected reaction, helps her up to a sitting position.

The two inseparable friends face each other. Hazel confused and Jane with a shattered heart.

Hazel speaks to her in an apologetic voice and tries to quell the sorrow surrounding her best friend.

                    HAZEL
          I didn't know that you and Mr.
          Caldwell had been so close.

Jane bows her head and closes her eyes in painful grief and then lifts up her chin.

                    JANE
          Hazel, don't you know who he was?

                    HAZEL
          Of course I do... he was John
          Caldwell as I've told you.

Jane shakes her head.

                    JANE
          As selfish as it sounds, I wish it
          were true... but it's not.

                    HAZEL
          Jane, whatever do you mean? Please
          tell me.

Jane covers her face in anguish.

                    JANE
          O God, how can this be?

She takes hold of Hazel's hands.

                    JANE
          That man in the picture is Tarzan --
          the one I wrote to you about... the
          man I loved.

                    HAZEL
          You can't be serious, Jane! Are
          you sure?

Jane nods, in her conviction.

                    JANE
          I could never forget his face...
          there's no one else like him.

A light goes off in Hazel's mind.

                    HAZEL
          It all makes sense now.   Him being
          born in Africa and his knowledge of
          African wildlife... and that
          American accent when it should have
          been British... but how could I
          have known?

                    JANE
               (in a daze)
          How did it happen?

Hazel hesitates a moment as she studies Jane's face.

                    HAZEL
          I saw something fall past my port
          window one night... but not hearing
          a cry or any alarm I assumed it to
          be refuse being thrown overboard.

Tears slide down Jane's blanched cheeks as she listens.

Hazel begins to choke up, but Jane's steady stare draws the
rest out of her.

                    HAZEL
          The next day I noticed his absence
          and notified the captain... after a
          search he was pronounced lost at
          sea... the captain believed it was
          murder.

Jane cups her hands over her mouth in mourning.

                    JANE
               (crying softly)
          Oh, my God, no... no.

                    HAZEL
          Forgive me, Jane... if only I'd
          said something but....

She shakes her head looking for forgiveness and understanding.

Through her sorrow, Jane's kindness still shines forth.

>   JANE
>   You didn't know, Hazel... how could
>   you? You're not to blame.

>   HAZEL
>   (tearing)
>   Oh, Jane, I couldn't believe he was
>   gone either... he was so alive...
>   so --

Hazel begins to weep.

Jane embraces her and both girls cry together.

EXT. LADY ALICE - STERN - DAY (NEXT DAY)

Jane leans over on the taffrail.

Behind her, sitting around one of the tables equipped with a parasol, are Prof. Porter, Esmeralda -- vigorously fanning herself -- and Tennington.

Their conversation is muffled.

Over the side Jane dangles the golden, diamond-studded locket trying to decide whether or not to let it go.

IN SLOW MOTION

Like a pendulum it swings a tad from side to side. From above, Jane's lovely yet sad face looks down upon it. She closes her eyes.

She can't let it go. She reopens her eyes, clinches the locket with the other hand, looks out towards the horizon like a lost soul, drops her chin and her shoulders begin to shake lightly as she silently cries.

BACK TO NORMAL SPEED

>   ESMERALDA (O.S.)
>   (in black Southern accent)
>   Oh, my poor honey child!

In a moment the big woman is beside her Jane and, gathering her under her wings, begins to escort her away.

                         TENNINGTON
                 I say, anything we can do?

Esmeralda stops and smiles gratefully at Tennington.

                         ESMERALDA
                   (in Southern black accent)
                 Thank you, Lord Tennington... but
                 only the good Lord and time can
                 help her now. I'm taking her down
                 below. She'll be alright.

EXT. LADY ALICE - FORECASTLE - DAY

The bow of the yacht rises and falls slowly.

Among several gathered crew members a fight breaks out
between two of them.

Oaths and curses burst from their lips and WILSON knifes the
other, pulls the blade out from the man's belly and punches
his face to the deck.

The first mate jumps him from behind but gets slashed in the
arm and shoved against the rail.

Wilson follows up the push and throws the first mate
overboard.

                         HAND
                   Man overboard!

A life preserver is quickly tossed over the side.

The whistle blasts several times.

The alarm bells begin to ring as Wilson is subdued by the
rest of the crew.

INT. LADY ALICE - DINING ROOM - EVENING

Silence hangs like a black shroud over the dinner table.

The sounds of silverware, drinking and eating substitute for
normal conversation.

All are occupied with private thoughts. Even the usually
oblivious pair of Prof. Porter and Mr. Philander are affected
by the somber mood.

Only the fearful Esmeralda has the temerity to whisper her
thoughts.

In a low voice she confides in Mr. Philander.

> ESMERALDA
> (in Southern black accent)
> We should've stayed in Baltimore.

Without turning his head, Mr. Philander stops slurping the
steaming soup and nods.

Satisfied with his agreement, Esmeralda goes back to her
dinner and Mr. Philander resumes his soup slurping.

                                        FADE TO BLACK:

The slurping sound transforms into a rending, crashing sound.

INT. LADY ALICE - WEE HOURS OF THE MORNING

The sudden, violent shock knocks several of the passengers
from their beds.

EXT. LADY ALICE - NIGHT

The crew along with the passengers rush out onto the deck
that's listing starboard.

Slowly, the Lady Alice creaks backwards and levels off again.

Soon, the deck lights are turned on by the crew.

Off the port bow the WATCH OFFICER discovers the cause.

The half-moon hanging in the star-riddled sky, looks down
upon a massive wreckage of a derelict rising up from the
surface like a black mountain accompanied by a host of
entangled flotsam.

> WATCH OFFICER
> Captain, we've struck a derelict!

A grimy, panicky sailor comes running up to CAPTAIN JERROLD
and Lord Tennington.

> SAILOR
> Captain, she's ripped open! She's
> going down, Sir -- straight to the
> bloomin' bottom!

> TENNINGTON
> Shut up, man, and control yourself!
> (to captain)
> (MORE)

> TENNINGTON (CONT'D)
> Have the engineer determine the
> extent of the damage and have the
> lifeboats provisioned immediately.
> Ensure that all the weapons and
> ammunition are placed in my boat.

Tennington stops the captain from carrying out his orders with a hand on his shoulder.

> TENNINGTON
> And, Captain, empty all the
> cupboards. Get as much food,
> utensils and tools into the
> lifeboats as you can. There's
> nothing wrong with being crowded by
> food and items we're sure to need.

Captain Jerrold gives him curt but understanding nod and moving out, he galvanizes the crew into instant action.

In a steady and calm manner, Tennington speaks to his guests.

> TENNINGTON
> I want you all to gather your
> belongings and be prepared... we
> may have to abandon ship.

The passengers hurry away to their cabins.

EXT. LADY ALICE - 10 MINUTES LATER

A composed but concerned ENGINEER stops before Captain Jerrold, searching for the right words.

> CAPTAIN JERROLD
> Well, man, spit it out.

He glances at Tennington and at the other passengers standing together around the captain all eager to hear his report.

> ENGINEER
> I don't wish to frighten anyone,
> but she's got a hole in her big
> enough to drive an oxcart
> through... we have fifteen --
> perhaps twenty minutes before she
> goes down.

The bow of the Lady Alice dips lower as her stern rises affecting somewhat the balance of those on the deck.

Captain Jerrold does the only thing he can do.

220.

                    CAPTAIN JERROLD
          Abandon ship! Everyone get your
          gear and get into the lifeboats --
          she's going down!

The passengers hasten to their cabins to retrieve their
belongings while the crew continues loading the boats with
stores, tools, utensils, weapons and ammunition.

EXT. LADY ALICE - 15 MINUTES LATER

The four lifeboats, three heavily laden, take turns splashing
down into the dark waters of the Atlantic.

The remaining sailors slide down the ropes to their
respective lifeboat, abandoning the Lady Alice.

EXT. ATLANTIC - NIGHT (30 MINUTES LATER)

Jane watches, as the Lady Alice, like a vertical monolith, is
consumed by the fluid mouth of the ocean.

The four lifeboats, fanned-out but near each other, watch the
final moments of the Lady Alice from a safe distance.

In another lifeboat, a saddened Lord Tennington follows her
as the stern vanishes beneath the surface.

                     TENNINGTON
                    (whispers)
               Goodbye, Lady Alice.

EXT. ATLANTIC - LIFEBOAT - MORNING

The combination of light and heat from the rays of the sun
bore into the angelic face of Jane Porter.

Her head moves. Her nose and brow wrinkle.

As if stung, she starts up wide-awake at the end of the
lifeboat instinctively throwing a hand over her forehead as a
shield against the abusive, blasting sun.

Before her, five men lie asleep in different places and
positions composed of Clayton, Rokoff, and British sailors
SPIDER, TOMPKINS, and Wilson.

Luggage, a metal bucket, a pair of canteens, several tin
cups, bags, and two knapsacks are strewn about the boat.

She scans the ocean in every direction for signs of the other lifeboats, but her desperate, troubled eyes search in vain.

They are alone in the gigantic pool of the Atlantic Ocean.

EXT. LIFEBOAT - MORNING (10 MINUTES LATER)

Clayton stirs and awakens from the bottom of the boat to find Jane sitting astern.

He's a little groggy but in good spirits.

> CLAYTON
> Good morning.

> JANE
> We're alone, Cecil.

> CLAYTON
> I say, old girl, what do you mean?
> There's six of --

Jane gestures with her eyes and chin over the side of the boat.

Clayton catches on.

Fully awake now, he searches in all directions, but nothing.

> CLAYTON
> Blast! The ocean's been calm --
> they couldn't have gone down -- not
> all three.

He proceeds to shake the men awake.

> SPIDER
> Blimey! Can't a man nap in peace?

Clayton tries to awaken Wilson.

> WILSON
> (still dreaming)
> It wasn't me! I swear!

> CLAYTON
> (still shaking him)
> Get up.

Wilson awakens disoriented.

> WILSON
> What?

Wilson grins at Spider.

                    WILSON
          Almost gave myself away, didn't I?

With Rokoff and Tompkins finally awake Clayton explains.

                    CLAYTON
          A bit of bad news, I'm afraid. We
          seem to have lost sight of the
          other boats which doesn't bode well
          for any of us.

                    TOMPKINS
          Is that why you woke us? On the
          contrary, mate, that's good news.
          If we were together our chances of
          being found would be lessened. But
          separate, means there's a better
          chance of finding at least one of
          us which would lead to a search for
          the rest.

                    WILSON
          He's right. It's common practice.

                    ROKOFF
               (in a French accent)
          That may be, but may I suggest we
          start moving east... towards the
          continent, yes?

                    TOMPKINS
          And the sooner the better. You two
          best --

Tompkins' face becomes flushed with alarm.

                    TOMPKINS
          The oars? Where are they?

                    SPIDER
          Bollocks! It's gone!

                    WILSON
          Mine's too! Bloody rot!

Rokoff shakes his head in disbelief.

                    ROKOFF
               (in French)
          Sapristi!

                    TOMPKINS
          You two ninnies. You lost the
          oars?

                    SPIDER
               (angry)
          Didn't I tell you to keep an eye
          out for me in case I dozed?

                    WILSON
          Me, your keeper? Why didn't you
          keep an eye on me?!

                    TOMPKINS
          Listen, mates! There's no sense in
          arguin'. If they're gone, they're
          gone -- wait. Did anyone have a
          look-see over the sides?

Everyone looks over the sides, but the oars are long gone.

Tompkins attempts optimism.

                    TOMPKINS
          It was worth a try. Oars aside, I
          say lets eat. I'm famished.

                    ROKOFF
               (in a French accent)
          That's the most sensible thing I've
          heard thus far.

Rokoff glances at Wilson.

                    ROKOFF
               (in a French accent)
          Pass me one of the tins, would you?

Wilson snarls like a junkyard dog.

                    WILSON
          Get it yourself, Frenchman. I'm
          not your lackey.

                    CLAYTON
          Gentleman, please. Let's be civil,
          why don't we.

Clayton lifts the tin and carries it over to Rokoff.

                    SPIDER
          Eh? What's with you two? Hogging
          the food for yourselves?
               (MORE)

                          SPIDER (CONT'D)
              Is that it? Well, we'll have none
              of that, see --

Jane, unable to bear the discordant behavior any longer, cuts
in.

                          JANE
              -- Please. This pettiness must
              stop. One of you will have to take
              charge or this arguing will never
              cease. And I for one don't relish
              the thought of being in a
              belligerent atmosphere aboard this
              small vessel.

                          TOMPKINS
              The lady's right.

Clayton, looking from Spider to Wilson.

                          CLAYTON
              I have an idea. Since you two
              don't trust us, lets divide the
              food and water between us.

The sailors look at each in agreement.

                          CLAYTON
              All opposed?

None are opposed and two large kegs of water and four tins of
food are divided among them.

The sailors immediately open up a tin and a clear, viscous
liquid appears.

They are dumbstruck!

                          SPIDER
              Blow me!

                          WILSON
              Bollocks and bloody hell!

Tompkins is speechless.

Their sudden and unexpected exclamations draw attention.

                          CLAYTON
                    (annoyed)
              What is it, now?

                          SPIDER
              Coal oil! That's what!

                         WILSON (O.S.)
                    Curse the bloomin' idiots!

Clayton and Rokoff quickly open one of theirs and it too is
filled with coal oil.

The last two are opened with the same results -- coal oil!

Wilson takes Spider's tin cup, turns the brass spigot on the
metal-banded water keg and begins to fill it, as Tompkins
speaks.

                         TOMPKINS
                    Well, we're lucky it wasn't the
                    water. Thank God, for that. We
                    can live without food for weeks,
                    but without water we don't stand a
                    chance.

Wilson hands Spider the filled cup and starts filling another
one.

                         CLAYTON
                    I highly recommend we conserve the
                    water. There's no telling how long
                    we'll be out here.

                         WILSON
                    Let us worry about that, guv.

                         SPIDER
                    No oars, no food....

Spider sits back down dejected and drinks.

His eyes scan the horizon intently and then he lifts up his
tin cup in a dark toast.

                         SPIDER
                    Here's to land or to Davy Jones'
                    locker... whichever comes first.

Spider throws back his head and drains the cup.

The others look at one another, uncomfortably.

                         JANE
                    May God help us.

                                        FADE TO BLACK:

SUPER: "2 DAYS LATER"

EXT. ATLANTIC - LIFEBOAT - DAY

On one of the thwarts a leather belt is being sliced and diced with a fixed blade.

                    SPIDER (O.S.)
          It's gonna mangle your insides.

                    ROKOFF
               (in a French accent)
          He's right, you know.

                    TOMPKINS
               (still cutting the belt
                into pieces)
          Not if I make'em small enough.

                    SPIDER
          Suit yourself.

Tompkins starts to chew his leather lunch, a piece at a time.

Spider scans the horizon with a hopeless, gaunt stare.

                              FADE TO BLACK:

SUPER: "4 DAYS LATER"

Prolonged agonizing screams and shrieks ensue.

Then silence.

EXT. ATLANTIC - LIFEBOAT - DAY

Tompkins' crazed upside-down eyes, surrounded by a convulsed face, glare at Jane. His dead eyes see Jane inverted.

His dead body lies fallen backwards over a thwart across from her.

The leer upon his face is disquieting.

Jane turns her head to one side to avoid the ghastly stare.

                    JANE
          Cecil, please... throw the body
          overboard.

Though wasted in strength, Clayton manages to push the body near the side of the boat but is too feeble to lift and throw it overboard.

Wilson and Spider watch him struggle with the body with sunken eyes embedded in dead faces.

Claytons stops, exhausted and looks at the sailors.

>   CLAYTON
>   (out of breath)
>   Wilson... give me a hand... I can't
>   do it alone.

>   WILSON
>   What for?

>   CLAYTON
>   What? The last thing we need... is
>   a rotting corpse in the boat.

He squints up at the sun.

>   CLAYTON
>   And with this blistering sun, it
>   won't be long.

With wolfish eyes and a malevolent tone.

>   WILSON
>   Best leave him be. He's more use
>   to us now.

At first Clayton seems not to understand him, but then the meaning settles in.

>   CLAYTON
>   You don't mean -- you're joking,
>   I'm sure.

Wilson licks his chapped lips and shakes his head.

>   CLAYTON
>   (to Rokoff)
>   Thuran, help me with this body...
>   before the unthinkable happens.

A weak Wilson rises to intervene but is blocked bodily by Spider who gives him a meaningful, steady stare.

>   SPIDER
>   Don't even try.

With the odds against him he sits back down on the thwart and watches like a ravenous jackal as the three men lift the body over the side.

His gleaming, demented eyes target Clayton.

EXT. ATLANTIC - LIFEBOAT - NEAR SUNSET

A half vanished sun basks the starving castaways in its weak orange light. The lifeboat rocks gently on the undulating surface.

SUPER: "7 DAYS LATER"

Hunched over on a thwart, Wilson gibbers and giggles with his eyes full upon Clayton.

Claytons keeps tabs on the madman but begins to doze off until he finally succumbs to sleep.

EXT. ATLANTIC - LIFEBOAT - NIGHT

Slow, dragging footsteps creep in the light of the rising full moon.

Clayton's eyes suddenly open, forewarned by the dull sound of shambling footsteps.

Creeping towards Clayton is Wilson wearing a pair of glassy eyes, that reflect the moonlight, and a gaping mouth.

Jane also is awakened by the mummy-like shuffling.

She takes one look at what is about to happen and screams!

Wilson drops on Clayton and like a beast of prey goes for the throat with bared teeth.

Thuran and Spider awakened by Jane's scream crawl to Clayton's aid.

The three men overpower the madman and throw him to the bottom of the lifeboat.

Curled up like a nautilus, Wilson cackles maniacally.

Worn out by the tussle, the three men rest against the sides of the lifeboat breathing heavily.

Wilson expels a piercing shriek and leaps overboard.

The men are too weak to attempt a rescue, but soon overwhelmed by their predicament and the loss of another member of their party, they all react.

Spider crumbles and cries like a child.

Clayton manages to regain enough strength to crawl to the
edge of the boat and look over the side for signs of Wilson.

Only the reflection of the silvery orb in the night sky is
there to greet him.

> CLAYTON
> Poor, chap... may God rest his
> soul.

Jane utters a desperate, silent prayer under her breath.

Rokoff struggles to sit on a thwart, at one end of the boat,
and drops his chin on his chest as the gears in his mind
begin to churn.

EXT. ATLANTIC - LIFEBOAT - DAY (NEXT DAY)

A tin cup is filled with water and then another.

Spider lets rear of the large keg fall back into place and
Clayton makes his way, like a drunk man, to Jane who is too
weak to rise.

Their clothes hang loosely upon their starving frames.

All suffer from sunken eyes with the men fully bearded and
mustachioed.

Clayton squats down unsteadily and hands her a cup.

Jane, a shadow of her former self, gives him a fragile smile.

> ROKOFF (O.S.)
> (in a French accent)
> We must do something soon or our
> fates will be similar to Wilson's
> if not worse.

Clayton turns towards him while Jane lowers her lips to the
cup.

Rokoff and Spider sip their water.

> ROKOFF
> (in a French accent)
> I mean something drastic.

Clayton does not like the direction of the conversation.

> CLAYTON
> Drastic?

                    ROKOFF
            (in a French accent;
             tapping on the keg)
        This one's almost empty, but even
        with the remaining keg of water,
        under these conditions, none of us
        will survive much longer without
        food.

                    SPIDER
            (suspicious)
        What's on your mind?

Rokoff's methodical eyes move from Spider to Clayton.

                    ROKOFF
            (in a French accent)
        Excluding the lady, we men can come
        to an understanding... a pact, let
        us say.

Spider's and Clayton's eyes stay fixed on the Russian.

                    ROKOFF
            (in a French accent)
        I propose a lottery... one of us
        will have to make the ultimate
        sacrifice for the sake of the
        others.

Jane stops sipping and looks up repulsed by Rokoff's
proposition.

                    CLAYTON
        I will not be a party to such a
        horrific act! Better death than
        what you ask.

Rokoff replies with a half-wicked smile made worse by his
unkempt, bearded face.

                    ROKOFF
            (in a French accent)
        You have no choice. You must vote
        in this or you will become the
        sacrifice by default.

                    CLAYTON
        There's still a chance we may yet
        sight a ship -- even land. We
        can't give --

                    ROKOFF
               (in a French accent)
          -- We haven't sighted a sail or
          smoke on the horizon since the
          yacht sank... and as for land, look
          around you. My plan is the only
          real chance we have.

                    SPIDER
          He's right, guv, so let's be done
          with it.

Clayton stands down and listens.

                    ROKOFF
               (in a French accent)
          I of course am in favor of the
          lottery. And you, Spider?

                    SPIDER
          I'm in.

Rokoff eyes Clayton.

                    ROKOFF
               (in French accent)
          Well gentleman, it's official...
          the count is two to one in favor of
          the lottery.

Rokoff turns around and rummages through life preservers and
luggage until he finds his coat.

He then digs into a pants pocket and draws out a handful of
coins and after selecting six francs, he returns the rest
back into his pocket.

After examining them he drops them all into Spider's anxious
hands.

                    ROKOFF
               (in a French accent)
          It's quite simple. I'll place the
          six francs under my coat and the
          first one to draw the 1875 franc
          will be the one.

Clayton shakes his head when he's offered the coins for
perusal by Spider, who then hands them back to Rokoff.

                    ROKOFF
               (in a French accent)
          We need to establish the order.

                         SPIDER
              I'll go last.

Rokoff glances at the silent and reluctant Englishman.

                         ROKOFF
                    (in a French accent)
              It seems, it's up to me to begin
              the lottery.

Jane watches, stupefied, as it unfolds before her.

Like a snake, his hand darts beneath the coat. Within
seconds he withdraws it holding an 1888 franc.

Clayton inserts his hand.

Jane inclines forward, breathless -- apprehensive.

Clayton's hand comes out in a fist. He opens it up but is
unable to glance down into his palm.

Rokoff looks at it and then meets Clayton's tired eyes and
shakes his head.

Jane closes her eyes and drops back in relief with an audible
exhale.

Rokoff turns to Spider.

                         ROKOFF
                    (in a French accent)
              Your turn.

                         SPIDER
                    (whispers to self)
              Spider, you bloomin' idiot. Serves
              you right for being last.

The perspiration of fear breaks out on his forehead as his
unsteady hand goes under the coat.

A shakier hand comes out and Spider opens it up just enough
to see.

Exhausted by the mental torment, he gulps and falls back onto
the floor of the lifeboat breathing heavily.

His fist opens and the coin rolls out and drops.

It's an 1879 piece.

Clayton picks it up, glances at it and then shows it to
Rokoff.

                         ROKOFF
                  (in a French accent)
               We go again.

Rokoff doesn't hesitate and delves for another franc.

He shows the selected coin to Clayton and then to Spider.
It's not the 1875 franc.

Spider rises with his eyes intent upon Clayton.

Clayton inserts his hand under the coat.

Jane cups her mouth as she watches in dreadful anticipation.

Clayton pulls back his arm with a clenched fist.

A frantic Spider opens the fist for him and eyes the coin.

Clayton turns his head to gaze at the poor distraught girl
and then drops his head and his hand along his side, while
Spider crawls to the edge of the boat.

Rokoff takes the coin from Clayton's hand.

The year is 1900.

SPLASH!

All faces turn towards the sound.

Spider is gone.

The two remaining men, taxed to their limits, lie exhausted
unable to continue the lottery.

EXT. WAZIRI VILLAGE - DAWN

A lone, lion's roar blends with the morning twilight as a
column of fifty Waziri warriors files out from the village.

EXT. JUNGLE - LATE MORNING

Spread out like a fan, the warriors move like spectres in
search of their prey.

Tarzan, a head taller than the tallest, is armed like one of
them.

A warrior further ahead discovers a wide fresh trodden trail
and signals the others.

HALF AN HOUR LATER

Moving cautiously in a single column the warriors follow the trail until Tarzan signals that the quarry is near.

Waziri, accompanied by Busuli, trots towards the ape-man.

                    WAZIRI
          I see nothing... I hear nothing.

                    TARZAN
          I smell them. They're not far off.

Busuli and the chief exchange doubtful glances as do a few others at his elbow.

                    WAZIRI
          How can you, a man, smell them and
          know their distance?

                    TARZAN
          If you believe not my words,
          believe your eyes. Send someone to
          follow me.

Tarzan drops the shield, impales the ground with his spear and leaps into a tree with the rapidity and agility surpassing that of a monkey to stop high upon a large branch.

Waziri points to one of his men, who leaving his weapons behind, eventually reaches Tarzan's side.

Grinning, Tarzan points.

The warrior follows Tarzan's hand for a few hundred yards and makes out a group of elephants congregated within a large, grassy bai.

The warrior, amazed, looks at Tarzan and then back again at the herd of pachyderms. Then, with a few hand signals to the men below, he confirms Tarzan's words.

EXT. JUNGLE - NOON

From the treetops Tarzan takes in the view of the bai.

A segmented trunk, with heavy, straight tusks on either side, wraps around some tall grasses and yanks them from the ground.

Another bull elephant, near it, sways gently with a gurgling rumble that vibrates the air around it.

Youngsters jostle back and forth trumpeting while the females rest or reach for the tender twigs in different areas of the bai.

Forty-nine pairs of eyes watch from the ground below, behind the veil of the jungle wall.

At a signal from the chief, the warriors rise with their heavy steel-shod spears and running into the

BAI

launch them into the pair of bull elephants.

Twenty-four drive deep into the flesh of the one eating grass and twenty-five impale the swaying giant.

The grass-eater collapses to the ground dead.

The other wounded, raging bull elephant charges after the warriors who dart into the jungle to escape the trumpeting and roaring inferno at their heels.

EXT. JUNGLE - CONTINUOUS

As it crashes through the forest wall it snaps off spears, blood streaming from its stricken side.

Busuli sprints down the jungle trail but he's no match for the gray behemoth towering behind him as he swiftly closes the gap between them, booming in pain and madness.

Flying through the trees above the screaming pachyderm, Tarzan yells with his powerful lungs to stop the frenzied rampage.

                    TARZAN   SUBTITLED
Tantor! Poogat, Tantor!   Tantor! Stop, Tantor!

But the furious beast is deaf to all sounds, its concentration focused solely on Busuli.

Tarzan blazes ahead of the bull elephant and with only a small interval between Busuli and certain death, Tarzan drops out of the air before the charging freight train.

The bull elephant turns in the nick of time to engage the newcomer, but with spear already in hand and faster than lightning, Tarzan leaps from the path of the bellowing bull.

The bull tusks and stomps empty ground as Tarzan, with mighty thews, drives the spear behind the left shoulder deep into the savage heart of the bewildered beast.

With one last thunderous roar, the bull elephant crumbles to the earth like a toppled tower.

Busuli sprinting for his life does not see Tarzan's heroic deed, but Waziri and many of the other warriors witness the incredible feat.

Tarzan is soon surrounded by a mob of celebrating and cheering Waziri warriors.

Tarzan springs onto the carcass of the elephant and raising his lips to the sky, rips the airwaves with the horrific victory cry of the bull-ape.

The warriors are taken aback and slowly move backwards from ape-man.

After the last note of his victory cry, Tarzan looks down and grins at the superstitious and apprehensive Waziri warriors from atop the gray mountain of flesh.

Enheartened by Tarzan's friendly demeanor the warriors regroup and prepare to move out, when from out in the distance, dull, POPPING sounds arrest their attention.

Tarzan's keen ears are the first to interpret the noise.

> TARZAN
> Gunfire! The village is under
> attack.

Stern, stalwart eyes turn toward the chief.

The chief's eyes glow with a burning fire as righteous anger covers his wrinkled face.

> WAZIRI
> Prepare for battle! The Arab
> raiders and their cannibal slaves
> have returned.

EXT. JUNGLE - AFTERNOON

The warriors dog-trot along a meandering trail in two columns.

The earlier fusillade of weaponry is now replaced by an occasional report from a rifle.

A few miles from the village the hunting party encounters a small group of frantic and frightened women with children who managed to escape the raided village.

Incoherent babbling follows but Waziri admonishes them to silence. He looks at one, an attractive young woman.

> WAZIRI
> Tell me woman... what has happened?

The young RATTLED WOMAN needs no prodding and lets loose.

> RATTLED WOMAN
> They attacked without warning --
> many Arabs and Manyuema -- all of
> them with guns! They rushed the
> village shouting and began killing
> everyone...

The lovely girl begins to cry.

> RATTLED WOMAN
> ... There was no mercy.

The other women try to comfort her.

Waziri gives her a moment to recover.

> WAZIRI
> Did they take any prisoners?

> RATTLED WOMAN
> I do not know... we fled and the
> Manyuema yelled after us that they
> would eat us all.

Waziri puts a comforting hand on her arm and nods indicating that she may go.

He summons one of his men.

> WAZIRI
> Take the women and children to the
> bai. Set-up camp and protect them.

The warrior corrals the traumatized women and children and leads them slowly away.

EXT. JUNGLE - AFTERNOON (MUCH LATER)

The hunting party pushes forward in stealth mode.

The noise of many desperate feet in flight, frightens monkeys
and birds who dart off screaming and squawking.

A group of more than a hundred suddenly comes face-to-face
with their chief.

More than half of them are men and most of them are armed
with either a spear and shield, bow and arrows or both.

Waziri, standing between Busuli and Tarzan, quickly issues
orders and the women and children are sent to the bai with an
escort of two warriors.

EXT. JUNGLE - LATE AFTERNOON

From the concealment of the jungle fringes, a Waziri scouting
party scrutinizes their sacked village.

EXT. JUNGLE - WAZIRI CAMP - LATE AFTERNOON

                    WAZIRI SCOUT
          ... No, they are inside the
          village, My Waziri.

                    WAZIRI
          Were you seen?

The warrior shakes his head.

A vindictive smile ensnares the chief's countenance.

Waziri raises his heavy war spear and spreads his eyes among
his men in satisfaction.

                    WAZIRI
          Vengeance!

All the warriors shoot up their spear arms.

                    WAZIRI WARRIORS
          Vengeance!

                    WAZIRI
          When you see me charge, then we as
          one, will fall upon them and avenge
          the blood of our slain!

The warriors begin to chant HAAOOT over and over again as
they begin to form into two columns of fifty each.

Tarzan, at Waziri's side and doubtful of the chief's plan,
pitches his own.

                    TARZAN
          Waziri, wait. Your scouts did not
          see within the village.

Waziri turns and raises up his hand to his anxious warriors
for them to standby and then confers with the ape-man.

                    WAZIRI
          Speak your mind, Tarzan.

                    TARZAN
          If what the woman said is true and
          they are all armed, you and your
          warriors will all be slaughtered
          uselessly. From the trees I will
          be able to see. Let me go and
          bring you word of their true
          strength and numbers.

Waziri looks into the keen, grey eyes of the ape-man. Slowly
he nods as he considers Tarzan's suggestion.

                    WAZIRI
          Your words are wise... I will wait
          for your return.

Waziri strikes the ground with the butt of his spear,
finalizing his decision.

Tarzan drops his shield and spear and with a quick spring
vanishes into realm of the jungle giants.

EXT. JUNGLE - LATE AFTERNOON (MINUTES LATER)

Like a wraith, Tarzan flies through the upper highways of the
canopy, swinging and leaping across yawning heights without
hesitation.

Soon he spies the palisaded Waziri village and begins his
descent.

EXT. WAZIRI VILLAGE - LATE AFTERNOON

Tarzan creeps along a giant limb overhanging the village
palisade and finding a spot with a view, sits down on his
haunches.

From his aerial vantage point, he makes out about fifty Arabs
and 250 Manyuema cannibals -- all armed.

Tarzan is intrigued by the Manyuema who like the Waziri are a handsome race in symmetry and countenance. Their faces are clean-cut with straight noses.

They're attired with loincloths covering the back and front with the front ending in a tapered triangle.

Their unusual coiffeurs consist of two chignons atop their heads split evenly down the middle with a single chignon decorated with one to three red, tail feathers from a parrot inserted at an angle or horizontally.

Around the rest of their fine heads, the braided hair falls down to their shoulders.

Some of the Arabs are busy abusing and fettering the prisoners.

A few Arabs eat around a low fire.

Others converse and clean their weapons.

Directed by Arabs, cannibal slaves collect and concentrate a great quantity of ivory near the gate entrance.

Near them, the majority of the savage cannibals cram themselves with the flesh of the dead. Most draw their meat from the fleshpots while a few prefer to eat their share raw.

Cooking pots are everywhere. Entrails and body parts are strewn all about the grisly feast. A pile of feet here -- a pile of heads there.

Headless bodies, minus hands and feet, slowly roast over large blazing fires handled by pairs of cannibals. Others busy themselves with the butchering.

Gleaning the information he needed, Tarzan zips away as quietly and invisibly as he arrived.

EXT. JUNGLE - WAZIRI CAMP - LATE AFTERNOON

Tarzan's powerful, lithe body lands in the midst of the waiting Waziri warriors.

A fiery Waziri is barking out orders to his men.

Busuli runs to Tarzan's side, concern writ upon his clean-cut features.

                    BUSULI
          Waziri has just learned that his
          wife was hacked to pieces and
          reason has left him -- he means to
          attack as soon as we reach the
          clearing.

Tarzan, dead-set on stopping the suicide mission moves to
confront the chief, only to be held back by Busuli.

Busuli drops his hand from Tarzan's shoulder and shakes his
head.

                    BUSULI
          It is useless, Tarzan. His blood
          has become fire... he hears nothing
          and sees nothing. He will not
          listen to you.

                    TARZAN
          But it's madness! He'll never be
          able to rescue the captives this
          way.

                    BUSULI
          How many?

                    TARZAN
          I didn't count them, but they're
          quite a few -- but it won't matter
          if he goes through with his plan,
          because there are close to 300
          raiders behind those gates.
          Everyone of them, armed with a
          rifle.

Holding Tarzan with his dark eyes...

                    BUSULI
          Even if they numbered a thousand,
          he would not listen. Therefore,
          hastens and hopes only to salvage
          the body of his wife and the rest
          before they are eaten by the --

Tarzan's solemn eyes and negligible head shake relay the
truth.

                    BUSULI
              (astounded)
          They have begun already?

Tarzan nods, inflaming Busuli's eyes.

                    BUSULI
          I will enjoy killing them!

MOMENTS LATER

At the head of a two column formation of a hundred, sleek,
ebon warriors, Waziri yells out a violent, curt command and
the war march begins.

Tarzan bringing up the rear with Busuli, chafes at the
chief's reckless decision and in a blink of an eye he
disappears, from the startled eyes of Busuli, into the trees.

EXT. JUNGLE - LATE AFTERNOON

Behind the jungle curtain, a long rank of a hundred Waziri
warriors are at the ready.

Waziri, with burning eyes, raises his spear, cries out and
charges!

EXT. CLEARING - LATE AFTERNOON

As one, they take-off across the open clearing brandishing
war spears, bow and arrows and uttering savage war cries as
they race towards their ravaged village.

The skirmish line swiftly transforms into a "V" formation
with Waziri at the tip of the spear.

EXT. WAZIRI VILLAGE - DAY

Galvanized by the war whoops, Arabs and the Manyuema
cannibals run to their protective positions behind the walls.

Rifles from behind the crowded walls rise to a horde of
shoulders awaiting the command of their Arab lord.

A brilliant and implacable sun stares down in dismay and as
the Waziri warriors reach the middle of the clearing, the

ARAB LEADER

yells and bullets fly.

IN SLOW MOTION

A bullet travels inexorably through the air rising and
falling almost imperceptibly and then bores through Waziri's

FOREHEAD

and exits the rear of the skull dragging with it a chunk of
gray matter in its wake.

Waziri's arms go up, the spear slips from his grasp and he
lands on his back dead with his lifeless eyes still open.

BACK TO NORMAL SPEED

Smoke rises above the walls, as another barrage of bullets
finds its way through the wall openings of the palisade and
speeds across the clearing taking down many more brave souls.

A small group reaches the gate only to be slaughtered by the
waiting raiders.

The merciless fire from the marauders forces the rest of the
warriors back behind the cover of the jungle wall.

GATES

open and a swarm of cannibals led by Arabs run out in pursuit
of the retreating Waziri warriors.

As the savage horde rushes across the

CLEARING

an

ARROW

whizzes through the air and into the

THROAT

of screaming cannibal. Another

ARROW

flies and penetrates deep into the

CHEST

of a hawk-nosed Arab.

From the edge of the forest fastness, high up in the trees,

TARZAN

quickly dispatches a few more of the rushing enemy and then
descends to the leaderless warriors prepared to fight -- to
the last man -- the coming onslaught of Arabs and cannibals.

In a commanding voice and demeanor, Tarzan addresses them.

> TARZAN
> We cannot fight them head-on.
> Scatter and use stealth to kill
> them one at a time when you can and
> let us meet where we killed the
> elephants -- and don't worry about
> the captives, I will bring them.

Taking Tarzan's advice to heart, the seventy-five remaining
Waziri warriors melt into the forest.

Tarzan sprints down the trail at just over forty miles per
hour, and leaps into the trees just as the horde crashes past
the wall and into the gloomy jungle.

EXT. WAZIRI VILLAGE - SUNSET

A lone Manyuema guard, armed with a rifle and a bandolier of
ammunition strapped across his chest, gazes out through the
large open gate across the clearing towards the vast forest
before the village.

His attention is held by the faint, sporadic gunfire in the
distance.

Directly behind him near the rear of the village, fifty
captives -- women and children -- fettered together by their
necks with a chain sit in abject misery.

IN SLOW MOTION

Leaping out from high up in the trees with a notched arrow
pulled far back on the bow, a poetic, savage Tarzan releases
a shaft as he hangs in mid-air. The upturned faces of the
captives watch below him in amazement.

BACK TO NORMAL SPEED

The

ARROW

plows through, a foot out from the cannibal's chest.

TARZAN

lands running without breaking his forward momentum.

The dumbfounded

CANNIBAL

stares down, round-eyed and aghast at the protruding arrow. Blood oozes from his open mouth. He attempts to clutch the shaft, but it's abruptly yanked from his body.

His eyes roll up and with a painful GRUNT he keels over dead.

TARZAN

wipes the bloody arrow on the dead man's loincloth, drops it as a second thought into his quiver and searching him briskly, finds a group of keys.

EXT. BAI - NIGHT

Near the carcass of the dead elephant, a huge fire burns within a large boma.

Big chunks of elephant meat hang over the fire.

The remnants of men, women and children are spread out eating and resting from the long day's ordeal.

The sound of many feet is the first intimation the warriors within the boma have that they're not alone.

A booming voice calls out to them.

                    TARZAN (O.S.)
          Do not be troubled, it is I,
          Tarzan. Let us in.

Armed with the dead sentry's rifle and ammunition belt
strapped across his magnificent chest, Tarzan leads a train
of weary Waziri women and children into the safety of the
boma.

Exclamations of joy and relief are expressed at Tarzan's
return and for the ones thought to have perished.

EXT. WAZIRI VILLAGE - DAY

A silent shaft cuts through the air and punches through a
cannibal's chest.

The cannibal grasps the arrow deep within him. He opens his
mouth, but death stifles his cry.

Like a hornets nest struck by a stone, a multitude of Arabs
and Manyuemas gather about the body.

Finding the arrow, angry shouts follow with every eye
scanning the fringes of the jungle walls, but they can see
nothing.

After a quick huddle among the Arabs, a command is given and
the gate is opened.

A large group comes out of the village and is divided into
patrols that begin to search the perimeter of the palisade.

Two patrols go in opposite directions into the jungle
surrounding the village, while the third crosses the clearing
toward the further forest wall.

CLEARING

As the third patrol crosses, two arrows are unleashed. An
Arab and a Manyuema fall.

Cursing and shouting, the Arabs hurry the patrol into the
safety of the jungle but not before another arrow drills deep
into the back of the last cannibal who collapses, screaming
to his death, on the forest fringe.

EXT. WAZIRI VILLAGE - TREES - DAY

Hidden on the sides and rear of the village, are the Waziri
archers with their powerful bows.

Each warrior has line of sight with each other along their
embracing tree-siege of the village, but are invisible to the
marauders below.

JUNGLE

From above, Tarzan overshadows a group of raiders like a grim
spectre.

MONTAGE - JUNGLE TACTICS

1) An arrow plunges into a point man. The crumbled body is
found by his patrol of angry Arabs and fearful Manyuemas.

2) A straggler is snatched up into the trees by a grass rope.

3) Strong, ebon arms yank a cannibal off the trail. A knife
falls and rises repeatedly until the muffled cries cease.

4) Up in the trees, a Waziri warrior gives a go-ahead nod to
another, who pops his head out from behind the bole and sends
a piercing messenger through the heart of a Manyuema cannibal
in the village.

EXT. WAZIRI VILLAGE - DAY

Furious Arab raiders reenter the village with terror-stricken
cannibals eager to leave the devastating jungle.

One of the yelling Arab's neck is suddenly transfixed by an
arrow and falls, gurgling blood.

Spooked, the cannibals clamor and mill in abject fear.

The Arabs with much shouting and rifle threats, order
everyone into the beehive huts and the Manyuema disappear
like electrical charges.

The Arabs with ready weapons, while conning the forest walls
above the palisades, slip into their huts, backwards.

From a high overhanging limb above the huts, Tarzan waits for
all the Arabs to take cover.

He then unslings his short, heavy spear and throwing back his
powerful arm rolling with muscles, he hurls it through the
thatched rooftop eliciting curses and an agonizing cry of
pain.

A grim smile upon his lips, Tarzan leaps out into the arms of
the jungle and zooms away through the trees.

EXT. BAI - NIGHT

A healthy fire burns in the middle of the boma. A lone
Waziri sentry stands near it.

The remnants of the village sleep on their grass beds
scattered throughout the interior of the boma.

Tarzan awakens fully alert and arms himself with bow and a
quiver filled with arrows.

He leaps over the boma without a sound and after several
quick strides disappears into the tar-black jungle.

EXT. WAZIRI VILLAGE - NIGHT

Firelight within the village plays above the upright, pointed
posts of the palisade.

A pair of hands cache a bow and quiver in the crotch of the
ancient tree.

Stealthy feet steal along a large limb that infiltrates the
rear of the village.

Tarzan peers through the foliage and spies a drowsy Manyuema
sentry sitting before an ebbing fire.

He drops like a ghost into the village proper and unsheaths
his Waziri long blade.

Moving with deadly silence and keen focus Tarzan nears the
nodding man from behind.

Just shy of his target, the cannibal warned by the mysterious
sixth sense, leaps up and wheels around!

Before him stands a bronze-muscled giant with firelight
playing off his mighty chest and the Waziri long blade.

The cannibal's eyes bulge.

He forgets the rifle strapped to his back and he forgets to
cry out.

Before the horrified man can turn in flight, Tarzan's hand
strikes faster than a Gabon viper, his steely fingers
crunching the man's throat.

Like a rock python, Tarzan's forearm muscles rip and bulge as
with his sinewy hand he lifts the man-eater off the ground
and looks into the suffocating cannibal's face.

The cannibal's face is a wreck as he tries desperately to
loosen the crushing grip upon his neck.

Tarzan tightens the squeeze and the cannibal's neck snaps
like a twig.

His legs stop quivering.

His arms fall to his side.

Tarzan tosses him over his shoulder and, with a short run and
a leap, is back in the tree that gave him ingress.

He strips the body and adds them to the tree crotch. He
grabs the man's rifle and walks out further into the village
along the monstrous branch.

He takes careful aim at an Arab beehive and FIRES.

Tarzan chuckles as a man shrieks in pain.

Silence reigns.

But soon the village is flooded by the horde of raiders.

Confusion and babbling take control of the pillagers.

The ARAB LEADER, tall and lean, fires a shot into the air. A
measure of quiet is restored as he draws all eyes to himself
and addresses them in the same language of the Waziri.

                    ARAB LEADER
              Where's the guard?!

Murmuring ensues among the mass of frightened and on-edge
cannibals. Yet, no one can answer the Arab Leader.

Fooled by the dancing shadows on the gate and seized by fear,
a cannibal begins to fire wildly at the barred entrance and
is quickly joined by both Arab and Manyuema.

As the rifles senselessly begin to pop and smoke, Tarzan
joins in the fusillade by targeting them in the rear.

A cannibal collapses.

Another drops with a bullet in his brains.

A Manyuema watches another crumble beside him and seized by
unbounded fear, screams at the top of his lungs.

The chaotic firing stops and the cannibal, with a fear-filled
face, points a shaky finger at the dead body.

The other corpses are found and the fear-bitten, jabbering cannibals rush as one to the unbar the gate and flee.

The Arabs shout, threaten and brandish their weapons and barely manage to stop the stampede from the village.

The Manyuema panic is subdued, yet their apprehensive eyes scan everyone and everything around them.

EXT. WAZIRI VILLAGE - NIGHT (A HALF-HOUR LATER)

Many more campfires illuminate the village and with the ample light, the marauders seem more at ease.

A weird, floating MOAN from above instantly draws over a hundred, unsteady rifles towards the frightful emanation.

The subdued fear resurfaces. Low, fearful voices fill the air.

Harried, unblinking eyes stare upwards into the jungle giant.

Tarzan lifts the dead body above his head and chucks it at the fearful gathering below him.

From below, the tremendous crashing noise of breaking and snapping branches is enough to scatter many towards the palisade walls.

For the others with more temerity, the body breaks through the foliage and lands with a heavy thud in disarray blowing dust and dirt in all directions.

Howls, shrieks, and screams strive to outdo each other as with unbridled fright the cannibals explode in all directions.

Many scale the walls and disappear into the blackness of the jungle.

Even more vanish pell-mell into the jungle after the gate is opened, rather than face the unnatural presence within the village.

Some take refuge within the beehive huts but the majority cower against the palisade wall opposite the unidentified mass lying inert before them.

After the dust settles, the Arab Leader moves cautiously to the body and crouching next to it turns it over.

He scowls and looks back at his men.

                    ARAB LEADER
              It's the missing guard!

The Arab Leader squints and looks upward towards the tree.

EXT. JUNGLE - NIGHT

As Tarzan's silhouette sails high through the canopy, infused
by copious rays of moon light, a sudden barrage of gun fire
erupts in the distance, peppering the night in his wake.

EXT. WAZIRI VILLAGE - DAY

Outside the gate the Arabs are loading up their slaves with
the large quantity of ivory tusks found in the village.

Within the center of the village, a dying fire is stoked and
torches lit.

The cannibals approach the huts to light them up, but before
anything is even singed...

                    TARZAN (O.S.)
              If you set the village on fire you
              shall all die!

The shaken cannibals don't wait for the ominous voice to
repeat the warning.

The lit torches are dropped into the fire.

But their Arab overseer, witnessing their defection, comes
roaring at them.

As he yells, hurling curses upon the cannibals, an arrow digs
into his chest. His lifeless corpse falls into the flames
and his robes catch fire.

The cannibals fly from the village to the Arabs outside and
after an excited explanation, armed Arabs enter to find their
fellow a blazing inferno.

Unable to put it out and angered by the defilement of the
man's body, they begin to shoot indiscriminately into the
most probable trees, but Tarzan is no longer there.

EXT. JUNGLE - DAY

Through a restless and shadowy jungle, a vanguard leads fifty pairs of Manyuema, each carrying a single tusk, upon a trail wide enough to accommodate two slave columns that are brought up by the rear guard.

A mishmash of giant trees, vines, creepers, grasses, brush and bush create green walls that rise high up into canopy where the sunlight struggles to reach the trail below.

Through this gauntlet the browbeaten and overburdened cannibals trudge, dogged on both sides by Tarzan's invisible, deadly warriors.

A swift SWOOSHING arrow nails an ivory-carrying cannibal through the back.

His partner, unbalanced and unable to bear the weight alone, falls to the ground with the heavy burden.

The cannibals in the immediate area panic but the flanking Arabs quickly move in quickly to restore order. They replace the deadman and the disrupted columns begin to move north again.

MONTAGE - ENEMY ATTRITION

1) Tarzan pops his rifle and a flanking Arab goes down.

2) Two Waziri archers release their arrows in tandem, and a huge tusk drops on two dead Manyuema slaves.

3) Two arrows plunge into the two foremost tusk-carriers forcing the train to stop.

4) Only the trained weapons of the Arabs keep the fearful and superstitious cannibal slaves moving forward.

EXT. JUNGLE - CLEARING - SUNSET (3 DAYS LATER)

In a clearing near a river, the exhausted, harassed cannibals drop their loads to prepare a boma for the evening campsite.

Campfires are quickly lit and the Arabs set up guards and the rest -- not assigned to boma detail -- after making their grass beds, fall fast asleep.

EXT. JUNGLE - CLEARING - MORNING

Outside the boma, a demoralized and fearful Manyuema watch as the Arab Leader orders two dissenters tied to trees.

He nods toward his Arab firing squad and two cannibals slump and slide down to the base of the trees, bullet holes oozing.

He sweeps the cannibals with a merciless gaze.

                    ARAB LEADER
          Who else wishes to defy me?!

Most if not all avoid the eyes of their vicious master.

                    ARAB LEADER
          Good!
               (to the Arabs)
          Move them out!

The reluctant cannibals pair-up and lifting up the ivory begin to form into their columns.

From somewhere up in the trees a powerful and mysterious voice seeps into the marrow of their bones.

                    TARZAN (O.S.)
          You shall all die! None shall
          return home.

The tormented souls of both cannibals and Arabs scan the jungle walls to no avail.

                    TARZAN (O.S.)
          Drop the ivory and kill your Arab
          oppressors and we shall spare your
          lives. You are all armed and
          greatly outnumber them.

Though a shadow of their former selves, the Manyuema number 130 while the Arabs, only thirty.

The cannibals look from one to another seeking a leader.

                    TARZAN (O.S.)
          Turn upon them and we will help you
          slay them.

The Arabs instinctively begin to band together into a tight group.

Each group eyes the other and then a

CANNIBAL

unburdened with ivory, fires into the Arab band and a storm of

BULLETS

screams and flies in opposite directions.

ARROWS

from the jungle take a terrible toll on the sons of the desert and though they fight bravely, are soon annihilated.

A heap of dead men in robes lie perforated with bullets and arrows -- but not in vain.

Ten dead Manyuema will never eat human flesh again.

The victorious slaves look up into the trees uneasily and before they have time think the voice confronts them again.

                   TARZAN (O.S.)
          Pick up the ivory and return it to
          the village.

The cannibals grumble in disagreeable tones, loath to do as they are bid.

The CANNIBAL LEADER who took the first shot takes charge.

                  CANNIBAL LEADER
          Why should we obey? You'll only
          kill us once we've done your
          bidding.

                   TARZAN (O.S.)
          We could, but we won't. But, if
          you refuse to do as I say, all of
          you will surely die.

                  CANNIBAL LEADER
          Show yourself, that we may know
          whether you be man or spirit.

From a tree near them, Tarzan lands lightly on the ground sending a shockwave of fear through the throng of maneaters.

Towering before them stands a powerful white savage with an incredible physique.

Tarzan approaches the Cannibal Leader.

                              TARZAN
            Fear not. I speak the truth. Do
            as I command and you shall all
            live. Afterwards, you will be
            escorted from our land and allowed
            to return to your home. Resist...
                  (indicates the jungle)
            ... and this will be your home.

After a short huddle, a decision is reached.

                         CANNIBAL LEADER
            We have no choice. We must do as
            you say.

                                   FADE TO BLACK:

SUPER: "4 DAYS LATER"

EXT. ATLANTIC - LIFEBOAT - DAY

Three wasted bodies covered in ill-fitting clothes lie in the
lifeboat in wretched conditions.

Rokoff rises and crawls pitifully and stops next to Clayton.

                              ROKOFF
                  (in a French accent;
                   faint)
            We must... draw again... before
            we're too weak... to do anything.

Clayton nods weakly and is barely able to sit up.

Rokoff drags the coat between them.

Clayton turns his sunken face towards his fiancee.

Jane lies lifeless on the floor of the lifeboat.

Rokoff goes through his collection of coins and selects four
francs.

                              ROKOFF
                  (in a French accent)
            Only four this time... we'll use
            the same year.

He shows them to Clayton who nods in agreement.

Rokoff draws and shows it to Clayton, but it's not the one.

Clayton reaches in and draws out a coin.

He opens his palm and it's the 1875 piece.

Too weak and too tired to care, he shows it to Rokoff who starts digging through his pockets.

> CLAYTON
> When?

Rokoff pulls out a pocketknife and struggles to open it.

> ROKOFF
> (in a French accent)
> Now.

> CLAYTON
> Now? Can you not wait... until
> dark. It would be horrible... for
> her to awaken... to such a scene.

Rokoff's hungry eyes glare at Clayton.

> ROKOFF
> (in a French accent)
> I can wait.

Clayton puts a hand on Rokoff's arm.

> CLAYTON
> Thank you.

Clayton crawls toward the unconscious form of Jane Porter. He lifts her hand to his lacerated lips and then lies down beside her.

EXT. WAZIRI VILLAGE - DAY

Heavy laden and unarmed Manyuema, sandwiched between the Waziri warriors, march toward the village entrance.

Tarzan at the lead is met at the gate by the ecstatic remnants of the Waziri people.

When the people see the prisoners, the women yell and the entire populace moves as one to take revenge, but Tarzan intervenes.

> TARZAN
> Stop! No one is to hurt the
> prisoners in any way.
> (MORE)

                    TARZAN (CONT'D)
          I gave them my word that if they
          brought back your ivory we would
          escort them back to their
          country... unharmed. You have lost
          much, but so have they. Over a
          hundred of them have died at the
          hands of your brave warriors, but
          now my word must be kept.

Sullenly and reluctantly the people acquiesce and stand
aside.

                    TARZAN
          Busuli, lead the prisoners within
          and secure them. After you and the
          men have eaten and rested, feed
          them.

EXT. ATLANTIC - LIFEBOAT - NIGHT

Clayton awakens to the braying of a hoarse voice.

                    ROKOFF (O.S.)
               (in a French accent)
          Clayton! Clayton... it's time.

He glances at Jane, still in the same position.

                    CLAYTON
          I'm on my way.

Clayton fights to his hands and knees and crawls towards
Rokoff but after only a foot, he collapses.

He tries to rise, but cannot.

                    CLAYTON
          I can't make it... I'm too weak.
          You'll have to... make your way to
          me.

                    ROKOFF (O.S.)
               (in French; in a French
                accent)
          Sapristi! I gave you the time you
          wanted... and now you want to rob
          me!

                    CLAYTON
          I'm not trying to rob you... I'll
          give it another go. Perhaps if you
          and I both crawl... we'll be able
          to reach each other.

Clayton gets up again and he can hear Rokoff struggling to move as well.

Clayton slides one hand forward and falls flat on his face.

Rokoff's groans keep pace with his unsteady, faltering movements.

Clayton tries to recover but only ends up on his back unable to move any further.

Above him a myriad of stars are witnesses to the grim affair unfolding in the lifeboat.

Clayton hears Rokoff's strenuous breathing and broken shuffling moving closer.

Finally, Clayton can almost feel the breath of the butcher behind him.

A maniacal laughter escapes the lips of the Russian and Clayton blacks out.

EXT. WAZIRI VILLAGE - NIGHT

Moderate drum beats resonate throughout the village.

At the far end of the village, opposite the gate, a boma enclosure holds the cannibal prisoners in place with two armed sentries keeping watch.

They sit and eat their food around several campfires in mute silence.

Several of them approach the boma and watch the activities taking place in the center of the village.

Senior Waziri warriors sit around a small fire.

Around them are congregated the entire village. Tarzan is in the forefront with many others.

Busuli raises his spear and the drums stop. A deafening silence, then...

                    BUSULI
          The time has come to choose a new
          Waziri. Since the death of Waziri,
          one man led us to victory against
          the guns of the Arabs and their
          cannibal slaves... and we lost no
          one.

Busuli looks intently at the others seated with him. He can
see in their eyes that they all, are of one mind.

                    BUSULI
          There is only one man who is able
          and deserves to be our king.

Busuli suddenly jumps up into crouching position with his
spear held high over his head and begins to dance slowly and
to chant around Tarzan.

The others make room around Tarzan as Busuli continues the
ritual dance of selecting a new king.

                    BUSULI
               (chanting)
          Tarzan, Waziri... killer of lions,
          haaoot.

Another warrior springs up behind Busuli to dance and chant
around Tarzan

                    WARRIOR DANCER
          Tarzan, Waziri... killer of
          elephants, haaoot.

Two more, in turn, follow suit chanting the same but
expressing different exploits.

Together, the four dance in a circle slowly and rhythmically
around the ape-man.

The last man springs up and when he joins the other four, the
entire village as one yells...

                    WAZIRI VILLAGERS
          Tarzan, Waziri!

Busuli stops and the five warriors face the honored Tarzan.

Busuli raises his spear arm and when the spear butt strikes
the dirt, the drums initiate the official victory and
election celebration!

Fast paced booming fills the night. Roaring fires lick high
into the night sky.

Many warriors begin to dance silently around the ape-man.
Glistening black, lean bodies jump high into the air uttering
war cries.

Tarzan's supple body ripped and filled with rolling, powerful
muscles stands kingly among his subjects but only for a time
and then he too joins the wild dance of the jungle savages!

He jumps higher, yells more ferociously than any and all, as the fires bounce off his splendid, jungle-made physique.

With the celebration in full swing, men, women and children partake of the large feast spread before them.

Several fires cook or roast giant forest hogs and antelopes.

A veritable cornucopia of fruits, nuts, viands, and cassava cakes abound.

Voices and laughter mix with native beer.

Tarzan and many of his warriors tirelessly continue the primeval dance, the drums quickening their every move.

EXT. ATLANTIC - LIFEBOAT - NIGHT

Crumpled at the bottom of one end of the lifeboat, lies the motionless figure of Jane Porter of Baltimore, rocked gently by the swaying of the ocean waves.

                              FADE TO BLACK:

The sound of torrential rain interspersed with explosions of thunder.

EXT. ATLANTIC - LIFEBOAT - DAY

Clayton's face is bombarded by heavy rain.

Sheets of rain pelt the lifeboat.

He awakens enlivened by the tropical storm and rolls over onto his stomach and there before him is Rokoff facedown with the pocketknife still in his hand.

He pushes himself up, turns and faces the opposite direction, his eyes landing upon Jane Porter.

Jane's frail form is soaked by the deluge.

Her upturned face reacts involuntarily to the crashing shower.

Clayton crawls to Jane's body.

Though fearful that she's already dead, Clayton attempts to awaken her.

He rubs her starved cheeks and then her hands but there's no response.

Thunder pounds the heavens and lightning flashes spread like veins in an overcast sky.

William Cecil Clayton desperately cups both sides of her head and tries to yell above the noise of the downpour.

>   CLAYTON
>   Jane, wake up! Oh, my dear...
>   please don't die.

Resigned, he lowers his head beside hers in abject sorrow.

A sudden, tremendous thunder clap starts her eyes to tremble. Her eyes roll to-and-fro and then flutter open. To avoid the onslaught of the rain she averts her face in Clayton's direction.

Clayton's head rises, his face ransacked with indescribable relief. A haggard smile spreads across his face.

>   CLAYTON
>   Jane, you're alive! Thank God!

Jane is a little confused.

>   JANE
>   What's happened -- how long -- how
>   long have I been unconscious?

>   CLAYTON
>   A day, I think... I thought I'd
>   lost you.

Clayton helps her up to a sitting position with her back up against the side of the lifeboat.

Jane spots Rokoff.

>   JANE
>   What about him? Is he dead?

>   CLAYTON
>   I don't know. I'll try to revive
>   him.

Jane drops a weak hand on his arm.

>   JANE
>   (apprehensive)
>   No. Don't. He's wicked.

His joy turns to distress.

                    CLAYTON
          But, I must. I just can't --

                    JANE
          -- He'll try to kill you... and God
          only knows what he would do to me.

                    CLAYTON
               (torn)
          Jane... it's just not done, old
          girl.

                    JANE
          Cecil, for our sakes... please
          don't.

Her eyes plead with him.

He shakes his head trying to clear it and crawls over to
Rokoff's limp body.

As he's trying to decide, his eyes chance to shoot past the
gunwale and his face is struck by astonishment.

He staggers up on two shaky feet and pointing dead ahead he
looks at Jane.

                    CLAYTON
          Land! Jane, it's land!

Jane follows Clayton's outstretched arm and peers through
sheets of tropical rain about one-hundred yards out.

A light breeze nudges waves onto a white, sandy beach
embraced by the encroaching equatorial jungle.

Clayton drops his arm and kneels back down by Rokoff's body.

                    CLAYTON
               (to self)
          We're saved... thank God.

                    JANE
               (relieved; re: Rokoff)
          Cecil, it's okay.

Clayton nods and grabs hold of Rokoff's opposite shoulder and
with great effort turns him over on his back.

Rokoff looks dead.

EXT. BEACH - DAY

A light drizzle falls as Clayton, looking more like a
scarecrow than a man, makes a final pull on the painter
towards a group of palm trees near the edge of the water.

He ties it off on the nearest palm tree.

A hollow-eyed Rokoff is awake and disoriented.

Clayton rests against the gunwale, out of breath.

                    CLAYTON
              (to Jane)
          I'm going out... to find food.
          I'll be back... as soon as I can.

Jane registers his words, as the light rain streams down her
gaunt countenance, with a few nods.

EXT. CLEARING - DAY (1 HOUR LATER)

The rain has ceased and with the breaking of the clouds a
ferocious sun steams up the beach and the profuse jungle
vegetation.

Lazy columns of steam rise up slowly and majestically.

Clayton breaks the jungle wall and trudges towards the others
bearing fruits and viands.

EXT. BEACH - LIFEBOAT - DAY (30 MINUTES LATER)

Jane munches on some exotic fruit.

She glances up at the blazing sun shielding her eyes from its
merciless heat.

                    JANE
          Cecil, please help me off this
          boat. This heat is simply too
          much.

Clayton tosses a banana peel and follows it over the side and
helps her off the lifeboat.

Rokoff follows them into the welcome shade of the clearing.

EXT. CLEARING - DAY

The three, bellies filled, collapse onto the soft jungle
duff.

EXT. JUNGLE - DAY (A WEEK LATER)

Through a more open jungle the Manyuema are escorted by the
Waziri warriors.

The warriors stop at a small stream running parallel to a
range behind it and surround the cannibals.

A silent fear falls on the helpless cannibals until Tarzan
drops out of nowhere to land before them, tall and powerful.

Tarzan sweeps their frightened faces with steel-grey eyes.

                    TARZAN
          Our domain ends here. You are free
          to go... don't come back.

Tarzan is about to turn around and leave them when...

                    CANNIBAL LEADER
          Wait. What about weapons?

Tarzan and his warriors, besides their usual arms, have
rifles strapped to their backs.

                    TARZAN
          We have given you your lives...
          that is enough.

Tarzan signals his warriors and two columns are instantly
formed facing away from their enemies.

Tarzan jogs to the front and without looking back, leads them
into the fastness of the grim jungle at a steady dog-trot --
the warriors chanting HAAOOT in cadence.

EXT. CLEARING - SUNSET (A WEEK LATER)

Tarzan breaks through forest wall and moves across at an easy
pace followed closely behind by his stalwart warriors.

WAZIRI VILLAGE

At their approach the gate is opened and their two columns
become one.

Tarzan along with Busuli stop outside the gate while the train of tireless warriors enter.

Tarzan keeps his alert eyes on the end of the column.

> TARZAN
> In a few days I will leave to find
> the city of gold.

> BUSULI
> (grinning)
> I knew you would, Waziri.

As Tarzan's eyes follow the last man into the village, he turns his gaze at Busuli.

> TARZAN
> Find me fifty brave souls who would
> join me in a long and perilous
> journey.

Standing straight and noble.

> BUSULI
> Forty-nine, Waziri.

Tarzan lays a hand on his shoulder.

> TARZAN
> (breaking a smile)
> I knew you would be the first.

EXT. WAZIRI VILLAGE - PREDAWN (DAYS LATER)

A low, heavy fog, filled with fireflies, covers the entire clearing up to the village gate, resembling a lighted city.

Countless surreal lights, greet Tarzan and fifty sleek, stouthearted warriors armed with spears, bows and arrows and hunting knives, as they file out from the village.

As they cross the

LUMINESCENT FIELD

the fireflies before them and on their flanks take flight, filling the night sky with thousands of tiny, glittering stars.

SERIES OF SHOTS - QUEST FOR THE CITY OF GOLD

1) Through unfamiliar jungles they follow a river that flows into green, open country and towards a hazy mountain range far in the distance.

2) At the base of the mountain range they begin the gradual ascent up through forgotten trails. Upon the other side of the range, the river becomes a rivulet that traverses similar terrain only to find themselves entering another vast, foreboding jungle.

3) As they continue through the forest the rivulet becomes a large river that runs down the middle of an expansive wooded valley. Before them, barely discernable, is another range of mountains.

4) At sunset on the edge of the forest, near the end of the river, they come to a final mountain range corrugated with draws, spurs and bulging with crags. Here the Waziri warriors make camp.

EXT. MOUNTAIN PASS - MORNING

Tarzan and his warriors inch up, like a long line of mountaineering ants, as they work their way up a steep crag towards the summit of the pass.

SUPER: "DAY 25"

Tarzan, well in the lead, is the first to top the summit onto a plateau.

On either side of the pass, mountain peaks climb thousands of feet above him like massive towers vying for the heavens.

He turns to monitor the progress of his men and then skims over the terrain already conquered.

Satisfied, he turns his attention to a narrow and barren valley littered with enormous boulders and short, stout trees.

Standing tall and majestic with his black hair long again, his keen, grey eyes canvass the valley and are soon rewarded by a sight situated to one side of the forsaken valley.

Enthralled, a smile of satisfaction creeps into his solemn countenance as his eyes take in a gleaming, fiery city reflecting a golden and dazzling light from its walls, domes and towers.

A huge wall encircles the ancient city with towers and spires rising in different parts of the long forgotten, magnificent metropolis.

EXT. BARREN VALLEY - DAY (HOURS LATER)

Through inhospitable terrain Tarzan leads his sleek, ebon warriors towards the mysterious city.

EXT. CITY OF GOLD - LATE AFTERNOON

As they near the city the change is dramatic as the ruins become discernable.

A colossal wall of fifty feet towers above them and though ten to twenty feet of the wall has fallen in a few places, it's still an imposing and powerful fortress.

Above it all hangs an eerie, disquieting silence. Unnatural and unclean.

Subtle sounds and shadows attract the ape-man's attention but he's unable to pinpoint the source, yet he says nothing to his men who are deaf to them.

                    TARZAN
          Busuli, have the men prepare camp.
          We'll sleep here tonight.

EXT. CITY OF GOLD - WAZIRI CAMP - MIDNIGHT

A shrill, high-pitched, shrieking scream awakens the Waziri warriors, like ice-cold buckets of water.

Tarzan, with drawn knife, is up on his feet and ready, but seeing it for what it is, he drops back into his makeshift bed.

The long maniacal shriek slowly becomes a moaning groan which disappears into the night.

The superstitious warriors, frozen in stark terror, dare to look from one to another in unfeigned fear.

EXT. CITY OF GOLD - WAZIRI CAMP - MORNING

Still shaken by the episode of the previous night the men are gathered around Busuli, in deep consultation.

Tarzan, untroubled, is some distance away from them examining
strange markings on the great wall.

EXT. CITY OF GOLD - WAZIRI CAMP - MORNING (LATER)

A hush falls upon the men as Tarzan enters the camp. It
doesn't escape him but he pretends to ignore them.

The men goad Busuli to confront the ape-man.

Busuli approaches Tarzan.

>   BUSULI
>   Waziri, let us leave this evil
>   place. The men will not stay.

Tarzan stares past Busuli towards his disconcerted men. He
searches their faces and is disappointed that a sound could
produce such fear in them.

>   TARZAN
>   Are you children to be frightened
>   by the sounds of the night?

None dares reply.

>   TARZAN
>   Then, your king will go alone.

Tarzan picks up his weapons and without further regard for
them, moves towards the huge wall.

Busuli's eyes follow his Waziri and facing the men, he tries
to encourage them.

>   BUSULI
>   This is not good. We are Waziri
>   warriors and we cannot abandon our
>   king to unknown dangers. I
>   cannot... you cannot.

The warriors hang their heads, shame-faced.

EXT. OUTER WALL - MORNING

Tarzan, focused on following the wall, is aware that his men
are close behind. He turns to look at them but none can look
him in eye and turning his face forwards again, he smiles to
himself.

EXT. OUTER WALL - MORNING (20 MINUTES LATER)

With his men in tow, Tarzan finds a narrow crevice in the
wall, no more than twenty inches wide.

Looking into the murky interior he discerns a flight of
heavily worn, concrete stairs that disappears around a turn.

                    TARZAN
          Follow me.

Holding his weapons in his hands and packed with mass and
muscle, Tarzan is barely able to squeeze through sideways.

Encouraged by their king's fearless attitude, but with
troubled demeanors, they follow after him.

INT. OUTER WALL - MORNING

They ascend the stairs and after making the turn, they zigzag
along a dim passage that suddenly angles off and opens up
into a courtyard.

EXT. CITY OF GOLD - COURTYARD - MORNING

Before them stands another wall almost as high. The entire
top of the wall is interspersed with small, round towers that
rise into turrets.

A similar entrance, framed in the inner wall, beckons Tarzan.

EXT. CITY OF GOLD - MORNING

Tarzan and his men exit the inner wall passage and find
themselves on a wide avenue and marvel at the sight.

Across the avenue are imposing granite buildings in various
states of preservation.

A few of the buildings suffer from crumbling facades with
plants and tree limbs weaving in and out of gawking windows.

A prodigious domed temple on a massive foundation appears to
have weathered the ravages of time.

Tall columns on either side of its large entrance are topped
with vile looking birds carved from the same stone.

A few of them catch glimpses of quick, fleeting shadows
within the domed structure.

Tarzan indicates the temple.

                    TARZAN
          We'll search that one first.

Tarzan crosses the avenue and starts up the wide stairs,
without a backward glance, followed by a tightly packed and
terrified group of warriors.

INT. TEMPLE - DOME CHAMBER - MORNING

A faint light swirls within.

A rough, misshapen hand disappears from the embrasure
centered in the dome above them and stealthy naked feet
scatter within a nearby gloomy corridor.

Figures of man and beast are carved on granite walls and
yellow tablets inset within the masonry, attract Tarzan's
attention.

Upon a concrete floor Tarzan saunters over to one of them to
find hieroglyphics written on a tablet of pure gold!

Soft, shuffling feet attract their ears and barely audible
voices vanish before they can be pinpointed.

Tarzan's senses are alive while his Waziri warriors follow
him huddled together like frightened children.

Beyond, Tarzan can make out other chambers and as he goes
through the next chamber he's met by

SEVEN PILLARS

of solid gold and in the next chamber he finds the entire

FLOOR

covered in the precious metal.

Past the chambers, the building branches out into two
enormous wings and here Tarzan pauses.

Surreal, stealthy sounds and voices seem to come at them from
every direction, yet whenever they look, there's nothing.

The sweating blacks begin to grumble and Busuli moves to
Tarzan's side.

                         BUSULI
          Please, Waziri, leave this terrible
          place. Only the spirits of the
          dead live here.

                         TARZAN
          Whoever or whatever they are...
          they're not dead.

                         BUSULI
            (shakes head)
          If they were alive we would be able
          to see them, but we cannot because
          they are of the spirit world.

Tarzan indulges Busuli's sense of reasoning.

                         BUSULI
          Our great witch doctor has taught
          us that these spirits will rip a
          man to pieces with their teeth once
          he has entered into their resting
          places.

Tarzan glances at the tense, desperate faces and almost all
in unison quickly nod to affirm Busuli's words.

Tarzan smiling, struggles to stifle an outburst of laughter.

                         TARZAN
          You may all go. I will remain and
          search for the gold alone.

Before he finishes, two-thirds of his men disappear leaving
behind Busuli and fourteen others wavering on whether to
remain or desert their king.

A chilling, piercing shriek fills the wide corridor and
Tarzan with spear in hand, finds himself alone.

Nothing can be seen, but Tarzan hears naked feet scurrying
all around him.

INT. TEMPLE - RIGHT WING - DAY

Along the smooth concrete floor Tarzan goes from room to room
searching for the gold until he comes to one room with a
barred door.

Here a screaming symphony bombards the ape-man.

Tarzan, motivated by the increased crescendo of the warning shrieks echoing throughout the great shadowy wing, rams the door open with a mighty shoulder.

The angry maelstrom of shrieks and screams cease.

Pitch blackness stares out at Tarzan from within the chamber.

Like a blind man using a walking stick, Tarzan with his spear to guide him enters the black void.

Once past the threshold the door slams shut!

DARK CHAMBER

A mighty battle ensues!

The sounds of breaking bones and cracking skulls coincide with agonizing cries of pain and death.

Soon the struggle is over and only the heavy panting and breathing of many bodies is audible.

INT. TEMPLE - INNER COURTYARD - MORNING

High walls, stacked with galleries that reach just below the ceiling, surround the entire small courtyard and several corridors bore into its granite surfaces.

A chamber door opens and a great number of man-creatures pour out into the courtyard with four of them carrying Tarzan bound and stripped of his weapons.

The dead, the dying and the badly maimed are carried through and out of the courtyard. Others not as badly injured, follow with limps and dreadful flesh wounds.

They are squat and grotesque in appearance and look more like cavemen than anything else.

Their white bodies are covered with loin cloths made of either lion or leopard skins and circling their thick necks are necklaces with the claws of the same animals.

They stand awkwardly on short, crooked, thick legs and their long, strong arms -- like their legs -- are encircled with huge bracelets of pure gold.

Each, wields a hefty, gnarled club and strapped to their hips are long, frightening knives.

Raveled hair falls down their backs and shoulders but only down to their receding foreheads.

Great, long beards rest on hirsute chests, covering most of their repulsive faces imbedded with close-set eyes and a savage mouth equipped with fangs.

They drop Tarzan unceremoniously on the hard surface, surrounded by nearly one-hundred of these strange man-creatures.

After a few words are exchanged between two of them in a strange and laconic tongue, they all lope off into the depths of the temple leaving the ape-man alone.

Lying on his back, Tarzan sees a shaft up in the ceiling directly above him revealing blue sky.

Tarzan tries the strength of the bonds around his wrists but prying eyes, under mops of tangled hair that watch from the higher galleries above, prevent him from trying to break free.

A single embrasure on one of the walls is the only other window-like opening in the entire courtyard. Through it, Tarzan's grey eyes catch vegetation.

INT. TEMPLE - INNER COURTYARD - HIGH NOON

Suffering in silence Tarzan lays on the rough floor patiently bidding his time.

As he lays there, the rays of the sun creep over the edge of the ceiling shaft and instantly he's deluged with light from the waist up.

Tarzan hears the scuffling approach of many naked feet and, squinting to minimize the shower of light, he watches the higher galleries begin to fill with the man-creatures while into the courtyard stream in a solid twenty of their number.

Whether in the galleries or in the courtyard the eyes of the brutish creatures are upturned towards the opening above.

A slow, eerie chant emerges from their throats and the ones in the courtyard begin to move to the solemn chant around the ape-man with their eyes glued to the ball of fire above them.

For a few moments more they continue the ritual and then suddenly the man-creatures, as one, turn with raised clubs to face their captive.

They charge him with hideous faces coupled with shrieks and howls yet, out of nowhere, a female dashes in striking in all directions and scatters the man-creatures, with a smaller golden club, away from Tarzan.

Beaten back from their prize by the woman, the man-creatures resume the chant and movement around him while the woman recites, mechanically, in the same strange language.

After finishing, the girl cuts the bonds from Tarzan's ankles and as he gets to his feet, the chant and dance end.

One of the man-creatures blurts out a few words and points to Tarzan with a massive club.

The girl gives him the go-ahead nod.

After four of them drop leather ropes around the ape-man's neck, the girl beckons him to follow with a motion of a hand.

Tarzan scans the corridor entrances beyond the girl and glancing back, witnesses a growing entourage of heavily armed man-creatures lining up behind him in two columns.

One of the rope holders jams a club into the small of his back and Tarzan is forced, like a wild animal, to follow the girl.

SERIES OF SHOTS - CORRIDORS

1) Tarzan is led deeper into the temple.

2) They move through a maze of shadowy, serpentine corridors illuminated occasionally by torches along the way.

3) Through some passages they are barely discernable, resembling disembodied spirits rather than living beings.

4) Finally, they near the end of a long corridor, its mouth bathed with daylight.

INT. TEMPLE - ALTAR CHAMBER - AFTERNOON

From the corridor they emerge into a huge chamber.

Grinning skulls embedded within innumerable nooks in the lofty walls, greet the ape-man.

Like the inner courtyard, it too is stacked with galleries.

Many spaced skylights in the ceiling and embrasures along the walls criss-cross to provide ample light.

Sconces holding lit torches at intervals along all the walls, scatter any of the remaining shadows.

The girl leads Tarzan to the center of the chamber before the foot of an altar.

A tall, golden cup rests on the altar and the dry bloodstains on it and around its immediate vicinity are apparent.

As the galleries begin to fill, a file of women holding two golden cups each, enters the chamber from an ornate, arched entrance across from the foot of the altar.

The women have beautiful symmetry and are attractive with large, black, doe eyes.

Like the other, they are dressed the same.

Wrapped around their bodies like serpents is a single piece of soft antelope skin.

It depends from a single shoulder, wraps around their breasts, angles down around their back, encircles their waist leaving their midsection, to include the navel, visible.

The soft skin continues to wrap loosely around their hips ending a few inches above the knees.

On their heads covered with long, thick, black hair rests a net-like cap made of interconnected light chains and oval discs of gold.

From this net-crown, fall, on either side of them, long, fine chains of gold mixed with oval discs down to their waists which is surrounded by an intricate chain-belt of gold.

Their feet are shod with leather sandals secured above the ankles by crossed leather thongs.

Like the men, they wear armlets and anklets of gold but are instead, delicate and very ornate.

The procession stops a few feet behind Tarzan at the foot of the altar and then turns left to form a rank, facing the opposite wall.

A corresponding number of man-creatures lines up opposite the females and advancing, take a cup from their counter-part and return to their position.

The male rank turns left to form a file and the female rank turns right to do likewise -- both facing the foot of the altar.

The eerie chant rises from their lips and fills the chamber with it's rhythmic vibration.

Behind the altar, a partially lit staircase disappears into the depths of the chamber.

From it, a BEAUTIFUL FACE emerges into the light.

As she glides up the stone staircase the voluptuous curves of her lithe figure become incrementally visible.

She is dressed similarly to the other women but instead of an antelope leather skin, she's covered with the fine, soft skin of a leopard.

Her head raiment besides the gold, glitters with diamonds and her arms and legs are almost completely covered with fine and elaborate bracelets sparkling with priceless jewels.

At one side of her flaring hips, resides a long jeweled knife and in her hand she carries a golden wand.

Like a sinuous cat, she moves up behind the head of altar.

The chanting ceases into the echoing corners of the chamber and the man-creatures and the women kneel before her.

She extends her arm out before them and recites a prayer with a sweet, soothing, beautiful voice.

She ends the prayer and slowly drops her arm back to her side and the cupbearers rise.

Her eyes take in Tarzan for the first time.

Curious, as the cat she embodies, she moves around him slowly and eyes him from head to toe.

She then speaks to Tarzan in the strange language.

                    TARZAN
          I do understand your language.

She shakes her head in annoyance.

Tarzan tries French and then Bantu but she again shakes her head.

In a disappointed tone of voice she gives the man-creatures a command and they begin to chant and dance around the ape-man as before.

Her eyes never leave the tall and powerful figure of the ape-man.

The resplendent young girl gives another command that puts an end to the chant and dance portion of the ceremony.

With the slight gesture of her chin the man-creatures force him to the ground and bind his ankles anew.

Then, they grab Tarzan with their powerful arms and after raising him high into the air, they stretch him out upon the altar with his head and legs hanging over the edges.

Finished with their portion of the ceremony, the entourage leaves to take their places in the galleries.

Once they're gone, the incredible beauty raises the jeweled knife ever so slowly above Tarzan's giant chest, when a disturbance takes place on the male side of the line.

A BURLY BRUTE, a more bestial looking man-creature, forces himself to the front of the line. The weaker one pushed out of his place, complains.

With the long, slim, sharp knife still held high above the ape-man, she orders the ugly brute to the end of the line who growls and grumbles all the way there.

The knife begins to descend matching the speed of her ritual prayer.

BURLY BRUTE

now at the end of the line, continues to growl and grumble.

BEAUTIFUL FACE

stops the sacrificial blade right above Tarzan's chest to give the troublemaker a nasty look. The

FEMALE

opposite Burly Brute, scolds him to be silent and

BURLY BRUTE

crushes her head with his club.

Then like a madman, Burly Brute attacks anyone and everyone within his blind-rage.

The altar chamber quickly empties and except for the few unfortunate ones who were not fast enough to escape his cudgel, only Tarzan and the woman remain in the chamber.

The blood-lust spent, he licks his foul chops as he suddenly spots Beautiful Face.

                    BURLY BRUTE   SUBTITLED
Gak beglak tan poogat kan   No one can stop me now. You
dooan. Gru tadan meeda!   are mine!

Tarzan is surprised to hear the man-creature speaking the Mangani language of the great anthropoid apes!

                    BEAUTIFUL FACE   SUBTITLED
Mee tam gat zeea. Gru zandu   I am the high priestess. You
ag tondat kan!   dare not touch me!

Burly Brute disregards her admonition, abandons his club, and creeps towards her with outstretched rakes.

Beautiful Face forgets all about Tarzan as horror takes over her regal countenance.

Tarzan's veins and muscles bulge as he strains to break free.

As Burly Brute rushes past the altar to seize Beautiful Face, Tarzan's last, extreme effort at breaking his bonds, sends him rolling off the altar and onto the cold, concrete floor.

A moment later Tarzan is up on his feet, free, but Burly Brute and Beautiful Face are gone.

A smothered scream sends Tarzan sprinting down the staircase and into the large dark opening, from where Beautiful Face emerged.

INT. TEMPLE - VAULT - DAY

Tarzan speeds down the descending steps with traces of light from the chamber above following him partially down into a low vault and finds various dark passages guarded by lit torches on either side of them.

The dancing light of the torches weaves an unnatural aura producing grotesque contrasts.

To one side he finds the man-creature on top of the struggling, frantic girl, choking the life out of her.

Tarzan knocks the man-creature off the girl with a sweep of his arm, sending him rolling near the entrance of one of the dark passages.

Instantly, Burly Brute is on his feet growling and drooling from his gapping mouth, his flashing fangs dripping saliva in the fiery glow of the vault.

Burning eyes of hate, bore into the ape-man, from a contorted bestial face and, overtaken by bestial madness, he forgets the knife at his side and charges Tarzan with the strength of a maniac!

Tarzan meets him head-on.

His roars drown out the creature's growls, reverberating throughout the vault like rolling thunder.

Crashing together they fall to the ground fighting like two jungle beasts.

The girl, pressed against a wall, is captivated as she watches with horrified eyes the savage fury unfolding only a few feet from her.

Tarzan much bigger and much more powerful, pounds a series of lightning blows into the ugly face of Burly Brute like a sledgehammer, crushing it and his skull into a sickly pulp.

It's quickly over.

Tarzan rises from the quivering corpse and shakes his head with its shock of black long hair, like the mane of a lion.

He puts a foot on the squat man-creature, upturns his face to let out the victory cry of the bull-ape, but his eyes catching the light from above entering down the staircase, warns him against it.

She watches Tarzan remove the deadly dagger from the dead body.

The blade reflecting the torch light, awakens Beautiful Face from her trance and replaces it with fear, as she comes to grips with her current predicament.

At that very moment Tarzan's eyes fall upon her.

She attempts a quick dash for one of the dark passages but Tarzan, in a blur, is at her side restraining her before she's taken a full stride.

In vain the girl tries to disengage herself from his grip on her arm.

                    TARZAN   SUBTITLED
Da ag magat dagan. Mee   Do not be afraid. I won't
panatz ehgat gru.   hurt you.

Amazed, the girl ceases struggling against Tarzan, forgetting the grip on her arm.

              BEAUTIFUL FACE   SUBTITLED
Kapo tadan gru? Beh leh ga   Who are you? And how is it
ita gru budat gani ooh idato   that you speak the language
mangani?   of the apes?

Tarzan releases her arm.

The dialogue transitions from Mangani into English.

                  TARZAN
          I am Tarzan. I know the language
          because I was raised by them. How
          is it that you know it?

Focused on gathering information, she skips Tarzan's question.

                BEAUTIFUL FACE
          Why did you save me from Tha?

Tarzan's brows knit together.

                  TARZAN
          You're a woman... I could not let
          him kill you.

She stares at him in wonder and shakes her head, not understanding his reasoning.

                BEAUTIFUL FACE
          I tried to kill you.

                  TARZAN
          (smiling)
          Yes, I remember... but you did it
          from a false belief.
              (indicating the corpse)
          He didn't.

She studies his face.

                BEAUTIFUL FACE
          I am in your power now. What is
          your will?

She bows her head awaiting his answer.

                  TARZAN
          All I want is your help.

She raises her exquisite countenance towards him.

                    BEAUTIFUL FACE
        What is your will, Tarzan?

                    TARZAN
        Show me the way out of your city.

Her hungry, cat-eyes devour the ape-man as she closes the
space between them.

Her soothing voice oozes with honey.

                    BEAUTIFUL FACE
        Nothing more?

Tarzan doesn't miss her look but shakes his head in
agreement.

                    BEAUTIFUL FACE
        You are the most magnificent man I
        have ever seen. You are the type
        of man I've seen only in my
        sleep...

A longing sadness reaches into her almond eyes.

                    BEAUTIFUL FACE
        ... Images which vanish when I
        awaken to this dreadful world.
        Once, men like you inhabited this
        great city. But that was long ago.

Her voice trails off in thought.

Curious, Tarzan considers her for a moment. Her beauty, even
in the poor light, cannot be overlooked.

                    TARZAN
        Who are you and what is this place?

                    BEAUTIFUL FACE
        My name is La and I am the high
        priestess of the Temple of the Sun.
            (with outstretched arms)
        And you are in the city of Opar.

LA, 20, kneels sitting on her heels and looks up at Tarzan.

                    LA/BEAUTIFUL FACE
        Sit Tarzan and let me tell you
        about my city and its people.

Tarzan, in no hurry, gets comfortable on the floor beside
her.

                    LA
          We are all that remains of a once
          mighty race of people who lived far
          north of here in the ocean 10,000
          years ago. They came here seeking
          gold and their empire of cities
          stretched from the rising of the
          sun to the setting of the same. It
          was a very powerful and wealthy
          nation. Then one day when most of
          the people were back in the mother
          land, a great catastrophe struck
          and pulled our nation into the
          depths of the sea. In the blink of
          an eye all that we were vanished in
          a single night. A few survived who
          were found by our searching ships,
          but not enough to sustain us.

                    TARZAN
          We, from the outside, have heard of
          your country and it's sinking. Yet
          many believe it to be only a fable.

                    LA
          What do you believe? Is the city
          of Opar a fable? Am I? Are my
          priests and priestesses you
          encountered a fable?

                    TARZAN
          I believe you. But many of my
          people have trouble believing the
          truth even when they come face-to-
          face with it.

                    LA
          I can understand the unbelief.
          Time has a way of erasing the
          past... after the fall, we could no
          longer maintain the empire of
          cities in this savage land. Most
          of our cities were destroyed,
          abandoned or overcome by savage
          tribes from the north and the
          south. What remained of our people
          took refuge here in this great
          fortress, high in the mountains and
          away from those who would
          annihilate us.

La rubs her sore neck.

                    TARZAN
          You don't have to continue if it
          bothers you. You can finish your
          story when I return someday.

She gives him a gentle smile rubbing her slender long neck
gingerly with a sleek hand.

                    LA
          I'm alright, thanks to you... it's
          a little sore, but I can finish.

Tarzan's attention is turned by stealthy footfalls still some
distance away.

La lays a soft touch on one of his sinewy forearms to regain
his attention.

                    LA
          They won't come in here yet.

                    TARZAN
          You can hear them?

                    LA
          No, but I know their habits and
          they won't be entering here for
          some time -- where did I stop?

                    TARZAN
          Your people had just taken refuge
          in Opar.

                    LA
          Yes, and that's when our
          degeneration began. Only apes
          inhabited this place. No humans
          dared come here. In time all the
          knowledge we had amassed
          disappeared and except for our
          religion we are a shadow of a once
          proud people. Then began the cross-
          breeding with the apes. These we
          exiled, but the damage was already
          done. We learned the language of
          the apes long ago. We use our own
          language only for the temple
          ceremonies but in time we'll speak
          only Mangani.

                    TARZAN
          But how do you explain the
          degeneration of the men but not of
          the women.

              LA
I'm not certain. Perhaps it was
our breeding of thousands of years
that has kept our line thus far
unstained. Priestesses were of the
noble class and were bred only with
the noblest of our race, especially
the high priestess which descended
from mother to daughter. In truth,
it is as much a mystery to me as to
you.

A sudden thought grabs Tarzan and he can't stop a grin from
crossing his face.

              TARZAN
You're telling me that those
priests I saw today including the
one I killed are the best you can
hope for?

La reproves him to caution with her soft voice.

              LA
Do not profane these men. They are
my holy priests.

No longer grinning.

              TARZAN
Don't you have better men to choose
from?

              LA
The priests are the best men we
have. The others are much worse to
look upon.

In the gloom, La doesn't notice Tarzan's involuntary cringe
at her fate.

              TARZAN
Now would be a good time to show me
the way out.

La stands up and takes a few steps stopping at the foot of
the stairs and gazes up into the light above.

              LA
Once you've been touched by the
light of the flaming god there is
nothing I can do, if they should
find you.
             (MORE)

                    LA (CONT'D)
          For saving my life, I will make
          certain that does not happen. It
          may take some time, perhaps even
          days, but I will find a way to lead
          you beyond the walls.

La walks back to the now standing ape-man.

                    LA
          Come, Tarzan. We must leave this
          place, for soon they will be
          looking for me and should they find
          us together, they will kill us
          both.

                    TARZAN
          Then you must not chance it. I
          will try to escape alone.

                    LA
               (shaking head)
          You are deep in the temple and
          though you are unmatched in
          strength, they would only capture
          you again by their sheer numbers.
          I'll hide you and return this very
          night.

                    TARZAN
          What about you? Will you be
          alright?

                    LA
          They'll believe the story I shall
          tell them... there's no need to
          fear for my safety. Follow me.

SERIES OF SHOTS - BASEMENT CORRIDORS

1) Tarzan follows La's lovely figure through a dismal
passage.

2) La pauses at an intersection briefly, then swiftly leads
Tarzan into another vein of Opar.

3) She leads him through a maze of dim corridors lighted
sometimes by the light coming through grills in the ceiling
or by scones bearing lit torches set at intervals throughout
the passages.

4) They stop at a door and enter the chamber.

INT. TEMPLE - CHAMBER OF THE DEAD - DAY

A stone grating above permits a meager amount of light to enter the small chamber furnished with an altar.

                    LA
          Here you must stay until I return
          for you tonight. They will not
          look in here.

La turns to leave but Tarzan stops her.

                    TARZAN
          Why wouldn't they search here?
          What's to stop them?

                    LA
               (looking back)
          They would never search here. It
          is forbidden for any to enter the
          Chamber of the Dead, except for the
          high priestess.

La hurries out leaving Tarzan alone in the Chamber of the Dead.

EXT. JANE CAMPSITE (CLEARING) - TREE SHELTER - DAY

SUPER: "SPRING 1910"

An improvised ladder climbs high into a large, rude shelter built into the crotch of an old, enormous tree. The entrance is over six feet in height facing southward and covered with a canvas that can be thrown over the top.

INT. TREE SHELTER - DAY

Through the long slits of the walls a soft light illuminates the interior.

The large shelter is divided in half by a wall of canvas dangling from a long horizontal sapling. On one side are two grass beds and on the other a single grass bed with an ulster used as a pillow.

Luggage and other bags are stacked in the corners.

EXT. JANE CAMPSITE - DAY

Hung out to dry on a vine tied between two small trees, are
articles of male and female clothing. Some are in good
condition while other items are torn or tattered.

Near the treehouse are three logs in a u-formation. At the
ends of two of them sit the horizontal water kegs. In the
middle is a circular pit filled with rocks with spent ashes
from a previous campfire.

From the edge of the forest Clayton and Rokoff enter the
clearing. Rokoff's arms are filled with various types of
fruits and viands and Clayton carries several large rodents
in both hands.

                    CLAYTON
          Jane!

He and Rokoff both look around for her as they walk towards
the campfire.

The men have regained most if not all their previous strength
and, except for tears in their trousers and shirts, appear in
good health.

CAMPFIRE

They drop their loads within the logs. Rokoff sits down on a
log and wipes the heavy sweat from his face. Clayton remains
standing, his eyes searching for Jane.

                    CLAYTON
          Jane, where are you?!

EXT. SHORE - DAY

Jane, dressed in a light dress down to her knees and cinched
around her waist with a vine, stands barefooted in an
isolated pool abandoned by the low tide -- hunting.

In one hand she carries a sack and in the other she holds a
medium-sized crab harmlessly clawing away.

                    CLAYTON (O.S.)
          Jane, we're back!

Jane freezes in the act of trying to force the crab into the
sack and smiles, her natural beauty fully restored -- healthy
and vibrant!

She succeeds in shoving the crab into the sack and jogs back
to camp.

EXT. JANE CAMPSITE - CAMPFIRE - DAY

The men watch as she jogs trampling through the brush towards
them.

Jane stops in front of them holding up the squirming bag in
one triumphant hand with a grin on her face.

              JANE
    Fish and crabs!

              CLAYTON
    Mmm, sounds delicious.

Rokoff is busy devouring Jane's beautiful legs.

              ROKOFF
      (in a French accent)
    Very.

Jane and Clayton miss his lustful stare.

Clayton points to the rodents and the fruits.

              CLAYTON
    Look.

              JANE
      (giggling)
    A feast for kings.

She drops the bag -- with the crabs and fish still moving
inside -- next to the small mammals.

              JANE
    While you two get dinner ready,
    I'll go and gather some firewood --
    we've run out.

Rokoff glues his eyes to Jane's back as she ambles off with
her small waist and flaring hips, heaping fires on his
burning lust.

              ROKOFF
      (in a French accent;
      chuckling)
    That, is a feast for any king.

Clayton stops skinning one of the rodents to follow Rokoff's
stare.

Jane is bent at the waist with her knees slightly bent
picking up firewood.

                    CLAYTON
          How many times must I remind you
          that she is my fiancee?

Rokoff with his base soul bared, faces Clayton with a wicked,
lustful smile.

                    ROKOFF
               (in a French accent)
          She's your fiancee, not your wife.

Rokoff, ignoring Clayton, turns his burning eyes towards
Jane's lithe figure.

                    ROKOFF
               (in a French accent)
          And a man has needs.

Clayton, the taller of the two and furious, grabs Rokoff by
the collar of his shirt and yanks him with both hands towards
him and looks dead into the rogue's sneering face.

                    CLAYTON
          You will respect my fiancee or I
          will --

                    ROKOFF
               (in a French accent)
          -- What? Hit me? Don't let your
          size underestimate me, my friend.

                    CLAYTON
          One more remark, like that, and
          we'll find out if my size doesn't
          matter. As for my estimation of --

Unseen, Jane shows up with her arms brimming with firewood.

                    JANE
          -- What's this?

Rokoff pulls Clayton's hands from his collar with effort and
then turns a sardonic smile towards the girl.

                    ROKOFF
               (in a French accent)
          Only, a little misunderstanding,
          Miss Porter... nothing more.

Rokoff turns away and grumbling in French begins to adjust
his shirt collar.

Jane looks from Rokoff to Clayton, comprehending.

                    JANE
               (mouths)
          Again?

Clayton nods.

Clayton gets back to the business of skinning and Jane starts prepping the campfire.

Rokoff sits down with an evil grin stamped on his face.

EXT. JANE CAMPSITE - CAMPFIRE - DAY (LATER)

Clayton places Tompkin's fixed blade on one of the logs.

                    CLAYTON
          I'll get rid of these and get some
          water.

He gathers up the skins along with the offal and a pail and marches off towards the far side of the clearing.

Rokoff watches him disappear into the jungle and turns his attention to Jane.

Her back is to him as she prepares the fire.

He places both hands on her shoulders and begins to massage.

Jane's face is horrified and disgusted with his shameless act but she turns and meets him with only disdain.

Rokoff laughs and retracts his hands with a shrug in expiation.

                    JANE
          You're probably one of the most
          offensive men I have ever met. Let
          this be the last time you put your
          hands on me or Clayton will hear of
          it.

Jane strikes the back of Tompkin's knife against a flint rock over a ball of tinder.

                    ROKOFF
               (in a French accent; in
                French)
          Come, my sweet. Can you hold it
          against me? Sapristi, but you are
          irresistible!

She stops and glares at Rokoff.

                    JANE
          Resist, Monsieur Thuran!

She resumes and sparks shower over the tinder. She blows
gently and a little fire comes to life.

                    ROKOFF
               (in a French accent)
          You may as well ask me to stop
          breathing.

Rokoff bursts into unadulterated laughter.

Jane quickly feeds twigs and larger pieces of wood to the
nascent fire and speaks her thoughts aloud.

                    JANE
          If only Tarzan were here.

Rokoff's laughter ceases and an angry light flashes in his
dark eyes. He cannot conceal his all consuming hatred for
Tarzan and doesn't care.

                    ROKOFF
               (in a French accent)
          Eh? You knew this worthless, pig
          of a man?

                    JANE
          On the contrary, Monsieur Thuran,
          Tarzan was the complete opposite of
          you -- he was manful.

                    ROKOFF
               (in a French accent)
          Careful, my sweet.

                    JANE
          You see? Tarzan would never have
          threatened a woman.

Caught with his own words he lashes out.

                    ROKOFF
               (in a French accent)
          He was a coward! Why do you think
          he was aboard the steamer that
          carried me and Miss Strong, hmm?
          After wooing a married woman, your
          brave Tarzan rather than meet the
          husband in a duel, fled aboard the
          ship not knowing of my presence.

Jane bites her lower lip to keep a smile and more from surfacing.

>   ROKOFF
>   (in a French accent)
>   The woman in question was my sister
>   and when I recognized him and swore
>   to expose him to everyone onboard
>   if he would not meet me in a hand-
>   to-hand duel in my stateroom, he
>   jumped overboard!

Jane bursts and her beautiful, melodic laughter fills the clearing.

The outburst spooks several colorful, plumed birds who take to the air along with an African fish eagle which sails into the sky screeching its displeasure.

Other birds including the monkeys, take part in the hilarity.

Rokoff's dark visage, darkens even more as he realizes his story has backfired.

Jane, with tears in her eyes, manages to quell her laughter.

>   JANE
>   (grinning)
>   Thank you, Monsieur Thuran, for the
>   tall tale. I haven't laughed like
>   this in ages. No one, who had ever
>   met Tarzan and then you, would ever
>   believe it.

She starts to laugh again, but this time it's muffled somewhat.

Rokoff with his arms crossed is not amused and waits for her laughter to subside.

>   ROKOFF
>   (in a French accent)
>   Then why was he travelling under an
>   assumed name?

Jane wipes away tears from the edges of her eyes.

>   JANE
>   Many people travel incognito. I'm
>   sure he had a good reason.

>   ROKOFF
>   (in a French accent)
>   He certainly did.

By this time Rokoff's true hair color has made inroads complemented by the return of his Vandyke beard and thin mustache.

                    JANE
          As I'm sure you did, in changing
          the color of your hair.

Vexed, Rokoff tramps off towards the shelter.

Jane sniffles and wipes away a few more tears of laughter as she watches him climb the rickety ladder and disappear into the treehouse.

The humor leaves her just as suddenly as it began.

Jane's eyes mirror her troubled mind. She casts her gaze downward pondering Rokoff's words.

                    ROKOFF (V.O)
              (in a French accent)
          After wooing a married woman --

Jane shakes her head of unpleasant thoughts and adds more wood to the growing fire.

EXT. COASTLINE - DAY

The irritated African fish eagle flies north and low along the coast.

Its huge dark wings contrast sharply with its white nape, head and chest.

Five miles up the coast it drops down to perch on a low branch in a clearing facing the jungle.

Its robotic glances and turns, angle this way and that. Then it cries out and throws back its majestic head.

There before it stands Tarzan's cabin. Playful monkeys scurry on its rooftop chasing each other in ever direction.

A lone lioness prowls the vicinity and growls hungrily and then lopes off into the jungle.

Another scream and the eagle is off into the sky.

The wind shifts its body as it wills, the eagle adjusting its wings and tail feathers.

Several miles further north along the coast, the eagle, still flying low, looks down and spots three boats on the shore and several humans.

EXT. BEACH - DAY

Near a clearing, three lifeboats lie side-by-side on the sandy shore. They're tied off and leaning against one of them is an armed sailor. He yawns keeping his eyes towards the shore as feminine voices reach his ears.

Sitting at the shore line are three women with their legs stretched out before them, hands back, their feet being lapped by the gently, incoming waves.

The three are wearing hats blocking out the equatorial sun. Their conversation is interrupted by the appearance of a circling eagle.

                    HAZEL
              (pointing up)
          Look!

The eagle circles low over the water with its head turned downward, its eyes focused below.

The other women follow her hand.

                    ESMERALDA
              (in Southern black accent)
          It kind'a reminds me of the osprey
          back home.

                    MRS. STRONG
          Yes, it does... but is it?

                    HAZEL
          It's similar, but it's much too big
          to be an osprey... its head is
          different.

The eagle folds its wings.

                    HAZEL
          It's diving!

The raptor levels out and skims the surface, dips its talons into the water and rips out a large fish.

                    MRS. STRONG
          My, that was breathtaking!

                    HAZEL
          It's amazing what these creatures
          can do.

                    ESMERALDA
              (in Southern black accent;
               smiling)
          Just like the osprey.

                    PROF. PORTER (O.S.)
          Haliaeetus Vocifer, my dear
          Esmeralda.

Without looking back she responds pretending to be annoyed.

                    ESMERALDA
              (in Southern black accent)
          Now, Professor, you know I don't
          understand Latin.

Prof. Porter moves in line next to them beside Esmeralda.

The other two greet the erudite scholar AD LIB.

Prof. Porter leans down a bit and pats Esmeralda on one of
her large shoulders.

Esmeralda greets him with a childlike smile.

                    PROF. PORTER
          It's an African fish eagle, my
          dear... very common.

                    HAZEL
              (impressed)
          How can you possibly know that?

The professor gives her an affable smile.

                    PROF. PORTER
          Books, my dear... books!

Mother and daughter glance at each other and grin.

                    MRS. STRONG
          I've told you... he's a walking
          encyclopedia.

Prof. Porter bows in acknowledgment.

                    PROF. PORTER
          My dear lady, that's the kindest
          thing anyone has said to me all
          day.

Prof. Porter turns to leave but remembering something wheels about.

> PROF. PORTER
> Also, ladies, Lord Tennington
> informs me that lunch will be
> served shortly and that you are all
> invited.

He lifts his top hat -- which has seen better days -- and treks back towards the clearing with his hands behind his frock coat.

EXT. TENNINGTON CAMPSITE (CLEARING) - AFTERNOON

Large shady trees decorate the clearing under which six rugged huts have been built.

Across from each other and ranged side-by-side, three face south and three face north. Between the huts is a spacious area where a large campfire with a low fire, burns.

Around the campfire are a combination of long and short logs. Low, rough tables, made from the forest, stand before the logs and simple wooden stools. A smaller table holds three of the kegs of water.

Surrounding the entire encampment is a high boma protecting the eighteen castaways of the Lady Alice from the wild and savage denizens of the primeval, equatorial jungle.

Captain Jerrold and the sailors are scattered about employed in work or relaxation. Some are building new furniture or improving the huts, others are cleaning weapons while the sounds of others at the beach carries into the camp.

CAMPFIRE

Lord Tennington, his guests and the COOK are the only ones still around the campfire.

Tennington is drinking coffee and puffing his pipe.

The cook is stoking the fire and adding new wood.

On one of the long logs, the women are sitting together and eating their late lunch.

Prof. Porter and Mr. Philander straddle a log with the chessboard balanced between them.

Mr. Philander taps his fingers on the log waiting for Prof.
Porter.

                    MR. PHILANDER
          It's your move.

                    PROF. PORTER
          Will you please stop that
          confounded drumming.

Mr. Philander stops drumming.

                    PROF. PORTER
          Anyway, we're not playing a timed
          game.

                    MR. PHILANDER
          I realize that, Professor, but we
          don't have forever.

Prof. Porter lets out a sigh and makes a move and then takes
a bite out of his banana.

Tennington notices the arrival of two armed sailors bearing a
large, plump red river hog on a pole between them.

                    TENNINGTON
               (grinning)
          Looks like pork chops for tonight.

The Cook looks up from the campfire towards the men carrying
the hog to the far side of the campsite.

                    COOK
          It's too big, Your Lordship...
          perhaps tomorrow.

Tennington releases a few pipe puffs.

                    TENNINGTON
          You're the cook.

                    ESMERALDA
               (in Southern black accent)
          Tomorrow? Not if I help you.

                    COOK
          Aren't you on vacation?

                    ESMERALDA
          Does it look like I'm on vacation?

Except for Prof. Porter and Mr. Philander who are lost in the chess game, everyone around the campfire, including the Cook, burst into laughter.

> COOK
> My Lord, it seems we'll be having
> pork chops tonight, after all.

EXT. TENNINGTON CAMPSITE - TREE STUMP - AFTERNOON

At one of end the enclosure, between the huts, Hazel tries her hand at chopping wood on a sawed-off stump. She takes a swing at one of the pieces but misses and instead the axe bites the stump.

She tries to extricate the axe but is unable. Perspiration beads her lovely forehead as she struggles to free the axe.

Lord Tennington, pipe in his mouth, strolls in, in his leisure manner.

Hazel is so absorbed, she's unaware of his presence.

He stands there puffing on his pipe and regards the young beauty.

> TENNINGTON
> Would you allow me, Miss Strong?

> HAZEL
> (out of breath)
> Oh, thank you... you're just in
> time. I was just about to give up
> on it.

> TENNINGTON
> What? With me around? You'll do
> no such thing, my dear lady.

He takes hold of the axe handle, gives it a quick tug and it's out.

Tennington extends the liberated axe to Hazel.

> TENNINGTON
> Here you are.

> HAZEL
> (smiles)
> My knight in shining armor.

                              TENNINGTON
                         (bowing playfully)
                    Your wish is my command, as they
                    say.

After the bow he points to the axe with the end of his pipe.

                              TENNINGTON
                    Need any help?

                              HAZEL
                    Thank you...

She wipes the perspiration from her brow with the back of her
hand.

                              HAZEL
                    ... But the exercise will do me
                    good... I need to keep busy, you
                    know.

                              TENNINGTON
                         (puffing pipe)
                    I completely agree... and
                    commiserate with you.

Hazel grins and her eyes lock with Tennington's.

Tennington drops his gaze for a moment, pulls the pipe from
his mouth and clears his throat.

                              TENNINGTON
                         (looking back up)
                    I've been meaning to tell you how
                    sorry I am about your future fiance
                    and --

                              HAZEL
                         (almost laughing)
                    -- My what?

                              TENNINGTON
                         (confused)
                    Monsieur Thuran? Were you and he
                    not to be engaged once you arrived
                    in America?

Hazel sits on the stump and leans the axe against the same.

                              HAZEL
                    Who told you this?

                              TENNINGTON
                    Why, he did.

Hazel shakes her head as she stretches her legs forward.

>   HAZEL
>   He lied to you, Lord Tennington.
>   It is true that he proposed to me,
>   but I told him I'd have to think
>   about it...

She smiles.

>   HAZEL
>   ... And the answer is no.

Lord Tennington is captivated by her vivacious smile.

>   TENNINGTON
>   That being the case, allow me to
>   introduce myself... I am Lord
>   Tennington.

>   HAZEL
>   Yes, I know.

Hazel drops her eyes for a moment still smiling and then
raises them again to meet his kind, steady gaze.

She stands up and curtsies in a playful manner.

>   HAZEL
>   And I'm Hazel Strong.

>   TENNINGTON
>   I know.

He puts the pipe back in his mouth and grasps the axe handle
and swings it easily to his shoulder and Hazel seeing his
intention moves aside and watches with more than a casual
interest as he brings it down swiftly to chop the wood in
half.

EXT. TENNINGTON CAMPSITE - CAMPFIRE - AFTERNOON (LATER)

A low fire burns in the abandoned fireplace. A coffee pot
simmers.

Mrs. Strong and Hazel enter and kneel by the fire and pour
themselves coffee.

They sit on one of the shorter logs and after a few sips Mrs.
Strong interrupts Hazel's thoughts.

>   MRS. STRONG
>   I knew he was fond of you.

                    HAZEL
          Who?

                    MRS. STRONG
          Lord Tennington, of course -- now
          don't play ignorant with your
          mother.

                    HAZEL
                (remembering)
          Oh, you saw?

She nods.

                    MRS. STRONG
          I saw and I'm surprised it took him
          this long to begin.

Hazel sips her coffee.

                    HAZEL
          I like him.

                    MRS. STRONG
          I've known it for some time, my
          dear.

                    HAZEL
                (exasperated)
          What don't you know, Mother?

Mrs. Strong chuckles and gives her daughter a hug with one of
her arms.

                    MRS. STRONG
          Please don't be annoyed with me. I
          may not be an encyclopedia, but a
          mother notices these things.

Hazel is galvanized by a sudden recollection and places a
hand on her mother's free arm.

                    HAZEL
          You were right!

                    MRS. STRONG
          About you and Lord --

                    HAZEL
          -- No, about Monsieur Thuran. He
          told Lord Tennington that he and I
          were to be engaged once we arrived
          in Baltimore.

Mrs. Strong puts her cup of coffee on the table.

                    MRS. STRONG
          I knew he was a scoundrel! I could
          feel it! That explains Lord
          Tennington's reserved manner
          towards you. That vile creature!

                    HAZEL
          Now, Mother, please don't get upset
          over nothing. He's not worth it.

She nods towards her mother's lonely cup of coffee and nudges
her affectionately.

                    HAZEL
          Join me?

Mrs. Strong, 39 and an attractive woman, looks at her lovely
daughter's cheerful face and forsaking her just anger,
finally succumbs to Hazel's contagious smile and picks up the
cup and sips.

                    MRS. STRONG
          I think you two make a fine pair.

Chuckling, Hazel shakes her head at her incorrigible mother,
and tries to sip the still steaming coffee.

INT. TEMPLE - CHAMBER OF THE DEAD - NIGHT

Through the grate above the chamber, the equatorial moon
sprays the darkness with a mist of light.

Tarzan sits patiently, head bowed, with his back to the wall.

His head suddenly pops up and after a few moments, the sound
of delicate footsteps.

The light of a torch outlines the door from within and
outside the door the footsteps stop. He hears something
being placed on the floor, then the door opens.

The low burning torch highlights La's jewels and her inviting
figure with a warm glow.

She places the torch in a sconce inside the chamber and
returns to the door, squats down and picks up a medium,
wooden bowl and a pitcher and hands them to the ape-man.

Tarzan sits on the altar and wolf's down the food.

> LA
> It's all I could bring you.

Tarzan glances up at her briefly, smiles and then goes back to finishing his repast.

> LA
> The priests are mad with rage.
> Never before has a sacrifice
> escaped... and except for this
> chamber, the entire temple has been
> searched.

Tarzan gulps and then pauses with a thought.

> TARZAN
> Are they still searching for me?

> LA
> Not in the temple. However, fifty
> priests are at this moment looking
> for you outside the city walls.

Tarzan picks up the pitcher and takes a huge draught and then wipes his mouth with a shoulder.

> TARZAN
> I don't understand... why do they
> fear this chamber?

> LA
> The altar you sit on is used by the
> dead to sacrifice the living. That
> is why none dare enter.

A subtle grin strikes the ape-man as his eyes meet those of the high priestess.

> TARZAN
> If this is true, then why am I
> still alive?

La enjoys the ape-man's look and doesn't turn away.

> LA
> No one knows more about our
> religion than I. Yet, what I was
> taught and what I believe are not
> the same. I know that the dead are
> harmless... they do not.

Tarzan drains the pitcher, puts it on the altar, and gets up.

                         TARZAN
          I'm ready.

                         LA
              (grabbing the torch)
          Come then, we don't have much time.
          I'll take you as far as I can
          tonight.

Tarzan exits following La.

The door closes on an empty bowl and pitcher atop the altar.

SERIES OF SHOTS - BASEMENT CORRIDORS

1) La's torch is the only light through several unlighted
corridors.

2) Through many torch-lit corridors she moves cautiously, the
union of torches covering them in an amber glow.

3) With Tarzan in her wake, she enters the vault once more.

INT. TEMPLE - VAULT - NIGHT

La pauses looking from one corridor to another. Deciding
upon one, she leads Tarzan into it, the light of the torch
fading in their wake as they move further away from the vault
and into the murkier passageways of Opar.

INT. TEMPLE - BASEMENT CORRIDOR - NIGHT

At a chamber door, La hands Tarzan the torch. From her hip
she loosens a leather strap to produce a large, ancient key.

She turns the key with some effort until the bolt finally
gives and pulls the heavy chamber door open -- disturbing the
silence -- and bids Tarzan enter.

Tarzan hands the torch back to her and enters.

INT. TEMPLE - PRISON CHAMBER - NIGHT

Tarzan turns around and faces the personification of ancient
beauty.

Standing there framed by the doorway, her almond eyes burn
with a low, smouldering fire as she regards the ape-man.

                    LA
          For now you must stay here, Tarzan.
          Tomorrow night I will lead you
          further from the city... I'll
          return for you then.

She screeches the door shut and Tarzan is plunged into sudden
and utter darkness. Not even the light of the torch
penetrates.

Tarzan hears her lock the door and then her footsteps slip
away.

In the Stygian blackness, Tarzan cases the chamber feeling
and tapping the walls with the fingers and palms of his
hands. The SOUNDS of his efforts follow him around the room.

After several moments he stops exploring. Only his strong,
steady BREATHING is audible.

The gritty sound of sliding masonry masks his breathing. In
a blink of an eye a few, fine lines of light penetrate the
blackness of the chamber.

Another push and an instant rush of moonlight fills the room
as does the sound of a heavy object striking the concrete
floor with a dull thud.

Like a mini window, a rectangular opening, ten inches wide,
four inches high and six inches deep, frames a portion of the
wall opposite the door.

Tarzan's pupils shrink at the shock of light as he looks
beyond the opening into a tunnel.

Working slowly to minimize sound, Tarzan begins to remove
other loose slabs of stone that make up the wall until he's
made enough room for his body to pass through.

Before switching sides, he passes the stone slabs into the
tunnel.

INT. TEMPLE - WELL TUNNEL - NIGHT

Tarzan replaces the flawlessly cut stone slabs back into
place.

The last stone slab is the one that fell when he pushed it
in. He inserts it with the damaged corner facing him.

Tarzan makes a survey of the large tunnel deluged with the
eerie light of the moon.

Stacked neatly to one side is a score or so of extra stone slabs.

He moves towards the other end and descries what looks like another opening further down the tunnel when he's forced to an abrupt stop by a dark pit yawning at his feet.

He gets on fours and, grabbing the edge with his hands, leans over and looks down.

At the bottom the shimmering reflection of the moonlight dancing on the surface of the water stares back up at him.

Tarzan looks upwards and above him is a shaft narrowing as it goes up and capped by a large circular opening with the mysterious and majestic full moon hanging high above it.

It's an ancient well.

Tarzan takes a few steps back and easily leaps across the fifteen foot shaft opening.

Ahead of him, through a wall, the tunnel continues.

The light diminishes the further along Tarzan moves through the tunnel until he comes to a flight of stairs leading into the belly of the earth.

Tarzan descends the tenebrous staircase and before he touches bottom, it's pitch black once again.

INT. TEMPLE - SUBTERRANEAN TUNNEL

Tarzan's bare feet are the only sounds in the unspeakable darkness.

His feet stop and the sound of knocking on wood is heard.

Tarzan struggles with a scraping, heavy wooden object and sets it down.

He takes a deep breath and then the sound of ancient hinges screeching and grinding as they're forced to swing open with an ugly cry, overwhelms the darkness of the tunnel.

Tarzan's labored breathing is the only reward for his efforts.

His footsteps move on.

INT. TEMPLE - SUBTERRANEAN METAL CHAMBER

Once inside Tarzan bumps into something causing an avalanche
of metal items to crash unto the floor and against each
other.

Tarzan emits a low, angry growl.

The clinking of metal on metal is heard.

Tarzan begins to move again, but then pauses, takes a deep
breath and sneezes loudly.

He continues and after a considerable amount of paces another
door blocks his path with hinges that scream to the very end.

Tarzan's breathing is heftier as he listens for the effects
of the screaming hinges.

INT. TEMPLE - SUBTERRANEAN TUNNEL

After a few moments, he begins to move again. His footsteps
fade away as he continues his passage through the inky
blackness.

EXT. BARREN VALLEY - CLEFT - NIGHT

The moon, surrounded by its hosts of stars, illuminates the
first few steps of a staircase that spiral straight down into
a large hole in the earth.

From these stairs Tarzan's face emerges bathed by moonlight.

He finds himself in a wide cleft between granite walls that
come together several yards behind the vertical tunnel.

Before him lies a path that inclines upwards and with nowhere
to go but forward, Tarzan follows it towards the top of a
gigantic boulder.

EXT. BARREN VALLEY - GIGANTIC BOULDER - NIGHT

Tarzan faces out towards the ruined and yet resplendent city
embraced by the pale light of the moon -- now a mile away in
the distance. Its domes and towers greet the ruler of the
night sky -- its majestic spires and turrets, high and proud,
reach for the moon.

He examines his find in one of his hands. It's an ingot with
concave ends. He bounces the twenty-five pound bar in his
hand a few times, like a grapefruit.

With both hands he holds it against the light of the full moon and the unmistakable yellow proclaims it for what it is.

Tarzan smiles.

> TARZAN
>> Opar...

He lowers the ingot to his side like a book and looks out towards the ancient city once more.

> TARZAN
>> ... The City of Gold.

Tarzan turns his attention towards the mountain barrier in the distance and then descends the steep but manageable boulder into the lifeless valley.

EXT. BARREN VALLEY - NIGHT

The moon lights the long forgotten, narrow valley.

Long, lithe and powerful legs move quickly through the rugged landscape.

Tarzan dogtrots straight for the mountain pass at an easy clip of fifteen miles an hour.

EXT. MOUNTAIN PASS - SUNRISE

A weak, orange ball rises behind the ape-man as he watches steady streams of smoke rising into the early morning air from the forest below.

> TARZAN
>> Priests?

An appreciable smile surfaces and he descends.

EXT. FOREST - MORNING

A makeshift boma encircles fifty black ebon warriors.

A giant forest hog hangs over an ebbing fire with very little of its flesh remaining.

They sit in groups around morning fires eating a meal of meat and other jungle fare.

A strong voice breaks up the quiet breakfast.

                         TARZAN (O.S.)
                Fear not, it is I, your Waziri.

Caught off-guard, some of the men prepare to flee, while
others -- with notched bows -- look above and about them for
the origin of the voice.

Tarzan drops down out of a tree, materializing suddenly
before his startled warriors.

They fall back with faces reflecting their superstitious
fears, regarding him as a phantom rather than as a man.

                         BUSULI
                Is it truly you, Waziri?

                         TARZAN
                What do you think, Busuli?

Busuli studies him for signs of the supernatural until Tarzan
begins to grin.

Busuli, realizing that it's truly their king, lets out a cry
of joy and is joined by a relieved but happy group of Waziri
warriors who gather in a semi-circle about their king.

Busuli, stands before his Waziri, his joy somewhat dampened.

                         BUSULI
                We are ashamed of leaving you,
                Waziri. We acted like children
                instead of like men... we are
                cowards.

Tarzan is touched by their humbleness. He puts a hand on
Busuli's shoulder, makes eye contact with him and shakes his
head in disagreement and then sweeps the rest of his fighting
men with steel-grey eyes.

                         TARZAN
                None of you are cowards. I've seen
                you hunt and fight. You are all
                brave men. Your only weakness is
                your false beliefs. Use your reason
                to free yourselves from these fears
                and superstitions.

                         BUSULI
                We are beginning to do so. We
                returned and camped here last night
                and today we planned to search for
                you... to free you or to avenge
                you.

                    TARZAN
          I have something else for you to do
          -- but first...

Tarzan looks at his men, their faces no longer filled with
fear but with determination.

                    TARZAN
          ... Did you see a group of strange,
          hairy men with long beards, descend
          from the mountain pass?

Busuli nods.

                    BUSULI
          Yesterday. We heard them before we
          saw them, Waziri. When they came
          we hid ourselves. They are as you
          say, strange... and ugly.

Busuli looks around at the rest of the men for confirmation
and they all nod their heads in agreement.

                    BUSULI
          They're the ugliest men we have
          ever seen.

Tarzan can't repress a chuckle at Busuli's brutal honesty and
the humor is not lost on his men.

                    BUSULI
          They were more beast than men.
          Some of them would walk on all
          fours like a gorilla.

The humor fades from Tarzan's face, as he refocuses.

                    TARZAN
          I'm glad you avoided them. We may
          have to fight them some day -- but
          now, I need your help.

He pauses to arrest their attention.

                    TARZAN
          I found the gold.

SERIES OF SHOTS - GOLD QUEST

1) Tarzan and his men climb the steep granite, oblong-shaped
boulder.

2) Down the spiral staircase Tarzan descends followed by his Waziri warriors.

3) Tarzan steps out onto the cradle of the cleft and each of his men in like manner resurfaces bearing an ingot of pure gold.

4) In two columns with Tarzan at their head, they trek across the lifeless valley of Opar towards the mountains with the precious cargo.

EXT. JUNGLE - WAZIRI CAMP - DAY

SUPER: "33 DAYS LATER"

Fifty-one gold ingots lie neatly stacked in the center of the campsite.

The Waziri warriors, meanwhile, are busy breaking camp and preparing to leave.

Busuli calls for the men to form up and the men quickly obey forming their signature two column formation.

Stoically, the sleek proud warriors wait for the order to march.

Busuli, nods his head in satisfaction, and leaving them reports to his king.

>   BUSULI
>   Are you certain, you will not need
>   us, Waziri?

Tarzan nods.

>   TARZAN
>   It's time you and the men were back
>   home with your wives and families.
>   You've done enough.

Tarzan gestures with his chin towards the pile of riches.

>   TARZAN
>   I'll take care of the rest.

>   BUSULI
>   As you will, Waziri.

Busuli hands his bow to Tarzan and then removes his quiver and knife and gives these to the ape-man as well.

                  BUSULI
              (grinning)
        You'll need these more than I, My
        King.

Tarzan accepts them with a grateful smile.

                  TARZAN
        Go now, and await my return.

Busuli turns at a quick trot and simultaneously yelling a
command, the two columns fall in behind him.

Tarzan's steady gaze follows them as they jog into the
primeval fastness and disappear with their unison chant of
HAAOOT.

Tarzan moves to the pile, grabs one and leaps into the trees.

He swings, leaps, and runs along the limbs and branches of a
constricted area of the jungle.

EXT. JUNGLE - AMPHITHEATHER - MORNING (AN HOUR LATER)

The soft light filtered by the trees strikes a stacked pile
of glistening gold ingots.

Tarzan, with the last ingot in hand, lands abruptly within
the quiet and empty arena.

After placing it among the others he walks to the hollow of a
dead tree and pulls out a familiar spade and begins to dig.

EXT. JUNGLE - AMPHITHEATHER - MORNING (LATER)

A pair of stamping feet move along a filled trench.

Tarzan inspects and approves of his handiwork with a few
nods. He walks over to the dead tree and drops the spade
into the darkness of the hollow.

EXT. JUNGLE - MORNING (NEXT DAY)

Tarzan's long and powerful form swings through the mind-
boggling heights of ancient giants.

Monkeys dart out of his way as he cruises along the aerial
highway.

Soon, though, he begins to descend and leaping from a tree he lands in a familiar clearing adorned by the cabin of his late father.

EXT. CLEARING - CABIN - MORNING

Tarzan stops before the door and his deft fingers quickly disengage the latch of the door.

He sticks his head in to have a look-see and then secures the door and takes to the trees.

EXT. JUNGLE - LATE MORNING

Five miles south of the cabin near the coast Tarzan travels leisurely through the middle terraces of the trees.

He lands on a mammoth limb and sifts the air with his sensitive nostrils for signs of game.

Not picking up anything he drops like a rock twenty feet at a time until he's lands on a narrow meandering jungle trail.

Crouched in hunting mode, Tarzan glides along the well trodden path silently with his senses on full alert for any telltale sign of prey.

He drops to all fours and sniffs the ground and as he comes up a light wind finds him, disturbing the leaves and his equanimity.

A whiff assails his keen sense of smell. He sniffs and then blows out -- his nostrils dilating for confirmation.

His grey eyes become electrified with a glint of surprise and sudden apprehension.

In a flash, the ape-man leaps into the branches above and plows recklessly through the trees towards the source.

INT. TREE SHELTER - LATE MORNING

Rokoff lies helpless tormented by jungle fever. Profuse sweat covers his heavily bearded face and forehead as he raves and jerks his head in every direction.

SUPER: "LATE SPRING 1910"

EXT. JANE CAMPSITE - CAMPFIRE - LATE MORNING

Jane is crouched by the fire roasting rodents. She tries to
ignore the suffering sounds reaching her from the shelter but
cannot.

She shoots a helpless glance towards the shelter and then
returns her focus to the task at hand.

A sound draws her attention and from the jungle wall emerges
Clayton carrying a long, sharpened, wooden staff and a limp
guinea fowl in the other.

Tired but pleased with his catch he holds it up in triumph.

Jane smiles at his antics and gets up to go meet him.

JANE CAMPSITE

She wipes her hands on her torn and worn skirt as she
approaches him.

Clayton reaches her about a hundred feet from the jungle
edge.

Jane is about to greet him when an enormous head of a maned

LION

pops out of the jungle wall behind Clayton.

JANE'S

lovely countenance morphs into frozen horror.

CLAYTON

wheels about following her stricken stare to witness the
deadly rending machine crouching low to the ground and moving
towards them.

                    CLAYTON
              (eyes glued on the lion)
          Run!

But Jane cannot. Paralyzed by the creature before them, her
body refuses to obey! The great

BEAST

opens its huge maw exposing four long fangs and pausing, shudders the air and ground with several tremendous roars.

Then, with its high shoulder blades alternating and its head low to the ground, it advances.

ROKOFF'S

haggard face appears at the entrance of the shelter -- a hundred feet away -- at the sound of the commotion and spying the threat...

> ROKOFF
> (in a French accent)
> Get to the shelter, quickly! Hurry,
> you fools, before it's too late!
> (in a weak breaking voice)
> Or I'll die alone, in this wretched
> jungle.

With all his energy spent, Rokoff collapses whimpering like a child. The

LION

stops with a lifted paw and glances up towards the shelter, its focus momentarily interrupted by Rokoff's ravings, it's tail twitching in curiosity.

Unable to face death head-on, Clayton turns his back on the confused lion. He then lets the useless staff fall at his side and then the guinea fowl.

JANE

is left confounded at Clayton's incomprehensible resignation.

She drops to her knees and bows her head in prayer, her eyes clenched.

EXT. JUNGLE - SAME TIME

Tarzan lands on a massive limb, at the edge of the jungle and immediately spots the events taking place in the clearing.

Bow and arrow spring to life in his hands. The

LION

begins to move again with an increased gait towards its easy prey.

TARZAN

draws the notched arrow far back. The

LION

crouching low, prepares to spring.

TARZAN

lets the arrow fly.

IN SLOW MOTION

The

ARROW

splits the air with its incredible speed and SWOOSHING sound and dives deep into the lion's rump!

It turns, maddened by the stinging pain driven into its body and tries to bite at it roaring terribly, when another arrow plunges deep into its hide next to the first one.

BACK TO NORMAL SPEED

JANE'S AND CLAYTON'S

bodies shake uncontrollably at the thunderous roars of the raging beast near them. Another

ARROW

finds its way into the lion's corrugated face. The

LION

turns its flank towards the jungle wall and two more fleet arrows, in swift succession, bury themselves into it.

TARZAN

notches another arrow and taking careful aim releases it.

IN SLOW MOTION

The

ARROW

streaks through the air and penetrates skin, flesh and bone
to burst the lion's huge ferocious heart. The

LION'S

voluminous roars cease. It's rear legs wobble and then
crumble as it struggles to remain standing with it's front
legs and then the mighty beast slumps dead a few yards from
Clayton.

EXT. JANE CAMPSITE - MOMENTS LATER

Dead calm. A man. A woman. A dead lion.

Jane opens her fear-filled eyes expecting to witness the
unthinkable -- the lion devouring Clayton.

To her supreme relief, Clayton is standing across from her.
His shoulders are hunched, his eyes still closed with a
slight tremor in his legs.

Taken aback, she presses her hand against her bosom at the
sight beyond Clayton -- the lion's lifeless body.

She puts a hand to her forehead, confused as to just what
happened. Her eyes turn back to the frozen man.

                    JANE
          Cecil!

Clayton opens his eyes, gingerly, uncertain of what to expect
and is met by Jane's spectacular eyes staring up at him in
wonder. She gestures with her face and eyes towards the
fallen lion.

                    JANE
          Look!

Her eyes return to watch his reaction.

Clayton turns around slowly and there a few yards behind him is the large carcass of the lion riddled with arrows.

Blood oozes from the area where the arrow penetrated the heart forming a pool of blood on the ground.

Clayton, dumbfounded, shakes his head as if awakened from an incredible dream.

EXT. JUNGLE - SAME TIME

Tarzan watches from the concealment of the edge of the jungle, still standing upon the huge limb, tall and powerful with his shock of pure black hair below the nape of his neck.

Then his sharp grey eyes squint and zoom in on the girl.

Tarzan is mystified -- stunned!

                    TARZAN
               (in a subdued voice)
          Jane.

Grey eyes then quickly track for the identity of the man.

A terrible snarl escapes the ape-man's throat. The red scar suddenly materializes upon his forehead as he recognizes Clayton.

Instinctively, in one motion, he nocks an arrow, pulls back the deadly shaft and puts a bead on the man, as Clayton helps Jane up from the ground.

His fierce, steel-grey eyes are merciless in their intent but just as quickly reason intervenes and he relaxes the bow string, the animal madness disappearing from his eyes.

He watches as Jane holds onto Clayton, a little unbalanced after rising from the ground.

Clayton draws her close and kisses her as he tries to comfort her.

Tarzan drops his chin slowly to his massive chest.

Without vouchsafing them another glance, he returns the arrow to the quiver, straps the bow to his wide muscular back and leaps into the branches above, vanishing into the gloom of the equatorial jungle.

EXT. JANE CAMPSITE - LATE MORNING

Clayton attempts to kiss her again but Jane places a hand to
the side of his face and gently pushes him away.

                    JANE
          Please don't.

Hurt and confused, he searches her eyes for an answer.

Jane is tired and overwrought yet her voice and eyes are
steady and determined.

                    JANE
          Our engagement is over. I could
          never marry you. Not --

She lowers her eyes and shakes her head.

                    JANE
               (raising eyes)
          Not after today.

                    CLAYTON
               (with a nervous smile)
          Jane, you're not yourself --
          tomorrow --

                    JANE
          -- Tomorrow, Cecil? I've finally
          come to my senses. I'm finally
          myself again, after all this time.

Clayton is desperate to salvage the situation.

                    CLAYTON
          Surely, you don't mean it. You're
          simply distraught after this
          terrible ordeal.

Jane continues, ignoring his pleading words.

                    JANE
          After denying my love to a brave
          man, how could I ever give myself
          to a man who was otherwise?

Shame covers Clayton suddenly and his eyes fall short of her
gaze as he slowly nods in understanding.

                    JANE
          He's dead now... and I shall never
          marry.

She walks up to the dead lion and is quietly joined by her former fiance.

She stares down at the huge carcass, perplexed.

                    JANE
          Who do you suppose did this?

Clayton's mind is elsewhere, still stunned by Jane's rejection.

                    CLAYTON
          I don't know. Your guess would be
          as good as mine.

                    JANE
          Perhaps if we call out?

Clayton shrugs, cups his hands alongside his mouth and calls out.

                    CLAYTON
          Hello! Hello! Is anyone there?!
          Is anyone out there?! Hello!

Clayton stops and looks at Jane.

                    CLAYTON
          Whoever it is was, more than likely
          has long since gone by now. And
          even if he'd come out, it's highly
          doubtful we would have understood
          each other.

Jane scans the thick entanglements of the jungle wall lined by huge trees like giant soldiers standing shoulder to shoulder with the constant hum of insects and animal life and becomes disheartened at the vastness of it all.

                    JANE
               (sighing)
          You're right, of course. It was
          silly of me to even suggest it.

                    CLAYTON
          I think it wise, to make for the
          shelter. Lord knows, I can't
          protect you.

Jane hears the wounded pride in his voice and tries to atone.

                    JANE
               (sorry)
          It's not true.
               (MORE)

                    JANE (CONT'D)
          You've done your very best for
          me... we all have our limits.

She lays a light hand on his arm.

His hurt eyes take in her breathless beauty that not even her
disheveled look can conceal. This and her torn clothing only
serve to enhance her natural beauty.

                    JANE
          The words I used were not very
          kind... especially after all you've
          done for me -- I'm sorry -- please
          forgive.

He breaks a weak smile, throws an arm around her back and
hugs her shoulders.

                    CLAYTON
          Let's forget about it, hmm -- at
          least until we're back in
          civilization.

Jane doesn't respond but turns around and heads back to the
treehouse.

Clayton searches the ground and picks up his staff and then
the guinea fowl and tags behind her.

INT. TREE SHELTER - NEXT DAY

Incoherent yells and screams from the delirious Rokoff fill
the shelter with their violence.

Jane tries to keep his face cool with a wet cloth but his
wild and unpredictable sudden movements make it all but
impossible.

EXT. TREE SHELTER - DAY

Jane descends the ladder, with Rokoff's mad and
unintelligible ravings spooking the wildlife all around her,
and moves towards the campfire area.

CAMPFIRE

She sits on the larger log with her back to the jungle and
looks out past the trees of the clearing towards the sea.

Quiet waves wash over the white sands as she searches the
horizon for signs of any ship.

EXT. JUNGLE - DAY

Fifty pairs of close-set eyes watch the unsuspecting woman
behind the curtain of creepers, vines and trees.

Their eyes move from her to the shelter from where Rokoff's
disturbing sounds continue unabated. Their wicked eyes scan
the rest of the clearing for signs of others and then vanish.

EXT. JANE CAMPSITE - DAY

From the jungle wall fifty misshapen manlike creatures step
out together like a lynch mob.

The squat ape-like men are almost upon her before she becomes
aware of their presence.

CAMPFIRE

Twisting about, Jane beholds fifty repulsive priests from the
city of Opar and she screams for all the world to hear.

Three of them rush her. Jane tries to resist and her screams
fall on deaf ears.

Overwhelmed by the assault of these monstrous men, by
shattered nerves and hopelessness, she loses consciousness.

One of the Neanderthals throws her limp body over a thick
shoulder and together the fifty Oparian priests melt into
jungle.

EXT. JANE CAMPSITE - DAY (HOURS LATER)

Clayton enters the clearing and except for the staff, is
empty-handed.

His eyes search for the girl at the campfire but it's empty.
He then looks up towards the tree shelter but all is too
quiet.

                    CLAYTON
               (alarmed)
          Jane!

Clayton hustles to the treehouse.

INT. TREE SHELTER - DAY

Clayton finds Rokoff awake, alert and free of the jungle
fever.

                         CLAYTON
              Where's Jane?

Rokoff is extremely weak.

                         ROKOFF
                  (in a French accent; raspy
                   voice)
              I don't know. You're the first...
              person... I've seen in days.

SERIES OF SHOTS - CLAYTON SEARCHES FOR JANE

1) Clayton inspects every square inch of the clearing.

2) On the beach, except for waves, nothing stirs.

3) At the nearby river there's no sign of her.

4) Clayton drinks from his canteen as he trudges through the
jungle calling out her name.

5) A lion forces him into a large tree.

6) At dusk it departs but Clayton remains in the tree and
finding a comfortable spot goes to sleep.

                                        FADE TO BLACK:

CRACKLING fire.

GRUNTS and indistinct GUTTURAL exchanges.

Sloppy CRUNCHING and MUNCHING.

EXT. JUNGLE - NIGHT

Jane's eyes open to a large campfire.

Burning on a spit is a large, overdone bush pig with a
crushed skull.

She gathers her legs underneath her and sits up, suddenly
cognizant of her predicament.

One of the priests noticing that the girl has awakened goes to the pig and cuts out a good chunk and tosses it before the startled woman.

                    PRIEST   SUBTITLED
Grombat!   Eat!

Famished she digs in with strong white teeth.

The priest grunts and sits back down with the others.

As she chews, she scans the horrid faces all around her.

She shuts her eyes in utter helplessness.

EXT. JANE CAMPSITE - MORNING (NEXT DAY)

A golden light fills the clearing in varying degrees. Mellow and mottled as it passes through the uncrowded, overhead canopy. In other places, angled rays of light strike the ground like giant fingers coming down from the heavens.

Through these rays, a weary, heavy-hearted Clayton enters the clearing.

CAMPFIRE

He sits on one of the logs and holding onto his staff for support, lowers his head and his shoulders shake in sorrow.

EXT. JUNGLE - DAY

Jane is herded like an animal through the interminable maze of the dense forest.

She's pushed by gnarled cudgels or dragged by the inhuman hands of her ruthless and wicked abductors when she fails to keep up.

As she struggles to maintain the pace, she trips and falls exhausted.

She's immediately kicked by the nearest priest.

Jane's face is covered in heavy sweat. Her hair is in shambles and her every breath is a gasp.

She's roughly yanked onto her feet and brutally cuffed and then kicked into a forced march.

Like a diamond in a cart of coal, Jane is forced mercilessly forward by the foul and horrid creatures banded with gold.

From up high, hidden by the profuse foliage of the jungle giants, two pairs of savage eyes witness Jane's misery and abuse at the hands of monstrous men.

Two anthropoid apes -- TEEGLAT, a large male and a smaller female-- squat side-by-side on a limb and watch as the strange company tramples past them announcing their every movement as they move deeper into the cruel and inhospitable fastness of the primeval jungle.

EXT. AMPHITHEATER - DAY (3 DAYS LATER)

A ripped and muscular body lounges on the lush green grass.

One of Tarzan's long, powerful, lithe legs is outstretched while the other has its knee up like a pyramid.

With both hands behind his long black mane and his eyes closed, his mighty chest rises and falls in idyllic comfort.

Alert, grey eyes open. His eyes glance straight ahead at the opposite side of the natural arena.

His acute ears hear many large bodies approaching, yet no sound has reached the amphitheater.

EXT. JUNGLE - DAY

Many long hairy arms swing through the congested aerial highway.

AMPHITHEATER

Tarzan sits up, yawns and stretches.

He stands up and tests the air with his nose and then he runs and leaps into the trees.

JUNGLE

Large black shaggy bodies sail through the gloom of the primeval African jungle, like a band of arboreal soldiers.

AMPHITHEATER

Concealed by the foliage of trees, Tarzan squats on a
generous limb, his attention focused on the opposite side of
the amphitheater.

Soon the SOUND of many large bodies moving through the trees
reaches the arena.

Then stillness.

A scouting ape breaks the plane of the jungle wall with his
ferocious face. Its blood-shot, beady eyes scan the
amphitheater for any signs of danger.

Not finding any, it vanishes into the jungle silently.

Indistinct, rough VOICES are heard in talks behind the veil
of the jungle wall.

A light smile materializes on the ape-man's noble features.

One by one they drop into the arena, like paratroopers.

Huge towering males first, then the females -- some with
infants -- and then the juveniles.

Nearly a hundred savage anthropoid apes in all come together
as one.

Fearlessly, Tarzan walks out on a large wide limb overhanging
the amphitheater in full view of the savage horde.

A watchful female spots the ape-man and instantly cries out
alerting the entire gathering.

Several massive bulls come to their full height and look up
growling and snarling, baring their awful fighting fangs at
the intruder.

Tarzan can see the full force of the males from the mighty
tribe preparing to launch itself against him -- the males
moving forward while the females with their nursing young and
juveniles moving behind the protection of the massive male
wall.

Tarzan addresses KARNATH, the largest of the males.

The dialogue transitions from Mangani into English.

                    TARZAN
          Karnath, have you forgotten Tarzan?
          Do you not remember that once I was
          your king?

And to another enormous ape.

> TARZAN
> Magor, do you not remember how we
> hunted together near the lake?

Then addressing them all.

> TARZAN
> It was I who killed the mighty
> Kerchak. I am Tarzan, great killer
> of apes and beasts!

The named and several others shuffle forward for a better
look at their former king.

Karnath and MAGOR cease their aggressive attitude, Tarzan's
voice and his appearance rekindling old memories.

Their heavy brows come together. Their minds are hard
pressed at first to recall, but it comes.

Karnath turns to Magor and the other males, and in a
makeshift huddle, they discuss Tarzan's presence and claim,
in gruff undertones.

After a brief moment, Karnath, an enormous ape at six feet,
seven inches tall, faces the former tribe member.

> KARNATH
> Yes, I remember you, Tarzan. Why
> have you come back?

> TARZAN
> I've come in peace to rejoin the
> tribe.

At this the apes confer together again for a longer span of
time, with few if any objecting.

> KARNATH
> Come, Tarzan, and join the tribe in
> peace.

From the tree limb Tarzan alights upon the thick, grassy
sward like a silent leopard.

Tarzan's identity established, most of the tribe goes back to
its daily routine, as if the ape-man had never left.

Two bold, young bulls unfamiliar with the ape-man scud
towards him on all fours to sniff him over.

One of them brashly threatens Tarzan with a vicious growl and bared fangs.

Too fast for the eyes to follow, Tarzan's fist pounds the side of the anthropoid's skull like a sledgehammer sending the large, daring ape tumbling across the arena.

Rolling onto its short powerful legs, the ape charges in full rage.

Like two battering rams they collide!

The bull tries to rend and rip with nails and fangs but Tarzan's lightning fast arm shoots to its throat, lifting it off the ground and then smashing the beast senseless back into it.

Steel sinews keep the throat in its crushing grip, but Tarzan not wanting to kill -- only educate -- releases him.

The ape cough's and sucks in air into its huge chest, but is too groggy to rise.

Tarzan is given a wide berth by the other young, but huge, bull as he moves among them, the fight already forgotten.

INT. TREE SHELTER - DAY

Clayton holds Rokoff's head raised so that he can drink from the tin cup.

He then props up his head using extra clothing and gives him portions of meat and various fruits and viands.

Rokoff, feeble, can barely bring the food to his mouth.

MONTAGE - THE GOOD SAMARITAN

1) Clayton feeds the emaciated Rokoff.

2) Rokoff manages to sit up and drink without any assistance.

3) Clayton turns several small rodents on a spit over a fire.

4) Clayton watches Rokoff devour every morsel of food.

5) Clayton enters the treehouse and finds Rokoff with his back leaning against one of the walls, shaving his once hollow cheeks that have now filled in.

6) Clayton sleeps in Jane's grass bed with the divider between him and Rokoff.

EXT. JANE CAMPSITE - TREE SHELTER - DAY

SUPER: "A WEEK LATER"

Rokoff descends the ladder and joins Clayton at the

CAMPFIRE

where the meat is almost ready.

They don't speak.

EXT. JUNGLE - TABLELAND - DAY (5 DAYS LATER)

Tarzan reclines with his wide back to a mammoth bole.

All about him, the apes are feeding or relaxing with the young apes roughhousing it.

Tarzan's mood is troubled and his conscience haunts him.

QUICK FLASHBACKS - JANE AND CLAYTON

- Jane prays as the lion prepares to spring.

- Clayton lifts her up, draws her close and kisses her.

BACK TO PRESENT

Tarzan's eyes blaze at the memory, but then...

TARZAN'S IMAGINATION - EXT. JUNGLE - DAY

A huge lion pulls Jane into the jungle by her leg. Jane screams and screams clawing at the ground before her.

EXT. TREE - DAY

Jane hangs from a tree limb wrapped in the coils of a gigantic rock python. Horrified, Jane tries to scream but cannot as the snake's cavernous mouth opens wide to engulf her.

BACK TO SCENE

Tarzan jumps up and shakes his long black mane.

He leaps into the tree and retrieves his hanging bow, quiver of arrows and rope -- his mind made-up.

Two apes suddenly jump in amongst them startling a few and provoking warning growls from nursing mothers.

Teeglat grabs his bride's arm and knuckle-runs to Karnath to show her off.

> TEEGLAT
> Look, Karnath! I have brought a new
> she to the tribe.

Karnath and a few other curious apes approach her to become familiar with her scent. The female remains very still until they're finished.

Tarzan drops down from the tree and begins to strap on his armament.

> TEEGLAT (O.S.)
> We saw many strange, short hairy
> white apes moving through the
> jungle with much noise...

Tarzan wheels about instantly and hastens to the little gathering to hear more.

> TEEGLAT
> ... And they dragged and beat a
> white she --
>   (points at Tarzan)
> The she was whiter than him. They
> kicked and they --

> TARZAN
> -- Did these apes wear shiny yellow
> bands around their arms and legs?

> TEEGLAT
> Yes and they carried large sticks.
> Sometimes they would walk --

> TARZAN
> -- The white she, did the she have
> long yellow hair like the sun?

> TEEGLAT
> It was very long and yellow like
> the sun.

Tarzan looks away, a wave of alarm and desperation shadowing his countenance.

>   TARZAN
>   (in a horrified whisper)
>   My, God. Jane.

Suppressing his overriding emotions he turns back to Teeglat.

>   TARZAN
>   Where did you see them?

>   TEEGLAT
>   By the second river.

>   TARZAN
>   And in what direction were they
>   moving?

>   TEEGLAT
>   (pointing east)
>   They followed the river towards the
>   rising sun.

>   TARZAN
>   And when? When did you see them?
>   How long ago?

Teeglat pauses for a moment and pats his bullet head. His
thick, black shaggy brows struggle for the memory and then
remembering he looks into the anxious face of the tribe's
former king.

>   TEEGLAT
>   A half moon has passed since we saw
>   those strange white apes with the
>   white she.

Teeglat continues, but the rest of his words are lost in an
empty void of soundless rabble as Tarzan sprints from Teeglat
blurring past the rest of the tribe and vanishing like a
sudden gust of wind into the trees leaving in his wake
disturbed foliage.

EXT. JUNGLE - DAY

Once outside the amphitheater and in the less dense jungle,
Tarzan pauses long enough to blaze a tree and hang his bow
and quiver in its branches keeping only his knife and rope.

In wild abandon he leaps out and races through the high
terraces of the jungle giants at breakneck speed like a
fierce storm, leaping huge gaps, dropping from dizzying
heights, heedless of all dangers and obstacles in his path.

EXT. JUNGLE - NIGHT

The glow of a full moon slips through the chinks of the canopy's armor.

A speeding shadow whooshes through the colossal ancients by the meager light of the moon.

Tarzan's eyes gleam as he passes underneath a swath of unobstructed moonlight, his inexorable determination driving him tirelessly forward towards Opar, the City of Gold.

EXT. JUNGLE - DAY (LIGHT RAIN)

Fifty ugly priests plow through a wet, steamy jungle.

Among them hobbles a woman with golden, long tangled hair. Her face evinces great discomfort, pain and exhaustion.

Her wet clothes are mere shreds of tattered cloths rent by the mobs of thorns and prickly plants.

Jane's milk-white skin bleeds from innumerable scratches, tiny cuts and pricks, the red blood mixing with the drizzle of the rainwater and contrasting sharply against her delicate skin.

The train of the march stops abruptly and up ahead two priests argue over something she cannot make out, nor does she care.

Jane removes her shoes and turns them over to look at the soles.

One is missing a heel and both soles are practically gone, so she drops them where she stands, wincing as her feet feel the jungle floor.

Constricted by the dense jungle, the long snake-like train of the monstrous men, begins to move again and Jane is shoved forward by a gnarled cudgel.

She grits her teeth as her sore feet move along the rough jungle floor without the hobble that her shoes had plagued her with.

EXT. JUNGLE - DAY

A knife cuts away at the joint of a plump hindquarter from a red river hog.

A large, strong hand rips the loosened rear leg from the hip socket of the hog.

Squatting on his haunches, Tarzan tears away, with his strong teeth, at the juicy, blood-dripping flesh.

EXT. JUNGLE - DAY

Flies buzz over the dead carcass of the hog and near it is an almost fleshless discarded leg bone.

The COUGHING sound of a nearby lion spurs several screeching monkeys to scramble into the safety of the trees.

EXT. JUNGLE - RIVER - DAY

At the river's edge Tarzan rushes cupped water into his thirsty body.

Two more handfuls and Tarzan springs into the trees leaving behind his masculine footprints in the soft mud -- one deeper than the other.

EXT. JUNGLE - DAY

A wall of mountains rear their high ridges, like giant barriers.

SUPER: "2 WEEKS LATER"

Fifty squat ogres tramp across an open jungle and through the foliage their ugly faces turn upwards towards the mountains that signal the coming completion of their long journey.

In their midst Jane, unconscious of everything, even of her pain, falters and falls.

Her body screams in agony as she struggles to get up, but cannot.

Her raw tender flesh trembles and her eyes are blurred from the torture of the forced march. She's reached the limit of her stamina, strength and endurance. She can go no further.

The condition of her clothes, if possible, have worsened almost to the point dispensing with propriety and decorum.

Jane is beyond caring and immune to the kicks that follow her fall.

A few more join in the abuse, but realizing that no amount of brutal goads will avail, a BIG PRIEST -- larger than the rest -- lifts the unconscious girl in his thick, hairy arms.

Blood drips from her lacerated soles leaving a trail of red as the fifty squat, repulsive men resume the tail end of the journey to the City of Gold.

EXT. BARREN VALLEY - MORNING (2 DAYS LATER)

Jane's feet are caked with blood.

On a lovely stained face, two long-suffering eyes slowly open. Everything is hazy and blurred, then her vision clears to behold the magnificent ruins of Opar standing in the distance before them.

But the grandeur of it does not register on the poor girl's suffering countenance as they advance ever closer to the outer walls enclosing the domes, spires, turrets and towers of the ancient city.

Jane closes her eyes, her fragile figure occasionally assaulted by tremors from the healing, raw wounds covering her tortured body.

EXT. OPAR/CITY OF GOLD - MORNING

A lone monkey steals a piece of fruit from one of the city orchards and scurry's up a bird-crowned pillar with its prize.

Nibbling on the fruit and unalert, the monkey watches below and is suddenly raked off the top of the pillar by the talons of a swift swooping raptor as the fifty monstrous men approach the temple with their captive.

INT. TEMPLE - INNER COURTYARD - MORNING

From one of the many doors, the fifty priests enter the courtyard with a retinue of priestesses awaiting them. Many others crowd around them with even more filling the galleries with wicked curiosity.

A shade of hope enlivens Jane's eyes as she catches sight of the priestesses.

Big Priest stops before the LEAD PRIESTESS with the captive in his arms.

The Lead Priestess inspects Jane from head to toe, annoyance marking her features.

At the indifferent treatment, Jane looks through them, and with a barely perceptible shake of her head, announces the return of her utter hopelessness.

The Lead Priestess addresses Big Priest imperiously.

>   LEAD PRIESTESS
>   Is this how you bring an offering
>   to the flaming god?

>   BIG PRIEST
>   She lives and there is still time.

She wheels about and looks at the waiting priestesses.

>   LEAD PRIESTESS
>   (pointing at Jane)
>   Bath her and treat her wounds.

As two of the priestesses approach, Big Priest puts Jane down unto the concrete floor and Jane cries out in agony and almost falls if not for the support of her two new escorts, who half carry and half walk her to one of the chamber doors held open by another of the female priests.

Once she's through the door, the remaining female priests enter and close the chamber door behind them. In moments, echoes of Jane's plaintive cries resound throughout the courtyard drawing emotionless glances from the male and female priests and then, silence.

INT. TEMPLE - GOLDEN CHAMBER - DAY

Jane awakens wrapped in the soft antelope skin worn by the women of Opar and lying upon plush soft animal furs of lions, leopards, giraffes and of other African fauna.

Her beautiful long and thick golden hair has been brought over her shoulder and rests across her bosom reaching down below her waist.

Her eyes slowly adjust to the soft light of the room entering through four embrasures.

The ceiling, walls, and floor are solid gold. She turns her head to one side and next to her are two golden bowls. Jane rises on her elbow and grits her teeth, her whole body afire with pain.

One bowl, the larger, has a roasted guinea fowl surrounded by fruits and nuts. The other is filled with water with a little golden cup submerged within the bowl.

She dips her hand in the bowl and retrieves the cup filled with water and drinks.

A few paces away near the center of the room stands an elaborate table and single chair, all of pure gold.

Even the door, she notices, is made of gold.

Jane slides back to rest her back against the wall and then grabs a small fruit.

She bites into it and notices for the first time that her feet are wrapped in leather with green plants and other herbs sticking out from them.

She moves her feet this way and that examining them, but does not remove the coverings, sensing that they're on there for her own good.

MONTAGE - JANE'S RECOVERY

1) Two female priests enter the golden chamber and escort Jane to the bathhouse to wash and retreat her wounds.

2) A priestess enters the golden chamber and tries to get Jane to stand on her feet. Jane attempts it, but shakes her head.

3) The female priests enter her chamber and this time the food and water are placed on the golden table. Jane crawls on all fours and heaves herself up onto the golden chair.

4) Another female priest enters Jane's chamber and motions for Jane to stand up, but Jane is still unable.

INT. TEMPLE - GOLDEN CHAMBER - DAY (5 DAYS LATER)

Jane sits at the table eating and drinking and appears much healthier.

Her lustrous, golden long hair is loosely braided and rests over one of her bare shoulders.

Her arms and legs are covered with pricks and cuts sustained during the relentless march, but moving no longer causes her any pain.

The heavy golden door glides open and the Lead Priestess enters and motions for Jane to stand.

Jane smiles and stands, her feet still covered with leather and herbs.

A hint of a knowing smile creases the lips of the Lead Priestess as she exits and two other females priests enter. One carries a pair of sandals.

They have her sit and then proceed to remove the leather coverings and the healing herbs and then examine her feet.

The lacerated soles are completely healed.

As one, they strap her feet up with the leather sandals and finished with their task, they leave the wondering girl alone to continue her meal.

EXT. MOUNTAIN PASS - LATE MORNING (2 DAYS LATER)

A light wind blows through Tarzan's long black mane.

His grey eyes stare far out across the barren valley encompassing the gigantic boulder, other rock outcroppings and Opar, the City of Gold and fiends.

SUPER: "SUMMER SOLSTICE 1910"

He drops down into a draw and quickly picks his way into the valley.

EXT. GIGANTIC BOULDER - LATE MORNING

Tarzan hastens down the steep path leading to the vertical underground staircase.

CLEFT

Tarzan vanishes down the spiral staircase.

INT. TEMPLE - GOLDEN CHAMBER - SAME TIME

The Lead Priestess, covered in a ceremonial headdress, enters the golden chamber to find Jane seated at the table adjusting her braided hair.

The usual smile she's greeted with is replaced by an unexplained solemn demeanor, as the priestess motions for Jane to follow.

INT. TEMPLE - CORRIDOR - LATE MORNING

Awaiting outside the chamber are six more female priests wearing the same ceremonial headdress.

Jane, like a sheep being led to slaughter, follows the Lead Priestess out the door with the votaries falling in behind and moving in unison to the Lead Priestess's measured step.

INT. TEMPLE - INNER COURTYARD - HIGH NOON

The ceremonial procession enters into a semi-crowded courtyard and half-filled galleries.

Jane's puzzled, crystal eyes follow the ritual with increased foreboding as she's positioned underneath the shaft high up in the ceiling, by the fair, dark-haired priestesses.

Her skepticism, as to their sanity, increases as she sees all their faces upturned towards something above her.

As Jane begins to raise her face and eyes upwards, she's showered by the powerful light of the noonday sun, diffused by the angled bottom of the ceiling shaft.

Jane, glowing like an angel in the sheet of encompassing light, turns her face away and downward, shading it was a hand.

Her misgivings rise as she's immediately surrounded by many revolting priests who begin to chant in a strange tongue as they dance awkwardly around her, their faces looking upwards.

Jane screams and shields her head and face with her hands and arms, as the madmen suddenly charge her with contorted faces and raised clubs.

The priestess bearing the light, golden club is suddenly upon them and drives them away from the frightened, startled girl.

Frightened and bewildered, Jane lowers both trembling hands upon her heaving chest as she attempts to recover her breath.

Just as suddenly as the light entered, it is snuffed out by the movement of the sun and Jane is led out from the courtyard by the priestess that saved her from the attacking monstrous priests.

Behind Jane a train of priests and priestesses follow, as she's led into the mouth of a yawning corridor.

INT. TEMPLE - ALTAR CHAMBER - AFTERNOON

At the reception of grinning skulls, Jane's fears are fully realized and her heart sinks as her despondent eyes fall upon the bloodstained altar mounted by a tall golden cup.

Jane attempts to flee but four priests grab her and drag her before the altar.

They tie her hands crossed at her lower belly with the leather thong secured behind her. Next her ankles are bond together.

Jane stands before the altar unable to move with the four priests in a semi-circle behind her. Escape is impossible.

Through the arched entrance the ceremonial procession of the dark-haired beauties begins as they make their way to the altar each bearing two golden cups.

At the altar, they're joined by the priests who take their golden cups and together they face the altar and begin the weird chant which creeps through the chamber reaching the galleries filled to capacity.

INT. OPAR - TEMPLE - WELL TUNNEL - SAME TIME

Tarzan's mighty form emerges from the depths of the earth, the meager light of the tunnel affording him a shadowy form.

As Tarzan nears the well shaft his form becomes more delineated and visible.

The faint, familiar eerie chant reaches Tarzan's ears and it quickens his savage eyes with alarm.

He leaps across the well chasm straight for the false wall and plows through with hands and arms, followed by his body as he forces himself into prison chamber.

PRISON CHAMBER

He tries the door but it's locked!

Tarzan snarls ferociously.

He rams it once! Twice! But it's no good, the heavy metal door is impervious to even his might.

He does a quick, one-handed pick-up of a stone slab and
dashes back to the well shaft.

INT. TEMPLE - ALTAR CHAMBER - SAME TIME

From the packed galleries, the close-set eyes on the bestial
faces of the men and the dark eyes of the women are all
riveted upon the scene below.

The priests and priestesses watch in anticipation past the
altar with their golden cups centered and chest-high.

La, as if by magic, ascends from the vault below.

Her shapely figure snails seductively towards the altar, her
hips jaunting left, and right.

INT. TEMPLE - WELL TUNNEL - SAME TIME

From twenty feet below Tarzan's upturned face looks up the
shaft with desperate, determined eyes.

He uncoils his grass rope and ties it fast about the slab.
He swings it out and up a few times to build momentum and
then with all the power of this mighty thews, he casts the
slab at a slight angle up and over the lip of the well.

Tarzan pulls the rope.

EXT. TEMPLE - OPEN COURTYARD - AFTERNOON

In a medium-sized, courtyard -- forsaken but untouched by
time -- a large slab grinds along the concrete floor towards
a stout well.

Centrally located, the well is elaborately carved with inlaid
reliefs of solid gold at intervals all around it.

A four-inch thick lip juts out six inches and is scarred with
cracks, crevices, splits and clefts.

The stone slab comes to an abrupt stop when the rope slips
into one of the tight clefts, that widens further back along
its length toward the inner rim.

INT. TEMPLE - WELL TUNNEL - AFTERNOON

Tarzan tugs a few times and then mounts the rope. It holds.
He begins to climb but stops as the rope begins to slip
downward in jerks.

The scraping sounds of the slab make their way down the well.

Tarzan peers into the dark void beneath him and then back up towards the top of the shaft, his eyes praying for the stone to catch.

The rope drops down once more with an impact sound and stops, and so does the unearthly ceremonial chant.

INT. TEMPLE - ALTAR CHAMBER - SAME TIME

La stands behind the head of the altar holding out a golden wand with an outstretched arm decorated with fine golden bands and many bracelets.

She lowers her arm with the sound of jostling bracelets ending at her side, the cupbearers rise with their eyes aglaze in anticipation of the bloodletting and, for the first time, La directs her eyes towards the young woman before the altar.

La, beautiful and resplendent in her attire and manner, is no match for the unbridled beauty standing before her.

Jane's small-waisted, lithe and supple figure is hugged by the soft antelope leather that accentuates her curves and firm apple-sized breasts.

Her very long, loosely braided golden hair falls down past her straight back and her brave jeweled eyes, encased in an oval face of astounding loveliness, return the appraisal.

La's eyes shift past the girl and to the priests behind her.

La raises a commanding hand, palm-up.

Instantly, Jane is lifted off the floor face up into the air, by the strong squat priests, and laid upon the altar.

Instinctively La's hand finds the jeweled pommel of the sacrificial blade.

She raises it high, with both of her hands, above her head.

Her smooth, pleasant voice spews out pagan prayers in a strange, unknown tongue.

Slowly the knife begins to descend to the tender breast of the helpless girl.

Jane watches, with terrified eyes, as the long, wicked blade inches down towards her falling and rising bosom, her full lips moving to a silent prayer.

Involuntarily she tries to break free of her bonds, but it's futile.

Overwhelmed by her inevitable end, she turns her face away unable to look any longer and swoons.

EXT. TEMPLE - OPEN COURTYARD - SAME TIME

The stone slab is jammed, mercifully, underneath the projecting outer lip of the well.

Manifold stress marks begin to crack the surface of the slab.

A large sinewy hand takes hold of the well's outer lip and the stone slab, free of the ape-man's weight, falls to the concrete floor and breaks into several pieces and the grass rope, dragged down by its own weight, is swallowed by the well shaft.

With a jerk of his powerful arm Tarzan is up and over the side of the well.

La's faint flowing voice seems to permeate the ancient open courtyard.

Surrounded by several corridor openings, Tarzan's ears move ever so slightly to determine the direction of La's voice.

With bent knees, bent elbows and arms slightly out, Tarzan does an almost 360 degree turn, ready to burst in whatever direction.

His ears lock on and Tarzan, like a bullet, disappears into one of the corridors.

INT. TEMPLE - AFTERNOON

CORRIDOR

A powerful back fills the arched entrance, light and shadow contrasting sharply to magnify his ripped, rolling muscles.

A Waziri knife hangs alongside his soft antelope loincloth that brandishes his powerful long legs.

ALTAR CHAMBER

All within are oblivious to the ape-man's presence, their eyes focused on the high priestess.

Before him are the two files of priests and priestesses
facing the altar.

Tarzan's eyes ignite and the scar on his forehead flames on
as he descries the slowly descending blade upon the inert
form of Jane Porter.

The full weight of the bull-ape, berserker rage, falls on the
ape-man. His face contorts. A vicious snarl draws back a
nobleman's lips exposing his strong white teeth and Tarzan
ROARS!

The unexpected roar of the bull-ape shatters the ceremony
freezing everyone in place.

He snatches a cudgel from the nearest petrified priest and
goes to town, laying waste to one and all priests that stand
in his way, crushing heads, arms and chests as he makes his
way towards the bloodstained altar in a fiery whirlwind of
destruction.

La's prayers become trapped in her slender throat, her dagger
freezes in time just above the fragile breast of Jane Porter,
as her stunned face witnesses rage incarnate rampaging
through her faithful priests, on his way towards her, with a
trail of bodies in his wake.

Fear and the fury of the slaughter scatters the remaining
occupants as fast as their legs can get them through the
exits of the bloodletting chamber.

Big Priest is the last to stand between Tarzan and the altar.

Like lightning, Tarzan's unabated rage clamps a sinewy hand
around its thick throat, raising him high above his black-
maned head.

A sudden twist of the wrist and he snaps his neck liked a
dried tree branch.

Tarzan looks straight at La.

He tosses the carcass, like a rag doll, to one side and drops
the blood smeared club.

Straight for the altar he continues and his fierce expression
recalls to La the blade so that she removes it from above
Jane's body and to her side in a trance-like motion.

At the altar, the scar upon his forehead begins to soften as
he lifts the lifeless form of the unconscious girl into his
mighty arms.

La's fear vanishes awakened by a tinge of jealousy and as
Tarzan faces her, she points at the girl.

                        LA
            Who is this woman?

The sounds of many bare feet, grunts and gruff voices reach
the altar.

                        TARZAN
            She is mine.

Tarzan glances quickly over his shoulder and then back to La.

                        TARZAN
            La, the key -- quickly.

La stares at him confused at the strange request.

                        TARZAN
            The key!

La cuts the leather thong holding the key to her side and
hands it to the ape-man.

Tarzan leaps down into the entrance to the vault just before
a large body of angry and armed priests move past the high
priestess in pursuit of the ape-man below.

Silence reigns in the large altar chamber.

La's blade falls from her fine white hand clattering on the
concrete floor.

Tears fill her beautiful, dark, almond eyes and with a
mournful cry she crumbles to the floor.

Her heart bleeds as she cries silently all alone in the
dreadful chamber of sacrifice.

INT. TEMPLE - VAULT - AFTERNOON

The priests cover the entire vault but Tarzan is nowhere to
be found. Only gloomy corridors greet their searching ugly
faces.

A priest is about to enter a corridor with a few others
when...

                        PRIEST 1
            Wait, we need not follow -- he is
            trapped. There is no escape from
            here.

Repelling smiles spread across many faces exposing small
fangs but PRIEST 2, holding a torch, is not convinced.

                    PRIEST 2
          You forget, he escaped last time.

                    PRIEST 1
          Yes, but we don't know how!

                    PRIEST 3
               (looking from one to the
                other)
          We will take no chances this time.
          You all, remain here. I will
          gather another group and march
          towards the mountain pass... just
          in case.

INT. TEMPLE - BASEMENT CORRIDOR - AFTERNOON

Tarzan hastens with Jane over his shoulder and a torch in his
other hand until he comes to the door of the prison chamber.

He inserts the torch into a sconce on the wall and unlocks
the door leaving the key in it.

He forces it open, grabs the torch and with his foot opens
the door wider to admit him and the girl.

INT. TEMPLE - WELL TUNNEL - AFTERNOON

Carefully, Tarzan enters into tunnel filled with the weakened
light of the sun.

He secures the torch into an empty sconce, lays Jane on the
floor ever-so gently and goes to work rebuilding the false
wall.

A gap is left by the missing slab he used to climb up through
the well shaft. Tarzan grabs another one from the neatly
stacked slabs near the wall and makes the replacement. A
perfect fit.

He looks it over to make sure that nothing has been
overlooked and then heaves Jane over a shoulder and takes the
torch.

He leaps the well shaft easily and disappears into the depths
of the subterranean world.

                                        FADE TO BLACK:

INT. TEMPLE - SUBTERRANEAN TREASURE VAULT

Tarzan's handsome, noble face is lit by the unstable light of
the torch.

His eyes rove upwards towards the ceiling and he smiles.

Tarzan, with the unconscious girl over his shoulder, holds
the torch high above his head to illuminate a great
rectangular chamber stacked with thousands upon thousands of
ingots!

Through the middle of the chamber a wide passage moves
between the entrances at each end, but to the left and to the
right of it, the great chamber is piled high and deep with
vast ingots of pure virgin gold.

As he walks slowly towards the other end, he spots the stack
he bumped into on his first visit.

The amount of gold filling the chamber is astronomical!

Tarzan looks down upon the angelic face of his sleeping
beauty. His acute ears tuning-in, can hear her steady
heartbeat and a warm smile spreads across his face.

Tarzan hastens through the large exit on the other side of
the treasure chamber leaving it again hidden by the
impenetrable darkness.

EXT. BARREN VALLEY - AFTERNOON

A large golden armlet gleams against the sunlight.

A band of lowbrowed, hairy monstrosities grunts and shuffles
on short warped legs through the narrow valley of Opar, their
long hair and beards, and partially covered necklaces of
savage claws, bouncing against their strong hirsute chests.

The fifty, wielding large knotted clubs, breath laboriously
unaccustomed to jogging.

Between them and the miles they need to cover to reach the
mountain pass, stands the immense granite boulder some three-
hundred yards ahead of them.

EXT. BARREN VALLEY - GIGANTIC BOULDER - AFTERNOON

Up the incline with Jane in both arms, Tarzan reaches the
summit of the granite boulder.

He glances back to the city of Opar with Jane resting her golden head upon his chest.

His grey eyes grow grim at the sight of the golden arm and leg bands glinting in the sun. Priests!

The cry of savage jubilation reaches the ape-man, as they spot him and the stolen sacrifice.

EXT. BARREN VALLEY - AFTERNOON

At fifteen mile per hour, Tarzan's long legs cruise the rough terrain easily eating up the miles.

Ahead of him in the distance rises the barrier ridge and within it, a flat plateau, that is the mountain pass.

EXT. BARREN VALLEY - AFTERNOON

Rounding the boulder, some of the exhausted, Oparian priests fall on all-fours -- apelike -- gasping for air.

Over a mile ahead of them only a trail of moving dust is their reward for their increased efforts.

Nevertheless, on crooked short legs, they renew the awkward, dogged jog in pursuit of the ape-man.

EXT. MOUNTAIN - DRAW - AFTERNOON

Up a deep draw Tarzan climbs carefully, Jane still immersed in deep repose.

EXT. MOUNTAIN PASS - LATE AFTERNOON

From the large plateau, Tarzan scans the hazy valley for signs of the monstrous men and is appraised of their location by the glint of their gold, still a few miles away.

He readjusts Jane in his arms and then carefully begins the descent for the waiting forest below.

EXT. JANE CAMPSITE - LATE AFTERNOON

Clayton enters the clearing carrying a bucket of water and two canteens slung over a shoulder.

As he nears the campfire his vision begins to blur and disorientation sets in, yet he holds on to the bucket, spilling water as he goes.

CAMPFIRE

Rokoff, sitting on one of logs, tracks him with the eyes of a jackal.

Once at the campfire, Clayton lowers the bucket and drops one of the canteens off his shoulder near one of the water kegs.

Clayton lumbers off towards the tree shelter and at the base of the shelter, he grabs the ladder for support with one hand his entire body shaking uncontrollably.

Up the ladder the stricken man climbs.

Rokoff watches him enter the shelter, a malicious smirk glowing on his dark countenance.

INT. TREE SHELTER - LATE AFTERNOON

Clayton drops the canteen to one side and collapses on his grass bed, his body shaking, his teeth chattering, his face and forehead a profusion of sweat.

EXT. JUNGLE - LATE AFTERNOON

Past the edge of the jungle, Tarzan carries the sleeping Jane to the rivulet and lays her down beside it.

He dips his hand into the gurgling cold water and dabs Jane's face and forehead with his wet fingers and hand, yet Jane does not respond to any of his ministrations.

EXT. MOUNTAIN PASS - LATE AFTERNOON

From the height of the pass, a dog-tired throng of bestial faces peer down the side of the mountain searching with their close-set wicked eyes for signs or traces of their quarry, but there is none.

Angry and disgruntled at the theft and then escape of their sacrifice they cry out in rage; yet, they dare not pursue and instead turn around to retrace their steps back to the ruins of Opar.

EXT. JUNGLE - LATE AFTERNOON

Through the never ending jungle, Tarzan pushes on with the
lovely Jane Porter still unconscious in his mighty arms.

Though asleep, Jane's eyes move erratically beneath her
eyelids.

NIGHTMARE FLASHES - BODY AND SOUL

-- La's hand melts into her chest and pulls out her heart.
La pricks it with the tip of the wicked, gleaming blade and
Jane's wounded heart begins to bleed.

-- Vines and creepers entangle Jane like a web while myriad
plants with thorns and sharp leaves surround her and cut and
prick her entire body mercilessly.

-- The surface of the bloodstained altar morphs into a pool
of blood and from within it a tall, golden cup rises out of
the blood with her name emblazoned upon it.

-- Jane is surrounded by fifty ugly, frothing priests with
eyes afire. Her whole body bleeds and trembles as she
struggles to dodge cudgels thrown at her at remarkable
speeds. Her body seizes up and a cudgel rams into her
stomach.

Jane's eyes abruptly open. The sensation of movement and the
wild jungle meet them. Her eyes shift and she sees a mighty
chest and arms bearing her through the awful forest.

Her eyes look a little further upwards and a beautiful smile
spreads across her face filling her wistful eyes with joy.

A sense of peace and tranquility blankets her and she sighs.

                    JANE
               (whispering in wonder)
          So this is heaven. Thank God, I'm
          dead. Tarzan... my Tarzan.

The coo of her voice pulls Tarzan's glad gaze upon her.

                    TARZAN
               (tenderly)
          Jane.

Tarzan raises her up and gives her a heartfelt embrace.

                    TARZAN
          You're back in my arms again.

Jane wraps her arms tightly around his muscular neck pressing her intoxicating face close to his, her eyes watching the trail behind them in a mesmerized state of mind.

                    JANE
          I'll never leave you again...
          never, my love.

Tarzan slows down and veers off the well-worn animal trail towards the stream running along side them.

He lowers her gently to the ground with her back against the bole of an enormous giant.

                    TARZAN
          I don't think your husband would
          approve.

Jane stands up slowly before the tall, ripped and muscled ape-man and raising one of her delicate hands she caresses one side of his face brushing back a bit of his long black mane.

Tarzan instinctively embraces her small waist and draws her closer to him.

Not looking at him, she rests both hands on his chest.

                    JANE
               (looks up)
          I never married him... I couldn't.
          It was always you and only you.
          And now that we're both dead, we
          can always be together.

Tarzan meets her joyous smile with puzzlement for just a moment and then smiles and begins to chuckle softly.

                    TARZAN
          You're not dead, Jane... and
          neither am I.

Jane is confused and completely thrown off her keel. She steps back and turns away from him with her hand on her forehead trying to assimilate the portent of Tarzan's words and then just as quickly she wheels about with a sudden recollection.

                    JANE
          But, you were killed! Hazel told
          me -- she said you had been thrown
          overboard. I have to be dead or
          I'm dreaming. The altar -- the
          knife --

Tarzan, with a polite smile, places both hands on her
shoulders shaking his head.

>   TARZAN
>   None of those things happened. I
>   wasn't killed and neither were you.
>   And as for your dreaming, I know
>   how you feel. It seems fantastic
>   that we're together again, yet we
>   are both very much alive.

Tarzan pinches her arm.

>   JANE
>   Ouch!

She pretends to be irked, scowling as she rubs the reddened
skin.

>   TARZAN
>   (grinning)
>   Well? Is it a dream?

She gives him an embarrassed smile and then throws her arms
around him.

>   TARZAN
>   So, you're not married. At the
>   clearing I thought you --

Jane releases him gingerly, her joy suddenly diminished.

>   JANE
>   (hurt)
>   It was you...

Tears begin to well up in her eyes as she searches his silent
face.

>   JANE
>   ... You who saved us that day at
>   our campsite... you who killed the
>   lion. Why, darling, did you leave
>   us... leave me?

In animal silence Tarzan holds her eyes with an unshakable,
solemn sadness.

She strikes his chest lightly with her closed fists looking
up into the ape-man's pained countenance, a few tears running
down her cheeks.

                    JANE
          My God, the misery and suffering I
          went through on that terrible
          march... Tarzan, I wanted to die.

She buries herself in his strong arms.

                    TARZAN
          You almost did. I thank God, I was
          in time.

He pulls her away and a grim face meets her poignant
features.

                    TARZAN
          I would have killed him... that's
          why I had to go. I almost did... I
          couldn't stand to see you in his
          arms. By the time I'd made my mind
          up to return to you, a bull-ape had
          informed me of your abduction.

Jane lets go of him. Feeling better and understanding
Tarzan's quandary she wipes the moisture from her eyes.

                    TARZAN
          Can you forgive me, Jane?

Tarzan's humble demeanor soothes the girl's heart.

                    JANE
          Forgive you? For saving my life
          any number of times?

Realization sets in.

                    JANE
          In the end, I'm to blame for all
          the unfortunate events that have
          befallen me.

She takes one of his large hands in both of hers and stares
at him sadly.

                    JANE
          When I learned that you had been
          killed...
               (chokes up)
          ... I didn't want to live
          anymore... I thought I had lost you
          forever.
               (crying softly)
          I couldn't bear it. God knows, I
          couldn't.

>   TARZAN
> Please don't cry, Jane. I'm alive.

>   JANE
> I know, my love, and that's the
> reason for my tears... because you
> are alive. And it's the most
> wonderful thing... to see your face
> again.

Silent tears flow from her doleful eyes.

>   JANE
> It should be me, asking you for
> forgiveness. For denying you and
> myself the love the Lord saw fit to
> give us. I was a coward and I've
> paid dearly... more than I could
> ever have imagined.

>   TARZAN
> We're human and we all make
> mistakes. But you and I are
> fortunate... we've been given a
> second chance.

Jane glances up at him with a recovering smile as she wipes
her watery eyes, a heavy burden lifted off her shoulders.

The past and fears forgotten, her mischievous side comes to
bear.

>   JANE
>   (sly eyes)
> And it's a second chance that I'm
> not going to waste... ever.

Her forgiveness and sudden playfulness draw a big smile from
the Tarzan.

>   JANE
> Kiss me, my big... strong...
> savage... ape-man.

Tarzan doesn't need to be coaxed twice as he takes her gently
in his powerful arms and smothers her with burning kisses.

After a moment of unbridled osculation, Jane pushes him
lightly away to catch her breath.

>   JANE
>   (panting)
> Oh, my goodness... you animal.

Rising on her toes, she encircles his corded neck in her
sleek arms and raises her full lips to his face and whispers.

                    JANE
          Again.

EXT. JUNGLE - NEXT DAY

Hand in hand, Tarzan and Jane stroll together along a wide
jungle trail.

Curious monkeys jump from tree to tree following them with
all the chatter in their noisy nature.

Tarzan notices that Jane is unusually silent.

                    TARZAN
          What's troubling you?

She looks up and confides in him.

                    JANE
          The last thing I remember was that
          awful knife about to plunge into my
          heart.

Tarzan pulls her close to him and comforts her.

                    TARZAN
          Yes, I remember. They paid a heavy
          price for it.

                    JANE
          Did you --

                    TARZAN
          Yes, I did.

She gives him a quick kiss on his face and then leans her
head against his arm.

                    JANE
          I'm glad. Those beasts!

Tarzan laughs at her whispered outburst.

She frees herself from his arm, suddenly alarmed by a
thought.

                    JANE
          Oh no! I'd almost forgotten about
          poor Clayton alone with another
          beast at this very moment.

Tarzan a little perplexed.

> TARZAN
> Are you telling me that one of
> those monstrosities stayed back to
> keep Clayton company?

Jane laughs outright.

> JANE
> No, but it's just as bad. It's
> another man who was marooned with
> us.

> TARZAN
> Who is he? I didn't see him that
> day.

Jane squints trying to recall the man's name.

> JANE
> His name is... oooh, it's just on
> the tip of my tongue.

She suddenly remembers and blurts it out.

> JANE
> Thuran! Monsieur Thuran... that's
> his name and...

Jane searches Tarzan's face.

> JANE
> ... He knows you.

> TARZAN
> Rokoff.

> JANE
> What?

> TARZAN
> That's his real name, Rokoff... and
> he's been a thorn in my side far
> too long.

Tarzan gives her a grin.

> TARZAN
> It was he and his associate who
> pitched me over the side of the
> steamer.

                    JANE
          He? But how?

                    TARZAN
          It was after midnight and I was
          leaning over the deck rail...
          thinking of you, when they charged
          me. It happened too quickly for me
          to do anything about it.

                    JANE
          The man is patently evil.

                    TARZAN
          In a word, very.

Jane gives him a full kiss.

                    TARZAN
          And that was for...

                    JANE
          ... Thinking of me.

                    TARZAN
          You're always on my mind.

                    JANE
               (playful)
          Even when you abandoned me at the
          campsite?

Tarzan nods.

                    TARZAN
          Even when you abandoned me for
          Clayton.

Jane frowns and Tarzan laughs as he smacks her backside for
good measure.

                    JANE
               (giggling)
          You -- you beast!

                    TARZAN
          That I am and you won't believe the
          things I did to try to forget you.
               (shaking head)
          But it was no good. It's as if you
          became part of me the moment I saw
          you.

Tarzan slides an arm around her slender waist and they stop walking.

> TARZAN
> And there's no way out... and I'm glad. I love you, Jane Porter.

He presses her lips with a single, slow kiss.

Jane responds afterward with a shy, girlish smile and as they continue their jungle stroll, she broods a bit.

> JANE
> Is it true?

> TARZAN
> About what?

> JANE
> About Thuran's sister... and you boarding the steamer to avoid a duel?

> TARZAN
> I see he lost no time in telling you his version -- an affair he planned. Her name is Olga de Coude and what passed between us entailed a kiss and an embrace... no more.

> JANE
> (worried)
> And you don't love her?

The stroll stops and they face each other.

> TARZAN
> No... and she doesn't love me. It was a moment's weakness and it was contrived by Rokoff so that we would be found together by her husband... as he did. And as for me avoiding the duel...

Tarzan points to the two bullet scars sustained in the duel.

> TARZAN
> ... I paid for my mistake too.

> JANE
> (indignant)
> That liar. The man is wicked to the core.

Jane kisses the scar on the shoulder and caresses the other one with her fingertips.

                    JANE
          There... is that better?

                    TARZAN
               (grinning)
          Much.

Throwing his arm around her they continue their jaunt through the now narrowing path and Jane with her head and eyes down...

                    Jane
          Is she beautiful?

Tarzan smiles and glances down at his lithesome, golden-haired belle.

                    TARZAN
          Yes, very beautiful...

Jane drops her chin at those words but Tarzan lifts it back up to look into her lovely jeweled eyes.

                    TARZAN
          ... Yet even so, not quite as
          beautiful as you.

Jane smiles, relieved. She takes his arm and resting her head on his shoulder, she takes a deep breath and then sighs. She's in heaven.

Their indistinct chatter is swallowed up by the buzz and jungle sounds surrounding them as they disappear from view at a tight turn on the trail.

EXT. JANE CAMPSITE - TREE SHELTER - LATE AFTERNOON (A WEEK LATER)

Clayton climbs down the rickety ladder. Half-way down he loses his grip and falls to the ground.

His face is soaked and delirious with merciless fever.

He struggles to his knees, picks up the dropped canteen and finally makes it to his feet.

An emaciated figure of a man and racked with tremors, he stumbles towards one of the kegs of water.

CAMPFIRE

Rokoff watches him indifferently as he stuffs his face with the catch of the day.

Clayton kneels before the keg and fills the canteen and then lumbers back to the tree shelter like a drunken man.

TREE SHELTER

He pauses at the ladder taking hold of one of the rungs to catch his breath and using every ounce of energy he climbs back up the ladder slowly -- one rung at a time.

CAMPFIRE

Rokoff wipes his greasy palms on his once white trousers and gulps down a bite with a cup of water.

> ROKOFF
> (in a French accent;
> laughing)
> Hurry, my friend, before it gets
> dark!

Thoroughly enjoying Clayton's suffering, he can't stop laughing as he cuts away another piece of burning flesh.

EXT. JUNGLE - LATE AFTERNOON

An alert Tarzan cautions Jane into silence.

His steel-grey eyes search far into the gloom of the jungle.

He sniffs the air and then listens.

Out of the blue, Tarzan sweeps Jane off the trail and springs ten feet into the air and with his free arm grips a branch his momentum swinging him forward to land on a humongous limb with his lovely cargo.

Jane, her breath taken away, searches Tarzan's noble smiling face in quest for an explanation.

> TARZAN
> Lion.

> JANE
> A lion? Where? I didn't see
> anything.

                    TARZAN
          In the jungle if you see a lion,
          it's too late.

                    JANE
          Where is he?

Tarzan points down the well-trodden trail about fifty yards.

Jane squints searching for the king of beasts but sees
nothing.

                    JANE
          There's nothing --

A large male lion comes trotting suddenly into view stopping
and sniffing the ground and then the air as he moves along
unaware of the two hidden in the tree.

Jane stares at Tarzan in wonder and admiration.

                    JANE
               (whispers)
          But how could you possibly know
          that he was coming?

                    TARZAN
          The eyes are not the only way to
          see.

Tarzan taps an ear.

                    JANE
          You heard him? From this far away?

                    TARZAN
          And much further. But I can smell
          them from even greater distances,
          if the wind is right.

                    JANE
               (awed)
          You're amazing.

Tarzan shrugs his shoulders.

                    TARZAN
          Not really. I was brought up by
          the apes who survive by their nose
          and ear. It came to me naturally.
          There was no choice, really. It
          was either adapt and learn, or fall
          prey to predators, like him.

The lion pauses underneath the tree sensing their presence and rumbles a ugly growl. The large beast paces a few times looking upward and then keeps moving down the trail.

Squatting next to each other like two children, Tarzan and Jane follow the lion until it jumps into the thick underbrush hemming the trail and vanishes from their sight.

Tarzan stands up.

> TARZAN
> After we reach Clayton, where would
> you like to go?

He proffers his hand to help Jane up. She takes it and stands beside him.

> JANE
> It doesn't matter, as long as I'm
> with you.

Tarzan considers her and smiles proudly.

> TARZAN
> That's my girl!

Tarzan taps his wide back and squats down a few inches and Jane eagerly complies.

Jane closes her eyes shut as Tarzan leaps out and taking a branch without so much as a jolt, propels himself and the girl higher and higher towards the dizzying heights near the canopy of the vast jungle.

Tarzan's mighty arms alternate like an untiring machine as his powerful hands unerringly take hold of unseen branches, in the eyes of the girl.

Jane's face is alive with amazement.

> TARZAN
> Hold on!

Tarzan let's go of a branch and flies a good twenty feet across empty space and Jane screams as they drop.

Tarzan catches a thick rope-like vine and as the fast momentum upward swing ends, he releases the vine to grasp a waiting branch to resume the cruise through the trees.

> JANE
> (laughing)
> You're crazy!

                    TARZAN
                  (grinning)
              Did you like it?!

                    JANE
              I loved it!

Jane looks down, her eyes aglow with wonder, as the ape-man
swings easily and quickly through the trees over a hundred
feet above the jungle floor.

EXT. TREE SHELTER - MORNING (2.5 WEEKS LATER)

A few remaining drops from an open canteen drip onto anxious
lips.

A wasted Clayton weakly shakes the canteen for a few more
drops, but it's empty.

Assailed by shakes he closes his eyes and grimaces in pain.
Clayton tries to rise but cannot and falls back helplessly
with a groan.

                    CLAYTON
                  (hoarse)
              Thuran! Thuraaaaan! Water...
              water!

Clayton's head moves from side to side as he fights against
the fever. He takes control and lies still, his feverish
eyes barely open, his ears listening.

At first only the jungle hum and the din of the untamed
prevail, but then the sound of the CREAKY ladder heralds
Rokoff's advent.

INT./EXT. TREE SHELTER - MORNING

                    ROKOFF (O.S.)
                  (in a French accent)
              What, English pig?

Clayton's eyes glance towards the entrance where Rokoff
stands holding a canteen in one hand and a sneer on his cruel
face.

                    CLAYTON
              Help me Thuran... I need water...
              I'm too weak to get up.

                          ROKOFF
                    (in a French accent)
               You denied me the girl and now you
               dare to ask me for help?

Clayton's eyes light up for a brief moment.

                          CLAYTON
               Have you no respect for the dead?!
                    (voice weakens)
               You lowest of men. I should have
               listened to her... I should have
               let you die.

                          ROKOFF
                    (in a French accent)
               Fear not, my dear Clayton, I'll not
               make the same mistake. Here's your
               water, dog!

Rokoff chugs the canteen. Water runs down the sides of his
mouth and onto his filthy shirt as he drinks. He swishes his
mouth with another lighter swig and spits it out on the
threshold of the entrance.

                          ROKOFF
                    (in a French accent)
               Drink that, pig, if you can.
               Crawl... drink, my friend. Not
               enough? Here, I'll pour some more
               for you.

He upends the canteen and empties it at the entrance and the
water quickly disappears through the thatched floor of the
hut.

Clayton turns his head away suffering from want of water and
as if on cue, Rokoff enters and lifts Clayton's empty
canteen.

                          ROKOFF
               This, I'll take... and anything
               else I want.

He opens up one of the knapsacks, inherited from the sailors,
and fills it with some clothes, a pair of shoes and,
rummaging for whatever he can find, he overturns one of
Jane's shoes and a golden chain partially falls out.

Rokoff's avaricious eyes are quick to spot it.

>   ROKOFF
>   (in a French accent)
>   And what, Mademoiselle, were you
>   hiding from me?

He reaches for the golden chain and pulls it up to reveal a diamond studded locket.

>   ROKOFF
>   (in a French accent)
>   Ah, a lady's treasure.

He slips it into his pocket without opening the locket and searches the other shoe and her other belongings for more baubles but comes up empty-handed.

He adds a few more miscellaneous items to the canvas knapsack and heads for the exit.

At the entrance, Rokoff glances back at Clayton one last time with a gleeful gleam of evil in his eyes, while a wicked smirk spreads across his face that suddenly erupts into merciless laughter.

The CREAKING of the ladder stirs Clayton into a state of pathos. He covers his face with the joint of his arm and sobs pitifully.

EXT. JANE CAMPSITE - CAMPFIRE - MORNING

Rokoff refills both canteens at one of the kegs and grabbing Clayton's sharpened staff sets out from the campsite and into the jungle.

EXT. JUNGLE - MORNING

Rokoff picks his way through the entanglements of the forest until he reaches a small game trail.

His clothes are a filthy disaster, yet serviceable. His normal hair color has all but grown back in and though kept short, it's much longer than the norm. His unwashed face is somewhat shaved and trimmed but still presents an untidy appearance.

On his back is the knapsack. On his shoulder are slung two canteens. In his hand is Clayton's staff and on his belt Tompkin's knife.

Rokoff steps out along the narrow path heading north, looking more like a hobo than a castaway.

365.

EXT. JUNGLE - AFTERNOON

Through an uncluttered wall of the jungle on the west side of
the trail, Rokoff makes out a little log cabin.

A triumphant smile spreads his thin mustache.

He pushes through the jungle wall and into the clearing.

EXT. CLEARING - CABIN - AFTERNOON

Rokoff enters the clearing upon the backside of the cabin.
Surreptitiously, he cases the cabin peeping through the
lattice windows for signs of life.

Finding none, he goes to the door and examines the locking
mechanism and after a moment, the door opens.

He enters and shuts the door.

EXT. JUNGLE - LATE AFTERNOON

A huge wide limb leads to Jane Porter who sits before an
arboreal bower built with one end against the mammoth bole of
the tree.

On top of plantain fronds and elephant ears, lies a
cornucopia of fruits, nuts and viands from the plentiful
jungle arrayed before the waiting girl.

Squawking birds and screaming monkeys announce Tarzan's
return as he alights onto the limb bearing a bundle of
grasses, strapped together and secured to his back with vines
and creepers.

Tarzan notices that the buffet hasn't been touched.

                    TARZAN
          Aren't you hungry? Or is there
          something wrong with the food?

                    JANE
          Neither. I was waiting for you, so
          we could eat together.

                    TARZAN
               (grins)
          A she-ape would have eaten all of
          it by now with no thought for her
          mate. Thank God, you're a woman.

Jane starts to laugh as Tarzan removes the large bundle from
his back and lays it on the monstrous limb.

                    JANE
          What have you there?

                    TARZAN
          Part of your bed. One more trip
          and you'll have a soft bed tonight.

Tarzan kneels with his back to Jane and retrieves from within
the bundle of grasses a beautiful bouquet of jungle blossoms.

As he turns, Jane's countenance stirs with a loving smile.

                    JANE
          For me?

Tarzan nods and hands her the bouquet of flowers.

Jane takes them and pulls his arm along to bring him to her
lips, and kisses him.

                    JANE
          They're beautiful... I love them.

Tarzan takes one of her hands and kisses it.

                    TARZAN
          You're the only flower I want.

Pretending to be disappointed.

                    JANE
          Is that all I'm worth, one kiss?

Tarzan wraps his strong arms about her and administers
several more kisses.

When he finishes, Jane is out of breath -- her lovely bosom
heaving.

                    TARZAN
          Is that better.

Jane picks up an available frond and fans herself and then
looking at the ape-man with a satisfied smile...

                    JANE
          Much.

Tarzan kisses her nose and gets up to leave for another jaunt
in the jungle. Like a panther he saunters for several paces
along the limb and glancing at Jane...

                    TARZAN
            You'll wait for me?

Jane blows him a kiss.

Tarzan places a hand over his heart as if pierced by an
arrow.

Still holding his heart, Tarzan falls over the edge and Jane
screams.

She rushes to the edge only to hear Tarzan's laughter as he
swings leisurely through the lower branches. He does a 360
degree turn and sends her a quick salute with Jane barely
able to wave back before he catches the next branch and sails
away.

Relieved, Jane collapses into a sitting posture and her
glittering eyes follow him until he slips past the thick
jungle veil and from her sight.

EXT. JUNGLE - NIGHT

A zenith moon stares out upon the jungle vastness and peers
down a generous opening in the canopy.

It's soft rays enter the rare breech to illuminate everything
below it, in a diffused spellbinding light.

Near the opening of the bower, Jane's face is caressed by the
creeping light of the moon as she sleeps.

A few feet from the bower, Tarzan lying on his back, is
bathed by the same light, his eyes glowing like a night
predator.

He yawns, his teeth glimmering in the moonlight, repositions
his long, sinewy body and closes his eyes.

EXT. CLEARING - CABIN - MORNING (3 DAYS LATER)

Rokoff steps out with only the staff and a canteen and
without looking back shuts the door. He's changed his filthy
shirt for one less filthy and thrown a worn and torn, white
blazer over it.

He scans the clearing for any sign of danger and then
proceeds to the back of the cabin and enters the jungle.

EXT. TENNINGTON CAMPSITE - LATE MORNING

A tall, lean and commanding figure, Lord Tennington stands
near the middle of the campsite with Captain Jerrold at his
side.

Before them are the remaining castaways listening to
Tennington.

                    TENNINGTON
          ... And while we wait for a rescue
          that may or may not come, Captain
          Jerrold and I have agreed that it
          would be prudent for us to begin
          work on a more permanent
          community... real cabins to replace
          our current huts.

The Engineer raises his hand.

                    TENNINGTON
          Yes?

                    ENGINEER
          Your Lordship, when do we begin?

Tennington gives the floor to Captain Jerrold.

                    CAPTAIN JERROLD
          We begin tomorrow, so I suggest you
          prepare yourselves mentally and
          sleep well tonight.

Prof. Porter, deep in thought, tries to break away from the
meeting but is held in check by the ubiquitous Mr. Philander.

                    TENNINGTON
          Afterwards, God willing, we'll send
          out an expedition northwards in
          hopes of finding a civilized
          outpost.

Tennington searches the other faces for more questions and
finding none continues.

                    TENNINGTON
          Well men, if you have any further
          questions please direct them to
          Captain Jerrold.

He smiles at the women and bows slightly.

                         TENNINGTON
          And of course I haven't forgotten
          the ladies. All I ask is that you
          continue helping the cook as need
          be to keep the men fed and hydrated
          while they work to create our
          little village.

Tennington looks at Captain Jerrold.

                         CAPTAIN JERROLD
          One more thing... the daily
          foraging parties and other duties
          will remain unchanged until further
          notice.
                  (to Tennington)
          That's all I have, My Lord.

                         TENNINGTON
          If there are no further questions,
          the remainder of the day, is yours.

Everyone branches off. Some to the front of their huts to
chat, other's to smoke and yet two others to the butchering
of an antelope.

Esmeralda and Mrs. Strong, together, enter their hut.

CAMPFIRE

Hazel sits alone on one of the logs facing south.

The sounds of Mr. Philander chasing Prof. Porter attract her
attention.

She turns her head to the right to watch Prof. Porter,
dressed in his usual but visibly worn top hat and frock coat,
as he marches across the beach with Mr. Philander close on
his heels struggling to keep him from walking into the surf.

She smiles sadly.

                         TENNINGTON (O.S.)
          He's quite a fellow, isn't he?

Hazel glances to her left to find Tennington watching the
pair on the beach.

                         HAZEL
          He's like a favorite uncle to me.
          I've known him all my life.
                  (MORE)

                    HAZEL (CONT'D)
He's eccentric, but I know that
Jane is as much on his mind as she
is on mine.

                    TENNINGTON
Closer than twin sisters... as you
mother put it.

Hazel nods.

                    HAZEL
I do miss her so. How sad that we
weren't all able to land here
together. Do you think they're
still alive?

                    TENNINGTON
It's possible. We are.

                    HAZEL
After all these months?

Tennington sits beside her.

                    TENNINGTON
I must say, you've been brave thus
far, don't give up now... there's
always hope.

                    HAZEL
          (looks towards the beach)
I just can't believe she and the
others are gone.

                    TENNINGTON
We don't know that, Miss Strong.

                    HAZEL
          (turns to Tennington)
Oh, I wish I had your strength, but
I don't.

                    TENNINGTON
You do. Like you, Esmeralda misses
Miss Porter terribly, and who's the
one who's comforted her? And your
mother? Who's given them strength
to endure these hardships? You
have.

                    HAZEL
          (smiles weakly)
Your optimism is catching.
                    (MORE)

                    HAZEL (CONT'D)
          If not for you, our little company
          would be in disarray.

                    TENNINGTON
          Oh, I don't know. I'm certain that
          all of you would have found your
          way around, so to speak. After
          all, I am, sort of responsible for
          all of you... it was my yacht --

                    HAZEL
          -- But it wasn't your fault.
          Still, I'm glad it was your
          yacht... and not someone else's.

Tennington and Hazel regard each other. He mesmerized by her
charm. She by his commanding, jovial nature.

                    TENNINGTON
          Miss Strong, I've been --

                    HAZEL
            (softly)
          -- Please, call me Hazel.

Tennington puffs his pipe a few more times nervously.

                    TENNINGTON
            (clears throat)
          Uh, Hazel... what I mean to say --

His face blushes ever so slightly.

Hazel smiles beautifully, her eyes aglow.

                    TENNINGTON
          What I want you to know is that --

He looks away from her and puffs his pipe and finishes lamely
with an evasion.

                    TENNINGTON
          We'll do our utmost to complete the
          cabins before the rainy season sets
          in.

Hazel lays an understanding hand on top of his looking at him
with tender eyes.

                    HAZEL
          You honor me.

He looks down at her hand, then at her and then straight
ahead again.

                    TENNINGTON
          I just wanted you to know.

                    HAZEL
               (softly)
          I know.

Suddenly, Tennington and Hazel see it at the same time.

Alarmed, he stops puffing and pulls the pipe from his mouth
and stands up with Hazel rising with him in complete
surprise.

Tennington pulls out his revolver keeping the girl slightly
behind him as a bedraggled man holding a sharpened staff
breaks into the clearing from the jungle.

Rokoff stops and stares, incredulity and joy filling his
unkept face and then starts to run towards them.

Tennington is further mystified when his named is called out
by this -- to him -- complete stranger.

                    ROKOFF
               (in a French accent)
          Lord Tennington! Lord
          Tennington... it's me... don't
          shoot!

Tennington lowers the weapon to his side as he and Hazel move
cautiously to the south entrance gate to meet the newcomer.

At the gate, Tennington eyes Rokoff with suspicion.

                    TENNINGTON
          Who are you and how do you know my
          name?

Rokoff is dismayed.

                    ROKOFF
               (in a French accent)
          I am Monsieur Thuran.

Tennington and Hazel exchange glances and take a harder look
at the rough looking man.

                    ROKOFF
               (in a French accent)
          Don't you recognize me?

Hazel's eyes open in astonishment.

                    HAZEL
          It is him!

The light of recognition finally enters Tennington's eyes.

                    TENNINGTON
               (holstering revolver)
          By Jove, it is you!

Tennington opens the gate and as Rokoff crosses the
threshold, Tennington extends a hand and Rokoff shakes it
vigorously.

                    ROKOFF
               (in a French accent)
          It's so good to see you! I never
          thought to see any of you again.

Hazel's eyes search expectantly over Rokoff's shoulder.

                    TENNINGTON
          It's good to see you too, old boy!
          We didn't know what to think -- we
          hadn't given up hope, but we
          certainly didn't expect to meet you
          and the others today.

                    HAZEL
          Where are the others? Are they
          further back?

Rokoff puts on a sad mask.

                    ROKOFF
               (in a French accent)
          I'm sorry to say, Miss Strong, that
          I am the only survivor.

                    HAZEL
               (in anguish)
          No!

Hazel buries her face in Tennington's chest and weeps and
Tennington's brief joy dissolves as he throws an arm about
the grief-stricken girl.

Rokoff's devious eyes follow their close interaction with
envy.

                    TENNINGTON
               (puffing pipe)
          What happened?

>   ROKOFF
>   (in a French accent)
>   The three sailors died before we
>   reached land... and we barely.
>   Jane disappeared while I lay in bed
>   with fever and Clayton only days
>   ago died from it. Then, finding
>   myself alone I decided to move
>   north to look for an outpost -- if
>   we'd only known you were less than
>   a day's journey north of us, they'd
>   be alive today.

EXT. JUNGLE - DAY

A pair of strong, dark-tanned feet land on a wide limb.

A pair of sandaled, milk-white feet slip down behind them.

A telltale wind blows agitating the foliage about them.

Tarzan stands motionless like a chiseled Greek statue with
his hand resting instinctively on his knife. His alert grey
eyes search and his nostrils dilate as they sample the air
for the intangible.

He blows out air vehemently through his nostrils and then
whiffs it back in.

Jane watches as Tarzan's entire body quickens automatically
into an alert posture.

She glances at his face and then follows his tunnel vision.

>   JANE
>   What is it?

He takes another whiff of the incoming wind to confirm and
then gazes at the lovely maiden standing at his side.

>   TARZAN
>   Men... black men. Friend or foe,
>   we'll soon see.

Tarzan crouches and Jane wraps her slender arms and shapely
legs about him and they're off in a blink of an eye.

EXT. JUNGLE - DAY (30 MINUTES LATER)

High above ten stalwart warriors Tarzan swings stealthily
with Jane securely attached to his back.

He presses swiftly ahead of them and then alights on a limb
near the trail to await their approach.

                    TARZAN
          They're my men.

                    JANE
          Your men?

                    TARZAN
          I'll explain later, but they're
          loyal and you need not fear them...

Jane nods, her upturned, stunning face radiating with love.

                    TARZAN
          ... You can trust them.

She looks into his eyes and, Tarzan unable to resist, kisses
her on the lips gently.

He then, reluctantly, focuses his attention to the bend at
the trail.

Soon, ten sleek handsome warriors come into view, their arms
and ankles adorned with bands of gold. Their backs are
strapped with bows and arrows and a knife hangs at their
side. In one hand they hold a short shield and in the other
a steel-bladed short spear.

                    TARZAN (O.S.)
          Busuli!

Instantly they form into a tight, defensive circle facing
outward, shields shielding their upper bodies and their
spears held high above shoulder level, their eyes searching
high and low for the caller.

                    BUSULI
          Who calls my name!

Like a panther Tarzan alights before them several yards away
with his feather-light burden in his arms.

He lowers her to the jungle trail and she takes hold of one
of his powerful arms.

                    TARZAN
          Your king!

Busuli's eyes almost pop from his head as his white teeth
shine with joy.

                         BUSULI
              Waziri!

Tarzan, with the bearing of a king, advances towards them
with Jane at his side.

With a warm smile Tarzan places a hand on his loyal
lieutenant.

                         TARZAN
              It is good to see you again.

                         BUSULI
              We have been searching for you for
              weeks and feared you lost. I am
              glad, very glad to see you again,
              My Waziri.

The normally stoic warriors are ecstatic to behold their king
once more but soon their eyes turn to the golden beauty
beside the ape-man with questioning eyes.

Tarzan puts a gentle arm about her shoulders and smiles at
her and then looking at his men...

                         TARZAN
              This is my woman.
                 (to Jane)
              I've just introduced you.

Jane waves and smiles graciously endearing her instantly to
Busuli and his men.

Busuli turns to the men.

                         BUSULI
              Our king and our queen!

Forming quickly behind Busuli, together they slap their
spears against their shields in salute to their sovereign.

They then kneel with their heads bowed, shields across their
chests and their spears standing erect upon the ground and to
the side and in unison they shout.

                         WARRIORS
              Command us!

                         TARZAN
              Rise, my loyal and brave warriors.
              I go to the aide of a friend. You
              may follow me or return to the
              village and await my return.

                    BUSULI
          We follow our king.

Tarzan nods his approval and with Jane beside him, leads the
way through the savage jungle.

EXT. JANE CAMPSITE - LATE AFTERNOON (NEXT DAY)

A stillness greets Tarzan, Jane and the ebony warriors upon
entering the clearing.

Jane's worried eyes search the campsite but all is deathly
quiet.

                    JANE
          Cecil! Monsieur Thuran!

TREE SHELTER

Tarzan clambers up the ladder and into the treehouse.

After a several moments, the anxious girl sees him reappear
at the threshold with a tin cup in his hand.

Tarzan jumps down to stand before the girl.

                    TARZAN
               (earnest)
          Is there water in the camp?

                    JANE
               (points)
          Yes, on the logs are two water
          kegs.

Tarzan moves with evident haste, with Jane following close
behind, to one of the

KEGS

and turning the brass spigot, water begins to flow into the
tin cup.

                    JANE
          Who is up there?

Tarzan's sad eyes look into Jane's worried face.

                    TARZAN
          Clayton. He's still alive but I'm
          afraid we're too late.

                         JANE
                    (distraught)
              Oh, no... please, no.

                         TARZAN
              Are you strong enough to follow me
              up?

Jane closes her eyes but when she reopens them to meet the
ape-man's questioning grey eyes, she nods.

TREE SHELTER

One-handed, the nimble ape-man climbs the ladder without
spilling a drop, Jane climbing up after him.

INT. TREE SHELTER - LATE AFTERNOON

In the gloomy interior a once handsome young man lies a
withered wretch upon a stale grass bed.

Dark hollows under closed eyes intimate his tribulation, his
wasted countenance portending no less than the death knell.

Clayton's chest barely rises and falls.

Tarzan kneels on one side and Jane on the other of the
emaciated figure.

Faced with Clayton's incredible suffering, Jane's eyes tear.

She watches Tarzan desperately work to revive the sleeping
man.

Tarzan rubs his forehead and then his skeletal arms with
water and finally he eases in a few drops of the precious
liquid onto a pair of parched and cracked lips.

Clayton's sunken eyes slowly open. At first there's an
emptiness in them. Then, he sees Jane's face hovering above
him and a lusterless smile wrinkles his drawn face.

                         CLAYTON
                    (weakly)
              Jane.

Aware of another, his eyes shift towards the ape-man and his
barely lit eyes open a little in amazement. Tarzan's
compassionate face stirs the dying nobleman.

                    CLAYTON
          Tarzan, I'm so glad... you're
          alive.

                    TARZAN
          You're going to be fine, Clayton.
          We got here just in time. Soon
          you'll be back on your feet again.

Clayton shakes his head.

                    CLAYTON
          It's over for me... and I'm glad.
          I couldn't bear to live... knowing
          what know and... knowing what I
          did.

                    JANE
          Where's Monsieur Thuran?

At the mention of the lowlife, Clayton's eyes ignite.

                    CLAYTON
          He left me here to die as I lay
          here shaking with fever. When I
          begged him for water he drank and
          then spat the water on the floor in
          front of me... and then laughed.

Angered by the memory of Rokoff, Clayton attempts to rise.

                    JANE
          No, Cecil. He's not worth the
          effort.

But Clayton cannot hear her.

                    CLAYTON
          I'll kill the monster if it's the
          last thing I do!

                    TARZAN
          Don't worry about Thuran. I'll
          take care of him for you and for
          me. He owes us both a great deal.

The sudden exertion leaves him even more depleted of energy
than before and he passes out.

Jane looks fearfully at Tarzan.

                    TARZAN
          He's not dead, but his heart is
          barely beating... he doesn't have
          much time left.

INT. TREE SHELTER - NEAR SUNSET

Tarzan and Jane sit beside the dying man each lost in their
own thoughts.

Clayton's eyelids flicker and then his eyes suddenly open as
if galvanized into wakefulness by an unseen force.

Jane is the first to notice and leans over him.

No tears fill Clayton's eyes but his face and voice fill with
sorrow as he speaks to her.

                    CLAYTON
               (in a hoarse whisper)
          My greed for your love... was
          insatiable... and because of it...
          I wronged not only you...

Clayton gestures with his eyes towards Tarzan.

                    CLAYTON
          ... But Tarzan as well.

He closes his eyes to gather strength and then reopens them
fighting to stay alive just a little longer.

                    CLAYTON
          Jane, I should have told you...
          long ago.

                    JANE
          Please, don't exert yourself... you
          need rest.

                    CLAYTON
          No, I must tell you.

Jane bows to his request.

                    JANE
               (softly)
          Tell me what?

He turns his head and faces the ulster he wore at the train
station.

> CLAYTON
> In one of the pockets... there's a
> piece of paper... that will
> explain, everything.

Jane reaches for the coat and pulls it next to her side.

Clayton turns his head to face Tarzan.

> CLAYTON
> Forgive me, Tarzan.

With great effort, he slides the ring of the House of Greystoke from his right, ring finger and places it in Tarzan's hand.

> CLAYTON
> Please take it... and honor it...
> as I could not.

He turns his head and eyes back to Jane.

> CLAYTON
> I don't deserve your forgiveness,
> my dear... but I do ask it.

> JANE
> (tearfully)
> I do forgive you, Cecil... please,
> forgive me.

Clayton raises a hand and Jane grips it in hers. The wane smile of a freed man, meets her poignant features.

Clayton lowers his hand and closes his eyes.

William Cecil Clayton's head slips to one side and a soft exhale announces the nobleman's death.

Jane crying softly raises her beautiful eyes to Tarzan's solemn countenance. She gets up and rushes around the body to Tarzan who stands, in time, to receive the mourning girl in his arms.

EXT. JANE CAMPSITE - CAMPFIRE - MORNING

A small boma encircles the campfire area.

A light smoke rises from an extinguished fire.

Outside the boma, wait the Waziri warriors and between four of them lies the body of Clayton.

TREE SHELTER

Tarzan is standing and looking up towards the tree shelter.

At the entrance Jane suddenly appears and waves down to the ape-man. She climbs down with the ulster over one shoulder and with a sad face stops before him.

> TARZAN
> What's wrong, Jane.

Without raising her head, Jane looks up at Tarzan with her eyes.

> JANE
> The locket you gave me... it's gone. I don't know where it is. I thought I left it in one of my shoes.

She shakes her head despondently.

Tarzan draws her next to him.

> TARZAN
> I'd forgotten about that. We'll come back tomorrow and search again. Perhaps together we'll have a better chance of finding it.

Jane, upset at the loss, nods silently in agreement.

> TARZAN
> Anyway my cabin is just a few miles from here and --

Jane is taken aback.

> JANE
> -- Your cabin?! My God, and we've been living here in danger all this time, when your cabin was just a few miles from here?

> TARZAN
> Yes, it's unfortunate... but what could you do... you didn't know. At any rate, now you'll be able to relax in comparative safety and we can bury Clayton's body next to his relatives.

Jane marvels at his thoughtfulness but Tarzan interrupts her.

                    TARZAN
          Are you ready to go?

                    JANE
          Oh, wait! Clayton said there was
          something important I needed to see
          in one of these pockets.

Jane searches one pocket but finding nothing moves on to the
next one and pulls out a worn yellow piece of paper.

She hangs the ulster on a rung, unfolds the paper, and reads.

INSERT - CABLEGRAM

          "The fingerprints confirm you're
          Greystoke. My sincerest
          congratulations!

          Your friend,

          Paul D'Arnot."

BACK TO SCENE

Jane's glittering eyes look at Tarzan in wonder.

                    JANE
          He knew and he didn't tell you.

Tarzan is intrigued by Jane's bewilderment.

                    TARZAN
          Tell me what?

Jane hands him the old cablegram.

                    JANE
              (in disbelief)
          That you're... Lord Greystoke.

Tarzan scans the cablegram and then looks into Jane's
astonished face.

                    TARZAN
          I knew... I just didn't know
          Clayton had become aware of it. I
          received this cablegram at the
          train station that evening... in
          the waiting room. I must have
          dropped it and Clayton obviously
          found it.

Jane is even more confused by his confession.

> JANE
> You knew? But then... why didn't
> you claim your birthright?

> TARZAN
> I received the news after you had
> decided to marry Clayton. Claiming
> the title would have taken
> everything from Clayton... and you.

Tarzan's great love for her overwhelms the girl.

> JANE
> You gave up your birthright --
> everything... for me?

> TARZAN
> You're all I wanted, Jane.
>   (indicating the jungle)
> I left this place because of you.
> My inheritance meant nothing,
> without you... so I let it go.

Jane closes the space between them and looking up into
Tarzan's noble face...

> JANE
> It's true what they say... fools
> throw away treasures.

She places both hands on his chiseled chest.

> JANE
>   (in a loving whisper)
> I am so fortunate to have your love
> and I thank God, for this second
> chance.

Tarzan meets her beautiful gaze with a gentle smile and
kisses her.

> TARZAN
> So do I.

Tarzan releases her.

> TARZAN
> Don't go away.

Jane smiles and shakes her head.

He then strides over to his Waziri warriors who are standing
straight and stoic.

>   TARZAN
>   (to Busuli)
>   You and two others take the lead.
>   I and my woman will follow behind
>   you... have the other three
>   warriors bring up the rear.

>   BUSULI
>   As you command, My Waziri.

Tarzan turns to rejoin Jane as Busuli orders the men
accordingly.

They enter the jungle with the four warriors carrying
Clayton's body, several paces behind Tarzan and Jane.

The jungle closes on the rear guard as they leave behind an
empty campsite with an ulster hanging on a rung.

EXT. JUNGLE - MORNING (3 MILES LATER)

Ten yards ahead of Tarzan, Busuli and the other two point men
suddenly stop.

Busuli looks back and signals for everyone to stop.

Busuli and the eyes of the other two warriors watch the trail
ahead of them with their spears at the ready.

A strange apparition dressed in a frock coat and a top hat
comes around the turn of the trail and into their view.

With his head bent down in deep scholastic thought, Professor
Archimedes Q. Porter walks slowly with his hands behind his
back, dead to the world.

Busuli and the two men lower their spears and look on in
wonderment at the strange man coming towards them.

Busuli glances backward and motions for them to come forward
as he points down the trail.

Prof. Porter stops in his tracks, still looking downward,
scratches the side of his face, shakes his head in
disagreement with his own mental conclusions and then
continues his stroll on the dangerous jungle trail.

>   JANE (O.S.)
>   Papa! Papa!

Startled back into the world, Prof. Porter stands up straight and looks ahead of him.

The old scholar's eyebrows rise and his jaw drops in the sudden and unexpected good fortune, leaving him momentarily speechless.

Jane, running ahead of the party, crashes into her father's arms nearly knocking him down in her unchecked exuberance.

>   PROF. PORTER
>   Jane! Oh, my dear, Jane! The Lord
>   is good to me.

Tears of joy stream down the old man's kind face as he embraces his daughter with all the joy and love of a father.

Jane pulls away from her father, her face red with emotion and teary eyes.

>   JANE
>   (almost crying)
>   I never thought I'd ever see you
>   again, Papa.

>   PROF. PORTER
>   (all choked up inside)
>   Neither did I.

They embrace again. Afterward, a smiling Prof. Porter kisses his happy daughter on the cheek and removes his spectacles.

He pulls out a handkerchief and as he cleans them, his myopic eyes notice for the first time a group of blurry individuals standing before them.

Realizing that they're not alone, he hurriedly puts his spectacles back on pushing them far back along the bridge of his nose.

Prof. Porter's eyebrows rise and his lower jaw drops again in utter amazement. He looks at his grinning daughter who watches him in unsuppressed anticipation.

>   PROF. PORTER
>   Tarzan?

Jane nods, her eyes radiant with joy.

Prof. Porter ganders another look at Tarzan, wrinkles his nose and pushes his sliding spectacles back up again.

                    PROF. PORTER
               (confused)
          It is you! I was misinformed. I
          thought you were dead, young man.

                    JANE
          We all did, Papa.

Jane gives her old man another affectionate hug.

Tarzan steps forward with a friendly smile and an
outstretched hand.

                    TARZAN
          I'm very much alive, Professor
          Porter.

Tarzan follows Prof. Porter's eyes as the distinguished
scholar studies the quiet but interested warriors.

                    TARZAN
          And these men are my warriors, of
          the Waziri tribe.

                    PROF. PORTER
          Fine looking men... friends of
          yours I take it?

                    TARZAN
          Very much so... I'm their king.

                    PROF. PORTER
          Interesting... very interesting,
          indeed. I've never heard of that
          tribe. I'd like to know more about
          them if --

                    JANE
          -- Papa, perhaps at another time?

                    PROF. PORTER
               (smiling)
          What? Oh, why of course, my dear.
          That can wait.

Prof. Porter's smile fades as he spots the body of Clayton
resting on the trail.

He looks at Tarzan and then at Jane with a sad countenance.

                    PROF. PORTER
          Yes, Monsieur Thuran informed us of
          his passing.

                         TARZAN
              He's with you now?

                         PROF. PORTER
              Yes. He arrived... two days ago.
              In fact, you'll be glad to know
              that he led us to your cabin.
                   (gazing at the body)
              I'm surprised he didn't bury the --

Prof. Porter's brows merge. He moves towards the pallbearers
and squats down to examine the body.

                         PROF. PORTER
                   (surprised)
              There's no decomposition and the
              body is still stiff. He must have
              recently died.
                   (still probing the body)
              But, Monsieur Thuran... said he
              died days ago... that can't be.

Tarzan looks at Jane, impressed at her father's deductions
and Jane nods in agreement.

                         JANE
              He died late yesterday.

Prof. Porter stands up.

                         PROF. PORTER
              I thought so. How unfortunate,
              though I don't understand it.

Then, lost in thought, Prof. Porter turns around and begins
heading in the opposite direction in his slow stroll, his
head down and hands behind his back, thinking out loud.

                         PROF. PORTER
                   (irritated)
              First I'm told, Tarzan's dead...
              and now I find he's alive. Then
              I'm told Clayton died days ago...
              and today, that he died yesterday.
              I wish people would learn to get
              their facts together before they
              trumpet them!

Grinning and shaking her head, Jane runs to her father's side
and taking his arm, frees him from his internal wranglings.

Tarzan sends his point men ahead, while he keeps a respectful
distance behind Jane and her father with the rest of the
warriors following in his wake.

EXT. CLEARING - CABIN - LATE MORNING

As they enter the clearing, Tarzan and his party find the cabin awash with activity -- French Navy sailors and castaways, like two lines of ants, moving two and fro.

Tarzan looks at Jane, who shrugs, and then at her father.

                    PROF. PORTER
          Ah, yes... I... forgot to mention
          them.

Tarzan scans the unfamiliar faces and unexpectedly his face lights up in amazement as his eyes alight on...

                    TARZAN
          Paul! Paul D'Arnot!

Paul D'Arnot hearing his name turns and is filled with joy and surprise at seeing his dear friend.

                    D'ARNOT
              (in a French accent; to
               self)
          Jean?

Tarzan strides up to him followed a few steps behind by Jane, Prof. Porter, and the Waziri warriors.

                    TARZAN
              (overjoyed)
          What in blazes are you doing here?!
          Either I'm dreaming or I've gone
          mad.

                    D'ARNOT
              (in a French accent;
               overjoyed)
          Then we are both mad, mon ami!

The two friends shake hands and then embrace until...

                    ESMERALDA (O.S.)
          Oh, my honey child! My baby!

Her shrieks startle the Waziri warriors, who instinctively take a step or two backward in self-defense.

All smiles, Tarzan, D'Arnot and Prof. Porter watch as Esmeralda thunders towards the smiling Jane who lightly runs into the big woman's arms.

Drawn by Esmeralda's excitement, Jane is soon mobbed -- with hugs and kisses -- by Hazel, Mrs. Strong and Mr. Philander in an, AD LIB, joyous reunion.

D'Arnot turns his attention back to his friend.

> D'ARNOT
> (in a French accent)
> They kept telling me that you were
> dead, but I would not believe
> them... and voila, just as I
> believed, so it is!

> TARZAN
> But how is it that you're here?
> You couldn't have known that --

> D'ARNOT
> (in a French accent)
> -- We didn't. It was purely
> chance, my friend. We were
> patrolling the coast when nostalgia
> set in and I suggested to the
> captain a visit to your cabin.
> (laughing)
> And deja vu... here we are again
> rescuing another party of
> castaways!

> TARZAN
> Your timing was perfect. Thank God
> for the French Navy.

> D'ARNOT
> (in a French accent)
> Yes, let us thank Him. Come Jean,
> I want you to meet my captain, who
> doubts that a man, such as
> yourself, exists.

Together they depart towards a little knot of officers in discussion, leaving behind Jane in her happy reunion with family, friends, and with the motionless Waziri warriors, interested spectators.

EXT. CLEARING - CABIN - LATER

As Tarzan leaves the officers to rejoin Jane, he's met by Hazel.

                    HAZEL
               (emotional)
          I'm so happy you're alive,
          Tarzan... not only for myself, but
          especially for Jane. God, how she
          loves you.

Hazel's eyes tear as she hugs the ape-man.

She pulls away and wipes a tear from an eye to meet Tarzan's
warm smile.

                    TARZAN
          And I, for one, could not be
          happier to see you again, Hazel
          Strong.

                    HAZEL
          I still can't believe it...
          suddenly, my mourning has turned
          into joy. Thank God for His mercy -
          - for this wonderful --
          inexplicable miracle.

Tarzan nods in agreement.

                    TARZAN
          You don't know how right you are.
          Jane and I are more than lucky to
          be alive... and so fortunate to
          have a friend like you.

Tarzan puts an arm around her shoulders and together they
walk back to Jane's reunion.

EXT. LANDLOCKED HARBOR - AFTERNOON

High on a halyard, the French flag flutters in a boisterous
sea breeze on an anchored cruiser.

Two large turrets with matching guns, one positioned on the
bow and the other on the stern, keep watch.

A manned lifeboat is lowered into the blue waters.

EXT. BEACH - AFTERNOON

Tarzan and Jane sit on the white shore underneath the shade
of several palm trees.

In the harbor a few lifeboats, propelled by the oars at the
hands of French sailors, glide towards the cruiser.

                    JANE
          ... And he's been after you ever
          since?

Tarzan nods.

                    JANE
          He's in for a terrible shock when
          he sees you.

                    TARZAN
               (grim)
          He's in for more than a shock.

The deadliness in Tarzan's tone draws worry into her eyes.
She sees the inexorable set of vengeance stamped on his noble
face, the gears of jungle justice turning in his mind.

Jane lays a delicate, fine hand on his arm.

                    JANE
               (gentle plea)
          Tarzan, please let the French
          authorities deal with him. You've
          already spoken to Captain Dufranne
          about him... leave it to them.

                    TARZAN
          He has to be killed.

                    JANE
          Why not let the French administer
          just punishment for his crimes?

                    TARZAN
          It would be better and much faster
          if I did it. This is my jungle...
          I rule here... not the French, nor
          anyone else. The authority lies
          with me.

                    JANE
          My love, they won't see it that
          way... they'll come after you.

Tarzan smiles.

                    TARZAN
          When they learn that he's a Russian
          spy working against them, that he
          tried to kill me by throwing me
          overboard and left Clayton to die,
          they'll thank me for saving them
          the trouble -- Count de Coude,
          himself, would no doubt decorate
          me.

In spite of herself, Jane chuckles.

                    JANE
          I wish you were right and that
          justice were that simple.

                    TARZAN
          And even if they did come after me,
          what then?

Jane considers him, concerned.

                    TARZAN
          Here, they would never be able to
          catch me... regardless of how many
          men they sent or how much money
          they spent or the resources they
          used. They would go bankrupt and
          still would have nothing to show
          for it.

Jane drops her head at the unpleasant picture being drawn for
her by the ape-man.

                    JANE
               (sadly)
          And what about us? Will you allow
          this fiend to keep us apart and
          win? I don't care about him. I
          love you, Tarzan... being with you
          is all that matters to me.

Tarzan grabs a chunk of bleached-white sand and lets it slip
through his fist and into the palm of his other hand, like
sand in an hourglass.

                    TARZAN
               (relenting)
          For your sake alone, I won't kill
          him.

Jane looks up with a relieved and grateful smile on her full
lips.

Tarzan cannot deny her and grins shaking his head slowly.

                    TARZAN
        But I believe you'll come to regret
        staying my hand. The French
        authorities won't be able to judge
        him as he deserves... he has too
        many friends in high places.

Tarzan looks deep into her eyes with grave concern.

                    TARZAN
        Rokoff never forgets... and he
        never forgives.

Jane, happy and content with her man, lowers her eyes and
then snuggles her golden head against his shoulder.

                    JANE
        (matter-of-factly)
        Well, if he comes for you again...
        then you'll have no choice.

Impressed, Tarzan glances down at her.

                    TARZAN
        (grinning)
        I knew you were half she-ape.

Jane laughs and strikes him playfully on his bulging shoulder
with a delicate fist, Tarzan pretending to be mortally
wounded.

He throws his arm about her like a blanket and kisses her
golden crown, she content to be at his side as Tarzan's alert
eyes shoot towards the ship anchored in the harbor as she
receives the arriving lifeboats.

EXT. CLEARING - CABIN - AFTERNOON (1 HOUR LATER)

The mood is relaxed.

Waziri warriors and a score of French sailors lounge around a
campfire eating and drinking. A few of the sailors and
warriors interact using sign language and some of the sailors
are able to manage a few words in Bantu.

Tarzan, D'Arnot, and CAPTAIN DUFRANNE are standing apart from
them and in discussion.

                    CAPTAIN DUFRANNE
               (in a French accent)
          ... How many days do you think you
          will need?

                    TARZAN
          Two, or three days should be enough
          for what I have in mind.

                    CAPTAIN DUFRANNE
               (in a French accent)
          Will you be needing men?

                    D'ARNOT
               (in a French accent)
          I'll go with him.

                    TARZAN
               (smiles gratefully)
          No, mon ami.
               (to captain)
          Thank you for your kind offer,
          Captain, but you all have done more
          than enough for us already. My men
          and I will go.

                    CAPTAIN DUFRANNE
               (in a French accent)
          Ah, but it's no trouble, My Lord.
          How far...

Their discussion continues indistinctly as Tennington and
Rokoff enter the clearing empty handed from an unsuccessful
hunt.

Tennington is the first to notice the Waziri warriors with
the French sailors and pulls the pipe from his mouth.

His surprised eyes fall on the lithe, ripped and powerful
figure of the ape-man towering over the two officers.

                    TENNINGTON
          By Jove, he's a big one. I wonder
          who he is.

Rokoff tired from the excursion does not notice the
newcomers, but prompted by the remarks he follows
Tennington's pointing pipe and staggers, falling back in
disbelief as his fearful eyes meet a pair of steel-grey eyes
boring into him.

                    ROKOFF
               (in French; in a French
                accent)
                    (MORE)

> ROKOFF (CONT'D)
> Sapristi! It's impossible! He
> cannot be alive!

Tennington, glances at Tarzan and then at Rokoff, concerned.

> TENNINGTON
> Steady, old boy.

SLOW MOTION

Rokoff throws the butt of his rifle to his shoulder and aims
straight for Tarzan.

> TENNINGTON
> (shocked)
> Noooo!

But before Rokoff can pull the trigger, Tennington strikes
the barrel upwards just as the hammer falls.

The bullet whizzes harmlessly above Tarzan's black mane.

BACK TO NORMAL SPEED

Faster than light, Tarzan is on him before he can even think
of engaging another round.

Tarzan snatches the weapon from him, as if from a child. He
extends the rifle to Tennington who takes it marveling at
Tarzan's prodigious strength as the ape-man raises the
gasping Rokoff off the ground with one arm.

He snarls up at the cringing man, with savage, penetrating
grey eyes but remembering his promise to Jane, he reluctantly
lowers the blue-faced Rokoff to the ground.

By this time Tarzan and Tennington are surrounded by the
officers, sailors and his loyal Waziri warriors.

> CPT. DUFRANNE
> (in a French accent;
> stern)
> This is Monsieur Rokoff, I take it?

Tarzan nods and shoves the choking man into the eager arms of
the sailors.

> CPT. DUFRANNE
> (in a French accent; to
> sailors)
> Put him in irons!

TARZAN
(remembering something)
A moment, Captain, if you would.

Captain Dufranne stays his men.

Tarzan approaches Rokoff who's breathing heavily and nursing a very sore neck.

TARZAN
I believe you have something that
belongs to me.

Tarzan inserts a hand into one of the inner pockets of the man's soiled blazer and pulls out a long, golden chain ending in a diamond studded locket.

Tarzan raises an eyebrow.

TARZAN
Now, this... I did not expect.

He then searches the other pocket and grins as he draws out the stolen documents.

Tarzan stares him in the face and his chest rumbles under a low snarl. Rokoff's head and shoulders tremble as he feels the emanating snarl and sees Tarzan's fierce face digging into his very soul.

Tarzan's wrath subsides.

TARZAN
For your sake, Rokoff, let this be
the last time our paths cross.
(to captain)
Thank you, Captain Dufranne.

The captain nods and then signals his men to incarcerate Rokoff aboard the ship.

Tarzan confers with Captain Dufranne regarding the papers taken off Rokoff in inaudible tones.

Jane and the others, silent spectators of the commotion, watch from near the entrance to the cabin, as Rokoff is led away to the beach.

From Tarzan and the captain, Jane's eyes rove and spy Lord Tennington.

JANE
(smiling and waving)
Lord Tennington, Lord Tennington!

Startled by her sudden appearance, Tennington's pipe falls
out of his mouth. He picks it up just as she arrives.

                        JANE
                  (all smiles)
            It's wonderful to see you again!

                    TENNINGTON
                  (amazed)
            My dear Miss Porter, thank God
            you're alive!
                  (nodding towards Rokoff)
            He told me you had been killed by
            some wild beast. I must say, this
            has been a day full of surprises...
            to say the least and I --

Good-naturedly, Tarzan saunters up to join them and Jane,
taking one of his arms in hers, introduces him to Tennington
who puffs unconsciously on his pipe, one hand rubbing the
back of his head and the other resting on his hip.

                        JANE
            Lord Tennington, allow me to
            introduce to you, John Clayton,
            Lord Greystoke.

Lord Tennington's pipe falls out of his mouth for a second
time.

Jane is unable to hold back her laughter as she squats down
to retrieve the stunned nobleman's pipe and hands it back to
him.

Tarzan, taking the initiative, shakes Tennington's
somnambulant hand while Tennington, for his part, finally
regains his composure, a little embarrassed at his own
reaction.

                                    FADE TO BLACK:

                    CPT. DUFRANNE (V.O.)
                  (in a French accent)
            "Naked came I out of my mother's
            womb, and naked shall I return
            thither:"

EXT. CLEARING - CABIN - NEXT DAY

A fresh mound of earth rises from the ground along side the
graves of the late Lord Greystoke and Lady Alice, a cross
imbedded at its head.

                    CPT. DUFRANNE
                (in a French accent)
            "the Lord gave, and the Lord hath
            taken away:"

An unusual gathering of French sailors, castaways, Waziri
warriors, and two British lords pay tribute to the late
William Cecil Clayton.

                    CPT. DUFRANNE
                (in a French accent)
            "as it has pleased the Lord so is
            it done: blessed be the name of
            the Lord."

Except for the Waziri warriors...

                    EVERYONE ELSE
            Amen.

A lieutenant does a sharp about-face towards a seven-man
honor guard.

Three times the lieutenant shouts a set of commands and three
times in precise, sharp movements seven shots are fired into
the sky in honor of the dead man.

Slowly the crowd disperses, the usual hugs, hand shakes and
comforting words are exchanged, but finally the new grave
finds itself alone alongside the other sleepers.

EXT. CLEARING - CABIN - DAY (2 DAYS LATER)

Tarzan and six sleek ebony warriors armed only with bows and
arrows strapped to their backs materialize from within the
jungle carrying the last seven ingots from the amphitheater.

Captain Dufranne, a few of his men and others watch as Tarzan
and his warriors lay them upon a large pile of forty-four
other solid gold ingots stacked against the wall beneath one
of the front windows of the cabin.

The six warriors leave to join the other four around a
campfire.

                    FRENCH SAILOR
                (in a French accent)
            Surely, you will share the secret
            of the gold with us... no, My Lord?

                    TARZAN
                (with a smile)
            No.

                    BRITISH SAILOR
                 (winking at others)
            Say now, that's a proper idea.
            Tell us, Your Lordship, and we
            promise to keep it a secret amongst
            ourselves. Won't we lads?

A bunch of smiling faces nod in agreement.

                    TARZAN
            I don't doubt it for a moment, but
            my answer is still no.

The others begin to laugh.

                    BRITISH SAILOR 2
            But wouldn't you feel better
            sharing it with the likes of us?

                    TARZAN
                 (grinning)
            Would you share the secret with
            them, if you were in my shoes?

British Sailor 2 takes a sweeping look at his mates and with
a toothy grin...

                    BRITISH SAILOR 2
            With these blokes? Not likely.
            They'd rather suck the monkey than
            be rich.

The others throw things at him and rowdy laughter ensues.

                    CPT. DUFRANNE
                 (in a French accent)
            I feel like the pirate, Levasseur,
            loaded with gold and anxious men...
            I'm glad you didn't tell them -- or
            me for that matter.

                    TARZAN
            There are thousands more like --

                    CPT. DUFRANNE
                 (in a French accent;
                  chuckling and raising a
                  hand)
            -- No, don't tell me... you'll turn
            me into a pirate on the high seas.

>   TARZAN
>   For the sake of your men and to
>   save you from a life of piracy,
>   I'll say no more.

With a grin and an inward chuckle, he takes leave of the
captain and enters the cabin.

EXT. CLEARING - SUNSET

Tarzan and Jane, holding hands, enter the clearing from the
beach.

Tarzan glances at the cabin some distance from them and
pauses.

>   TARZAN
>   It may be that after tomorrow you
>   and I may never see this place
>   again.

He takes hold of both of her hands, gently.

>   TARZAN
>   How do you feel about getting
>   married in the cabin... where I was
>   born, where my parents lived and
>   died... and where I first saw your
>   lovely face... here in the jungle
>   where I grew up and where you and I
>   first met?

Jane blinks her moist, loving eyes and a single tear slides
down a delicate cheek.

>   JANE
>   (emotional voice)
>   What could be more beautiful, my
>   darling?

She embraces Tarzan and as one hand slips away to caress his
neck, she looks at the cabin.

>   JANE
>   (smiles; whispers)
>   Where it all began.

INT./EXT. CABIN - MORNING

Tarzan and Jane stand before Captain Dufranne in a full
house.

Tarzan dressed in his loincloth with his blade at his side and Jane dressed with her soft leather garment and sandals -- her long locks braided.

D'Arnot, the best man, stands to Tarzan's immediate right and Hazel, the bridesmaid, stands to Jane's immediate left.

Others unable to enter, crane their necks through the door to witness the event while others watch through the latticed windows.

Captain Dufranne canvases the room and then looks at the groom and bride.

                    CPT. DUFRANNE
               (in a French accent)
          Shall we begin?

Tarzan and Jane glance at each other smiling and returning their eyes to Captain Dufranne, they both nod, yes.

                    CPT. DUFRANNE
               (in a French accent)
          Ladies and Gentlemen, we are
          gathered --

                    TENNINGTON (O.S.)
          -- Forgive me, Captain, for
          interrupting...

All eyes turn to the British lord.

                    TENNINGTON
          ... But a thought just occurred to
          me and I find it smashing. Why not
          make this a double wedding?

Tennington turns his attention to Mrs. Strong.

                    TENNINGTON
          I find, Mrs. Strong, that I
          cannot... in good conscience allow
          this moment to pass without asking
          for your daughter's hand in
          marriage.
               (to Hazel)
          Will you be my wife, Hazel?

Hazel's face and eyes light up like the sun as she presses both palms high up against her chest to catch her breath, taken away by the utter surprise and boldness of his request.

She glances from Tennington with a joyful face and welling
eyes towards her mother, who's even more shocked than her
daughter.

Hazel nods excitedly at her mother's questioning expression
and Mrs. Strong clasps her hands in joy, as Hazel runs into
Tennington's arms overcome with happiness.

She then rushes to her mother and no sooner is their embrace
finished, than Jane is their to congratulate her.

Jane and Hazel hold each other's arms, exchange joyful smiles
and consummate their happiness with a hug.

                    JANE
          God bless you, my dearest friend.

                    HAZEL
          And God bless you, my dearest,
          dearest Jane.

The two beauties come apart and wipe the tears of joy from
their eyes and with one more grinning look at each other,
they move excitedly to the sides of their future husbands.

The two couples stand beside each other with no bridesmaids
and only one best man amongst them.

Captain Dufranne smiles affably and the ceremony begins.

His voice fades as it travels from the cabin and into the
clearing where a crowd witnesses the union -- by either sight
or sound -- of two British lords and two American belles.

EXT. BEACH - LATE MORNING

A lifeboat rocking gently on the tranquil waves, stands fast
at the hands of the four oarsmen. In the craft are seated
LADY JANE, Prof. Porter and D'Arnot, their eyes riveted
towards the shore.

Tarzan stands before crestfallen Waziri warriors.

                    TARZAN
          ... I don't know when or if ever I
          will return.

                    BUSULI
          We will wait for you, Waziri.

With a light, grateful smile Tarzan places a hand on Busuli's
shoulder and then turns to board the lifeboat.

The Waziri warriors watch as the craft glides upon the tranquil harbor.

Tarzan looks back and raises his hand in farewell.

Busuli raises his spear and then lowers it in response.

Four oars move as one as they propel the boat towards the waiting cruiser.

EXT. ATLANTIC - CRUISER - DECK - NEAR SUNSET

Tarzan, dressed in flannel white ducks, and Jane in an elegant long dress, stand close together leaning on the rail as the French cruiser steams slowly northward, their eyes upon the setting sun.

Jane looks at her husband.

> JANE/LADY JANE
> Will you miss it, terribly?

Tarzan thinks for a moment and then nods.

> JANE
> Wherever you wish to live, my
> darling... is where I want to be.

Tarzan smiles, puts an arm around her and kisses one of her lovely cheeks.

> JANE
> I still can't get over it. It's
> like a dream come true.

She leans closer against him.

> JANE
> There's only one thing I regret...

She looks up at him and then begins to play with the end of his tie.

> JANE
> ... The loss of the locket you gave
> me.

She continues to play with the tie without looking up at him, a little upset at the memory of the lost locket.

> JANE
> It reminded me of that day... when
> you and I first met in the jungle.
> (MORE)

                    JANE (CONT'D)
          I'll never forget... it was
          terrible and wonderful... now it's
          gone for --

A golden chain with a diamond studded locket drops down
before her startled beautiful face. It glistens in the
waning light of the sun, the gleaming diamonds matching the
light in her eyes.

With a suppressed grin, Tarzan drops the heirloom into the
palm of her hand.

Jane, overcome with emotion is speechless. She places the
locket carefully around her neck and then opens it and
looking at the portraits of his parents, smiles warmly.

She then closes it and lets it rest on her bosom and gives
Tarzan a sudden emotional embrace.

She pulls away and looks up at him with moist, loving eyes
resting her hands on his arms.

Tarzan slides his hands down to her small waistline.

                    TARZAN
          Want to know where I found it?

Jane shakes her head ever so slowly, her jeweled eyes
beckoning him.

                    JANE
          Kiss me, darling.

Jane wraps her slender arms around his neck and covers his
lips with a long passionate kiss.

Tarzan doesn't complain.

                                        FADE TO BLACK.

                        The End

www.ingramcontent.com/pod-product-compliance
Lightning Source LLC
Chambersburg PA
CBHW080722020726
47503CB00010B/2756